Here Without You

Cooper's Ridge Series Book 2

JJ HARPER

Cover design by JC Clarke at The Graphics Shed
Edited by SJS Editorial Services
Formatted by JC Clarke

Prologue

MALLORY

You never believe when someone says goodbye to you, it might actually be goodbye, as in never see, never speak to, never hear, touch, and taste again. But it happens, it happens more times than you will ever realize. I know this because it happened to me.

"I'm off to work, Mal," Archer calls to me from the hallway.

"Hold up, mister. Not so fast. I want kisses before you leave me alone." I mock-pout at him, making him laugh.

"Oh, sugar, I will always give you kisses. Come here, hot lips." He laughs and drags me into his arms. Holding my face in his palms, he kisses me soundly. "There you go. Now, I love you, and I'll see you later."

"I love you too. Be careful, Arch."

"Always." He kisses me softly. "Goodbye, Mallory."

Two hours later, my life shattered around me, and I'm left alone.

Chapter

One

EIGHTEEN MONTHS EARLIER.

"Hey, hey! Hold up! What's the hurry?" A deep, rich, dark-brown voice calls to me as I try to dodge past the owner, clipping his shoulder. His hand reaches out and catches my arm.

"What? Shit, I'm sorry. I'm running late, and I can't be late today." I go to move off again when he drops hold of me.

"Where are you going?" Mr. Sounds-sexy-as-fuck asks me.

"My job, and I'll lose it if I'm late!" I shout at him over my shoulder and dart off again down the sidewalk.

I sneak into the kitchen of the coffee shop I work in and dump my bag and jacket in my locker. Phew! Just in time. I wash my hands, grab my apron, and walk out into the shop. The queue is out the door already, and I slide up to the counter to take my first order of probably hundreds today.

Eight hours making and serving coffee isn't really what I had planned for my life, but when my folks cut me off and stopped paying my tuition, I needed to earn enough to stay in college. My student loans help, but it's still not enough to live on. I need to keep this job. It's one of *the* places to get coffee and is always good for large tips too. Situated in an affluent area, lots of rich city kids and wealthy business people are more than happy to wait an extra few minutes to be served by the cute staff who work here. Not that I put myself in that bracket, I'm just happy to get what I can.

The next couple hours are crazy busy, and I hardly even get to look up. When I hear a cough and a deep chuckle, I raise my eyes up from the espresso machine. Shit! It's the gorgeous guy from this morning.

"Hello again." He smiles and looks at my name badge. "Good to see you made it, Mallory." His bright-green eyes sparkle mischievously when he says my name.

My eyes dart to my boss to see if he heard the comment, but he's too busy gawking at the table of cute college girls to be listening to the counter.

"Oops, sorry," he says and pretends to zip his mouth shut.

"What can I get you?" I ask, trying not to stare at him. God, he's hot! I take his order, and he moves down to pay the cashier. When I look up to find him again, I see him leaning against the wall watching me, making me nervous. His blond, carefully styled hair is just the right length to grab and tug, and his emerald-green eyes sparkle with glee. Everything about him exudes wealth and privilege; his suit alone must have cost a couple thousand dollars. His confident smirk when I hold up his coffee holder with the three cups already in place has me watching him as he saunters back to me.

"Thank you, Mallory. I'll see you around." This time he winks.

"I would have thought an important guy like you would have minions to fetch your coffee for you." I laugh as hot-coffee guy, as I now call him, comes up to the counter.

"I could, but then I wouldn't get to speak to you, now would I?" He winks. "I didn't see you here yesterday? I didn't get anywhere nearly as much foam on my cappuccino from the sullen girl."

"I don't work here every day. I'm in college so it just fits around my schoolwork." I blush as I didn't expect him to notice whether I was here or not.

"What time do you finish today?" he asks.

"Why?" I carry on making his order, knowing he won't move off until it's finished.

"I wondered if you'd like to grab a drink or maybe something to eat with me," he asks. I just stare at him; my mouth drops in surprise. "You're old enough to drink?" he queries and smiles, but it's not in condescension.

"Um, yeah, I am. But why do you want to have a drink with me? You don't even know me." Admittedly, I've seen him every day I've been here, *and* he does wait for me to serve him. Letting others past until I get to him.

He laughs, and it sends shivers through my body. "I guess that's why I would like to have a drink, to get to know you. So, what do you say?" His tongue darts out and dampens his bottom lip, and I follow the motion, unable to tear my eyes away.

"I can't tonight. I have a study group. I go straight from here." I hand him his drinks.

"Tomorrow then?" He leans forward and whispers, "I really would like to get to know you, Mallory." His voice is husky in my ear.

"I don't think it's a good idea, I'm sorry." I'm already kicking myself for turning him down.

"That's okay. I'll ask again tomorrow, and the day after. I'll get you to say yes in the end." With that, he winks and moves off to pay.

And he does just that, the next day, and the one after that. Then I have two days off, and when I get back to work, I look forward to seeing him again, but he doesn't show up. The day seems to drag on and on. Plus, summer has arrived, and the temperatures have rocketed, making every customer be in a bad mood. Hell, we're all in a bad mood. I finally look up at the clock and realize I can leave. I can't get out of there fast enough.

I rush out the kitchen door and straight into the furnace as the heat hits me in the face. Dragging my T-shirt over my head and tucking it into my back pocket, I walk away, then hear someone whistle and call out my name. Turning to the sound, I see hot-coffee guy standing outside the shop front.

"Mallory." He sounds breathless as his eyes roam over my bare chest. "What a pleasant surprise. I was just thinking about you."

"Really? It can hardly be a surprise considering I work here." I tip my head and look him over. He's not all dressed up in one of his fancy suits today. He's dressed in a cute pair of pale-blue shorts and a white polo shirt; his sunglasses are on the top of his head, pushing his blond hair away from his forehead. Giving him a much more approachable look, and a younger one too.

"Okay, you're right. I hoped to find you leaving and persuade you to come for a drink." He looks at me with puppy dog eyes, making me burst out laughing.

"Fine, but on one condition." I chuckle.

"Anything you want." He smiles and steps closer to me. Damn, if he doesn't smell amazing. I step back, realizing I probably don't smell too good.

"Well, you could tell me your name." I laugh as we walk next to each other.

"Shit! Haven't I told you? No wonder you wouldn't go out with me." He thumps his hand against his forehead, theatrically. "It's Archer, Archer Hawkins."

"Okay then, Archer, Archer Hawkins. We can go for a drink."

We walk into the nearest bar and find a table away from the bright sunlight pouring in through the large windows. I shrug my shirt back on over my head and watch him head over to the bar. He really is incredibly good looking and doesn't seem aware of the admiring glances he receives from both the men and the women having the same idea as us.

He turns back halfway over and asks if I want a beer. I nod and give him a thumbs-up. His smile floors me. I groan, wondering what the hell I've gotten myself into.

Chapter

Two

"Can I see you again, Mallory?" Archer asks as we stand at the intersection waiting for the WALK signal to light up. "And I don't mean just when I buy my coffee."

"I think I'd like that." I smile shyly. We've had a great evening. Archer is interesting and funny and wanted to know about me. I kept trying to deflect his questions, but he's very good at asking things in just the right way to get me to open up. Not enough to talk about all this recent shitstorm with my parents, but enough to make him laugh.

"When?" Archer's hand touches the back of mine. His fingers slide over my knuckles, making little sparks shoot up my arm.

"I'm not sure. I've got exams starting in a couple weeks and need to cram. I'm going to be busy a lot of nights with my study group and then in the library. I need to work hard, or I won't get my finance…" My words dry up when I see him frown.

"Don't you get help from home? Or a scholarship? Is this why you're working every spare hour in the coffee shop?" Archer sounds annoyed. No, not annoyed. Shocked.

I bristle, and I know he senses it because he apologizes immediately. "Shit, Mallory, I'm sorry. That was rude and out of place of me."

"Yeah, well, shit happens, and life doesn't always go the way it was supposed to. Look, I've gotta go. I've had a nice time, Archer. I'll see you around." I turn and walk away. I can get to the bus stop and be back on campus quicker. Maybe I can put all of this out of my head.

"Mallory! Mallory, please wait," Archer calls out, but I don't stop.

The next day, I work a late shift, allowing me to get some studying done in the morning. I just sit and stare at the same page in the book and think about Archer Hawkins, and how he is perfect for me. We like the same music, the same baseball team, the same books. It's just unfortunate we don't have the same choices in life available to us. When he told me he was a lawyer, I knew I was right about him having money. We would have six months ago, but not now. Not now that my family has cut all ties with me because of my "lifestyle choice" is how my stuck-up asshole father put it.

"Being gay isn't a choice, Dad. It's who I am. I was born this way. I didn't wake up and think 'Hey, gay looks fun. I'll give it a go!' For fuck's sake!"

"Language, Mallory!" my mother barks at me from the other side of the table.

"What is it you're saying then, Dad?" I look at him and see the sneer on his face.

"I'm saying that unless you stop this ridiculousness, I will stop paying your allowances, your tuition fees, and your apartment. I won't have you bring my name into disrepute. You'll make me a laughing stock. I can't believe after all the privileges you have had, you still act like some sort of lowlife." He uses his knife to point at me. "You won't be welcome here again. I don't want your type near your siblings."

"Unbelievable, you really are a shit! Fine, do that then because I won't lie. I have more self-respect than that. And I think the real lowlife here is you, turning

your child away because of who he is, and who he chooses to love." I pull my napkin off my lap and drop it on my plate.

"Self-respect? You think being queer makes you have self-respect. I don't know how you can look at yourself in the mirror." He grabs his glass of very expensive red wine and gulps the entire contents down before slamming the glass on the table, causing the stem to fracture.

"I do actually. You just carry on sleeping with your secretary as long as we all pretend we don't know about it, and you, Mother, can keep the bottle of vodka in the back of the pantry, and we can turn a blind eye. But I'm not allowed to choose the gender of the person I want to sleep with? You don't know the meaning of self-respect." My chair scrapes back over the floor, making my mother wince at the sound; it just makes me laugh even more.

Looking over at my dumbstruck brother and sister, I send them a smile. "Sorry, you two. Not for who I am, but for who they are. I hope you get out of here as soon as you can."

I walk out the door and out of the house.

Ten days later, I have a letter from my dad's lawyer telling me to leave my apartment and return my car. I preempted his callousness and have already spoken to the finance office and the housing office and have a dorm room and a grant for my fees. Luckily, I'm at the top of all my classes, and I only have one more year to go. So fuck him!

The next step was getting a job, and one of my buddies had heard about the job in the coffee shop, so I hot-footed it down there and grabbed an application.

My phone rings, making me jump. Looking down, I see an unknown number and decide to ignore it and let it go to voicemail. Then I get my head back into my book, and this time I focus enough to make some decent notes before having to go into work.

When I walk inside, I see Carl looking at me strangely. "What's up, dude?" I ask as I tie my apron around my waist.

"Your man over there has been waiting all morning for you." Carl nudges his head over to the corner. I look over and see Archer sitting there, looking so unhappy.

"What the hell!" I step out from behind the counter and walk up to him. My hands sink into the pockets on the front of my apron. "What's going on, Archer? Why've you been here all morning?"

"I wanted to see you. I needed to see you to apologize again." He reddens as he tries to reach out to me.

"You didn't need to do that. You said you were sorry last night." I look around and see my boss glowering at me. "Look, I need to get to work. Don't worry, Archer, it's okay."

"Can I see you again? Tonight? Please, Mallory, give me another chance." He smiles softly, making my heart skip a beat.

"I can't do tonight. I'm here 'til ten o'clock." I look over my shoulder, and my boss is scowling at me, his arms folded over his chest. "I've got to get to work. I'm sorry, Archer. Maybe another day." I scurry away, avoiding eye contact with my boss and serve the next customer.

"I'll be here at ten, Mallory," Archer calls out as he walks out.

"This isn't a pick-up joint, Halston. Get to work," Mr. Kowolski mutters to me before stomping back to his office.

Carl looks at me and gives me a smile. "He's a hot guy, rich too. You should go for him." He winks and carries on serving.

The day is long, and I'm hot and sweaty by the time I finish. All I want to do is go back to my room and get under a cold shower. The night has cooled down, but even in darkness, the heat is suffocating. I walk out the kitchen door and see Archer waiting for me. He smiles and pushes off from the wall. I look at his long legs clad in denim tonight, and a tight-fitting short-sleeved shirt shows off his broad chest, making me swallow hard.

"You shouldn't have come out again, Archer. I'm tired and in desperate need of a shower and my bed. Can we take a raincheck?" I ask quietly as he approaches me.

His green eyes darken as he looks me over. "I'm here now, and I can offer you both of those options if you'd like to come back to my place." His voice is deep and husky as he steps into my space.

"Huh? I don't think that's a good idea. We don't know each other." I struggle to speak as I inhale the crisp citrus scent of his cologne.

"What better way to find out more." His mouth is so close to mine I can feel his warm breath washing over my dry lips. I slide my tongue over my lower lip, dampening it or maybe trying to capture his flavor. My eyes flutter as I feel his mouth brush over mine, a touch so light I could have almost believed I imagined it until I hear him sigh.

"Shit," I mutter under my breath. My heart beats frantically in my chest as I crave for his touch.

"Come back with me, Mallory." His words resonate in my chest, making my refusal impossible. I nod my head and let him take my hand. "Thank you," he whispers.

We walk slowly towards a tall and very impressive apartment building. Even more exclusive than my parents' home and that takes some beating.

"Nice address," I comment with a chuckle.

"Yeah, it's not bad." Archer catches my eye and winks.

We walk through the door being held open by a doorman man who smiles and greets Archer by name. Then still with my hand in his, he strides to the concierge desk.

"Good evening, Winter. I'd like to introduce Mallory Halston. He has access to my home at any time."

I turn my head and gawp at him, but he carries on smiling.

"Of course, Mr. Hawkins. Good evening, Mr. Halston."

"This way, come on." Archer leads me towards an elevator and pressing the call button, the door immediately slides silently open and we step inside. Archer opens a key pad and enters a code.

"It's 47531. You'll need to remember that, Mallory." He smirks.

"I'm not sure that's necessary right now," I mutter, making him laugh.

"Oh, Mallory, I'm not letting you go that easily. I want you. I've made that perfectly obvious." His thumb strokes the back of my hand the whole time as he watches me.

"Do you always get what you want?" I ask, feeling not nervous but maybe apprehensive.

"Yes." His eyes darken as he stares at me.

"Have I made this too easy for you? Should I turn around and go back home?" I ask jokingly.

"Easy? Shit, I've asked you every day for a couple weeks and then after one date, you bolt off into the night. Hell, Mallory, you are anything but easy. And please don't leave yet."

The elevator slides open again, allowing Archer to pull me out towards his doorway. He drops my hand to reach for his key and slides it into the lock. The door swings open into a large open-plan room, and Archer reaches out his arm, letting me enter first. I look around at the expensively decorated but very stylish and lived-in room. A small smile breaks out. I like it here.

"Let me show you where my shower is. Would you like me to get you something to eat? I can order pizza?" Archer walks ahead of me and down a hallway to his room. I can't help but stare at his bedroom. The bed is the biggest I've ever seen and has crisp white and navy bedding and cushions. The floor is a light polished wood, giving such a light airiness to the room. But the floor-to-ceiling window is the real showpiece.

"Wow! Archer, that's some view!" I step over to look out and see the city laid out before me, blanketed in darkness, but the lights glitter like stars. I look up and see Archer in the reflection as he watches me.

He looks so beautiful. I know I may be making a mistake, but in this moment, I want him. I want him as much as the lust in his eyes proves he wants me.

Chapter
Three

We continue to stare at each other, neither making a move until I blink and turn around.

"Where's this shower then, hotshot!" I try to lighten the mood, but I don't think it's working as he swallows hard.

"This way. Can I lend you some shorts and a T-shirt? I'm guessing you don't want to put the clothes you're wearing back on."

"That would be great, thank you." I follow him into another room and see the shower is more of a wet room than an enclosed space.

"There's towels and everything you'll need already in there. Take your time, Mallory. I'll order some food." Archer turns and walks out. I strip out of my clothes and turn on the shower. The water powers out, and I know I'm never going to want to shower anywhere else ever again. Definitely not in the weak version my dorm has to offer. I scrub the sweat and coffee from my body and wash my hair, enjoying the products I can no longer afford but used to have. Then I just stand with my head tipped back and my eyes closed, letting the water hit my chest.

Eventually, I turn off the water and run my hands through my hair and then down my body, shucking the water away. Stepping out, I reach for the towel. When I look up, I see Archer standing in the doorway. His hand seems to be squeezing his dick through his jeans. I watch as he walks towards me and takes the towel from my hand.

"Let me." His voice is rough and hard, but his hand is soft and gentle as he wipes the towel down my neck and slowly over my chest. My breathing gets quicker as he circles my pecs, slowly, lazily as if it's his hand not the fabric caressing me. "I have never wanted anyone the way I want you."

His hand moves lower, and I grasp his wrist, stopping him from going any further. His eyes widen in surprise.

"Why?" I ask him, still stopping him from touching me.

"I don't know. I just know I can't leave you alone." He leans closer, letting his forehead rest on my own—a touch I have always found very sensual.

His mouth moves over and stills, waiting for me to agree. I know I'm lost to him as my head slowly nods. As his mouth presses firmly over mine, I know this is going to be like no kiss I've ever experienced before. The softness of his lips surprises me as his tongue slides over the seam of mine, seeking entry. This is a take-no-prisoners kiss. He's in total control as his tongue delves into my mouth. He explores every part of my mouth, stroking against my tongue before pulling back out to suck on my tongue.

Fuck! My hand lets go of his wrist, and I grab at his hips, pushing my naked and aroused body against his. I can feel his erection through the rough fabric of his jeans against mine. I wish it wasn't between us. Archer's hands are in my hair now as he continues fucking my mouth with his tongue. He tightens his fingers as his kiss slows down and we break apart, panting as we draw heaving gulps of air into our lungs. He kisses me again, softer this time but still so controlling. I never want it to stop.

"I need you, Mallory. I need to taste you," he whispers, then lets go of my hair and drops down to his knees. "Fuck, look at you. So hard, weeping for me, your cock aches for me."

I groan as his hot breath washes over the sensitive swollen head of my dick. My head lolls back as he runs his nose up and down my length, breathing in deeply as he reaches the juncture of my groin and thigh. My hands reach out into his hair, and it's even softer than I imagined. I stroke my fingers lazily over his scalp as his tongue licks back up the crease to the base of my dick. Long flat strokes of his tongue travel up my length until I think I can't bear anymore.

Then his mouth closes over my crown and sucks. The tip of his tongue flicks over the slit, and I can feel more precum bursting out. Archer moans and then sinks down, taking my whole length deep inside the warm, wet cavern of his mouth. I feel the back of his throat, but he keeps going, and I slip deep inside, and he swallows around me.

"Fuck! You need to stop! I'm gonna come if you do that again." I pull on his hair, but he is relentless, sucking my dick as one hand plays with my balls and the other skims up and down my ass crack, just teasing as he gets close to my hole. Then he sucks hard and tugs on my balls before releasing them to draw up inside my body. As my knees shake, my orgasm fires through me, and I pour my load into his mouth and throat. Unrelenting, he swallows me. As I finish and soften, he licks me and scrapes his teeth over the tip of my cock, making me flinch at the sensitivity.

"Wow! Fuck, Mallory. Wow!" Archer stands, his hands cup my face. His lips are red and swollen but still so fucking sexy. I lick across his bottom lip, making him moan as I tug it between my teeth, then release it to dive into his mouth. I taste myself and suck on his tongue. He growls and increases his grip on my ass.

"I need you to fuck me," I pant into his mouth.

Archer's groan sends shivers through my body. I can hear and feel his need.

"Get on my bed. Fuck, Mallory! I want you so much."

We rush through to his room, and I clamber up onto his mammoth bed, pushing cushions to the floor and kicking down the duvet with my feet. Then I settle back and watch as Archer takes off his clothes. His shirt drops down to the floor, then he pops the button on his fly before dragging down the zipper. My hand slides down my stomach over my tight muscles and back onto my now, once again, very hard dick.

"God, you look stunning." I moan shamelessly.

"Open the drawer, sugar. Get the lube and condoms out, then bend your knees up, open your legs," Archer orders. I comply, loving the instructions.

I dart across the bed and reach into the drawer. I look at him just as he drops his pants. "Condoms? Plural?" I raise an eyebrow.

"Hell, yeah, plural. We've got all night, Mallory." He stalks over to me, his hand wrapped around the impressive length of his dick. "It's Friday night, and you have no college, and you aren't working tomorrow. Now lie back down, I want to explore your body."

Archer maps my body with his fingers and his tongue, sending me higher and higher. "You taste divine, Mallory. Your skin is so soft, and it loves my touch."

He's right too. My skin feels alive as he traces every line and contour. I feel goose bumps break out as he scrapes his teeth over my nipple. I can't hold back my moan as my back arches into him.

"Oh, honey, I can't wait to feel you clamped tight around me. You are so receptive to my touch. I knew we'd be perfect together," he murmurs as his mouth covers my other nipple.

"Then do it, Archer. I need you inside me. Take me, please God, take me," I puff out my words as he pushes my legs back, folding them over my chest.

"Christ, you're perfect." He slides his tongue over my hole and up over my taint then down again. "Hold your legs, Mal. Don't move them." His breath is warm over my skin. His finger is there, circling my pucker. I watch as he sucks the digit into his mouth, making it wet before pressing it down on my hole. "Let me in. I'll make you feel so good."

Slowly, he pushes inside me and hell, yeah, it feels good, but it's not enough. I need more.

"Fuck, Archer, give me more. I need you inside me." The grip on my thighs is punishing as I hold on tight, not wanting him to stop. As his finger slips out, a moan escapes me, but soon he adds another finger and pumps in and out of me, stretching me. "Enough! I'm ready."

I hear the rip of the condom wrapper, and then his hands are gone. Opening my eyes, I watch, mesmerized as he rolls the thin latex down his rock-hard dick. Then he squeezes the lube bottle and coats his dick and drips some over my hole. I feel the tip of his cock press against my pucker as he slips slowly inside.

"Fuck, you're so damn hot. You ready for more?" Archer moans.

"Yes, God, yes." I bear down and feel him slip through the tight ring of muscles, then still again. "Don't stop," I beg.

Then pulling back just slightly, Archer looks at me, then pushes completely inside me. "Mine!" he groans. "I need to know you're mine, Mallory Halston."

I have never felt so full, not just with him inside me but also in my head and my heart. Everything about him consumes me. "Yes, yours," I cry out as he pulls back and plunges deep inside me.

Leaning over my body, he kisses me, his tongue mimicking the actions going on in my ass. Pulling his mouth away, Archer grips my ankles and pounds inside me. It's not enough.

"More! Harder! Give it to me!" I cry out. My hand wraps around my dick, and I tug hard, working myself at the same punishing pace as him.

"Christ, I'm not going to last. I want you to come. Come for me, Mallory," he cries out and can't stop.

"FUCK! ARCHER! FUUUUUUUUUUUCK!" I scream out his name as I come. Ropes of cum pelt my stomach and chest. I don't know how I produced so much after I'd come already. But then I feel Archer stiffen further, and he roars out my name. The heat of his orgasm fills me. Even through the condom, I can feel him pouring his load.

He collapses on top of me, and I feel my cum squish between us, but I don't care. I want his skin on mine. As I gaze into his still-unfocused eyes, I watch the haze clear, and he sees me. Dipping his head down, he kisses me tenderly, almost reverently.

"Shit, Mallory, I knew you'd be good, but I hadn't imagined just how good. I'm never going to let you go. You get that, right?" He kisses me again before I can answer. As he lifts his weight off me, I feel him slip out of me. He stands, drags the condom off his now-flaccid dick and throws it in the trash. "I'll get a washcloth, honey. Stay still."

Just moments later, Archer comes back from the bathroom and kneels back on the bed, wiping me down, cleaning off the residue all sticky on my stomach before cleaning between my legs. Throwing the cloth back in the direction of the bathroom, he flops next to me. Turning my head to him, I chuckle. He catches my eye and joins me; soon we are laughing hard.

"Shit, Archer, you sure don't hold back!" I laugh.

"No, no, I don't. Are you okay with that? I meant every word of it. You're mine, and I won't let go of you." His head faces me, and I can see the honesty. Surprisingly, I find myself nodding, agreeing with him.

We lie quietly until my stomach growls, making some terrible noises. "I guess I'd better order that pizza now." Archer laughs and slides off the bed again. "Anything you don't like on your pizza?"

I shake my head. "Nope, I'm happy to take whatever you want."

Smiling again, Archer's eyes sparkle. "Good to know, sugar. That's good to know."

When I wake, it's still dark outside, but I'm not sure what time it is. I look across at Archer. He really is beautiful, but this is all too much for me. I can't let this move on this quickly. I need to keep my head down and my grades up, or I'll lose my college grants. I know what we both said to each other, but I'm going with it just being in the heat of the moment. He's not really that into me; claiming me as his wasn't a serious demand.

Slipping slowly out of the bed, I grab my clothes and quickly pull them on. I must feel about on the floor for my Converse but find them and tiptoe out of the room.

I look at my phone now and see it's three thirty. Shoving my feet into my shoes, I head out of the apartment. I hurry for the elevator to arrive, suddenly panicking that Archer could wake and notice me gone.

He really is an amazing man, and damn, he knows how to fuck, but I can't get this involved. He'll end up bored of the college kid, and I'll be the one broken hearted.

The doorman nods at me, but I don't say anything. Breaking out into a jog, I make quick work of getting back to my dorm.

As I collapse into my lumpy, uncomfortable bed, I close my eyes and let sleep capture me again.

Chapter

Four

Waking up slowly, my brain confused yet again, I try to work out why I'm here. I remember bolting form Archer's apartment. I don't have work today, but I've got a study group this afternoon and an essay to write. I drag myself out of bed and into the bathroom. As I stand and pee, I hear my phone ringing, but I ignore it. Looking in the mirror, I take in my features. My shaggy black hair that could do with a cut, my dark-blue eyes so similar to my father and brothers but now so separate from them. I look the same as always, but today I feel so different. Last night, with Archer, was something so real, so life altering. Is that why I bolted? I don't believe in love at first sight, but the tug in my heart when I think of him waking up alone this morning contradicts my head. Will he be angry, or will he be relieved? Spared the embarrassment of getting me out of his apartment? Then, under the hot water from the shower, I wash the remnants of last night's sex. I can still feel him in my ass; he was that good. Maybe I was wrong. If so, it's too late to change anything now.

I'm sure he'll understand why I had to leave, or maybe he got what he wanted and won't be back again. That thought bothers me more than I thought it would. I can always try to reach out to him again and explain.

As I switch off the shower, I can hear my phone again. I can't think who needs to get hold of me unless it's work needing me in. I don't want to go in, so I ignore it again. Pulling on some clothes, I grab my bag with my laptop and all my notes, ready to make my way to the library. It's busy in here today. I guess exams are coming up, and everyone is cramming. I find a table at the back in the corner and sit with my back to the window. The sun is warm, making me ditch my hoodie. I flick open my laptop and pull out my notes and textbook. I can feel my phone buzzing again, but at least it's on silent now. I can ignore it for now. It's easy to lose track of time when I'm immersed in my work. I love this course and doing this instead of the business degree my father expected from me was my first act of rebellion.

The second was admitting who I am, and I guess that one didn't work out too well for me. I'm happy now though, happier than I was living a lie. I may not have the luxuries I was used to, but this feels more real. I know I'm working hard at school, and I have a job that pays me well enough to eat.

My phone buzzes again. I'm ready to throw it out of the window. I need to get this essay finished before study group. I'm in the coffee shop all day tomorrow on a double shift.

An hour later, I'm finished. I've checked and double-checked, and all I need to do is email it to my professor and I'm done. When I stand and stretch, I feel all the muscles in my back flex and contract. With my arms over my head, I stretch the kinks out. My stomach rumbles now, so I head out of the library and wander down to the cafeteria to grab something to eat.

By the time I turn in for the night, my head is buzzing. I've had so much to think about today. The guys in my study group are awesome and so bright. We bounce ideas and answers off each other. It's just not the best thing to do before bed. My head is so full of information I know I won't sleep. I dig my earbuds out for my phone and switch on some music.

I tune out everything and relax. As I drift off to sleep, I think of Archer again and wonder if I'll ever see him again. Somehow, the thought of that saddens me. Have I missed out on something good?

The next morning brings the joys of ten hours of serving coffee to every kind of person there is. I'll get the orders that are a yard long with venti-iced skinny hazelnut macchiato, sugar-free syrup, extra shot, light ice, no whip or grande chai tea latte, three pump, skim milk, lite water, no foam, extra hot. What the hell is lite water? These people really need to get a grasp of what's important in life. Shit, would they make that shit at home for themselves? Fuck no!

So, with that in mind, I head into work. I walk through to the serving area from the kitchen and see the place is already swamped. Tying my apron around my waist, I walk over and stand next to Carl.

"Hey, bud, you okay?" I ask as he looks up and smiles.

"Yeah, it's been crazy since we opened. You here all day?" He grins because he already knows the answer.

"Fucker!" I mutter under my breath, but I smile at him.

I'm busy, hell scratch that, I'm rushed off my damn feet for the next few hours. Then there's a lull before the crazy lunchtime crowd. I lean back against the counter behind me, not paying any attention because Jessie is there. Carl had finished his shift, saying a quick goodbye as Jessie took over.

"Mallory, there's a man asking for you." Jessie nudges me, making me look up. There looking so stunningly handsome, but also so incredibly pissed is Archer Hawkins. My heart beats faster at the sight of him, something I didn't expect. His grim face soon turns any happy feeling off.

"Archer, it's good to see you. What can I get you? Your usual?" I know I'm talking shit, but his eyes bore into me.

"Fuck coffee. I would like a moment of your time, please," he speaks pleasantly, but I can tell he's angry. Shit, hasn't he ever gotten up and left in the middle of the night? I'll bet he has.

"I can't, Archer. I'm on a double shift. I haven't got time today." I look as apologetic as I can. I reckon I could take a break. It's quiet for now, but he's too intense for me to deal with now.

"You owe me, Mallory. You owe me an explanation. Why didn't you answer your phone yesterday?"

"That was you? How did you get my number? Y'know what, never mind. I'm sorry, Archer, but I'm busy here today. I can't talk now."

"What time do you finish?"

"Nine," I answer reluctantly. I know he's not going to leave me until he knows.

"Then I will see you at nine." He turns and stalks out.

"Wow! That was intense. What did you do, kick his puppy?" Jessie asks.

"I left him in the middle of the night," I mutter.

"Ouch! No wonder he's pissed. He's hot! Why d'you leave?"

"It seemed like a good idea at the time. Y'know, the whole walk of shame the next morning? I didn't want to do that."

"Not so much now though, right?"

"What d'you reckon?" I get back to work and get rushed through the two hours that's lunchtime and then again through the evening post-day coffee to get them home. Some of these guys are in here three times a day and at six or seven bucks a cup, they throw their money away. Idiots.

At last, I can take off my apron and hand it over to the night staff. I say a general goodbye and head out through the kitchen to the staff entrance. I can't decide if I want him, Archer, there or not. I want him to want me enough to fight for me, but I'm not sure I'm up for his anger simply because he was left. I grab my hoodie from the clothes hook and pull it over my head.

I see him as soon as I push the door open. Archer leans against the wall. I can see the tension pouring from his body. Every tendon and sinew seems so tightly strung, so ready to snap.

"Archer," I greet him as he pushes himself away from the wall.

"Really? That's all you've got to say? You left our bed, Mallory. In the middle of the night, according to the night porter. Is that your usual M.O? Because when I closed my eyes that night, I felt so complete. So happy that I had found the one, the man that would change my life. Was I just a hookup to you?"

I'm astounded at his passion and hurt. I never took his words that seriously. I thought he was doing the Big I Am. Here's my code to my floor and all that shit. So, what do I say? Do I apologize? No, that doesn't sit comfortably. I guess the truth is the only way forward.

"When I woke up, it suddenly felt too much, too overpowering. You told me I was yours. You kept saying 'you're mine.' I guess when I lay there in the dark, it all scared the crap out of me. I didn't know how much of it was true, or how much of it was a way for you to tap my ass. Fuck. Archer! I don't know, it was all too intense."

"So, you thought it was better to leave than to wake me and talk to me? Shit, Mallory, how could you have dismissed everything we shared so easily, so callously? Fuck, I woke feeling so damn good until I saw the empty side of the bed. Damn, you hurt me, Mallory."

"Hey, hold on! How come this is all about you? Have you never woken and sneaked out?" I see a shimmer of guilt slide over his face. "Yeah, you have. I'm guessing you just thought I'd better get outta here because, shit, you may have to have the awkward conversation in the morning. The one where both of you pretend to have something important going on. Of course, you have, so think of this from my point of view for a moment, will you?"

I watch him sag back against the wall and shake his head. "Don't you feel anything for me, Mallory? Did you not mean it?"

"Archer, I meant everything I said, I just needed a breather, a space to collect my thoughts. I knew this would go one of two ways. You would either ignore me and never see me again, and I would put the night down to us being horny and willing. Or, you would come back and fight me over it."

"Which one did you expect? Which one do you want?" he asks me quietly.

"Honestly, Archer, I expected to never see you again, but that's very different from what I want." I look at him and see him tense again. "I want you to want me again. I want you to mean what you said because I meant it. I want to see you want me, for me, for who I am." It's my turn to fall back against the wall, exhausted, not just from standing on my feet for ten hours, but from trying to decipher my feelings and how I would react to seeing him.

"Oh, honey, I meant every fucking word of it. I have never felt anything like the way you make me feel. I want you, Mallory, but more importantly, I want you to want me the same way. I won't do this if we're not both in this for real."

"Then I'm with you. I'm in this with you, for the whole nine yards." I smile shyly at him, but it soon turns into a gasp as he stalks towards me, predator-like.

"I want to kiss you, Mallory, but only if you mean it. Only if you're prepared to stay the night, the whole night?"

"I won't leave again, Archer, not until you tell me." I squirm as he leans into my body, melding his to mine.

"That's fucking good to know. I'm never going to tell you to leave." His emerald-green eyes have darkened as he lowers his head to mine. The moment his lips touch mine his eyelids flicker shut as he presses harder against my lips. Then it's darkness as mine close and I'm lost in his kiss. The sweet slip of his tongue over the seam of my lips has my blood pressure rising and my heart pounding. My hands reach out for his hips as I clutch him to me. The air is full of a deep groan, but I don't know if it's from him or me. I feel the bulge in his jeans swell and harden as he pushes into me.

There's a clatter of a dumpster lid being opened and shut that brings us both back into the present. "We need to get out of here. Where do you want to go, Mallory?"

"Your place," I mumble against his neck.

"Our place," he counters me.

"Not yet, Archer. Don't push me."

"Okay, I won't. Much." I feel his grin on my neck as he answers me. "Let's go." He clasps my hand and looks at me. "Are you with me, Mallory?"

"I'm with you," I answer confidently.

Chapter

Five

"Hey, sugar, what time do you want me to come over?" Archer's deep voice sends shivers through my body. Even over the phone, he affects me. We've been together for three months now, seeing each other every spare moment we can. His work is crazy hectic at times, especially in the run-up to him going to court. Right now, he's just working his normal hours, so he has been pestering me to move in with him every spare minute he can.

"Anytime, baby. I'm all packed up and ready for you." Okay, so I caved. I want to be with him just as much but thought we were moving too fast and held off, until now. Now I'm ready to be with him.

"Awesome, I'm on my way. See you in twenty." He blows a kiss down the phone and ends the call.

I look around my room and see everything important to me packed up. When I left the apartment my father provided, I just took what was personal to me. The only reminders of my family are the photos of my brother and sister. I miss them but haven't been able to reach out to them. All ties have been severed by my parents. They could've moved away for all I know. I wish I could say I didn't care, but it's not true. It still fucking kills me to know they turned me away because of my sexuality. Something as simple as who I choose to love has wrecked a family, all for appearances.

I hear a knock on the door and open it to the most gorgeous sight, Archer. I softly sigh as he leans in to capture my mouth with his.

"Have you missed me?" His hands grip my hips as he walks me backwards into the dorm room.

"Actually, you've caught me at a bad time, I've got a hookup from Grindr on his way. Sorry, we'll have to do this another time." I bite my lip so I don't smile.

"Really, I'm sure I'd be better than him. I bet he can't make you come as I quickly as I can or torture you slowly until you beg for release. Choose wisely, Mallory."

"Fuck, you've got me so damn hard!" I moan.

"Good!" He winks and steps away.

"What? No… wait, you've gotta do something about it. I can't carry heavy boxes with a stiffy. I could damage it."

"Hmm, maybe you shouldn't have teased me." Archer grins but steps closer to me again. His hand snakes down my body and cups the bulge in my pants. "Would be a shame to waste this, I suppose," he murmurs dirtily in my ear before biting down sharply on the lobe.

Archer is on his knees and has me out and in his mouth so quickly, I almost step back in surprise. I'm engulfed in his mouth and in his throat in seconds. My fingers grip his hair as he works me frantically with his fist and mouth, and he's so damn right. I know I'm going to explode so damn quickly.

"Fuck, yes. Yes, don't stop, baby. Take me deep," I groan as his hand leaves my dick and grabs my ass cheeks, separating them so he can push his finger inside me. I know the moment he does that, he'll go for my prostate and then it's game over.

I throw my head back and roar out my orgasm as he sucks and strokes me through the aftershocks. Then standing, he pulls my pants up and zips me closed before giving me a wink and picking up the first box.

"You're welcome." He laughs loudly as I stand still, my mind in a daze. "You gonna help me?"

I shake my head and drag myself back into the present and then follow his lead and pick up a box.

"That is all away, are you sure you don't want more of it out?" Archer looks at me. I think he was surprised at the lack of it all, eight or ten boxes isn't much to sum up over twenty-two years of life.

"Nah, most of it's shit anyway. You've got my vinyls out, and that's good enough for me." We've flopped down on his sofa and have a pizza order on its way.

"Don't just think of this as my place, Mal. It's yours too. Do what you want with your stuff. It'll be nice to see someone else's shit all over the place." He grins. The buzzer at the door goes off. "That'll be dinner. You want to grab a couple beers?"

I wander down to the kitchen, and I hear him open the door, but it doesn't sound like a conversation going on between a delivery guy and a paying customer. I push the door of the fridge shut and walk back to the living room, uncapping both bottles as I go.

"Look, it's just not a good time. No, nothing is wrong. In fact, everything is most definitely very right." Archer sounds strained, but I still smile at the everything's right comment. "Okay, yeah, fine. Sunday brunch is doable. We'll be there. Yes, both of us. I'm not messing around anymore."

I can't hear anymore, and then the door closes, only for the buzzer to go again. At least this time, it's gotta be our dinner.

We chat comfortably about nothing much, but I can tell Archer is pissed at something, and it must be whoever was at the door. I'm not having that ruin our first night living together. Sitting up, I swing my leg over his so I'm straddling him. Looking down, I give him a smile and watch as his tongue dampens his lip in expectation of a kiss.

"You wanna tell me what got you pissed, babe? Or am I gonna have to fuck your bad mood away?" I pitch my hips forward, grinding against him. His eyes darken when I keep my hips rolling. He grips my ass hard, holding me against him. I can feel his erection pressing up to mine, making us both moan.

"Hmm, I think I'd like you to fuck it away," he murmurs.

"Yeah? You're gonna let me top?" I've taken him a few times before, but I love him in my ass so much, I tend to bottom more. I know Archer loves to top.

"Yeah, I want that fat cock of yours in my ass." He bites down on his lip as I run my hands through his hair.

"I think I want you bent over this sofa," I whisper.

"Fuck, yeah!"

I clamber off him and reach in the drawer in the coffee table. We worked out early on that we need supplies in every room. I grab the lube and a condom, then shuck out of my sweat shorts and T-shirt. Archer is the fastest stripper going and is naked by the time I turn back to him.

"Get in position, baby. I fancy it hard and fast." I run my hand softly down his back as he leans on the sofa, feeling the muscles bunch under my fingers as he writhes. With his knees on the cushions, resting his elbows on the leather, he looks at me. His pupils are so dark I can hardly see any of the vibrant green I love so much.

"Spread your legs, Archer. I wanna see that hole." I pant, desperate to be inside him.

Widening his stance, he leans his chest on the couch and pulls his cheeks apart. I can see his tight hole, and I fucking love it.

"Ready, baby?" I tip the bottle of lube and let it stream down his crack to his ring. I watch as it runs over his pucker, making it twitch. My finger follows and pushes inside him, making him groan loudly. Pumping it in and out a couple times, I add a second.

"I'm ready, Mallory. Fuck me now," Archer cries out needily. I pull out my fingers and reach for the condom as Archer turns his head. "No condom, we've been tested. I want to feel you, all of you."

"Y'sure? I don't mind carrying on using them." I'm shocked he wants to go bareback.

"Just fuck me, Mallory. Get that gorgeous dick in my ass now!"

I'm not going to argue. I squeeze more lube into my hand and stroke it over my dick. Then lining the head up to his hole, I push in. "Oh, God! I have never felt anything this damn good. Shit, Archer, you are so hot and tight. Fuck!"

"God! Yes, yes," Archer cries out as I thrust all the way inside him. This feels so damn good.

Picking up speed, I grip his hips and piston in and out of his ass. Leaning over him, I lick at the sweat beading on his neck. I scrape my teeth over his tender spot behind his ear, knowing this will tip him over. I suck hard, bruising his skin. I feel him shudder as his orgasm builds. Sliding one hand from his hip, I grasp his dick and stroke him hard and fast, matching it to my thrusts.

As Archer cries out, his cum fills my hand, and his ass tightens around me, gripping me hard and making my own climax explode inside him. I feel the heat of my release flooding him as he shudders and flexes around me.

Collapsing down on his back, we slide down, lying half on, half off the sofa. My dick slides out as he falls into my lap, and I hold him tight to my chest. Kissing his face and hair as I wipe the sweat from his forehead.

"I fucking love you, Archer Hawkins." Tipping his head up to my face, I pour my feelings into a kiss.

When Archer pulls away from me, his voice is shaky. "Not as much as I love you."

"More," I whisper. "Forever and always."

Standing on shaky legs, we stumble to the bedroom and flop down on the bed. "We should shower. I'm all sweaty, and so are you."

"You like me sweaty." Archer laughs.

"I do, but I'm sure you'd like to wash the cum off your body." I laugh. "C'mon I'll help with all the hard to reach places."

It doesn't take us long, and we get back into bed. I'm lying with my head on Archer's chest, and our legs are entwined. I can tell he's back to brooding about his visitor.

"Talk to me, baby. What's going on?" I tip my head up to look at him as he sighs.

"It was my mother at the door. She bugs me at the best of times, and she knows I hate when she turns up unannounced. I'll have to remind the desk to let me know if she's on her way up."

"What did she want? Does she know about me?" I'm worried now that I may have made his life more complicated. His mother is a difficult woman, a woman of power. As a Supreme Court Judge, she's important, and she knows it. She thrives on it. Just like my father—a passive-aggressive bully.

"She knows, but my mother doesn't like to admit I'm gay. She thinks if she doesn't acknowledge it, it will just go away. I've never hidden it, and I'm not ashamed of it. I won't hide you, and I'm sure as fuck not ashamed of you." Archer dips his head down and kisses my hair.

"At least she didn't disown you like mine did. One minute, I was the pride of the family. The next, I was out on my ass. No apartment, no car, and no college fund." I match his sigh. "But I got you, and you make it all worth it. If I hadn't had to get a job, I would never have met you."

"I've agreed to go to brunch on Sunday, so be ready to be subjected to her interrogation."

"What? Why am I going? Shit, Arch. I don't want to make it worse. I can stay here."

"No way! If I've got to put up with her, so do you. You can't leave me alone with her." Archer wraps his arm around my neck, laughing. "We're a team, sugar!"

"What's your dad like? Is he cool with who you are? You don't talk about him much," I question.

"My dad is okay, but my mother is in charge in that house." He snorts. "Please come."

"Fine, but only because I love you."

I feel his breathing even out as he falls asleep. My head is full of a woman I have yet to meet but I'm sure is going to dislike me. I wonder if she'll know who I am, or more interestingly, who my father is. Hell, they probably know each other.

Chapter
Six

"You ready for this?" Archer holds my hand, and I know he's not happy about doing this. He says we can walk out at any time, if she gets to be too much.

"Nope, not one bit, so let's do it!" I let out a shaky laugh.

Archer rings the doorbell on the large impressive oak door, then steps back. I look at him quizzically.

"You don't have a key?"

"Oh, I do, but she prefers it if I knock. Just don't ask." He smiles.

As the door swings open, I come face to face with Archer's mother. They look alike. Both have blond hair and green eyes, and chiseled cheekbones. Archer's eyes sparkle bright with glee and mischief most of the time. His mother's are cold and sharp as they look us over. Archer's hair is soft and messy. I love running my fingers through it. Hers is stiff and lacquered in a rigid knot at the base of her neck, making her skin look too tight. I'm pretty sure there's some major

Botox going on, and I doubt she can crack a smile. Her tailored linen cream pants and silk lilac blouse are so smart and wrinkle-free, there's no way she has made brunch.

"Archer, you're late." She sneers.

"Good morning to you too, Mother. And no, I'm not. I'm on time." He looks at his watch and taps it. "You said eleven, and it's ten fifty-nine."

"Then you should have been here five minutes ago." She steps back and opens the door further. "You didn't say you were bringing a friend, Archer. How typical of you."

"Yes, I did. You just chose to ignore it. This is Mallory Halston, my boyfriend, not just my friend." Archer's hand still holds on firmly to mine. I'm not sure if it's to stop me from bolting or him.

"Halston as in Martin Halston's son?" Her eyes sharp fix on mine.

"Yes." Then mutter, "Unfortunately," under my breath.

"Hmm, I thought I recognized the name. You're not much like him, are you?" she declares rather than question.

"I try not to be. My father is a difficult man, Mrs. Hawkins."

"Are we actually going to get some brunch, Mother? Or just have twenty questions here?" Archer is pissed, I can tell. I squeeze his hand, and he returns it.

"Of course, this way." The infamous Supreme Court Judge Valerie Hawkins leads the way through the kitchen and out into the immaculate garden. The large wooden table is laden down with every kind of breakfast product known to man, by the look of things.

A man stands and smiles at Archer. This must be his father. Walking swiftly to Archer, he embraces him. "Good to see you, Archer. It's been too long." He turns to look at me, his smile still in place. "Hello, young man. Who's this, Archie?"

"Dad, this is Mallory, my boyfriend." Archer smiles.

"Very nice to meet you, sir." I offer my hand, and he shakes it firmly.

"Welcome, Mallory. Please call me Warwick. Come now, let's eat."

We take our seats and Archer loads my plate with pancakes and bacon. He knows what I like, and we're all soon eating in an uncomfortable silence.

"So, Mallory, do you intend to follow in your father's footsteps and take up a place next to him in commerce?" Valerie asks.

"No, I'm in my final year in college studying engineering."

"Really? How disappointing for your father. Always so sad when a child doesn't want to emulate his father." She's back to sneering again.

"Unfortunately, I disappoint my father in more ways than not joining his firm." I look at Archer as he grips my hand in support.

"Yes, I can imagine."

"Mother, stop this now. You invited us here so at least have the decency to be polite, or we'll leave," Archer snaps.

"For goodness sake, Archer, stop making such a drama. I'm just asking," she snaps back. It turns into a staring competition.

"Valerie, that's enough," Mr. Hawkins speaks for the first time, and she breaks her eyes away from her son.

The next ninety minutes are painful. I just want to whisk Archer away back to his apartment and wrap my arms around him. Finally, Archer places his knife and fork down and lifts his napkin from his lap to place on the table.

"Thank you for a delicious brunch, Mother. We really need to be going." He stands, and I follow suit. "Dad, I'll speak to you later in the week."

"Yes, I expect you have things to do. I'm sure you can see yourselves out." Valerie waves her hand derisively.

"Warwick, it's been a pleasure to meet you, and Mrs. Hawkins, thank you for your hospitality." I offer my hand to Archer's father, and we shake again.

"I'll walk with you both," he offers as we move back into the house. As soon as we are inside, he speaks again. "Mallory, thank you for coming with Archer today. You both look very happy together. I hope you and your family reconnect soon."

"Oh, you all know what happened?" I feel myself redden with embarrassment.

"Don't be embarrassed, Mallory. I know how difficult your father is. I wish you both happiness together."

"Thanks, Dad. I'll call you in the week," Archer replies for me.

As soon as we walk outside, Archer heaves a huge sigh of relief. "C'mon, sugar, let's get out of here."

"Jesus, Archer. How do you cope with her?" I pull him into a hug, and we stand together for a few minutes just reconnecting.

We settle into a routine quickly. I've finished this year in college and have picked up some extra daytime shifts at the coffee shop. I'm banking as much as I can so I'm not living off Archer's salary, even if it is a huge one. In fact, our first argument was over me paying my way. Archer is more than happy to let me keep all my own money and he carries on with all the utility bills and grocery shopping.

"I've done it for so long now, sugar. It doesn't matter. It's only food. I'd rather you saved your money. That way you can pay off your student loans." Archer looks at me and smiles.

"That's ridiculous, Archer. I need to pay my way. I'm not living off you. We're a partnership. Please let me do this." I stare at him, not smiling.

"Fine, you can buy the groceries one week, and I'll do it the next. But, once you're back in college, you don't pay. Your hours at the coffee shop will go down again, and it's an important year. Your final year will be hard enough without you busting a gut at work."

"Okay, now come here and kiss me."

"Now you're talking." Archer steps into my arms and kisses me hard.

Chapter
Seven

"No! I've told you at least three times. Don't do this, Mother, it will only make you look stupid! Stop trying to pretend it isn't happening." Archer paces the room, scowling, his phone is up to his ear. "You will look like a fool, Mother. The Urquharts know exactly who I am. Marcus is in my firm, for fuck's sake!"

He continues to listen for a few short minutes before he stops. He must sense me looking at him. His eyes raise from looking at the floor to meet mine. He grimaces and shakes his head at me.

"Mallory will be attending the gala with me. Whatever you choose to do will only make you look foolish. Don't do it, I mean that."

Archer throws his cell onto the sofa where it bounces off and hits the floor.

"You wanna talk about it?" I ask quietly.

"No, it's not important. My mother is being her usual overbearing self. There's nothing we need to worry about, I promise." He pops a

43

kiss on my mouth.

"Okay, but I'm guessing this has something to do with the date you need to bring with you on Saturday night? Am I right?" I joke.

"You got that, did you?" He shakes his head dryly. "It seems she's arranged a date for me in the shape of Cecily Urquhart. The sad thing is I've been her beard, as it were, in the past but we have both realized that at thirty, we need to man up to our parents and move past our sexuality."

"Yeah, but that always works out well." I give a dry chuckle, thinking back to my own parents' rationalization of what *their* truth was.

"Honey, there's no way I'm going to this incredibly stuffy, boring night without you holding my hand. I can't wait to get you in a tuxedo." His eyes darken as he scans my body. "Then out of it at the end of the night."

"Is that so? I'd better rent one then. You can practice then if you'd like." I bite my lip, knowing it drives him crazy.

"There will be plenty of nights out that will need you in a tux. We might as well buy one. Let's go now."

"I'm not sure I can afford to buy one, Arch." I know what he's going to say. Any arguments we have, which aren't many, are over money.

"I'm buying it, Mal. It's because of me that you need one, which means it's up to me to buy it. Don't argue with me. It's not worth it."

"Fine."

Of course, it's a stunningly tailor-made suit that fits like a dream. I smooth the fabric down over my chest as I take a final check in the mirror. I see Archer walk up behind me. Wrapping his arms around my waist, he leans in and drops a kiss on my neck.

Breathing in deeply, he groans. "Fuck, you look and smell divine. Let's not go. We can stay here and fuck all night."

It's my turn to moan when his teeth scrape over my heated skin. "No, but we don't need to stay too long. We don't, do we?" Our eyes meet as we look at our reflections.

"Mallory, we can leave straight after dinner."

"Let's go then."

Archer drives us, and we're soon pulling up outside the Hilton, and he hands the car over to the valet. "Don't bury it in the middle; we're not staying too long," he informs the young lad and hands him a fifty-dollar bill.

"I'm sure you didn't need to tip him that much, Arch," I grumble at his extravagance.

"I know that, but he will do as I asked because of it. Come on, I really want this night over with."

I know the minute we walk in this is a mistake. Valerie Hawkins is waiting in the foyer with Warwick, another equally uptight couple, and two very beautiful women.

"I knew you'd do this, Archer. Why do you have to be so defiant?" she snarls, not even looking at me.

"It's not defiance, Mother. It's me bringing the man I love just as I said I would." Archer walks up to his father and shakes his hand then turns to the woman I assume is Cecily. "It's lovely to see you, Cecily, and you too, Miranda." He kisses both of their cheeks and then tugs me gently forward.

"This must be Mallory." Cecily smiles at me warmly. "I've heard so much about you." She kisses my cheek. "Don't let the witch get to you," she whispers, making me cough out a nervous laugh.

45

"Well, I suppose this dreadful situation can be salvaged. Archer, your date can go in with the other women, then you can follow with Cecily." Valerie sneers.

"No, Mother. I will walk in with Mallory holding my hand. I am not hiding him. Most of the people in there know I'm gay and have a boyfriend. It's just you making a scene about it. Get over it. I mean it, it stops now."

I watch her face turn the most dreadful puce color as she looks ready to explode as they stare at each other.

"It's good to see you again, Mallory." Warwick shakes my hand then gives his wife a glare that gives away his displeasure with her. "Valerie, let's go inside now. Everyone is here."

The night is surprisingly fun. Cecily and Miranda are a brilliantly funny couple who are so in love, it's beautiful to see. We ignore Valerie just as much as she ignores us. Dancing with Archer's arms around me is an amazing feeling. Very different than his usual grinding I get when we are in clubs.

"What are you smiling about?" he asks as he twirls me around.

"I was thinking this is a very different way of dancing for us, not our usual hot and sweaty routine." I pull him closer. "Just as fucking sexy though." I let him feel my arousal as I press our hips together.

"Maybe it's time for us to leave then?" he murmurs, then licks the shell of my ear.

"Fuck, yes." I sigh.

We say a brief good night to Cecily, promising to have dinner together soon. Archer doesn't even bother to seek his parents out. I notice Warwick watching us with a minute smile on his face. I mouth "good night" to him and he nods.

When we get home, Archer does everything he promised me—stripping me slowly out of my tuxedo, kissing every patch of bare skin as he reveals it. My dick is painfully hard, and I can feel the dampness of my precum as it leaks onto my underwear.

"Oh, my ever-loving Lord." He moans as my pants slide down my legs, leaving me standing in a black jock strap. "Thank God I didn't see this before, or we would've never left the house."

Kneeling in front of me, he sucks on the head of my dick through the damp fabric. His hands are tight on my ass, kneading the tight globes. A finger traces down my crack then back up again, teasing me as he never quite reaches my needy hole.

"Archer, I need you inside me. I need it hard tonight," I whimper as his teeth tease the fabric down, exposing my dark-red, weeping cock.

"You got it, my love." His teeth scrape over the mushroom head then his tongue laps at the slit, before sucking on the precum beading there.

I step away and clamber up onto our bed, pulling my underwear off as I wait for him. With no regard for the expensive clothes, Archer undresses so quickly it's seconds before he climbs up between my legs.

"Turn over then, on your hands and knees."

As soon as I'm in position, his mouth is on me. I love him rimming me; he's a master at it and can keep me on the brink of an orgasm with just his tongue.

I shamelessly grind onto his tongue, but soon he pulls away, making me cry out for more. His hand comes down hard on my ass cheek, making me yelp, begging for more rather than to stop. The coldness of the lube he pours slides down my crack to my hole as he spanks me again and again.

"Get inside me, Archer," I growl, looking at him over my shoulder.

"I haven't stretched you yet, lover."

"No, rough and hard! Get inside me and pound," I bark at him.

Then it's the head of his cock at the entrance to my body that makes me shudder in expectation. He slams inside me, balls deep in the first thrust. My back dips as I arch my ass up to him. Yes, this is what I want.

"I'm good. Go, baby. Fuck me," I say, giving him the green light.

Dammit, he does exactly that. Plunging hard and fast, his hips like pistons as he fucks me. Sweat pours over my body as he slaps my ass again. This sets off my orgasm.

"Oh, God, Archer. So good, so, so good. I'm gonna come, baby. You ready?" I pant as my arms collapse, leaving my ass in the air and my head on the sheet.

"Fuck yes, you're so fucking hot. Squeeze me tight, Mallory." He sounds like he's gritting his teeth as he still powers into me.

As I clench around him, he hits my prostate, and I groan loudly. Without even touching my dick, my orgasm shoots from me. Archer stiffens, then I feel the white heat of his release filling my channel as he pumps more and more inside me.

Collapsing down on top of me, I feel his lips over my neck as he kisses, sucks, and bites me. His dick finally stops twitching inside me, and he tenderly pulls out of me. Damn, I'm going to feel this for days, I think happily.

After he falls over to lie next to me, I turn my face to look at him. His eyes are glazed, and he has a sex-drunk grin on his face.

"You are one fucking hot piece of ass, Mallory, my love." He sniggers, making me join in.

"We need to shower, babe. We're all sweaty." I reach up and cup his face. Turning into my palm, he showers it with kisses.

"I like you sweaty." He smiles.

Chapter
Eight

At last a day off. I've worked seven days straight after Carl went sick. I plan to do absolutely nothing today. Archer is at work and has given me strict instructions to rest, so who am I to argue.

Dressed in just sweatpants, I lounge on the sofa watching Netflix when the buzzer on the door sounds. I'm not expecting anyone or any deliveries. I'm tempted to ignore it. It goes off again.

"Fuck it!" I pause the program on the TV and stride over to the door, pulling it open. Shit! Valerie Hawkins stands there with her permanent sneer on her Botox-frozen face.

"Mrs. Hawkins, Archer isn't here. He's at work." I just want her gone.

"I know that, Mallory. It was you I wanted to talk to." She steps past me, even though I haven't invited her in.

"So, what do you want?" I ask as I shut the door behind her.

"You. I want you out of here and out of my son's life. You're not good enough for him." She casts her eye around the room, which luckily is clean and tidy, looking for something to criticize.

"Excuse me?" I can't believe what she's saying to me. "Archer is a grown man, a very intelligent and successful man. I think he's capable of making a decision on his life. Archer loves me as much I love him. You have no say in this. I think you should leave." I cross my hands over my chest as she looks me up and down.

"Don't be ridiculous. Archer has a hugely successful career ahead of him, and he needs to snap out of the gay stupidity and get real. He needs a wife and family. Do you really think he'll make it to being a judge with you hanging around? You made a complete spectacle of yourself, embarrassing Archer and all of his friends and superiors at the gala last month. I've spoken to his bosses to assure them it won't happen again. You're not the one for him, so this is what I am prepared to do."

I watch her reach into her bag and pull out an envelope. She smirks as she offers it to me.

"In here is a check for twenty-five thousand dollars. Take it and leave him. I don't care where you go. Just leave this city and never see my son again. If you don't accept this, I will be speaking to your college professors, and I'm sure I can persuade them to fail you in your final exams. Don't mess with me, boy. You're not big enough to play my games. Take the money, Halston, and leave."

I stare at her as she holds out the envelope. Her hand is steady, and she locks her eyes on me. Without saying another word, I turn on my heels and open the front door again.

"Get out!" I growl. "You are an evil bitch. You get out of here."

"Fine, fifty thousand. I'm sure that will be enough for you to forget about him." She pulls out another envelope.

"I told you to leave." I shake my head at her.

She takes a step closer and hisses at me. "You won't win this, Halston. I will ruin you." Dropping the second envelope on the table by the door, she struts past me.

"I will be telling your son all about your visit. Expect a call from him later. Get out of here now and don't come back."

I slam the door as hard as I can the moment she's out of the door. "FUUUUUCK!!!!" I shout aloud and storm back to the sofa. I need to text Archer. Grabbing my phone, I swipe it open and hit my contacts list. My fingers shake as they hover over his number. I'm desperate to call him, but I know he's busy. A text will have to do.

Hey Baby,
Please come straight home.
We need to talk.
ILY
Xxx

I immediately get a message back

Mallory,
What's happened?
Have I done something wrong?
I love you, honey.
Xxx

Shit! I don't want him to think that.

No, baby.
It's not you.
It could never be you.
I need you.
Xxx

I get another.

I'm on my way now.
Xxx

Damn, I didn't want to scare him, but I need him. I need him to hold me and tell me it's going to be all right. It will only take him ten minutes or so to get here, and I pace the floor, waiting, trying to ignore the envelope that seems so ominous.

The door swings open wide, and Archer stands in front of me. He's red in the face from running, by the look of it. Storming up to me, he drags me into his arms. As I duck my head into his neck, I break down.

Our relationship has been full on from the start. I have given myself totally to him. My heart lives for him, and I know he feels the same way. He has loved me from the beginning. He tells me every day. Even when we are fucking hard and dirty, I can feel his love for me. For me, he is my forever. I can't imagine not having him with me for the rest of my life.

"Tell me what's happened, Mallory. What has you so upset? You're scaring me, my love." Archer holds me close. I can feel him sway as he rocks me.

"Archer"—I lift my head up to see his face—"am I holding you back? Is you being with me going to damage your career?"

I watch the shocked expression on his face turn to anger. "What the fuck has gone on? Of course, you're not holding me back. I love you. We're a team, you and me." I look as his eyes skim around the room and then fix on the envelope, his mother's handwriting on the front. "What is that, Mallory?"

"That is a check for fifty K," I answer, my voice shaking.

"I think we need to sit and you start from the beginning." His eyes are still fixed on the envelope. Then he drops his head and kisses me softly.

I sit next to him, but he pulls me onto his lap with his arms wrapped around my waist, keeping me close and centered.

"Your mother paid me a visit. She said I had embarrassed you and your friends. That she had spoken to your bosses." I continue to run through everything that was said. I feel his hand tighten around me as he gets more pissed off.

"That damn woman! God, she has gone too far this time." Archer lets go of me, and I slide off him. He paces the room in an instant as he tries to comprehend what has happened. He pulls his phone out of his pocket and swipes it open.

He looks at me as he waits for it to be answered. "Mother, how fucking dare you! You have no damn idea what is right for me. You need to back the fuck off out of my life! I know you haven't spoken to my boss because he told me how happy I look with Mallory."

I cringe at the rift I have caused in his family.

"You do this every time I meet someone, but this time you've gone too far. I'm gay, Mom. Nothing is going to change that. Mallory is the most important man in my life. I'd marry him today if I could. He is my future. Not some blond empty-headed woman you approve of. I'm gay. I like men. I like fucking men! You can get out of my life, I'm done with you. Don't call and don't come any fucking where close to Mallory." Archer ends the call before she can reply and strides back to me, pulling me up and against him.

"I love you, Mallory. She can't change that, I promise."

The next call Archer makes is to his best friend. I haven't met him because he lives a couple states away, but they talk all the time. This time Archer moves away and speaks quietly to his friend, not letting me know what he's talking about. I trust him completely.

Later, when we're lying in bed and I'm curled over him in my usual position, Archer runs his fingers through my hair.

"I meant it, y'know." His voice is low. "About marrying you."

"Is this a proposal?" I chuckle. "'cos it was crap." I laugh and turn my head to kiss his chest. I feel his laughter bubbling up.

"Yeah, I guess it was. I'll think how to do it properly. I want you to say yes." He laughs.

"Baby, I promise you I will say yes however you do it." I kiss him again.

"Even after everything my mother has said?"

"Your mother scares the shit out of me. The thought of her wrecking my exam results and therefore my future just to stop us from being together baffles me. Why is she so against us being together?"

"My mother hates me being gay. She ignores it most of the time and still thinks I should hide back in the closet. She says it's okay to fuck whoever I want as long as I go home to a wife afterwards." Archer's chuckle is dry and painful.

"Oh, Archer, I don't know what to say." I push myself up to look into his eyes and see such pain there.

"Just love me, Mallory. Make love to me," he whispers back.

"Always and anytime." So even though he came home to ease me, it is Archer that is suffering the most.

We make love all night, pouring everything we have into each kiss, each caress, each sigh. In the morning, we're exhausted but peaceful. Archer calls into the office and cancels all his appointments, allowing us to stay together.

We have no further contact with Valerie Hawkins. Archer has spoken to his father, and I don't think that went down too well because he was stomping around the apartment muttering under his breath. I wonder if we will get through this.

Chapter

Nine

It's my graduation day. Valerie's threats were unfounded. Whether the professors ignored her, or she didn't attempt to sabotage my life, I guess I won't ever know.

Archer is still wonderful. I have never been so happy. I look around the auditorium searching for his face and then see him. His whole face lights up, and he gives me two thumbs-ups, making me blush. I keep my eyes on him through the whole ceremony until I get nudged and it's my turn to collect my degree. I manage to get up onto the stage without falling on my ass as I still look at my man. I can hear his cheers as he whoops and hollers at me.

As I step past all the other graduates, weaving in and around them, I seek out Archer. Stopping dead in my tracks when I see him leaning against a motorcycle. There's a huge red bow wrapped around the handlebars.

"What's this?" I smile and step into his arms.

"Congratulations, Mallory. It's a graduation gift, I've seen you eye it in the bike shop for months. I love you, sugar, and I wanted to give you something special." Archer gives me his 1000w smile, and I match it. Then he steps away, and in front of everyone, he drops to his knee.

"Mallory Carter Halston, will you please do me the absolute honor of becoming my husband? I love you and promise to keep loving you for the rest of our lives," he pronounces proudly.

I look around, and it's as if the world has stopped turning. Nobody moves as they watch Archer hold out his hand and offers me a light-blue box. I can feel the tears building in my eyes as I nod.

"Yes. Oh, my God, yes!" I can see the shake in my hand as I reach out for the box. Archer stands and lifts the lid. Inside is a platinum band with an onyx band in the middle. It's elegantly perfect and timeless in its beauty.

As Archer slides the ring down my finger, the crowd around us cheers and claps. I can see phones being held up as they film or photograph us. I bet this gets on to social media, and I don't care. I want to see this moment over and over again.

"I love you, Archer. I seriously fucking love you," I whisper as my lips press up to his.

"Yeah? I reckon I love you more." Then his mouth is back on mine, and this kiss is pure ownership. Archer claims me in front of my friends and peers.

Breaking apart, I look around him to the bike. "You ready to get out of here?" I ask, looking at him as I run my hand down the sleek black paintwork and leather seat.

"Hell, yeah." Archer steps around to the other side of the bike, lifts two helmets, and offers one to me.

In minutes, we're away and racing down the wide campus roads and onto the highway. Archer has his hands on my waist, but he's not clutching at me. I can tell he feels comfortable and at ease with me riding away. Twisting and turning through the city streets, I bring us back to our apartment building. I wait at the barrier for the underground parking to lift, then drive us down to the space next to Archer's BMW.

Letting Archer climb off the bike first, I lift my helmet off and lift my leg over the bike to stand next to him. "Wow! That was awesome. Dammit, Archer, you're about to get so lucky." I grin and wrap my hand around the back of his neck, tugging him up to my body. "I can't wait to see you in leathers!"

His laughter fills me with so much happiness. The sparkle in his bright-green eyes so full of promise sends shivers over my body.

"We need to get inside and get naked. I think we've got some celebrating to do." Archer grabs my hand and drags me to the elevator.

As the door slides shut behind us, Archer pushes me against the cool steel wall and tangles his hands in my hair. "You have made me the happiest man alive. Not just because you said yes, but every minute of every day."

Leaning in to kiss me, I feel so complete. His tongue slips between my lips, tangling and dancing with my own. I'm vaguely aware of the clunk as my helmet hits the floor, and I drag him against my body. I can feel his erection pressing, rubbing my own. The ping of the elevator arriving at our floor breaks us apart. The doors slide open, and this time, it's me rushing forward to our door. Archer crowds from behind as I fumble with my key.

"Get the door open, Mallory, unless you want me to fuck you out here? I will, you know. I want inside you so damn much."

The key slips into the lock, and I push the door open. We stumble inside and pull our clothes off.

"When do you want to get married?" I ask as we lie together in the huge tub. The warm water washes over me as Archer runs his hands over my abs and down to my junk.

"Anytime, the sooner the better. I want you to have my name. I want to show the world you are mine and I am yours," Archer whispers into my ear as I lie back, my back to his chest.

"Then we need to get to City Hall and get a license. I'm happy to marry you tomorrow, or as soon as we can."

"Me too." His mouth is so close I can feel the heat of his breath on my damp skin.

"What about your mother? Will you tell her?" I hate bringing her up. Archer hasn't seen or spoken to her since her visit to me. He still speaks to his father so I guess Valerie knows we are still very much together.

"My mother is nothing to me. I won't let her anywhere near us. Us being together is what's important to me, that's all that matters." Archer leans down and kisses my neck. "

Chapter
Ten

Breakfast is lazy today. I've been given the task of getting the marriage license since Archer needs to be across town today and I'm not working. I've finally given in and handed in my notice. Now that I've got my degree, I need to look for engineering positions. Something I should have done before now, but the threat of not passing my finals has put me off searching. An honors degree should be enough to get my foot in the door somewhere good.

"I'm off to work, Mal," Archer calls to me from the hallway.

"Hold up, mister. Not so fast. I want kisses before you leave me alone." I mock-pout at him, making him laugh.

"Oh, sugar. I will always give you kisses. Come here, hot lips." He laughs and drags me into his arms. Holding my face in his palms, he kisses me soundly. "There you go. Now, I love you, and I'll see you later."

"I love you too. Be careful, Arch."

"Always." He kisses me softly. "Goodbye, Mallory."

I watch him walk out of the door, and I still can't believe my luck. This amazing, beautiful man wants me. Sighing as he shuts the door, I turn and head back to the bedroom to shower. My head is filled with promises of a good life to come.

I get back from getting the license and some lunch. I search through the job sites on the internet when there's a knock on the door. My first thought is of Valerie Hawkins, but it's two cops standing in front of me. Both of their faces look fierce.

"Can I help you?" I can't work out what they're doing here.

"Mallory Halston?" the taller of the two men ask. I nod to reply.

"Can we come in?" The taller dark-haired cop takes a small step closer, encouraging me to open the door.

"Of course." I shake my head bewildered.

When they step inside, I close the door behind them. I lead them through to the lounge and offer them a seat.

"What can I do for you?" I sit opposite them and watch as the taller man looks at his partner before he speaks.

"Mr. Halston, unfortunately we have bad news for you. Mr. Archer Hawkins was involved in a road traffic accident this morning. A semi jumped a light and hit Mr. Hawkins' vehicle."

I stand, shaking my head. "No, no way! He only had a short drive. Where is he? What hospital was he taken to?" I grab my shoes and shove my feet into them, ready to leave.

"I'm sorry, Mr. Halston, but Mr. Hawkins passed away at the scene. I'm really very sorry to have to tell you this." I look at his name on his uniform, telling me he's Williams. He carries on talking, but I just can't comprehend what he's telling me.

"Mallory?" His partner stands and walks towards me, but I back away.

"No, no! We're getting married! I got the license this morning. He can't be, he loves me. He wouldn't leave me."

"Is there someone we can call?" He asks again, but I shake my head.

"I need to go to him. Please take me to him." I can feel my body shut down as my brain tries to make sense out of all this.

"We can do that. Let's go." The men look at each other and nod. They don't look happy about it though.

The ride to the hospital is silent. I have no idea what to do or what to say, and I think they're feeling equally lost.

Pulling into the ER doors, I jump out and race inside, but I'm stopped. In front of me is a huge man blocking my way.

"Let me through. I have to get in. I need to see him." I push against this wall of a man, but he shakes his head.

"I'm sorry, Mr. Halston. You aren't allowed in here. Mr. and Mrs. Hawkins have asked for you to be refused entry here. This is for family only. You aren't family."

"But we're engaged. We're going to get married. I need to see him. I need him. He will want me here," I beg with tears pouring down my face as I claw at his chest.

The policemen have walked past me, and when I look, I can see them talking to Archer's parents. Valerie turns to me and sneers before stepping up to me.

"Get out of here. Get away, I warned you!" Her hand comes up, and she slaps my face.

Stunned, I step back. Walking backwards, I stumble and fall. Collapsing to the floor, my hands cover my face as I cry.

I feel hands lifting me up and lead me to the exit. I'm crying out I can't leave. I don't want to leave. Nooooooo!

I'm back alone in the apartment, and I have no idea how I got here.

Lying on our bed, I have Archer's pillow in my arms as I rock. The scent of him is all over it. I can't let it go.

Looking up and out of the huge window, I can see it is dark now. How long have I been here?

The door opens, making me turn towards it. Archer's mother stands in the doorway.

"Get out, Halston. I'm giving you fifteen minutes before I call the cops and have you arrested for trespassing."

Looking at her, I don't understand how her son, her own flesh and blood can be so amazing while she is so evil.

"What did I ever do to you to make you hate me so much? Why couldn't you be happy that your son had found someone to love, someone who made him so happy?" I look at her as she narrows her eyes at me. "Are you jealous? Have you never had someone who loves you so much he makes your heart sing?"

"I think I want you out right now. You have no right to talk to me like that. You are despicable. You stole him away. This gay idea he had would have gone away if you hadn't come into his life."

"You really are fucking crazy. You have no idea how to be a decent human being. The man I love with my whole heart is your son, and he has just died. He's been taken away from me. Everything we planned for, every dream we had has been stolen away from us, and all *YOU* can think about is hate!" Spinning away from her, I stalk away to the closet and grab a duffel bag and shove clothes into it. My vision is blinded by my tears, and I have no idea what clothes I'm taking.

I look at her cruel face again. "The only joy I have is knowing he loved me. He loved me more than anyone else in the world, and you have to live with that. *You have to* live with the fact he never wanted you. He never wanted to see you again. The last thing he said to me was that he loved me. The last thing he said to you was that he never wanted to see you again. And you're right, I want to be out of here. I hope to never see you again."

Storming around the room, I collect some photographs and some more of the special mementos of our life. Unable to bring myself to look at her again, I walk out of the room that has brought me so much joy and happiness. Lifting my leather jacket and taking Archer's helmet, knowing I must have this with me, I step out of the apartment, leaving every chance of happiness behind. I feel the tear in my heart cleaving me in two, but here isn't the place to fall apart. I can leave here knowing every day I spent here up to now has been filled with nothing but love, laughter, and joy. Something I don't expect to find again. I had my chance, and I've lost it.

Chapter
Eleven

STARTING OVER

MALLORY

As I wander up the high street, I can feel a good vibe about this place. It's quiet enough to keep my head straight, not full of the pain and sadness that have been wrenching my heart and soul. Maybe have a new start. Standing outside a bar, I notice it's got a vacancy for a bartender hanging in the window. I wonder if they would be interested in a new face in the town. Would they trust someone that looks like me?

It's closed, so I look to see if there's an opening hours' notice.

I see an incredibly good-looking man walking towards me "Hey, you okay?" he asks but has a smile on his face.

"Um, er yeah, I guess. I was just looking for the owner," I stammer, embarrassed to be questioned so suddenly.

"I'm the owner. I'm Kes. What can I do for you?" Kes smiles at me, then turns and looks over his shoulder. "I was just driving past and saw you. Are you interested in the position here?"

"Yeah, I am. I've not done bar work before, but I worked as a barista," I say, thinking that working in a coffee shop can't be that different from bar work. I try to stand straight. Losing Archer has made me shrink inside myself, but for him, I need to try to straighten myself out.

"Okay, are you local? I don't think I've seen you around." Kes sounds kind, but I still flinch at his question.

"No, I've just moved here. I'm Mal… I mean my name is Carter." I really need to stop stuttering.

"Okay, Carter. We open at twelve, but I won't be here till three. Can you come back then?" He looks at me and seems to be taking me seriously.

"Yeah, sure. Thanks, Kes. I'll see you then." I smile. Then he turns and walks back to the very smart, new pickup truck. I watch him drive away and wonder what to do with my time. I spy a coffee shop further down the street.

I sit quietly in the window of the cozy coffee shop. My first thought as always is to call Archer and tell him. The pain in my heart wrenches again, making my stomach twist in knots and my breath hitch in my throat. Will I ever feel any better?

I think back to over the last four weeks, the pain and emptiness inside me. Maybe here's the chance to start again now, to be a different me. That's why I gave the bar owner my middle name. I can be alone with my grief. Leaving the man I was with Archer behind me won't be easy, but what choice do I have? I need to start over.

Not knowing where to go or what to do, I just rode, putting miles and miles behind me, stopping only to crash out in a cheap motel. The first time I stopped, I stayed for four or five days, consumed with pain and loss. Even in sleep, I grieve for him, calling out, searching for him.

I race down corridors and through doors, never reaching him. I can see him always just out of my grasp.

At just before three, I make my way down to the bar again. Nerves race through me as I get closer. Pushing open the door, another gorgeous man looks at me and smiles.

"You here to see Kes?"

"Um, yeah. Is he here?" I look around and see Kes walk out from a door at the rear of the bar.

"Hi, Carter, thanks for coming back." We walk through to an office. He lets me step through before closing the door behind us.

I can't believe my luck; this guy seems so nice and genuine. I'm guessing he's about the same age as Archer but so very different. His shoulder-length hair is tied back at the nape of his neck. His eyes sparkle as he tells me about the position and hours available. I can hear the pride in his voice as he talks about the bar.

"What do you think, Carter? Do you think you would fit in here?" Kes asks. I'm still waiting for him to ask me why I'm here. I decide to let him know a little bit about me.

"Yes, I think I would like it here. Like I said, I'm new to the town, and I'm looking to settle somewhere that is quieter than the city. I've been through a bad time, and I'm trying to find myself again. This looks like a good place for that." I look at him and wonder if he's going to ask me anything else.

"I can tell you've had a hard time, but as long as you are clean and sober, I'm happy to give you a chance." He smiles again.

"I promise it is nothing like that. Just my personal life took a heavy blow, and I had to get away. I'm not much of a drinker, and I've never taken drugs. I can take tests if you would like?"

"No, that's not necessary. I will trust you. You don't look like a bad guy, Carter." Kes looks down, then back up at me. "Do you have anywhere to stay?"

This question surprises me. I didn't think this would be something he would care about.

"No, I'm going to see if I can get a motel while I find an apartment, or just a room. I hadn't expected to find a place to stay, let alone a job," I stammer again, not sure why I've suddenly become nervous again. Or it may be that he is about to turn me down until I find a place.

"Okay, there is a small apartment upstairs. It's nothing fancy, but it has a bedroom, kitchen, and living space as well. Of course, a bathroom. It's furnished, but again don't expect too much. If you would like to take it, you can."

Wow! I was not expecting that. I can feel my chest expanding as I fill with unexpected emotion. I must bite down on my cheek to stop myself from crying at the kindness of this stranger. I nod and try to find my voice to thank him.

"I would like that very much. Thank you, Kes. You're being very kind to me." I smile slowly, something I haven't done for a while.

"Okay then, that's settled. Come on, let me introduce you to the guys, and you can have a look around. I'll get Denver to show you the ropes. It's him you will be replacing. I'm sure we'll find more hours if you want them too."

"Um, what about rent for the apartment, I can give you a deposit if you would like?" I still have money in the bank. Valerie hasn't been able to get her hands on any of the accounts.

"Don't worry about it. It comes with the job. Trust me, Carter. I'll find you living on the premises very useful on early delivery days." Kes laughs again and stands, moving around his cluttered desk. "Let's go."

We walk back out and see the two guys that spoke to me first kissing. I tense. A quiet gasp escapes me as I wonder what Kes will think of his staff kissing at work. But he chuckles and walks behind the bar, kissing the guys with just as much tenderness. I know my eyes have widened, but then he introduces the men as his boyfriends and queries if I have a problem.

I stutter out my reply and know my cheeks are flaming. But the dude named Denver walks from behind the bar and offers to show me around.

There's a calmness to this man that comforts me. Although I'm sure he's interested in me, he keeps his conversation light and talks me through the typical sort of day I can expect here. I relax and even ask a few questions.

Chapter
Twelve

CARTER

Sometimes I think I'm happy. That I'm not still one nudge away from falling apart, and then the dreams come back and drag me back under. Cooper's Ridge is a good place to be. The people are so friendly and welcoming. Kes, East, and Denver are amazing men. They have let me be. They haven't pried but have listened when I let a piece of my past slip out.

I've been here for over six months now and have watched the three men learn and develop their relationship. I've watched as Denver bared his soul and was pulled back together by the men who love him the most. I've never even thought of a trio. I'm not naïve, but it's not something I expected to find in a town as closed as this one should be. But the acceptance of the townsfolk to these men has me feeling happy. The head count of gay men in this town is larger than I would have imagined. Maybe it's the acceptance of these three individuals that encourages people to be themselves. I'm not talking pride marches or the likes, but seeing a man hold another man's hand in the street isn't unusual. The bar is so open to everyone that it makes its mark not just here, but in the surrounding towns too.

I have friends here. I have Shelley who works with me and keeps everyone from me, especially on rowdy nights where I seem to be fair game. I have spoken more to her about where I come from, and she knows I have lost my love. And yet she has never asked me my sexual orientation, whether I'm gay or straight. I don't discuss it because at this time in my broken life, I can't imagine another man with me.

Archer still owns my heart, and until I feel at peace, I can't imagine anyone else making me feel anything.

But last night's dream was different. It started the same, with me racing through the corridors, but this time I found him. There he was standing tall and strong and so heartbreakingly beautiful. His blond hair stirred as if in a breeze, but I couldn't feel it. All I could feel was him reaching out to me. I stumbled forward into his arms and felt his embrace right through to my core. As his lips met mine, we both moaned softly.

"I miss you, Archer. I miss you every day. I didn't get to say goodbye. Your mother..." My words fade away as a look of deep pain flashes over his face.

"My mother will get what she deserves," Archer speaks bitterly. "That's not why we are here, baby." His voice and his eyes soften again as he looks at me again.

"What do you mean?" I get this feeling I'm not going to like the answer.

"I'm looking for you, Mallory. I never want to let you go. I will find you again, I promise. I love you, sugar. I will always love you. Just look after yourself until we are together again."

The pain in my chest burns through me. "I don't understand. I need you. I need to remember you. What if you're wrong? What if you never find me? That you were it for me? I need to keep you in my heart and my head." My chest heaves as I try to drag air into my lungs.

"Baby, I've seen it. I've seen us happy. Just promise me you'll wait." Archer's smile looks mischievously at me as his eyes twinkle.

Then he becomes more serious. "Mallory, I need to go. I love you. I will always want you. I just need more time. Wait for me."

His mouth touches mine again, and I can taste him again on my tongue. I can feel his hands in my hair as I deepen the kiss. With a sweet smile, he's gone.

My eyes fly open, and I'm panting. I can still smell his cologne and feel his touch. My tongue slips over my lower lip, and I can taste him, but for the first time I'm not crying. I feel peaceful, rested. The tear in my heart isn't ripping me apart. Being called Mallory again, by him, only him.

"Oh look, your fan club has arrived." Shelley nudges me in the ribs and winks.

I've been at work about three hours, and I'm closing tonight. I got a long way to go yet. I'm not in the mood for Shelley's games, but I look up and frown when I see Dan Mortimer and Conn Martinez. They're good friends of Kes and come in often. I know Shelley is messing with me, but it still makes me uncomfortable the way Dan looks at me.

Breaking from my reveries, I look up and see him smiling at me. His amber-colored eyes sparkle with mischief. "Good evening, Carter. You're looking good tonight."

"Thank you." I smile and place my hands on the pumps of the draught beer. "What can I get for you?"

"It's good to see a smile on your face, Carter. It suits you." Daniel smiles and looks around at his friend and shakes his head. I wait patiently for their private conversation to finish. "Sorry, can we have a bottle of Kes' merlot, please? We'll want to eat too. I think I can sort that out with your server when we're ready." He gives me a wink which surprises the hell out of me.

"Er... Okay, shall I bring it over to you?" I'm not sure what's going on here. He doesn't usually act like this, so I ignore it and smile again.

"That would be good. Thank you, Carter." With another smile, he turns away and walks over to his friend.

"Well, that was weird." Shelley stands next to me again after finishing serving.

"Oh good, I thought it was just me. What's going on there, d'you reckon?" I ask as I turn to the wine cabinet and open the door. I pull the red wine from the climate-controlled cabinet, then reach up for two of the decent wine glasses we keep for the good bottles, and the good customers. The tourists and rowdy gang get the sturdy cheap glasses. Kes would go off on one if I gave his friends the crappy ones.

When I look up, I can see them both talking, but Conn is the one now looking at me. Again, it feels like he's studying me, but then he smiles, and his face lights up, making me think they're still talking about me. Deciding not to think any more of it, I uncork the bottle and place it and the glasses on a tray with a dish of nuts. Holding it in one hand, I carry it over.

"Gentlemen, would you like me to pour?" I look at them and see them both swallow hard, then look to each other.

"No, thank you, Carter. We'll take it from here," Conn is the first to speak.

"Okay, then. Let the server know when you're ready to order. Enjoy." I walk quickly back behind the bar, wondering what the hell is going on with the two men. Somehow, I have a feeling it has to do with me.

But they leave me alone for the rest of the evening. Kes and East show up and have been sitting with them for most of it.

Chapter
Thirteen

CARTER

I look around the garden at the crowd of people I now consider my friends. As they laugh and joke, Kes spies me and calls out my name. Strolling over to him, I smile and hand over my contribution to the barbeque.

"You didn't need to bring anything, Carter." Kes laughs but accepts the bag. The invitation for a cookout came as a surprise to me. I don't usually have a Saturday off work, but Kes insisted I get out from behind the bar and arranged coverage for me.

"I can't turn up and not bring anything. That would be rude. It's only some ribs. I marinated them in my secret sauce." It's only recently that I've started cooking for myself again. Since Archer died I haven't bothered to prepare anything. I've lived on takeout and frozen TV dinners. Cooking again is making me feel more of my old self. I haven't dreamed of Archer again and have found myself sleeping through the whole night deeply and peacefully.

"I can't wait to try it, then. Come on, let's grab a beer and join the others." Kes walks over to a large plastic tub filled with ice and beer bottles. Following behind, I look to see who else is here. I see Dan joking about with East, but his eyes meet mine, and he smiles. I get an unsettled feeling in my stomach whenever I am around him. He says something to East and heads in my direction. Yep, the knots, or is it butterflies, make an appearance.

"Carter, how lovely to see you outside the bar." Dan steps up to me. His eyes roam my face, making me swallow hard when he lingers on my mouth. My tongue darts out to dampen my bottom lip, making Dan's eyes widen and his pupils dilate. "You're looking good."

"Um, yeah, thanks. It's good to see you too." I scan the groups of people looking for anyone else to talk to but him. He still watches me.

"Yeah, but the place is packed with friends." Dan's eyes dart around, searching. He laughs and winks at me. I can feel a blush rushing up and staining my face red. "Here comes one of them now."

I turn and watch Conn walk up to us. As he reaches me, his arm slides over my shoulder and hangs loosely there. I freeze, but he doesn't seem to notice. "How come you always get the best-looking man to talk to?" he jokes with Dan.

"I'm lucky that way," Dan jokes.

Conn grins and keeps his arm over me. "It's good to see you here, Carter."

"Thanks. Kes was keen for me to get out of the bar for a while," I answer, not comfortable with his arm on me.

"Let go of him, Conn." Dan nudges Conn away from me.

"Excuse me," I mutter and walk away, making my way to Denver.

"Hey, Carter. You okay?" Denver gives me a welcoming hug and clinks his beer bottle against mine. "Cheers, it's good to see you. What's going on with Dan? You looked uncomfortable there."

"I don't know. Dan seems to be flirting with me all the time, and I don't understand why or what he wants. Last week, he asked me to have dinner with him, but I'm not sure. It's confusing me though. Are he and Conn an item? Sometimes they look like they are but then others they are very separate." I look back and see them standing close together, but both men are watching me.

"They're not an item. I think they've messed about a bit, but no, they aren't together." Denver answers matter-of-factly. "I think Dan likes you, Carter. He's a good guy. He was a geeky guy at school but always friendly, someone good. He's looking at you again."

"What, like he wants to eat me? Because it seems that way to me."

Denver barks out a laugh. "Yeah, I guess that's one way to describe it. The question is do *you* want him? Because I know you've been through hell, but recently you've looked lighter and happier. I wondered if you might be looking for someone."

"I don't know. I'm not sure if I'm ready." I look at Denver and swallow hard. "My fiancé died. I was banished by his hateful mother and never got a chance to say goodbye. I'm not sure my heart can take any more hurt. And I think Dan could do me a whole load of damage."

"Oh, Carter, I had no idea. I mean, I guessed something had happened. You were so lost when you got here, but I wouldn't have guessed that." Denver rests his hand on my shoulder as I shudder at the pain I have just unleashed.

"I haven't spoken to anyone about it, but I'm beginning to feel human again. Whether I'm ready to be with someone else is hard to work out." I run my hand through my hair and look at Denver again.

"That's only something you can work out, but I think if you find it too much when he flirts with you, maybe you're not ready yet. There's no set time for grief, Carter. You will go through some very tough times. Maybe you could talk to someone about it. Have you thought about counseling?"

"I don't think I am. I'm not ready, he's a bit too intense. I'm not going to be used like that. Thanks though, Den. I appreciate your thoughts." I look around and see everyone having a good time. I realize my heart just isn't in it yet. I'm not as ready as I thought. "I'm gonna head off. I'm sorry, but I can't do this."

"Yeah, okay. Take it easy though, Carter. Don't let yourself forget what it's like to be happy." Denver smiles sadly at me and lets me walk away.

I step through to the kitchen and make my way down the hall to the front door, I left my helmet and jacket on a table just inside the door, making it easy for me to leave quickly. I have a feeling my admirer will notice I've gone soon enough.

I've just thrown my leg over my bike and started the engine when I see Dan coming through the front door. I'm sure he calls out to me, but I need to be away from him and the confusion he causes me. I knock the visor down on my helmet and drive away.

Chapter
Fourteen

CARTER

I keep quiet at work in the weeks since Kes' cookout. I know Kes has been watching me. I'm not sure what he's expecting me to do. I just want an easy life. Dan hasn't been in so much lately, and it's made me wonder if Denver had a word with him. I think not seeing him has been good for me. I've kinda missed his flirting as I've been thinking that maybe a dinner date with him wouldn't be such a bad thing to do. It doesn't have to go any further than being friends, but perhaps I can take a small step forward.

I haven't been able to stop thinking about what Denver said. Archer was my whole life, just as I was his. I can feel my frown across my forehead again, which isn't good when the bar is full of tourists all wanting a good time, not a scowling bartender. Just as I pull myself together and stop thinking, I look up as the door opens and Dan walks in. Fuck! What am I going to do now? I look around for Shelley or Kes. I can let them serve him; I'm due a break. Or I can man the fuck up and say hello to him.

He smiles at me hesitantly, and his eyes light up when he sees me break into a genuine smile in return. He's a very good-looking man. Tall, with strong legs and a broad chest. His amber eyes sparkle with laughter and mischief, making me smile properly. I don't get the massive buzz of excitement flooding my stomach I always had with Archer, but I can feel some attraction to him. The butterflies are fluttering.

"Good evening, Dan. What can I tempt you with tonight?" I ask jokingly and watch as his eyes widen and dilate.

"I was coming in to see you, and maybe get you to agree to dinner with me. C'mon, Carter, it's only dinner. I'm a nice guy, I promise." He gives me a wink.

"I'm free on Thursday, if that would suit you?" I reply and chuckle at the surprised look on his face. "What? Were you expecting me to turn you down?"

"I *am* surprised, Carter, but it's a very happy surprise. Thursday night is perfect for me. Thank you." His grin is contagious, and I match it. I hear a cough behind me and see Kes and Shelley with their eyebrows virtually disappearing into their hairline but grinning like loons.

"Cut it out, you two, and leave me alone." I laugh, but I feel the blush rising up my neck and cheeks.

Kes walks up and stands next to me, then slings his arm over my shoulder. "You'd better behave, Dan. I'd hate to have to take you down if you hurt my man here."

"I promise I will be the perfect gentleman. I'm a well-respected man around here, I'll have you know." Dan laughs and mock-punches Kes on his shoulder.

"Yeah, yeah. I'm sure you are." Kes laughs, then strides away back into the office.

"Okay, now that I've been embarrassed by my friends here, what would you like to drink, Dan?" I get my work head back on.

"A beer would be good tonight, Carter." Dan smiles and takes a seat at the bar. "You mind if I keep you company?"

"As long as your drinking or eating, you are more than welcome to stay." I smirk and find myself giving him a wink that has him blushing this time.

I get back to work. It's not too busy tonight, and I manage to get a chance to talk to Dan more than I thought. He is a nice guy. The conversation is easy going and more of a fact-finding mission. I'm surprised just how much we do have in common. He is the same age as Archer at thirty-one, but he doesn't seem to care about the nearly seven-year age gap. It's certainly not one that bothers me.

Dan leaves at around ten-thirty with a sweet smile and a squeeze of my hand. "I'll see you on Thursday, Carter. Is seven-thirty good for you?"

"That's great. Shall I meet you here?"

Dan nods then strolls out into the night. Shelley nudges her shoulder into my arm. "He's a nice guy, Carter. I wouldn't've encouraged you if I didn't like him."

"I know, Shell, but I've had such a tough time lately. It's difficult to look forward. I'm trying though, and I like him. I'm just not sure if I'm ready to take it any further than friendship."

"I don't think you should overthink this, Carter. I think it is exactly what he said, just a dinner."

The rest of the night passes quickly, and I'm ready to get upstairs and into my bed.

After seeing Shelley to her car, I go back inside, lock up, and take the internal stairs to my apartment. I like living here. It's small, but I've managed to put my mark on it. I have bought some extra furniture and put out the few pictures and mementos I managed to snatch up as I left. It's enough for me.

Stripping off my clothes, I dump them in the laundry hamper and step into my shower. As the hot water pounds over my head, I think of Archer again. I feel the tug in my chest as my heart hurts. But I'm feeling something else now, and I think it feels a bit like hope. I know I'm not over Archer, and I know I'm not ready to tempt my heart with someone else. But I'm so tired of being sad. I need some respite. I don't know how to get over him, but maybe I don't have to get over him. Maybe I simply need to accept a new chapter of my life.

I scrub my body as I contemplate and decide I'm not cheating on Archer, or with myself, by going on a date with Dan. It may turn out to be a disaster anyway. That brings a smile to my face as I get out of the shower and towel myself off.

Getting into bed, I lie back and try to clear my mind, allowing me to sleep peacefully. It only takes moments until I feel the heavy blanket of sleep come over me.

Chapter
Fifteen

ARCHER

My head feels so heavy, my eyelids are like cement as I try to open them. Coughing, when I feel a restriction in my throat, I panic. Then cool hands are on me and I hear my name being called.

"Archer, Archer. Can you open your eyes for me?" the quiet female voice asks.

I try to lift my arm to my mouth but it's too heavy. The panic rises again as I cough. Feeling like I'm choking, I try to dislodge whatever is in my mouth and throat.

"Okay, steady. I'm going to take the tube out of your throat. Try to relax, Archer. It will just take a moment."

I feel a hand on my mouth and throat, and then the slide of whatever tube is in my throat. I cough heavily as it slips up and out of my mouth. My throat feels like the roughest sandpaper and my mouth is too arid to make any lubrication for it.

"Thirsty," I croak as I try to lift my hand up, but nothing moves. "Where am I? What's going on?" My eyelids finally find the strength to open and I blink in the bright light, wincing in pain.

"Archer, relax. You're in hospital. You were in a car accident. Let me get the doctor. I'll tell your family you're awake."

"Mallory, where's Mallory?" I scan around me and don't see him.

"I don't know about a Mallory, but your mother is here. I'll let her know," the nurse replies, looking confused.

I hurt everywhere. Any movement feels like torture. As I look down at my body, I can see the extent of my injuries, but I really have no idea what happened. My eyes flutter shut again as pain shoots through my body, making me gasp.

"Archer," a male voice speaks my name, forcing me to open my gritty eyelids again.

"I hurt." I grimace as my voice scratches through my throat.

"Archer, my name is Dr. Cavanaugh. I'm the chief trauma surgeon here. We can sort your pain out for you. I want to run through your injuries and the treatment you have received so far, if you're up to it?"

I watch as the same nurse comes back and hands me a controller. "This will administer your pain relief, Archer. Just press the button, it will only administer the correct dose. You can't overdose on it, but it gives you more control."

I press the button and look back at the doctor. "What happened to me?"

"You were hit by a truck on your way to work. The driver had been drinking the night before and was still over the limit when he hit you. I'll start at the top. You have sustained cuts and lacerations on your face, neck, and scalp. This was caused by the glass breaking and the airbag, so it needed suturing. Your left arm is broken, both ulna and radius as well as your collarbone and wrist. We have had to pin both bones. How are you doing so far?" he asks kindly.

"I'm okay. The meds are kicking in. Please carry on." I want to get this over with. I need to see Mallory. He must be going out of his mind, which raises the question… how long have I been here? "When did this happen? When can I see my fiancé?"

"Please let me finish and we can sort out your visitors. You suffered a pneumothorax and the paramedic had to insert a chest drain as you were being transported here. Scans show that your spine is intact, but you will feel bruised. Scans also showed a ruptured spleen, so we had to remove it."

"Shit!" I'm not sure I can deal with much more, the quicker it's over the sooner I get to see Mallory. "Go on, what else?"

"I'm sorry, Archer. But you're very lucky to be alive. If you'd been in a smaller car, I don't think you would have made it. I don't have much more but it is still serious. Because you were hit from the side, the protection bars in the door shielded you, but the impact still snapped your femur and only just missed your femoral artery. I think if it had ruptured, you would have bled out before we reached you. Unfortunately, the bone has had to be pinned and plated and we have fitted an external fixator to hold everything in place. Your ankle was also broken. The right side of your body isn't as badly injured, but your ankle shattered and has had some serious work by our orthopedic guys. Have you any questions?"

"You haven't told me how long I've been here. When did this happen?" I'm seriously stressing at how long Mallory has been waiting.

"Five days ago. We kept you heavily sedated and intubated when you went into breathing difficulties. We reduced the level of sedation, allowing you to wake yourself up when you were ready. Now, your mother is here. Would you like her to come in now?"

"I don't give a shit about my mother, but I want to see Mallory, my fiancé."

"I don't think anyone of that name has been here. You will have to ask your mother."

"When can I go home?" I ask. I just want Mallory. He should be here holding my hand, listening to this, helping me understand what has happened. I don't understand why he isn't here.

"You're going to be here for a long while yet. I will go into more details later. Right now, you need to rest."

I close my eyes, giving in to the sedative effects of the pain meds.

I dream of hearing Mallory calling me, shouting out my name. I try to shout out, but I have no voice. Running through a maze of corridors, I can hear him getting further away as his voice fades away. Standing alone, I watch the walls come down, leaving me alone in an empty space, devoid of color or sound. I'm alone and all I can feel is the weight of my sadness.

A different voice drags me from my sleep, one I recognize but do not want to hear. My mother.

"Archer! Archer, can you hear me?" Her loud annoying whine burrs through my skull like a hammer drill.

"I think the hounds of hell can hear you, Mother. Shut the fuck up!" I pry my heavy eyes open and see her standing with her arms folded across her scrawny chest with her usual scowl on her spiteful face. "What are you doing here? Where's Mallory?"

"I'm here because I'm your mother. And as for that lowlife, who knows where he is. Good riddance to him."

"What do you mean, you don't know where he is? Did you see him? Have you told him what happened to me?" I'm panicking now. What if she hasn't bothered to tell him?

"Of course, he knows. I sent someone over to your apartment to tell him. I haven't seen or heard from him since. He obviously doesn't have any feelings for you. He was just after your money, darling. Everyone could see that."

"Get out, go and find him! I don't care what you think about him, what we had was real. We were going to get married. I don't want or need you here. Find him!" I try to move but the pain is too bad, making me cry out and reach for the button to administer more pain relief.

"Well, he already seems to have failed on the 'in sickness and in health' part of the vows, don't you think?" Her sneer makes me shudder as she scoffs derisively.

"Just get out and don't come back until you have him with you." I close my eyes as the tears build up. I won't cry in front of her. I won't give her the satisfaction of seeing how upset I am.

Chapter

Sixteen

ARCHER

"This is it, are you ready?" Mason Reynolds, my boss and friend is here along with his brother Austin to take me home.

"I've been here for three months. I'm damn sure I'm ready. Hell, I was ready three months ago." I laugh, then reach out to grab my crutches.

Austin picks up my bags, handing a couple over to his brother as I push myself up to stand. When we walk out of my room, I hear a cheer and see all my physical therapists and nurses all standing under a goodbye banner. I feel tears prickle my eyes as I look at the people who have helped me walk again, who have listened to me rant and cry as I struggle through the pain. The pain of my broken and battered body has been nothing compared to the pain of my broken and shattered heart.

The nurses would let me talk all night if I wanted to. They listened and never judged me or told me to move on. They knew to never let my mother in here. Even when she tried to show up with my dad, they would turn her away. I don't know what she did, but she did something or said something to Mallory to make him leave me. I believe my father when he says he doesn't know what happened. I hadn't allowed him any further visits.

Now it's time to go home and try to get my life back on track. I still have a long way to go to be healthy again with many more hours of physical therapy to get the strength back in my legs. I'm determined to get my life back on track. I will go back to work, and I will move forward.

"You shouldn't have done this." I smile as I make my way to the nurses' station where there are cards and gifts waiting for me. The other residents are all here too, and some of the men and women that have gone through this specialized rehabilitation center.

"We love you, Archer. How could we let you go without a send-off?" Malik, my favorite therapist, laughs and hugs me.

"Yeah, yeah. I've been a pain in your butt for the last twelve weeks. You can't wait to get me outta here."

It takes another thirty minutes of hugs and goodbyes before we make it out to Mason's SUV. It feels strange to be going home. I'm not sure what I'm going to do there by myself. I had the locks changed after I banned my mother from visiting me. Her poisonous vitriol was too much to bear. I haven't spoken to her for nearly five months. My recovery in the hospital was long and painful. I developed an infection in my thigh from the pins, and they had to operate again to clean it and replace them on the fixator. Then my lung collapsed again and that really fucking hurt! More tubes and more drains which led to more heavy painkillers and the loss of time as the days floated into each other.

Mason handled the case against the driver of the semi that hit me. He jumped a light and was over the legal limit for alcohol. He had already had previous DUIs and the last had expired only a few weeks before. The CCTV caught the moment he hit me and hell, I don't know how I survived. He got a lifetime driving ban and four years in jail. He was also made to pay damages to me, but the money is unimportant. I just wanted that asshole off the roads.

"Are you okay back there?" Mason asks as I try to sit comfortably while still keeping my leg straight. The fucker laughs as he looks quickly over his shoulder.

"Yeah, fucking awesome. I'm covered in dog hair and I'm sure the seats are covered in spit or juice." I laugh because although he has kids and a huge dog, his car is immaculate. "You been letting your lovely wife use your pride and joy again?"

"My wife and kids are my pride and joy," he growls back, "but if she's messed it up, she'll get her ass spanked."

Austin laughs hard. "That's why she's messed it up, bro!"

Minutes later, we pull up at my apartment building and I look up at the tall steel and glass structure. Suddenly filled with dread, I don't want to go inside. I don't want to see the empty spaces where Mallory has cleared all his stuff out. I'm going to sell it and find somewhere else to live. I might even move away. I need a few more weeks of work on my legs but I'm going to the rehab center in a local gym. They mainly deal with veterans with amputations, but Mason has sorted it with the guys who own it.

"Are you sure you want to go in, Arch? I've told you we've still got our apartments in the city you can have." Mason has swiveled in his chair to face me.

"No, maybe after I've been inside but I've got to get my shit together. Everything I own is in there. I need to look around. He may have left a note or a forwarding address, or maybe it's going to be cleared out of everything and he took the lot. I have no fucking clue what went on."

"Come on then, let's do it. Then we can take you out and get you drunk!" Austin claps his hands together then opens his door and steps out of the car.

I shuffle closer to the door and wrench the handle open and try to get out. My main problem is not having a dominant leg. The ankle on the right is so weak and any heavy pressure on my left makes my thigh throb. It takes a couple minutes and both of them helping me, but I get out and upright, and have my crutches again.

The doorman steps out to open the door. He smiles. "It's good to see you again, Mr. Hawkins. Welcome home."

"Thank you," I answer but this doesn't feel right. I really don't want to be here.

Mason takes the key from me and opens the door. I step inside my home, a place that I loved. As I look around, it looks like the last time I was in here. The magazine I was reading is still on the sofa. There's a vase with very dead flowers on the sideboard. I bought them for Mallory before he graduated.

Walking further inside, the air smells musty and unlived in. I can hardly breathe as the pain breaks free from my chest. I keep moving, my eyes looking for any evidence of him, and there are plenty of his things still here. Why would he leave his belongings if he left me?

At the entrance to our bedroom, I stagger. Mason's hands reach out to grab me. Our bed is unmade, but on the top of it is a marriage license. He got it! Confusion floods me as I look around. His clothes are still in the closet. His toiletries are still in the bathroom. Again, I'm lost at why he didn't pack his stuff up? As I look over the surfaces, I notice things missing. The photographs of us, the box he kept something from every date we went on. Silly mementos I would laugh at, but he never cared. *"I love them. We will always remember everything we do together,"* he told me.

"Something's wrong. This doesn't make sense." I look at my friends. "Why would he leave his clothes but take our pictures and trinkets?"

"I gotta agree. A guy that was leaving you wouldn't give a shit about his photos of you, but he'd want at least a couple sets of clothes." Mason gazes around the room, shaking his head.

"Why don't you get Lucas to look for him?" Austin asks. "You know he'd find him."

"I don't know. I'll think about it. I could be wrong, and he really did just walk out of my life. Do I really want to be faced with that again? Thanks, Austin."

"What do you want to do? Do you want to stay or come back with us?" Mason places his hand on my shoulder and gives it a squeeze.

"Yeah, there's nothing for me here. I'll decide what to do with it another time." I pick up the piece of paper that would have meant so much to us and place it in my pocket. I pull open a drawer and take out a small photo album, handing it to Mason. "Can you put that in my bag?"

With another glance around my happy place, I turn and hobble back to the front door and walk away from my past life.

Chapter
Seventeen

CARTER

I see Dan walking towards me, making the butterflies in my belly stir and rise, swirling around. He looks mighty fine tonight. This is our fifth date, and tonight, we're going to a club. Dan called me earlier with the change of plan, saying he's in the mood for dancing. I haven't danced in what seems like a lifetime, so I'm ready for it tonight.

"Hey, Carter, babe, you look amazing." Dan's eyes roam over my tight black T-shirt and down, gazing at the skinny black jeans. His hand touches my face, and he leans in for a kiss. As his lips touch mine, I can feel the need in him. We haven't done too much touching and have shared a few kisses. I like the boldness of his action tonight; it sets the scene for a night of hot bodies dancing to the same beat.

"So do you. I'm liking the fitted shirt." I slowly peruse his midnight-blue tailored shirt tucked neatly into a pair of grey slacks. My fingertips run down from his collarbone to his waist. I feel the tiny tremors that run over his skin.

"We need to go; otherwise, I'll be dragging you back to my place," he growls and grasps my hand.

"Shall we grab something to eat before we hit the club? I haven't eaten much today." I look over at him as the cab drives us into Denton.

"Good idea. What do you want?" Dan is still holding my hand, his fingers entwined with mine as his thumb strokes up and down my own.

"Pizza will do. I don't need fancy, just something easy."

Twenty minutes later, we're in a pizzeria tucking into a huge everything-added pizza. "What made you think about dancing tonight?" I wipe my hands on a napkin and lean back in the chair. I pick up my beer and wait for him to finish chewing and answer.

"I dunno. I was at work, and I've had a really tough case lately. I just thought what could be a better way of letting off some steam than having a hot guy grind against me while the music pounds." He smiles and picks up his beer. "Then the thought of you rubbing up to me as you get lost in the beat has had me hard all day long."

I cough hard after swallowing a huge gulp of beer. "Okay, I guess I asked for that. Well, I happen to agree with you, we'd better finish up here so we can get our groove on." I give him a sly smile that has him fixated on my mouth.

The club is full, and the music is pounding through my chest. I can feel the bass as it reverberates through my whole body. I can feel the vibes coming off all the male bodies as they writhe and dance, making me want to lose myself in the music.

Twenty One Pilots' *Lane boy* blasts out, and I can grind my way through this one with no problem. Dan still holds my hand, allowing me to drag him into the throng. It doesn't take much for him to get with it. With his hands on my hips, he moves to the beat. He's an amazing dancer, something I never would have expected from him. I soon let him take over. We dance and dance; I don't know how many tracks have been played. We seem lost in the music and the soft caresses we share.

Pulling me up against his body, he swings me around, and my back is against his chest. I lift my arms and wrap them over his head, letting my head drop back on his neck. Dan lowers his head, and I feel the heat of his mouth as he brushes long open kisses on my neck. Fuck! He is so hot! I can feel his hard dick pressed up to my butt. It feels like a nice thick dick. I hadn't realized how much I missed the soft touch of loving hands.

My head fills with memories of Archer, but that is all they are now. Memories, happy thoughts that deserve to be treasured. Dan runs his hands down my torso and rests them with his thumbs tucked just inside my front pockets. A true feeling of ownership, of possession. It's a feeling I love. My hips nudge back against his groin as I grind against him. I feel the hiss of his warm breath as I rub over his dick.

"Fuck, Carter, the things I want to do to you." His teeth scrape over my neck before he sucks on the tender skin. I know he's marking me, and I can't say I mind.

Twisting around to face him and wrapping my arms around his neck, I capture his mouth with mine and slip my tongue through the small gap made by his sigh. Our hips still sway to the rhythm, but our mouths dance by themselves. As my tongue curls around his, I can taste the faint mint flavor from the candy after the pizza and beer, but it's not just his taste I can't get enough of. As I hold his head close to mine, his hands roam down my back to cup my ass cheeks, and he pulls me even closer to him.

Moaning, I pull back and see his black pupils as his irises dilate, losing the sparkling amber colors, as his lust heightens.

"We need to get out of here." I moan as I press my mouth to his again.

I think we kiss the whole journey home, I hope Dan gave the driver a decent tip to put up with us making out like teenagers.

When we get inside, Dan steps back and looks at me. I can feel the waves of desire rolling off him. His tongue darts out and slides sensuously over his lip. Fuck, this is it!

Chapter
Eighteen

DAN

"I may regret saying this, but I need to just clear this up in my head." Reaching out to him, I step back into his space. "Are you sure you want to do this? We can go slow if you're not ready yet."

"Daniel, I wouldn't be here if I didn't want this. I'm not going to turn you down. Let's just take what we feel is right. Because right now, I want to see you naked. I want to touch and taste you. I want to be here, with you, doing this."

"Thank fuck! C'mon, let's get to my room. I want to peel you out of your clothes." I race up the stairs and hear Carter hot on my heels. This is so much more than I imagined, and I want so much more from him. I need to be inside him. He is perfect.

I wait for Carter to come in before I move behind him and close the door. Facing him, I drink in the sight of his thin but muscled body. His chest heaves with anticipation as he watches me. Taking a step closer, I reach for the hem of his shirt and slowly peel it up his body. The muscles I have only dreamed about seeing emerge as the fabric moves higher.

"Damn, you're beautiful, Carter. Every inch of you is perfect." I wait as he lifts his hands over his head, allowing me to pull his shirt off. As I drop it to the floor, I kneel and lay kisses over his chest and down to his abs. Each square inch of taut muscle gets its own share of adoration. I smile against his stomach as he clenches when I dip my tongue in his belly button.

Trailing my mouth from hip to hip, I reach up for his belt buckle and quickly unclasp it. I keep my mouth fixed to his skin. The quiet room is filled with the sound of his zipper being lowered.

I lift my eyes up to look at him and see him staring, slack-jawed with pent-up raw need back at me. Subtly, I request to carry on, and his acquiescence spurs me on. Reaching for the waistband, I tug the tight jeans down his thighs, leaving his snug black briefs in place. Carter takes over and rips his jeans down and toes off his shoes. As he tugs the tight denim from his legs, I take the moment to strip out of my clothes. In seconds, we're both standing in our briefs. Carter takes hold of his junk and tugs on it through the fabric, making me hold back a moan.

This time, it's his turn as Carter tugs me closer, stepping back until he reaches the bed. He pulls me between his spread legs. Raising his eyes up to me, I find I'm locked in the raw heat of his gaze. Running his hands slowly up my legs, I feel every hair on my body react to his touch as electricity races through my body, sparking every synapse inside me. I want to close my eyes and just feel, but his stare keeps me fixed. His dark-blue eyes are black now, shooting so much power I feel helpless.

The tips of Carter's fingers slide with the lightest touch up the inside of my thighs. I moan as my hips pitch forward. I want his mouth on me. Then grazing over the fabric holding my painfully hard dick trapped, he reaches the band and slowly lowers them. As the swollen crown escapes its confines, Carter keeps his eyes on me.

"Watch," he mouths to me as if I could look away. His tongue darts out and captures the bead of moisture escaping from the slit.

The loudest groan escapes me, then he tugs my briefs down, letting them drop as they reach my knees. Before my dick can bounce back against my stomach, it's in the scorching, wet heat of his mouth, I feel my legs buckle, but Carter's grip on my ass keeps me upright as he works on me. He sucks hard on the head, making me cry aloud before he takes me deeper. The sound of the slick, wet action fills the room so decadently I feel my balls tighten. But so does Carter, and he reaches between my legs and tugs on my balls, denying me any chance of release. Over and over, he edges me in the best blow job I have ever had until he takes me deep in his throat. Even with his nose pressed hard on my skin, his eyes stay fixed on mine. His hand tightens again on my sac as he swallows around me, my dick deep in his throat.

"Arggh, fuck! Carter! Let me come. Fuck, I'm so close!" I cry out as my eyes squeeze shut, and I pant through my need.

Then his mouth is gone, making me cry at the loss. Opening my eyes, I look down again, noticing that he has removed his briefs, and I get my first glimpse of him. What a beautiful sight it is.

Pushing him on the bed, he scoots further on, propping himself on bent arms. There is no hesitation or embarrassment in his eyes as I climb up his body.

"Top or bottom," I murmur, not that I give a shit either way right now.

"Bottom. I want you inside me. Take me, Dan, fuck me, own me." Shit! The hottest words ever.

Reaching over to the drawer, I grab the lube and a condom and throw them on the bed next to us.

"I want to explore every inch of your sexy body, but that can wait. Right now I need to be inside you," I growl in his ear, then trail my tongue over the shell to nip the lobe. I love how he's writhing beneath me as I suck and bite on his neck.

"Fuck, Dan. I need you, I need you now," he begs.

Kneeling up between his spread thighs, I grasp the underside and push his legs up to his chest. "Hold them, Carter."

He pulls on his legs, lifting his ass up higher to me, and I get to see his hole. Fuck, I'm not gonna last when I get inside him. Grabbing the bottle of lube, I squeeze it and generously coat my fingers, then drop it again. Shit, I'm nervous now. I look back up at Carter and see his flushed face and the damp sweat glistening on his skin.

"Please, Dan," he pants, giving me the go-ahead I need. I rub my finger over his hole and immediately feel him push down, and the tip slips inside him. Fuck! If I thought his mouth was hot, it's nothing to the feeling of his ass gripping my finger. Working it in and out a couple times, I feel him relax, and I add another, pumping him. I watch as his dick drips precum over his stomach.

"More?" I ask as a third finger nudges his hole.

"Fuck, yeah!"

After only a few more pumps and stretches, I know he's ready for me. I pull my fingers out, and he whimpers at the loss. I tear the condom wrapper and quickly suit up and tip more lube over the thin latex. As soon as I press against his pucker, I slip inside. I feel him tense up, making me halt.

"Tell me when you're ready, baby," I whisper, and he smiles at me.

"You feel amazing, and fucking huge!" He chuckles, the action making me slip further inside him. He nods. "I'm ready."

Pulling back just slightly, then sliding fully, I take my time to feel every ripple from his tight channel. As his muscles clench and release, allowing me to bury myself to the hilt, I watch as Carter's eyes roll back in his head. He groans so sensuously and deeply, I feel the vibrations over my dick, making my balls draw up again.

"More?" I ask as I pump smoothly inside.

"Everything," he murmurs back, giving me another smile. I feel my heart squeeze as I fall for him. I will do anything and everything to make this man mine.

"Always." I pull back and thrust deeper and deeper. Leaning over him, I capture his mouth and pour the depth of my emotions into him. When his legs wrap around my ass, forcing me deeper inside, I know I'm not going to last much longer.

"I can't hold on, Dan," he keens as his hands wrap around my neck.

"Nor me, let's do this together." I pull out of his embrace and kneel up again. "Stroke yourself, Carter," I order as I pick up speed. I watch as his hand beats up and down, and I feel the tension in his body build. I know he's close. Fuck, I can't hold on. "Yes, baby, yes! Oh fuck, I'm coming!"

As I stiffen and fire my load inside him, his stomach is coated with thick white ribbons. He comes so hard, it reaches up to hit my chest. I cry out and fire again. Carter's legs collapse down as he throws his arm over his eyes. His chest rises and falls as he drags deep gulps of air inside his lungs. I have never seen anything so beautiful.

I lower myself down and roll off him. As my exhausted dick slides out, I drag the condom off and dump it in the waste bin. Closing my eyes as my chest mirrors his, I come down from the greatest high I've ever had. When I turn my head, I see Carter looking at me. His smile is lazy and so hot. I lean over and kiss him.

"You okay?" I murmur.

"Yeah, I am. I really fucking am." He chuckles. Looking down at his chest and stomach, he laughs louder. "Damn, it looks like I needed that."

"Shower?"

"Yes, please, but only if you're coming too." He strokes his hand down my chest until he hits the sticky deposits of his release. "Shit, you got it too!"

After getting messy again in the shower, we get clean, and I wait hesitantly to see if Carter plans to leave. My stomach is in knots at the thought of him walking out. I don't realize I'm holding my breath until it whooshes out of my body when he climbs back into bed.

"You okay with me staying?"

"I would love for you to stay." Dropping my towel, I clamber in next to him and lie down. My heart beats faster when he turns into me and lays his head on my chest. As my fingers stroke through his damp hair, I feel him drift into sleep. It takes me a while longer, not just because I'm reliving every moment of this evening, but because I need to make sure I keep hold of this amazing young man.

Carter rolls in his sleep and turns his back, allowing me to spoon up against him. As he sighs, his hand tightens on mine, and he mutters good night again.

Chapter
Nineteen

CARTER

I can feel someone laying soft kisses over my shoulders, making me squirm. I open my eyes and twist around to see Dan watching me, with his head propped up in his hand. Smiling, he ducks his head down and drops a soft kiss on my mouth.

"Morning, baby," he whispers, and my stomach flutters as the butterflies unfurl their wings. His amber eyes shine bright with happiness and a glint of mischief as he gives me a little half smile that shows off a dimple I had never noticed before. The rough stubble on his face is new to me too as he's always clean shaven when I've seen him. I like the early morning Dan.

"Good morning," I murmur back as I wrap my hand around the back of his head. "I'll have another one, if you don't mind." I press my lips to his as he quickly parts his to let me in. I moan softly as he rolls me onto my back and deepens the kiss, sliding his body over mine. I open my legs to let him settle between them. As our dicks touch, another shameless mewl escapes me, making Dan chuckle and flex his hips into mine again.

As his hand reaches between us, he grasps both of our dicks stroking them against each other. It doesn't take long before we're spewing our loads.

"You can't beat a bit of frottage first thing in the morning!" Dan laughs, then surprises the hell out of me when he lifts his hand to his mouth and licks it. "What?" he says when he sees my eyes widen when he offers it to me. Who am I to turn that down? As my tongue flicks out, I hear Dan groan before attacking my mouth again. This guy is gonna wreck me, I can tell.

When we pull apart, I look around for a clock. "What time is it?" I don't have anywhere to go, but I'm curious as to how much time we have together.

"It's early, about eight. Do you have to leave?" He kisses my neck as he speaks.

"No, I'm good 'til this afternoon. Do you have to go into work?" It's my turn to let my tongue slide over his collarbone, reveling in the goose bumps that bloom over his body.

"No, I'm free today. Shall we get breakfast?"

"I thought we'd just had it, or at least a protein shake." I wink as he laughs and pushes himself off me.

"Let's eat and then see what else we can get up to." His grin is contagious as he pulls me from the bed.

When I walk into work, it looks like there's an intervention about to take place. Kes, East, and Denver are all here as well as Shelley and the new bartender, Paris.

"Hey, guys. What's up?" I step up to them and see the huge grins on their faces. "Why are you looking like goons?"

"We thought we'd come in and say hi. Y'know, just a catch-up." Kes keeps smiling as he laughs.

"Oh really, you just happened to drop by. Right, fine. I'll play along." I narrow my eyes because I damn well know why they are here. "How are you keeping, what's new?"

Denver smiles and looks me over. I remember I've got the same clothes on as last night, but I don't think they would know that. "Oh, we're all good, y'know. Getting along with the joys of parenting, what about you? What's new with you?" His grin is devilish.

"I'm good. Nothing much to say. I'll just get to the office and start on the banking." I walk past as East looks at me and catches hold of my arm and looks at my neck. His finger nudges the neckline of my shirt and drags it away.

I tug away from him as he laughs. "Fuck off, East!" I scowl and move on.

"He's got a hickey!" He smirks, and the rest of them all burst out laughing.

"Come on, Carter, spill the beans! What's going on with you and the hot lawyer?" Kes is still laughing but stops when I shoot him a back-off look.

But as I think of Dan and the amazing morning, I can't help grinning. "It's going well. That's all I'm going to say."

"Congratulations, Carter. Happiness looks good on you. And if it's Daniel who is making you happy embrace it, buddy." Kes smiles again.

"Yeah, we're only messing with you. It's been great to see you smile more." Shelley hugs me and drops a kiss on my cheek.

The rest of the day drags as I watch the door. Dan said he'd try to come in, but he didn't say when.

"Stop staring at the door. If he said he'll come, he will." Paris sighs at me and nudges me with his elbow.

"I'm not staring. I just glanced over when you happened to be looking at me," I grumble.

"You keep telling yourself that," he jokes, then looks up and smiles. "It looks like your man is here."

I whip my head around and gape as I take him in, striding towards me, his eyes fixed on me and only me. I gulp and stare. His dirty-blond hair is in its rough-and-ready state that just makes me want to run my fingers through it. His amber eyes blaze with gold flashes as he looks me over. I drink in the fitted white T-shirt stretched tight over muscles I have traced with my tongue. His blue, well-worn jeans mold his long, strong legs, the muscles flexing as he gets closer.

His eyes flicker down to my mouth as I dampen my bottom lip, making him copy my action. Fuck! He is hot as shit!

"Hey, baby," he murmurs as he reaches the bar.

"Hey, you," I whisper back as we both lean over the polished wood bar. Our mouths touch, and I hum against his soft, but oh so firm, lips. "I've missed you."

"I've missed you too."

When we pull apart, I notice the room has gone quiet as everyone stares. I look at Shelley, and she fans her face.

"Holy fuck, you two are hot as hell!" She looks around and laughs. "I think they just got their Hollywood moment, that was straight out of the movies."

I close the bar not much later. Paris has walked Shelley to her car, and Dan is waiting for me to finish locking up.

"Did you walk?" I ask as I look for his car.

"Yeah, I fancied a beer or two while I gazed at you and thought about all the things I want to do to you when we get home." His arm is wrapped around my waist with his thumb tucked into a belt hook as he tells me all of his thoughts. Damn it, I'm hard by the time I get to his place.

Chapter
Twenty

DAN

These last couple months, or nearly three, I've been with Carter have been the best I've ever had. I'm so close to telling him my feelings, that I have fallen in love with him, but I'm still not sure he's ready to hear it, even though I think he feels it too.

We've spoken very little about his past. He's told me his fiancé was killed in a car accident, but we don't talk too much about it. I for one, I don't want to talk about a man I can see meant everything to him. I've been watching him since he turned up here, and the damaged man he was then is nothing like the beautiful, funny, caring man he is now. I'm not going to remind him of that time again.

I can see how he feels about me, and not just when we make love. If he can't stay over, he'll leave me notes around the house to make me smile when I find them. He remembers the things I like, and he's a great cook. He said he had to learn, so why just learn the basics, learn how to do it properly.

I watch him now as he moves around my kitchen. He's comfortable here. He knows his way around, allowing me to let him get on with it and deal with the clearing up afterwards.

"What are you making tonight, baby?" I sit on one of the stools at the island in the middle of my large kitchen. I've poured us both a glass of Pinot Noir, and I swirl the dark-red liquid around in the glass.

"Chicken Marsala. It shouldn't be much longer. How hungry are you?" He struts towards me. I swing around on my seat and part my legs in time for him to step between them.

"Hmm, that's a loaded question. What are you offering?" I tug on his waist, pulling him closer as I wait for his mouth to touch mine. The taste of wine mixed with pure Carter makes my head swim as I lazily stroke my tongue against his. I love it when his hands slide up my neck and into my hair, fisting it to the perfect level of pleasure and pain. I groan as he tugs and devours my mouth.

Releasing me from his clutches, he steps back and wipes his thumb over his lip, a sight that is always so freaking sexy.

"I've made enough for you to freeze some for when your friend comes to visit. I know you'll eat pizza every night if I don't." He laughs.

"We've talked about this, Carter. You don't have to stay away. I want you here. I want to show you off." I sigh. This is a discussion that hasn't been resolved yet.

"I will. I can't stay away from you for too long." He winks. "But your friend has had a shit time, and I think maybe he would like some downtime with his best friend. He won't want me here while he's hurting and needs to talk it over with you."

"Dammit, Carter. I hate it when you make sense. Fine, but not too long. I hate not having you in my bed," I grumble.

My best friend from college is coming to stay for a while. I've offered him a partnership at my place if he wants or needs a change. He was in a horrific car accident that should've killed him, but he survived only to find out his boyfriend dumped him and ran while he was still unconscious. He'll be here in a couple days, so I'd better get my fill of Carter before he leaves me with my friend.

"You'd better be staying with me for the next couple days, baby. Or I'll be tying you to the bed when you sleep." I watch his eyes flare and think he kinda likes that idea. "Or maybe I'll just tie you to it tonight. What do you think?"

Carter flushes, and his eyes dilate as he nods. "Fuck, yeah, you can tie me up anytime. I love that."

"That's good to know, baby. Good to know." I watch and burst out laughing as he adjusts his junk in his jeans.

"Fuck off!" He laughs. "Asshole."

"Yeah, baby, yours, all open and begging for me." Damn, now my dick's getting hard. "How long 'til that's ready?"

As we lie exhausted, breathless, and panting, I turn my head to face him. It's now or never. His eyes meet mine, and I can see love blazing out of them.

"I love you, Carter. I know it's soon…" He stops me by placing his finger over my lips.

"I love you too, Dan, and it's not too soon. It's perfect."

Chapter

Twenty-One

ARCHER

"So what time does your flight get in? I'll come pick you up."

I listen to my best friend and sigh. "I've told you. I've got a rental car. I'll need some wheels when I'm with you. I'll call you when I land." I hear a car horn. "Look, the cab's here. I gotta go. I'll see you in a few hours." Laughing, I cut him off. I walk out of the guest house Mason has kindly let me rent from him for the last couple months.

I got signed off by the doctors, and as long as I keep exercising and building up the strength in both legs, I'm good to go. I've accepted an extended holiday with my best friend. I know he's hoping I'll like it and join his practice. Who knows, maybe I will?

I've upgraded on the flight to first class. I still need the leg room so I can stretch out. If I sit too long, it aches, and then I find myself limping when I walk again. I don't want to look like I'm an invalid anymore and have worked hard at the gym to improve my stance and gait.

The last nine months have been a living hell. I never thought I could lose a near-perfect life. I had a job I loved and excelled at, a home I was very happy with, and then I found the perfect man. The age difference never bothered me. Seven years is fine. I'm only thirty-one, and Mallory always seemed older than he really was. We just fit. It worked. It worked so damn well I still don't understand why he left, and I guess I never will. My family was the only fly in the ointment, but that part is shut down now. My mother will get what she deserves in the end.

And now I'm doing something for myself. Mason has told me I will always have a job there if I want one, and I hope to go back there, but not yet. A change of scenery is what I really need now, and I'm excited about it.

When I collect my vehicle from the car hire, I laugh at the size of it. It's like a monster truck but it's got a good-living-in-the-country feel about it. Setting up the GPS takes a couple seconds, and I pull out and head off down the highway. I've got Imagine Dragons blaring out of the speakers, and I've got a stupid damn smile on my face.

It takes me just over an hour to pull into the town I haven't visited since we were in college together. I see how much it has grown and prospered. Well, by the look of the buildings and amenities, many looking new. The number of expensive cars driving past me shows there's still money to be made on ranches. As I turn into the last street, I slow down to check the numbers. Soon, I'm pulling up into a driveway in front of a smart two-story house. Beeping the horn, I laugh and switch off the engine, opening the door and climbing down as the front door opens and my friend races out.

"Hawkins, you fucker! Look at you, standing on your own two feet. It's damn good to see you, buddy. It's good to know you're still living and breathing." His arms wrap around me, and I'm hugged hard, his fist pounding on my back. "You really fucking scared me, Archer. Don't go getting nearly killed again, y'hear me?"

"Dan Mortimer, you ugly bastard. Get your hands off me and let me breathe." I smile hard, and I'm glad I'm not the only one to have a sheen in my eyes. "I promise no more fighting with trucks."

"Let's grab your bags and get inside. There's a beer with your name on it." Dan chuckles.

"I've not brought too much. I wasn't sure how long you're prepared to put up with me. I'm not much fun lately."

"Dude, you can stay for as long as you want. I've got the room, and I think a bit of R and R is just what you need. I'm here if you want to talk about it, but I get it if you don't. Whatever you need, Archer, you know that."

"I do and thank you. I think a beer is just what I need. Can I grab a shower first? Flying first class is good, but I've still got the whole airplane funk going on."

Dan laughs and grabs my bag. "I'll show you to your room. It's got a bathroom attached."

"This is a great place you've got here, Dan. You can't regret coming back here?"

We're sitting on a gorgeous deck looking out over a huge backyard, including a large pond and wooded area. The sun is setting, and the only other sounds are the cicadas chirping in the trees, and the hiss of a beer bottle being uncapped.

"This is so the opposite of what I'm used to. I've never been anywhere so peaceful. You're a lucky man, Dan." I smile at him as he lies out on a lounger.

"I am, though it was tough at first. I had to deal with the death of my father and the expectancy of me stepping into his shoes. I never hated the thought of being here again. I just wasn't planning on it as soon as I qualified. But it's good here now, I'm happy." He looks over at me and grins. "This place was a bargain, and I snapped it up. It had been empty for a while. The old guy who lived here went into a nursing home after a stroke. After he died, his family just wanted to get rid of it. It needed to be gutted, but there's a great guy here that runs his own construction company, and he did all the work. I'll have to introduce you to him and his partners." He chuckles as I raise my eyebrows.

"Partners?" I ask. "As in plural?"

"Oh yeah, and they're hot as hell. East and his boyfriend Kes. He owns a great bar on the high street. They have been together for a few years now. It raised a few eyebrows to begin with, but then everyone got used to it. The fact they didn't give a shit what anyone thought helped, I think. Then a guy we all knew from school came back to live here, and after a couple months, two became three. He's a hotshot surgeon and comes from a very well-respected family. Again, a few of the oldies grumbled, but they ignored it, and it's great to see them all so happy. I envy them. I thought I would be happily married by now, but the right guy has never come along. Until now."

"Wow! That's so cool, lucky them." I look over at Dan, and he's got a smirk on his face, making me grin. "I know what you're thinking about, you dog!"

He laughs hard and scrubs his hand down his face. "I think that was one of the best nights ever. Something I've never repeated but wouldn't turn down again."

"I haven't thought about that in years, dammit." Thinking back to when Dan and I were together during college and the very cute boy who tempted us both into his bed. How can I have forgotten about that? Then Mallory's beautiful face fills my mind, and I'm back to being hurt again.

"Yeah? Well, I have. I think when it's in your face, you tend to think about it. Not sure if Carter is up for that." Dan laughs and grins wide as he thinks of his lover.

"So, what's he like, your man? When do I get to meet him? I thought you were joined at the hip."

"He's being a stubborn ass and staying away so that we can spend some time together. He didn't want to tread on our time catching up and on me persuading you to stay and join me at work." Dan laughs, and I can see the love he has for Carter pouring from him. "He's a good man. A keeper for sure."

"Yeah, I thought I had that, but it turns out he wasn't the man I thought he was." I push my hurt away again and stand, stretching. I see Dan looking at me, or more looking at my leg. I put loose-fitting sweat shorts on after my shower. The scars are vivid and red, running from my knee to almost my hip. I've got support bandages on both ankles. They tend to ache and swell when I've been on my feet too long. "Not a pretty sight, is it?" I state, my voice sounding hollow.

"Shit, Archer. I'm sorry. I didn't mean to look. You've been through so much, I'm sorry I didn't visit, I was stuck in a case from hell and couldn't leave. I should've come to you." Dan reaches out to me, and I step up closer as he stands and wraps his arms around me and holds me tight. "It will right itself, Arch. I promise you. You'll get your happy ending."

I pull away. "Yeah, I'm sure I'll have a long line of hot men wanting to love me." I snort.

"Then you aren't seeing what I see. I see an amazing man, someone that survived the most awful car accident. You've been through so much pain and look at you. You're walking again. Your ankles must be more titanium than bone, and I can't imagine the hours of painful physical therapy you've endured. Archer, my man, you're an amazing, beautiful man. Any man should be honored to have you." Dan laughs but looks embarrassed at his outburst.

"Would you?" I ask tentatively. It's been years since we were together, but we had a good time and ended it still being great friends.

"In a heartbeat, Archer. But I'm not the man you have in your heart."

"Thank you, but now you have a new man in your heart," I whisper quietly and lean forward to kiss his forehead. "I'm going to turn in. It's been a long day. You can show me the sights tomorrow."

"I'll do that. It will take about twenty minutes but hey, why not." He laughs. "Sleep well, Archer. I'm happy you're here."

"Me too, g'night."

My eyes open as the bright sunlight streams through the curtains. A warm breeze washes over me as I try to work out where I am. I can hear birds but nothing else. I rarely had my windows open in my apartment, all except the balcony doors. The sound of birds was never a prominent noise.

Then I smell coffee, and that is something I'm used to. I push myself upright and look about the room. Dan has done a good job of decorating it. The walls are a soft green, and the furniture a distressed grey making it look elegant. The large king bed was extremely comfortable, making sleep come very quickly last night. But now my stomach rumbles, and I need food and coffee.

Finishing in the bathroom, I wash my hands, looking at myself in the mirror. I still have scars on my cheek and forehead, although the vitamin E cream I use is helping them to fade. I should probably shave but decide against it. I quite like the stubble now. I'm more tanned than I used to be after spending my time at Mason's place, and it suits me. I have changed since the accident. Apart from the obvious pain at losing Mallory, I think I've grown as a person. I've had to toughen up and face all my challenges head on, and I've won so far. I just need to get my heart and my head in the same place. Maybe I'll believe Dan's words from last night.

Walking back downstairs, I can hear Dan talking. He's either on the phone, or he has a visitor. When I reach the kitchen, I can see him pacing the floor with his phone at his ear. He must have heard me. He turns and smiles, pointing at the coffeepot. I nod and pour the hot, dark, and divine-smelling liquid into the two mugs.

"Yeah, baby. I miss you too. Yeah, he's good too. Just woken up by the look of him. He's searching for the coffee. Yeah, Carter, I will. Call me later. I love you, too." Dan ends the call and drops the phone on the white marble breakfast bar. "Sorry about that."

"No worries. This is your place. You want anything in this?" I hold up the mug.

"Nah, I'm good with this." He takes it from me and puts it next to his phone. "You hungry?"

"Yep, starved. Whatcha got?" I take a sip of coffee as he ambles to the huge black-lacquered fridge.

"I've got the lot." He smirks and pulls food out. Fifteen minutes later, we're tucking into the bacon, eggs, and waffles.

"Damn, that was good. I'm gonna need to exercise that off!" I rub my stomach and chuckle.

"How about we take a walk? I can show you around," Dan says as he picks up the plates and moves over to the dishwasher.

"Sounds good. How far are we talking about? Am I gonna need my cane?" I flush at the thought of him seeing me with a prop to help me.

"We'll do as much or as little as you can manage. It's getting cooler now, so we're not going to be ruled by the heat. But why don't you take it, y'know, just in case."

"You don't mind?"

"Mind what?" Confusion washes over his face. "What, you with a cane? Of course not. Don't be dumb."

After thirty minutes of Dan pointing out everything new and where his friends live, we walk into the town and stroll easily up the high street. I can see there are a lot of new businesses here.

"The tourist trade has taken off hugely here, and many of the ranches offer hiking, horseback trekking, and hunting holidays, and have had cabins built on their land. The guy, East, I told you about last night, he has done most of them and has a large team of workers now. We really are a thriving town all year round because the skiing is great here too."

"It looks it, too." I look up and down and spy a bar across the street. "The Last Drop Inn, cool name! Is that the bar you were telling me about?" I point up the street.

"Yeah, that's Kes' place. Come on, he may be in. Carter is away in the city today speaking to a new supplier, so unfortunately you won't get to meet him." Dan laughs and slaps me on the back.

I step inside the cool bar and look around, taking in the polished oak bar with brass rails and tall stools that seem to have a person sitting on every one of them. It's a popular place, and I can see why. The walls have prints of cool cars and iconic actors and actresses all over them. The booths look cozy and inviting. I can see a stage in the back corner, so I'm guessing they have live music here too.

"This is a great place," I enthuse as we make our way to the bar.

"You wanna grab a seat, Arch? I'll bring it over." Dan points over to one of the tables rather than a booth.

"Sure." I feel my ankle give way, and I must use my cane to stop me from slipping. "Ow, fuck!" I hobble gracelessly to the table and pull out the chair, collapsing down.

"You okay?" Dan asks as he places two tall glasses of beer down, the drops of water already beading on the outside of the glass.

"Yeah, maybe a bit too much walking. My ankle gave out."

"You gonna be okay to walk back? I can get us a ride from Kes." Dan looks at me, with worry lines all over his forehead.

"Stop worrying, you old woman. It happens sometimes. I'll be fine when I've sat for a while. It's a great place. I'm used to sports bars." I like it here. Better than the typical bar I would go to with friends. I watch Dan's eyebrows shoot up under his hairline, questioning me. "Yeah, yeah, I know. I like sports, especially baseball. Those tight pants are hot! But the guys I work with are straight, so we got used to going there after work."

"Did you go there with your man?" Dan takes a gulp of his beer and sighs. "That's good beer."

"Yeah, sometimes. He got on well with everyone. We liked to spend our time together. We'd hit the gay bars, have a few drinks, and dance. Damn, he was a good dancer. I guess he still is, but just not with me." I feel a wave of longing and loneliness wash over me.

"Hey, I'm sorry. I shouldn't've brought it up. I won't again."

"No, no, it's okay. Look, I got used to the idea months ago, but it seems more real now than before. I guess it's because I'm getting my life together now. Being here is good, it's new. I have no demons here. No one to constantly ask how I'm doing. Except you, you big girl." I nudge him as he picks up his glass and make him choke on his drink.

"Fine! I'll let you fall on your ass next time. Asshole," Dan mutters under his breath, making me laugh.

"This feels good. Thanks again, man." I grin at him. "Is this where you met Carter then? Where he kept turning you down?"

"Asshole! I only asked him out properly once, and he said yes! But dammit, I've been flirting since he showed up. About eight or more months ago now. He turned up on a shit-hot black custom bike, and Kes gave him a job and the apartment upstairs. He was quiet and looked so broken down, but he has been happier lately. He got the manager's job and is simply a genuinely great guy. You'll like him too."

"Jeez, you've got it bad." I laugh and change the topic, I don't really want to hear him talking about a guy he's in love with. It brings it all back to me. We finish our beer and decide not to have another and head home. As we walk out, I get the scent of a cologne I'm very used to. The same as Mallory wore. Turning my head, I look behind me and see the back of a very thin guy with dark wavy hair retreat through a door.

We laze about for the rest of the day, lying out in the afternoon sun, then grilling steaks outside for our dinner, making for a perfect day.

By ten, I'm done for and need to crash. I look over at Dan and see he's almost asleep too. I have forgotten how good looking he is, and it amazes me he hasn't been snapped up. His new boyfriend is damn lucky to have him. Hell, I would have considered it again if he hadn't been taken.

Damn that thought makes me realizes I've had one beer too many. "Hey, Dan, I'm gonna hit the sack. You want me to lock up?"

"Nah, you go. I'll be right up. Night, Arch."

But sleep doesn't come easily, although after the walking and the beers, I should be knocked out. Eventually, I feel myself slide away under the blanket of sleep. I dream of Mallory, but a different Mallory. The same man but so changed, so sad and lonely. I want to call out to him, but I know it's never worked in the past dreams. It morphs into something more, something so hot. Mallory is naked, but he has me and Dan teasing and torturing his body to the greatest climax. I wake in a sweat-soaked state, with the biggest hard-on I've had in months. Hell, since I was last over and inside Mallory.

I reach down to stroke myself, knowing there's no way I'll get back to sleep with this bastard. It takes just a few strokes before my back arches on the bed and a fountain of cum shoots over my chest. I breathe hard but manage to chuckle when I look down and see the stripes of my release over my stomach and chest.

"Dammit!" I whisper in the dark but drift off to sleep again, not awake long enough to wipe the stickiness from my body.

Chapter
Twenty-Two

DAN

I can't believe how easily Archer has settled into life here. We haven't been out much. I think he's still in recuperation mode and has spent a lot of time relaxing in the sunshine. I'm getting used to the vivid scars on his body, and I'm amazed at his strength and determination to get full strength again. Knowing his ankles have both been fractured and he has more metalwork holding him together, I don't know how he manages to walk so well.

"Hey, what's got you all quiet and pensive? You okay?" Archer looks at me and cocks his head to the side. "Am I outstaying my welcome?" He laughs and bumps his fist against my shoulder.

"What? God, no! It's great having you here. It's only been a week, so you're good for a while longer. I'm gonna have to go into work after the weekend. You want to come with me, or are you happy hanging out here?" I stop myself from running my eyes over his naked chest. He's still ripped, and his tan looks too damn good. I can still see the scars on the side of his ribs where he had to have drains inserted to inflate his lung again.

"I'll stay here. I'm trying not to think about work yet. You've got a great setup here. I like the dynamics you've got going on there."

I'd taken Archer into my offices a couple days ago. I wanted to see how easy it would be for him to fit in here. I've built up a great reputation and pull in work from all the surrounding towns. There's plenty for him to do if he decides to join me.

"I dreamed about you the other night, about us together." Archer looks at me, and I watch his bright-green eyes dilate as he roams over my body.

"Fuck! I guess I should tell you that I've had a couple since you got here too." I let myself peruse his half-naked body now.

"Yeah? Did yours involve a third? Because mine did, but we had been reminiscing. I guess it was just an errant thought." A pale-pink blush covers his neck and face.

"Who was the third?"

"Who do you reckon? He's always in my dreams, but this was the first time like that. The first time it was good."

"Yeah, well, mine had Carter with us." I smirk and walk up to him. I sigh when his tongue darts out and slicks his bottom lip.

His face looks as flushed as I feel. His green eyes soften as his pupils narrow. A slow, lazy smile spreads over his face as he licks his lips, as if he's tasting mine. I mirror his action and smile. A chuckle builds in my chest

"I'm here for you. You're my best friend, Archer." I lean in and pull him against me. He runs his hands down my arms to clasp my hands.

"Daniel, I don't know what I would do if you weren't my friend. You're stuck with me. Whatever happens will happen, but I'm not looking too deeply into my life or looking too far ahead. I'm adjusting to a life I never thought I would have and being here, with you, is helping me. Thank you for being here for me." His mouth presses briefly up to mine then he pulls away.

My cell phone rings halting any further conversation.

"Hey, whassup?" I grin when Archer rolls his eyes at my greeting but listen to my caller. "Hold up, he's here. I'll ask him." I lower my phone. "Kes wants to know if we fancy going out tonight. Dinner then a club. You wanna go?"

I wait while Archer thinks then nods. "Yeah, sure. Sounds good."

"Kes, we're in. Yep, cool. See you there later. Thanks, man."

"You should call Carter. Get him to meet us after dinner. I could finally get to meet him, *and* you get your jollies with your man." Archer looks over at me. We've just had a lazy lunch, and he's clearing away the detritus of turkey club sandwiches. We seem to have mayo and mustard on every surface.

"You sure? I don't mind not seeing him tonight," I lie blatantly and laugh when he raises his eyebrow at me. "Yeah, yeah, all right. I'm missing him like fucking crazy! I'll call him."

It turns out he's going out tonight with Paris, so he'll be there anyway. I take extra care getting ready. I want his jaw to drop when he sees me. Plus, I've prepped everywhere else too. I want him in my bed and my body tonight. It's been too long.

"Is it a gay bar or a gay-friendly bar?" Archer is nervous. I can tell, but he's playing it cool.

"It's a gay bar, y'know the type. Lots of leather and bare chests, hips grinding, blow jobs in the bathroom gay bar." I burst out laughing at the look of abject horror on his face. "I'm messing with you, Arch, just chill. It's a gay bar but a good place. Lots of space to chill out. It's got a decent dance floor and plenty of eye candy, but it's not full of bare-chested alpha bear types. You'll like it, I promise." I rest my hand on his thigh to calm him.

"And the guys we're meeting are the three you talk about; the bar owner is Kes?"

"Yep, and we're here now." I pull the car up outside the restaurant. I can see Denver's truck a couple cars ahead of mine. "The guys are already here, so let's hustle."

I laugh when Archer sighs. "I hate meeting new people. They always stare at the way I walk, and FYI, I'm not dancing."

"Oh, cheer up, you miserable asshole!"

We walk into the restaurant. It's a great Italian one that does a mean lasagna. My stomach growls, and Archer laughs. I look around and see my friends already at the table. Nudging Archer, I point, and we walk over.

"Damn, you're right. They're handsome fuckers!" Archer hisses at me.

After introductions, we sit and order. The conversation flows easily. I knew Archer would get on with them. I've been friends with East and Kes since high school, and it was great to meet up with Denver again too. We hang out regularly, and I like their company. Archer seems relaxed with them too, another plus sign and a tick in the box to make him move here.

"Dan said you had an accident recently. You look like you recovered well?" Denver asks Archer. "I run the trauma unit over at Charlottestown."

"Yeah, it's been a rough few months. It was touch and go for a while, but I had a good orthopedic surgeon. He got me fixed up. I'm very grateful for his hard work and determination to get me walking again. I broke my tib, fib, and talus. There's a heck of a lot of metalwork holding them together. I broke my femur too, and that had an external fixator. It's been a long road to get me walking this well. I had an amazing physical therapy team, and I'm good now. Plus, my arm and wrist broke and a collapsed lung, and I said goodbye to my spleen." I watch how Archer shrugs off something that almost killed him.

"Damn! That's seriously tough. Who was your bone man?"

"Alec Truman, he was amazing. Do you know of him?" Archer replies.

There's a pause in the conversation. I watch as Denver swallows hard and Kes and East reach out to him. Then Denver smiles. "You did good. He's an excellent doctor. I know him and know his dedication to getting everything perfect. I'm happy you had him."

"How long are you staying here, Archer? Hasn't Dan driven you crazy yet?" East changes the subject and lightens the mood.

"He's not too bad. I'm used to him. We were dorm mates and then shared a house. I can't believe it took me so long to get here to see him. To answer your question, I'm not sure. I've taken a sabbatical from my job, and I have great bosses who understand my need for a change."

"I'm trying to persuade him to come and join me. *Soooo*, the longer I can keep him the better!" I laugh and clap Archer on the back.

"Are we ready to hit the club?" Kes claps his hands together. We've had a lazy dinner and have just finished our coffees.

Ten minutes later, we walk into the club, and I'm hit by the sound of a heavy bass and the scent of hot male bodies. My dick twitches in my pants, and I wonder if Carter is here yet.

"Hey, Dan. If you want to find your man, that's cool. Get all your kissing over with before you find me," Archer whispers loudly over the noise and laughs.

"I think I will. Grab me a beer, and I'll be back in a few." I wink and head off in search of my man. I see him getting his groove on with Paris. I know they're good friends and nothing else. I don't feel jealous, apart from wanting him to grind against me again.

I walk up behind him and wrap my arms around his waist, drawing him close to my body. "Hey, baby, have you missed me?"

Carter twists in my arms and lunges for my mouth. His tongue delves into my mouth as his hands grip my head, holding me still. I let him control this because I'd have him in the bathroom and up against the wall if I could. I feel our dicks harden as he pushes his hips forward. We both moan and keep on kissing as if we're starving for each other, which I guess we are.

Slowing the kissing down, I lean back to look at his lust-drunk eyes. His heavy lids are hooded over the black of his glazed eyes.

"Fuck, it's been too long, Dan. Do we have to stay long?" He presses his forehead to mine and drops more kisses on my lips.

"No, we can say hi to the guys. I want you to meet my friend, then we can go." I kiss him again, then grab his hand and lead him back to the bar. As we get there, Archer has his back to us. I tap him on the shoulder. As he turns, I see his face turn to stone. His jaw is tight, and there's a muscle in his cheek pulsing. I've never seen such an angry look or stance on him.

"Archer, I'd like to introduce you to my man..." My voice dries up when Archer speaks.

"Mallory Halston," he spits out, his eyes blazing with fury.

Chapter

Twenty-Three

CARTER

"Yes, fine." I finally give in to Paris' demand to go to a club with him. He's a nice guy, but not my type, which is good because I'm not his either, but we get on well and have a laugh.

"Really? Yay! Awesome! That's great. We can go after work. It will be a laugh." Paris jumps up and hugs me.

"You ready to go, Car?" he asks, and I can see he's excited.

"Yep, come on. We'll go upstairs. You can shower and change if you want. I'm going to."

Paris has been here before. We have had Xbox marathons here where he's ended up crashing on the sofa. But there's nothing more there, and I'm grateful for a friend that doesn't ask too many questions. He knows the diluted version of my background. I mean, I've got pictures of Archer in here; it's bound to encourage questions.

"Go on, you get showered first. I've got some leftover pizza if you want some. Oh, and Dan called. He'll be out tonight with his buddy and Kes and his men. We can meet up with them if that's okay." I walk into the kitchen, pull the pizza box out of the fridge, and grab two slices to microwave them.

"I'm done!" Paris walks out, and I must admit he looks good. Tight, black, skinny jeans, ripped at the knees, and a tight vintage Sex Pistols T-shirt, with worn-out Converse on his feet.

"You're gonna be every man's wet dream tonight, Paris." I laugh as he blushes.

"Fuck off. Now go, get pretty. You'll want to look good for your man." He does the same as me and heats up some food.

Fifteen minutes later, I'm showered and dressed, and not far off what Paris is wearing. I'm in dark-grey skinny jeans with a fitted black shirt with the Rolling Stones tongue on the front. I step into my high-top Converse and run my hand through my hair. It's longer now than I used to keep it, but I like it this way. I put a black stud in my ear, and I have a stud in my nose. When I look in the mirror, I can see me, the me I am now, the me after Archer, and I like it. I like what Dan has brought out in me, and to be in love again is awesome.

"Come on, then, pretty boy. Let's go!" I wrap my arm around his shoulder and wonder where the desire for me to be happy has come from. For now, I'm gonna just roll with it.

The club is filling up nicely when we walk in. The beat of the music reverberates through my chest, reminding me how much I love dancing. The image of me grinding against Archer as he held my hips and whispered all the dirty things he would do to me when we got home, pops in my mind. He never let me down and always took me higher and higher every time he touched me. Now I get to do it with Dan, anytime we want.

I shake the thought away as we get up to the bar and wait for a bartender to reach us. The guys here are hot. It's got a good vibe here too. I look around the room once we've got our beers and check out who's here. There's a great mix of men, a few leather harnesses and collars but nothing too in your face. They would look but only touch if you invited them.

Imagine Dragons *Thunder* comes on, Paris grabs my hand, and we head into the clutch of heaving, swaying, and grinding hot male bodies. As my hips gyrate, I feel Paris place his arms loosely over my shoulders. l grin as we move in time together, and even though I know we're not each other's type, it feels amazing to grind against him. My arms rise as I dance harder. Paris moves his to grip my hips, and I throw my head back, singing out the words. I feel someone take hold of my shoulder as I'm pulled against a warm body.

Then I feel some arms wrap around my waist, and I smell a very familiar cologne. I know my man has found me. I need him, so I twist quickly in his arms and attack his mouth. As soon as our tongues connect, I get lightheaded, and I need more. I plunder his mouth, twisting our tongues together before sucking hard on it, making both of us groan. My dick hardens and rubs against his. Shit! We need to get out of here, or I'll be dropping to my knees in the bathroom.

"Fuck, it's been too long, Dan. Do we have to stay long?" I pant as my head rests against his.

"No, we can go say hi to the guys. I want you to meet my friend, then we can go." His voice equally as breathless.

"Let's go." I whisper as I cling onto Dan, still feeling dizzy from our kiss. I let Dan lead me through the gyrating hoards.

"Archer, I'd like to introduce you to my man…" Dan's words dry up as his friend turns to face me.

It's Archer standing in front of me, his eyes blazing, shooting flames of fury as his lips curl. "It didn't take you long to move on, did it? I lay in a hospital waiting for you to come to me, and you fuck off out of my life." He sneers.

I'm motionless. I feel like his hand has punched into my chest and ripped out my heart. The feeling of cold water drenches my body as he pushes me away and storms past me.

As I look around, I see Kes and his boyfriends. Dan has his arm wrapped around my waist. I feel him go rigid.

"What's going on, Carter? How does he know you?" The confusion on his face is apparent and heartbreaking. I don't know what to do.

"He's your best friend? Archer-fucking-Hawkins is your best friend? Jesus fucking Christ!" I go cold, freezing cold. Archer is alive and well and so fucking angry, and I'm in love with his best friend. Shit!

"We need to find him, Carter. Come on, baby, let's work this out." Dan's voice echoes in my head, but I'm so lost in the hows and whys, I barely register his words.

Chapter
Twenty-Four

ARCHER

The look of pain on his face confuses me. It's not the look I expected, not the look of a man who chose to walk away from me. It was a look of genuine distress and horror. I can't think anymore. I must get away from him. With no thought of the men I came with, I rush out of the club.

I lean against the wall, the heel of my palms pressed hard against my eyes as I drag deep, painful breaths into my aching, burning lungs. I wasn't even aware I'd been holding my breath until I gasp.

"Archer?" I hear Dan speaking softly. "What's going on? How do you know him?"

"Because that is my Mallory, the one that left me when I needed him the most." Running my hands through my hair, I tug hard, fisting it and pulling hard. "FUUUUUUUUUUUUUCK!!"

I can't stop the anguished cry from bursting from me. My chest heaves as the tears pour unchecked down my face.

"How can you not have known who he is? Fuck, Dan, I talked about him all the time. Shit!" I shout at him, ignoring the look of shock written all over his face.

"I had no idea, Arch. I promise you. His name is Carter to everyone here. He's my boyfriend. Shit, I've talked about how much I love him, and he's been yours all along."

"He's not fucking mine anymore though. He's yours. He loves you. You told me that. Fuck! I can't deal with this," I shout, then look past Dan and see Mallory standing further back, his arms wrapped tight around his body, tears streaming down his face. He looks so beautiful to me. He's been in my dreams for so long, and now I have him here standing before me, and I can't touch him.

All the anger leaves my body, and I slump back against the wall. It feels like it's the only thing holding me upright. I'm sure my legs aren't doing a very good job. "Dan, I'm sorry for yelling."

"I think we need to get back home." He looks over his shoulder and sees Mallory in pain, and he reaches out to him. I see the hesitation in Mallory's eyes as they flicker between the two of us. He steps tentatively to Dan and catches hold of his hand, the sight making me wince.

"We need to get home. We need to talk about this," Dan says determinedly. "We need to know what happened, and where we go from here."

The ride home is silent. Mallory sits in the front with Dan. I don't pay any attention to the ride, and soon we're outside Dan's house, the place I came to to try to rebuild my life and start again.

When we get inside, Dan walks straight over to his liquor shelf and reaches for the bourbon. Sloshing a couple fingers of the amber liquid into three glasses, he hands one to me, the second to Mallory. Taking only a sip, he sits.

I watch as Mallory chews on his thumbnail and leans on the chair Dan has just sat on. He looks at me like I'm a ghost. Fuck! What did she do to him?

"Mallory..." I try to talk.

"You died," he stutters, then reaches for Dan's hand. Again, it's like a knife in my heart how he turns to him. I really have lost him.

"No, I didn't. I could've easily, but I made it, just." My words dry up as I think back to the pain.

"Archer, I had two policemen at the door of our apartment. They told me you died." The pain in his voice is palpable.

I take a seat on the other sofa, and unlike Dan, I take a huge gulp and shudder as the fire hits my throat and stomach. Waiting for him to continue, my head drops back against the soft leather, and I close my eyes before I speak.

"I woke up five days after the accident. My mother told me you packed up and left me as soon as she told you." I sigh at the painful memory. "Nothing hurt more than the pain in my heart. I had a feeling my mother had done something, but for her to tell you I died, I can't forgive her for that." I look at Dan, and he is frowning. I know how analytical his mind is, and he's thinking hard. I wait for him to speak.

"Carter turned up about eight or nine months ago. I remember Kes looking out for him from the start. He was a very different man than the one you see tonight. His eyes were clouded and dull. He was so thin. I reckon he was at least twenty pounds lighter. He stepped into the bar position well and would talk and joke with the customers, but there was never any joy in him when he was by himself." Dan pauses and lifts Mallory's hand up to his mouth and kisses the back softly.

"I think it was a few months, maybe more like four, before I saw a change in him. He filled out. He relaxed around people and would open a conversation rather than just answering. That's probably when I started flirting with him."

Mallory laughs. "You were a pain in my ass, baby. Always embarrassing me."

"He would blush and shake his head when I asked him out. They were only flirty jokes, not a proper invitation. But whenever I did, I would see the shutters come down, and he closed himself off. He never gave me a reason, he just said no. Kes guarded him, and so did Shelley. They are very protective of him. So, I had to just be patient and keep trying to encourage him to take a chance."

"I'm really not that keen on how you made a play for my fiancé," I snap at him, and Mallory looks like I've slapped him.

"I had to stop being your fiancé when your mother told me I was a lowlife and had fifteen minutes to get out of *her* apartment, not ours, before she had me arrested for trespassing. I grabbed the few things I could, told her to get fucked and left."

"It's not her apartment. It never has been. It's always been mine and then ours. Why didn't you go to the hospital? You were down as my next of kin." I'm shouting now as my frustration and anger builds.

"I did. I fucking tried, but your mother had some huge motherfucker blocking me. She just sneered and said it was just family allowed," Mallory shouts back at me now. Dan has hold of him, stopping him from standing, but I'm already back on my feet.

"Hey! Come on! Cut it out, Archer. Calm the fuck down! This isn't what this is about. You two do not need to be hating each other right now. You need to find a way to talk to each other, to find out what the hell has been going on. And most importantly, to find a way to move on from here, to move forward.

"What are you expecting from this? That we all become friends?" I spit at him. "I can't see that happening."

Mallory stands and shoots daggers at me. "Y'know, I've had enough of this shit! I'm going to bed." He looks down at Dan, and what I see from him is the love that shines from him. "I'm gonna go home, okay?"

"No! No fucking way." Dan stands, and the two go chest to chest "You aren't walking out of here, Carter. Not without me."

"Let's go, then," Mallory replies without any further comment.

Dan looks at me "Think about it, Archer. Think about what you want. Think very carefully. We'll see you tomorrow."

I sit in silence as my best friend and the love of my life leave the house.

Chapter
Twenty-Five

CARTER

"What's going to happen, Dan? What the hell do we do now?" I pace the floor of my small living room. Dan looks around, and he spies a photo on my bookshelf.

"I don't know, baby. I'm as confused as you are. This is like something from a book or a film. It doesn't seem real." He picks up the picture of me and Archer. It's one of my favorites. We look so happy and so in love. I can see the pain on his face, and I reach out to him.

"I'm sorry, Dan. I feel that this is my fault. If I hadn't been so locked down in my grief, I would have mentioned his name, and we would have been able to work it out."

"I guess, but if you'd known he was alive, you wouldn't be with me. You would have gone back to him. We wouldn't be a 'we,' and as fucked up as this is, I love you, and I'm happy we got together."

"Oh, Dan, I love you too. I don't know how I should feel about Archer anymore. I'm happy he's alive, but I'm not the same man I was when we were together. I'm sure he has changed too." Although my heart squeezes when I think of him again.

"Why did you change your name? If you'd stayed with Mallory, maybe I would have worked out that you were Archer's boyfriend. It's an unusual name, and given how unhappy you were, I could've put two and two together." He shakes his head sadly.

I moan. "I changed it because I needed to be someone else. It's my middle name, so it was easy to do. See, it's still my fault."

"You can't blame yourself, Cart..." Dan's words dry up, and he takes a deep breath. "Would you rather I called you Mallory now?"

"No, I'm Carter now. I like it. It felt weird when Archer called me Mallory. It didn't feel like me." I lean into him and sigh as Dan's arms wrap around me.

"Let's go to bed, Carter. It will all seem better in the morning. Well, maybe not, but at least we won't be as tired. Y'know, I can't believe I haven't been in here before."

"I never thought about it. We're always at your place. I like it there. There's so much space. This place is small and too close to work."

As we undress and climb into my queen-sized bed, I snuggle up to Dan and rest my head on his chest. I can feel myself drifting off as Dan strokes up and down my back. A thought enters my mind. Shit!

"Dan, we need to go back to yours." I push myself up to look at him.

"What? Why?" His confusion apparent.

"What if he leaves? I mean, would you want to stay if you've just seen your best friend leave with your ex-boyfriend? We need to sort this out. I don't think he should be by himself."

"You're right. Come on, let's go."

In minutes, we're dressed and racing down the stairs. I know it will only take us ten minutes to get there, but I have the feeling of dread building up in my chest that we'll be too late and he will have already left.

"D'you think he'll be there?" I look to Dan as we walk hurriedly back to the house.

"I do. I think he'll realize he shouldn't be driving, after drinking this evening. I hope so anyway. C'mon."

Picking up speed, we jog back. I relax as his rental car comes into sight, still sitting on Dan's driveway. Slowing down again now, Dan reaches for my hand.

"Hopefully, he will have gone to bed, and we can talk in the morning." Dan sighs.

The lights are still on in the front room, negating Dan's hope. As Dan puts the key in the lock, the door swings open, and Archer stands with a bottle of Scotch in his hand. I can see him swaying as he brings the bottle up to his lips.

"Whatcha doing back here? Haven't you rubbed my nose in it enough today?" Archer slurs at us both.

"No, Archer. We came back because we didn't want you to be alone. I think we have got so much to talk about and deal with," I reply.

"Whatever." Archer turns and stumbles back to the living room, collapsing down on the sofa.

"I think we should all get some sleep. It's late now. I don't think we can work out anything tonight. Archer, leave the scotch and get some sleep." Dan takes hold of the bottle and takes it from Archer's grip.

Archer looks up at me, and I see tears build in his eyes. He looks so broken and lost, I want to wrap my arms around him.

"Archer, please don't cry," I beg and step up to him.

"I lost you, Mallory. I needed you so much, and you weren't there. You broke my heart. Now, just as I start to live again, I find you, and I've still lost you. I love you, and I can't have you." Tears stream down his face, and I can't hold back.

"Archer, I'm so sorry. I had no choice. I had no reason not to believe her. I should've questioned her. I shouldn't have believed her. I lost you too, and now, like you, I have started to live again. I love you, but I love Dan now, too." My arms wrap around him, and we hold each other. Tears fall from my eyes as I grieve for what we have lost.

I feel Dan's hand on my back. He soothes me, rubbing circles over my spine as I cry. I feel Archer's hands grip my waist as he continues to sob.

"I should've looked for you. I should have called you. I should've not trusted my mother. I thought she may have done something. I just never thought she would do something so abhorrent. I let you down, honey. I'm sorry." His fingers tighten on my hips as he blames himself.

"It's not your fault, Arch. I get that you're angry, and I understand why. Let's move on and see what we can do. I want you in my life, Archer. I hope you want me to be in yours." I feel him nod against my chest, and I can't stop myself from dropping a kiss on his hair. As I inhale the oh-so-familiar scent of him, I sigh softly.

Then, in what feels like slow motion, Archer lifts his head, and his mouth presses gently on mine. I hear Dan gasp, but he keeps his hand on my back, still stroking me. Is he okay with this? Fuck! What's going on? Then Archer moves back, away from me. His brilliant-green eyes are blazing. Is it the remnants of his tears or from the kiss?

"I'm going to bed," Archer speaks quietly. "Thank you, and yes, I want you in my life."

He walks past Dan and smiles sadly. "You're a very lucky man, Dan. I hope you know that."

"I do, and I still want you here. I love you, Archer. You know that, right?" Dan pulls Archer in for a hug, and they hold each other tightly for a few moments. Archer ambles his way out, and we stand silently as his heavy footsteps climb the staircase.

Dan reaches out to me, and I step willingly into his embrace. "You let him kiss me," I whisper.

"I did. I think you both needed it. I love you, Carter. I want you to be happy, and I think seeing Archer again will make you happy." Dan leans in and kisses me, a long slow burner of a kiss. Deep lazy licks as his tongue caresses mine, and a low moan escapes me as my fingers grip tightly to his shirt. "I want you, it's been too long. Take me to bed."

"Let's go." I whisper.

The door to the guest room at the front of the house is shut, and I hope Archer sleeps well, even with all the whiskey in his veins.

When we're inside the bedroom, Dan's eyes slide up and down my body. I feel my dick thicken as he gazes at me; the hunger in his eyes makes me shiver.

"Strip for me, baby." His voice low and husky, drips with the promise of dirty sex. My insides clench as he palms his own dick through the fabric of his slacks.

"Are you sure we should be doing this? Archer is just across the hallway. It feels weird." I look at him and see his hurt expression.

"You don't want to make love with me? We've been apart for over a week. I've missed you so much. Is he coming between us already?" The pain in his voice is palpable.

"No, Dan. He's not coming between us. I just wonder if he hears us it will hurt him even more, making him leave us before we have a chance to speak."

"Carter, I want you. I want to make love to you. Please, baby, I need you," Dan pleads. His hand strokes down my face and neck until it travels to rest over my heart. I can't deny him something I want too.

Kicking off my Converse first, I let my fingers hover over the hem of my T-shirt, slowly inching it up my torso. I keep my eyes fixed on Dan as he licks slowly over his lower lip before biting on it. Leisurely, I pull the shirt up and drag it over my head, throwing it in the same direction as my shoes.

My hands slide over my chest, pausing to tug on my nipples. The sensations make me moan and tug a bit harder. Leaving the reddened, pert nubs, I skim over my six-pack, making it flex under my touch. Dan is breathing hard now, his hands in fists at his side as he holds himself back.

My fingers slide down the groove of my oblique muscles and dip under the waistband of my jeans. Popping the button, I halt when he takes a step towards me. Standing still again, Dan gazes, mesmerized, at the zipper slowly being lowered. Then my hands slide down the back, pushing the denim down and over my ass.

Dan watches me silently as I strip out of my clothes. His eyes roam over my body. I love how his eyes darken and his breath quickens every time I take my clothes off. He loves me, and I love him, but my heart shifts and stutters as I realize that I love Archer also.

"You are perfect, Carter." He sighs, then he pulls off his clothes and strides up to me. As his body covers mine, his mouth captures my lips. Pulling my arms up over my head, he holds them in one hand as the other travels over my chest to tweak and tease my nipple, making me groan loudly as I squirm, desperate for more.

Chapter
Twenty-Six

ARCHER

As I lie here, I think about what just happened. I couldn't stop myself from kissing him. I needed one taste of his lips. But now I feel worse. I still want him, and it's killing me all over again. As his arms wrapped around me, I felt my heart beat again, pounding hard, sounding out to his, calling for him again.

Then I hear them come upstairs. Dan has the master room at the back of the house, but I still hear the door opening and shutting firmly. I squeeze my eyes tight, trying to block out the image of the two of them together. Concentrating on some deep, calming breaths, I try to relax, but then I hear a moan. Oh God, no! I can't hear them making love. I can't bear it!

It goes quiet, but now the image is in my mind. I imagine all the things they could be doing. My ears seem to be on high alert, so as much as I want to block them out, I lie still, waiting for the moment I hear them cry out their orgasms.

Then I hear it. First, I hear Mallory, and my dick instantly goes rock hard. Dan follows, his groan so guttural and passionate. I screw my eyes tight shut, trying to hold back the pain. Tears escape as I feel my heart shatter again. I can't stay here. I can't do this.

But then something inside me tells me to hold tight, that he doesn't have a choice if I take myself out of the equation. I know I won't try to win him back. That's not me. I don't do shitty things like that. I'm a good guy. Then I think of my dream and the three of us being together, something I know Dan has thought about too. Maybe we do need to have a talk.

I won't suggest it as that's not me, but I find myself wanting to be around them. The idea of staying here might be a good idea after all.

Or is it? And who would it hurt the most? I guess that would be me again. Oh, fuck! What am I going to do?

Eventually, sleep takes over, and I slip away, dreamlessly.

I wake with the most God-awful banging in my head. It feels like I've got an ax buried in my skull. My mouth feels like something crawled in there and died, and my eyes seem to be glued shut. What the fuck happened?

But then the memories come flooding back. Mallory is here. Mallory is Carter, and Mallory is fucking my best fucking friend! I pull one of the pillows over my head and silently scream into it.

I want to go home! I don't want to be here anymore! But I can't. I need to see him. We need to talk. Shit! I pull the pillow away and try to open my eyes. The sun shines brightly through a gap in the curtains, making me wince. Twisting my head around to the side, I grab my phone to see what time it is.

Whoa! Eleven-thirty. Wow, I never sleep this long. I think it was probably more a whiskey-induced coma. I never drink like that, not since college, and now I remember all too vividly why. I hate hangovers. They really knock me on my ass. Dragging myself out of bed, I stumble to the bathroom. I rest one hand on the wall while I pee. I'm not sure I'm sober yet because the room sways around me.

I need a shower. I switch it on and turn the heat up. I have to lean on the wall here too. I close my eyes and tip my face up to the spray, letting the scalding water seep through my whiskey-soaked pores. Turning around, I let the water pound over my neck and back. I can feel the tension in my muscles and bones, and I know the water will soothe me. More memories of last night come back to me, the most vivid was the sound of them fucking.

I sink down to the floor and wrap my arms around my bent legs. My head drops down to rest on my knees as I sob. Deep, heartbreaking, wretched sobs. This hurts too much. I love him. I still really fucking love him, and he doesn't love me that way anymore. And it hurts, it hurts so damn much.

Eventually, I notice that the water is cold, and I'm cried out. I force myself back up to my feet and turn off the water. Grabbing a towel, I scrub myself dry and stagger back to bed. Collapsing, I burrow under the duvet and let sleep take me away again. I don't need to see them today. I need to let my heart settle before facing them.

When I wake again, my headache has gone, but so has the sunlight. Shit, I've slept all day. I guess it doesn't matter. I didn't have any plans, so why the hell not? My stomach rumbles loudly, protesting at the lack of food in it. I guess I should get up and get something to eat. I can come back up here with it. Some grilled cheese sandwiches I think will do just fine.

Slinging on some sweatpants and a T-shirt, I make my way downstairs. I hope Dan and Mallory will be out, but I hear voices as I make my way to the kitchen. No such luck.

Chapter
Twenty-Seven

DAN

"Wow!" I slide out of Carter and pull off the condom. Swinging my legs off the bed, I get a cloth to clean him.

"How d'you feel about getting tested? Is it too soon for us?" He reaches for the cloth. "Here, gimme that. I'll do it."

"Really? Yeah, I want to, and I don't think it's too soon. We love each other. We're committed to each other, which leads me to ask you a question. Will you move in with me? I hate it when you're in your apartment. I want to wake up with you every day."

"Yes! Yes, I want to be here with you…" His voice fades, and I see him glance to the door. I know he's thinking of Archer. "What about Archer?"

"I think that's up to you, baby." I lie back and pull him against me. I love the way he tangles his legs with mine. "Did you know we dated at college, for a while actually."

"I did, but why did you break up? He never said."

"We were talking about it the other night, and we don't know. Maybe we just drifted apart, found other people we wanted to date. I still love him, y'know."

"Yeah, I know. I do too. Is it going to make it too difficult?"

"Would you consider him being a part of us?" I speak cautiously, just testing the water.

"What? As a threesome? Shit, Daniel, that's a lot to think about." Lifting his head up, Carter studies my face, searching for something, or maybe he's getting pissed. "Is that why you want me to move in? So, we are all together? Don't I satisfy you?"

"What? No, baby, you make me so complete. When we make love, it's everything I ever want. I want you to move in because I love you and want to be with you. Archer may still decide to leave or stay but find his own place. But I think he would only be leaving because it would be too hard for him to be here without you. If you still love him and still want him as much as you love and want me, maybe we should let him know." My hand trails lazily up and down his back, a motion I know he loves while I let him think.

"Can you really see the three of us together? I mean properly together, the whole sex thing?" Carter trails his fingers through the fine line of hair down to my dick.

"Fuck yeah, I can. I had a dream about it last week, and dammit, Carter, it was so hot."

"I think we need to be sure. I'm not sure that just giving it a try is fair on any of us. If we want to be committed to each other, there must be the trust that we aren't simply experimenting with him. I don't think it should be based on sex, simply because the thought of us in a ménage is hot. This must be because we love each other equally, that we want a relationship, all of us together. Not just a third because you had a sexy dream."

"I know that, Carter. Do we discuss this with him? Or maybe we should hear what he has to say first. This could all be theoretical if he decides to leave."

"I think what's important is if you love both me and Archer enough to want us in your bed and in your body."

"I know I don't want to not have him in my life. I know I love him, but I love you too, so much." Carter squirms as my finger rims his tight hole. "Dammit, Daniel, pack it in."

"No, I want inside you again, right now."

"Jesus, Dan." He sighs as my finger dips inside him.

Reaching across to the drawer, I grab another condom. The lube is still in the bed somewhere. Good, Carter has found it. I suit up quickly and slide deep inside him. We both groan loudly as I pound inside him. God, I can't wait to be free of the latex barrier and be bare inside him.

"Jesus, Dan. That was intense. Fuck!" Carter eases himself off me, and I slide gracelessly out of him. We both wrinkle our noses. "Testing tomorrow!!" He laughs and grabs the now-cold, wet cloth. Making me shriek, he cleans up his mess. He even disposes of the condom and cleans me.

"I'm never letting you go, y'know that, right?" I mumble. Sleep tries to drag me under.

"Good, because I'm not going anywhere."

I feel the covers pull up over me and sleep claims me.

The alarm on the table next to my bed goes off, and I hear Carter groan and pull a pillow over his head. Chuckling, I pull him into my body. "Not a morning person are you, baby?"

"Not when I don't have to be, no. I'm not scheduled to work 'til later this afternoon, so I plan to sleep this morning," he mumbles but turns his head to face me, opening one eye to just a slit. "I'd be fine if you hadn't kept me up all night fucking my brains out. This is your fault."

"But, Carter, baby, you loved it." I grin and kiss his pouting mouth. "I have to go to work today. Will you be all right here with Archer?"

This makes him open his eyes wider, and a frown wrinkles his brow. "I guess so, maybe it would be good for us to talk, y'know clear the air a bit."

"I don't want you discussing what we talked about last night, not until we can all be together. You okay with that?"

"That's fine with me. It's going to be hard enough to ask him to be with both of us. Like hell am I doing that on my own." He sighs, concentrating on something.

"What's going on in there, Carter?"

"Do you still want me to move in? And get tested?" He frowns again.

"Hell, yes to both of them. I'll make the appointment. We may be able to go at lunch. I'll see what I can do." I kiss him again. "Go back to sleep, I'll call you later. I love you."

"Love you too," he mumbles and drifts back to sleep.

Chapter
Twenty-Eight

CARTER

I think it must be an hour later when I wake up again, feeling a lot more human now. I think back to everything that went down yesterday, and I still can't get my head around it. Archer is alive! Not just alive but sleeping down the hallway. Dan wanting to stop using condoms. Dan asking me to move in with him. Dan asking me to consider us having a three-way relationship. Jesus, what a mindfuck!

I get out of bed and hit the shower, my head still full of all the things that can go wrong with it all. Every scenario and disaster rush through my head as I soap my body, recognizing the ache in my well-used ass. At least that makes me smile.

As I wander down the hallway, I see that Archer's door is closed, but I'm not sure if that means he's in there or has gotten up and has gone downstairs. I'm torn between wanting him to be awake and wanting to hide from him until Dan is home. At least I've got work this afternoon, so I can be out of here and back to my place after a coffee.

Sitting and flipping my iPad open, I mess about on YouTube when the doorbell rings. I smile as I know this will be Kes, he's going to be going frantic thinking about what happened last night. He's so protective and I love that about him. I don't know which of his lovers he'll bring with him. Opening the door, I smile and see Kes and Denver bitching lightheartedly with each other. I know they don't mean it. I love how they're always touching each other. Even now, Denver has his thumb through Kes' belt loop.

"Hey, guys, quit your moaning." I laugh. "What are you doing here?"

"You look better!" Denver smiles. "We went to your place, and well, Kes, wanted to check up on you."

"Come on in. I've just made coffee. You want some?" I let them pass and close the door behind me.

"Has it sunk in yet, Carter? Can you believe what has happened?" Kes asks as he leans against one of the kitchen cupboards. "Are you happy with him being here at Dan's?"

"Yeah, it has. His mother is behind it all, I'm guessing. She's the one who made me leave." I walk away, leaving the coffee to brew. "I can't stop him from being here. He's Dan's best friend, and I'm not coming between them."

"He's a good guy, Carter. We really liked him when we met him last night. He's suffered some dreadful injuries, but he had a good surgeon." Denver looks at Kes who reaches out to squeeze his hand. "Actually, he had my ex operating on him, so I know he was treated well."

"I know he's a good guy, Denver. I was engaged to him for a very short time, before… well, you know what happened." I hand over their coffees and sit back down. "I'm glad you're here, I need your help."

Kes pulls out the stool next to me and sits himself down. "What's up?"

I let out a dry laugh. "Where do you want me to start? Okay, Dan asked me to move in with him last night, and I said yes. Before that, he asked if we could get tested so we don't have to keep using condoms. Again, I said yes. I hate those fuckers. I know I'm clean. I was clean when I was with Archer, and I haven't been near anyone else since. I'm happy to do it with him. I love him, and I want to be with him." I pause and take a deep breath.

"Go on, Carter, we're here for you. You're one of us, you're family." Kes places his hand over mine and gives it a squeeze.

"Yeah, well, here's where it gets complicated. I love Archer too. Dan knows this. He asked if I would consider having Archer as well."

I see the surprised look on both of their faces, and it raises a smile from me.

"And what did you say?" Denver asks as Kes just looks stunned.

"I said we should ask him. I would still be with him, guys, if his mother hadn't ruined our lives. I would be married to him by now. I'd picked up the marriage license the morning he died, of his accident, I mean. So, the feelings I have for him are still real, but, and this is a big but, I love Dan and won't have what we have now compromised. What do you think I should do?"

"Shit, Carter, what do you want us to say? We can't make that decision for you, only the three of you can. But, if you love them both and you think they love you the same way, I would say, what have you got to lose?"

"I could lose both of them. Even the thought of having Archer with me again excites me, but he may not feel the same way I do. Am I strong enough to accept him rejecting me? Will Dan still want me to live with him if Archer turns us down?" I run my hands through my hair and drag them down my face. "I don't have a fucking clue?" I look at Denver. "How did you know they were worth breaking your heart for? You'd just had a bad breakup, so what made you take the risk?"

"It took me a while, Carter. I didn't immediately jump into bed with them and think, 'WooHoo, I'm in love again.' I got to know them, just the same as when you started dating Dan. You must get to know each other as a new entity, a new unit. Don't just rush to have sex with them together. You and Archer have a lot to work through."

"I know, but where do you start? I know he's going to have masses of trust issues, and I know there's going to be some guilt."

Kes cocks his head. "If his mother played him, why should he feel guilty about it?"

"Think about it, Kes. I was told he had died, so I had no reason to try to call him. Dead men don't have cell phones. But he was told I left him, walked away without a backward glance, and yet he didn't try to call me. I mean, wouldn't you have tried, at least once? Even if it was to tell me what a bastard I was, but he didn't. Not once. This could've all been cleared up five days after his accident when he woke up and banished his mother if he'd tried to call me."

"Do you blame him for that?" Kes asks gently.

"I don't know, maybe." I shrug. "I can be found at fault too. If I'd used my first name, if I'd told Daniel that my boyfriend, Archer, had died, I could've had it cleared up." I sigh.

"I think this is why you need to reconnect before you can make any decisions. If I'm honest, I can see it working. I believe the three of you could be very happy. I just don't think it will be an overnight thing." Denver smiles sweetly, comforting me.

"Look, take a few days off work, starting today. Take it a day at a time and see what happens. As long as you're honest with each other from the start, you can only go forward." Kes stands and walks over to the sink, dropping his coffee cup, then turns to his lover. "Are you satisfied he's okay now?" He grins.

"Hey! It was you getting all stressed out, not me." Denver laughs and grabs his hand. "Let's leave him alone now."

"Thanks, guys, for checking up on me and for your advice."

"Anytime, Carter, you know that. Just don't rush this. If it's worth having, it will happen." Kes drops a kiss on my forehead as he walks past, heading for the door.

After they've gone, I tidy up the kitchen, putting the used mugs in the dishwasher. I can hear a shower running, so Archer is still here and awake. Maybe I'll see him soon. Crap, the knots in my stomach cramp at just the thought of him and me together here.

My phone rings, breaking my concentration. Dan's picture flashes up making me smile.

"Hey, baby. You okay?" he asks.

"Yeah, Kes and Denver have just been here. Kes was worried about me, apparently." I chuckle. "What's the call for? Not that I mind, of course."

"Yeah, Kes is a good man. Did you talk about us?" Dan questions, and I wonder if he'll be pissed I did.

"I did, do you mind?" I hesitate to ask then hold my breath.

"Of course not. He's your friend, and I'm sure he's got a lot of advice for you and for me. We can talk about it tonight. I called to say we can get tested this afternoon. Can you make it over in about an hour??"

"Y'know, I know I'm clean. I was tested with Archer, and I haven't been with anyone else. I've still got the proof."

"Yeah, I am too. I got checked before we got together. Are you saying you're okay with not being tested, especially if we do move forward with Archer?"

"Yes, I love you. I trust you, and fuck, I want you inside me with nothing between us."

"Shit, Carter, you can't say shit like that to me when I'm working.

Look, I've got to get back to it. I'll see you tonight. Love you."

"I love you too. See you later." I end the call and listen out for any movement upstairs. The shower is still running, and because I know Archer, I know he doesn't do hangovers.

Soon, it goes quiet, but Archer doesn't come out of his room. I give it thirty minutes, then decide to check on him. I slowly push the door open and look around. All I can see is a body-shaped bulge under the duvet. I can't see his head. He must be cocooned in there. The thought makes me smile as I fight the desire to climb in there with him and hold him tight.

Denying myself that right, I walk backwards out of the room and close the door softly behind me. I walk back down, not sure what to do with myself. I was supposed to be at work, and now with Dan gone, I'm at loose ends. I decide to take my bike out for a blast. I haven't ridden just for the sake of it in months. I walk over to my place to get my leathers.

This is what I need to clear my head. I race down the highway, not speeding so much but just enjoying the freedom. I find myself thinking about getting to know Archer again. I want to know everything that happened to him. I need to tell him what happened to me too. I hope he's prepared to stay and try a life here. It's a good place and being here without him has been so hard, but without having any memories of us here, everything has been new. I have found myself again. I want him to do the same. After this, I make my way back to the house and to Archer.

But when I get home, he's still not up. I take another peek, and he's still burrowed in the bed covers. At least it won't be long before Dan comes.

I'm waiting impatiently when Dan walks in. I watch as he dumps his briefcase by the door and removes his tie, undoing his top couple shirt buttons. He hasn't seen me yet, giving me time to gaze at him, taking in his long legs clad in dark-blue suit pants clinging to the rock-hard muscles of his thighs. The ones strong enough to hold me up against the wall as he fucks me. The curve of his ass, firm and high, ready to be grabbed and bitten. Shit! I need to stop. Just as I cup my dick, trying to calm it down, he turns to face me. He smirks and gives me a wink. The fucker, he knew I was watching!

"Hey, baby. Have you missed me?" He swaggers towards me, his eyes dark and heavy, full of promise.

"Hmm, not sure. Have you missed me?" I bite my lip as he reaches me.

"Oh, Carter, you've been on my fucking mind. All. Day. Long." Lowering his head, he grazes his mouth over mine, not giving me anywhere near what I want.

"What are you going to do about it?" I growl at him, then bite his lip.

He pulls back and grins wickedly. "I'm sure I can think of something. Let me get changed."

"You need any help with that?"

"Definitely."

We race up the stairs, scrabbling at our clothes as we go.

"Shower?" Dan questions, and I nod, laughing as we trip over ourselves to get in there quickly.

Sated and smiling, we're back in the kitchen squabbling about what to make to eat. Dan still keeps touching me anytime he can, and I love it.

"Have you seen Archer today? Did you manage to speak to him?" Dan kisses the back of my neck.

"No, he's been in bed all day."

"He's been sleeping all day? How do you know?" Dan asks.

"Because I looked in on him a couple times. I was worried about him. Archer doesn't drink much, and I know how much he hates hangovers. I just wanted to make sure he was okay. I care about him. I care a lot."

Then Archer walks in looking like shit, and I know exactly what he needs.

"Hey, guys."

"Archer, hi. How are you feeling?" Dan takes stock of what he's seeing.

"Pretty much like I look. Wrecked, ashamed, embarrassed. I'm sorry for my behavior last night. I shouldn't have gotten drunk."

"I think it was perfectly understandable, Arch. Yesterday was a clusterfuck of epic proportions. We're feeling a lot of those emotions too. C'mon, sit. I'll get you a coffee, and I'll do you a grilled cheese sandwich."

I set about making his favorite hangover food while Dan and he chat. I don't pay too much attention, but when I hand him his food, I instinctively drop a kiss on his head. I feel him freeze underneath my touch. Glancing over at Dan, he gives me a nod. It's showtime, I guess.

Dan stands next to me. Archer picks up his grilled cheese and smiles. "Okay, guys, out with it."

Dan has his arm slung casually over my shoulder, pulling me closer, giving me the reassurance and strength I need.

"We want you to stay. We want you to stay here. With us, the three of us together," I blurt out.

Dan groans and shakes his head. "Way to go, babe."

"You talk, then, Dan." I'm blushing brightly.

"What Carter means is that we would like you to think about staying and being with us, as in having a relationship with us. I know it's out of the blue, and maybe we have asked you way too early. Hell, you and

Carter have only just found each other again."

I look at Archer and see… Shock? Abhorrence? Bewilderment? Dan kisses the side of my head while we wait for some sort of response.

Chapter

Twenty-Nine

ARCHER

I look at them dumbfounded. I watch as Dan smiles and kisses my fiancé's temple, my ex-fiancé, and then smiles at me.

"We love you, Archer. And you've said you love us. What we want to know is if you love us enough to be with us? The whole nine yards of us."

"Why?" It's the first question that pops into my head. "Why would you think this is a good idea, or is it your idea of a joke?"

I look at them and see Mallory, fuck! Carter, chew on his lip as his face blanches. Dan tightens his grip on him as his eyes narrow at me.

"Okay, I guess we got it wrong. I'm sorry, Archer. I thought this would be something good. We each love you. Carter has grieved for you for months, and he's still in love with you as much as he is with me. We thought you loved us too."

Carter has tears in his eyes. I can see him trying to control them and not let them fall. Damn, that hurts my heart. I reach out to him but halt when I see him flinch. I've hurt him. After all that has happened, I have rejected him.

But am I really not even going to consider this? Do I want to be with them? Can I share myself with them? With all my scars, will Carter want me?

"I do, I do love you, but this is so… shit, so unexpected. I thought you were going to ask me to move out." I shake my head. I can't believe this. "You want us to be a threesome, or do you want me as a third? There's a huge difference." I know I'm not prepared to even think about this as a third.

Carter sucks in a sharp breath and shakes his head. "How could you even think that? This isn't a game. I want you. I've missed you so fucking much. I want to try, but the decision is up to you."

"Dan? Why? Why not just keep him to yourself? He is perfect."

"Because I love you too. I want you as much as I want Carter. Fuck, we've both admitted to dreaming about it. Be honest, man, can you see us all hot and sweaty, teasing and tasting each other. Fucking each other? Because I can, and so can Carter. Christ, I'm getting hard now just talking about it. I want your ass, Arch, and I want your cock in mine. I want to watch you fuck Carter. I want to see him take you. I want the whole fucking thing."

I draw in a long breath because that was hot. I can feel my dick twitching in my pants as it tries to overrule the logic in my head. "Carter, what do you think? You said you want me to be with you. Do you see us as a threesome? How do you expect this to happen, or how would you like it to happen?"

"Archer, I'm not going to go back over the past and what we suffered because you're here, and I think shit like this happens for a reason. We were meant to be together again. We should never have been apart, and now we have the chance. Not just to recapture what we had but to take it further and expand it.

"I love Dan. He has let me remember what it's like to be in love again, the new kind of love where everything is fresh. We're learning so much about each other, and I think we will have to go through the same thing. I think we have to get to know each other again. I want to know all about your accident. I want you to want to share everything with me again. And this is the important thing. I want to reacquaint myself with your divine body. I want us to grow and learn together, the three of us. I believe we have the chance of something very special, and that's because we are all in love with each other."

"Fuck! Carter, you've changed. You're a stronger, more mature man than you were nearly a year ago. I think we've all got a shit ton of stuff to talk about. Two days ago, I still believed you had left me. I still tried to hate you. Finding you in love with another man is hard for me to take. I believe you when you say you are in love with me because of the way you look at me. It's the same as before. I don't know if us all being together will work. I need to think about this." I shake my head, unsure of what to do. "Y'see, my heart is saying yes, but my brain is telling me I'm the one that will get hurt. I'll be the one that ends up alone."

Carter reaches out to me. I can see the concern and need etched on his face. As his hand touches mine, I feel the electricity rush through me again, the same as it always has.

"Oh, Archer, don't you think I'm having the same worries? You and Dan have so much in common. You're the same age. You both have successful careers. Hell, you both used to date. Where do I fit in with all of that?" His fingers draw circles on the back of my hand.

"You are and always have been a perfect fit for me, and I see it with you and Dan too."

"Then what is holding you back?" Dan questions me.

"Self-preservation." I look at them and see them flinch. "I'm going for a walk. Let me think about this, okay?"

"Okay," Dan murmurs as he pulls the man, I now must think of as Carter, against his chest. I feel a spark of envy as he kisses the top of his head. I want to be doing that.

Walking away from them is hard. I know I need to clear my head. The evening is warm, the violet sky is clear of clouds, unlike my head which is a shit-storm of turmoil. The hangover I started the evening with has receded to a dull ache, leaving me with only the thoughts and images of Dan and Carter. I can't stop it switching back to me and Carter. Fuck, I want to call him Mallory. I want to snatch him back and take him back home again. But he doesn't want that; he wants us both. Can I do that? I think of my dream and the three of us together. It was incredibly hot, but it was just a dream. It may not feel like that if we are together now. Kes and his boyfriends pop up in my head. The way they complete each other. I wonder how it was for them to adapt and become a threesome.

My thoughts veer away from the sexual aspect of a threesome, allowing me to imagine a more day-to-day life, and it seems easy. I want to work with Dan. I like it here. I want Mallory back in my bed. If I must call him by his middle name to have that, then I can do that. Now it comes down to having to share, not just him but myself, to have him back in my life. Can I do that?

I stop walking and close my eyes, thinking about how I feel about Dan. A warmth spreads through me as I see his smile when he looks at me. A dimple shows on his left cheek, and I remember I used to kiss that dimple, making him laugh. I think of what sex was like with each other. I'm sure we've both gained a lot more experience now. I think about how it felt sliding into him, something I haven't thought of in years but gets my dick twitching now. I smile to myself, chuckling at the thought.

I guess the bottom line is I want to try. I don't want to miss what could be the best thing that has ever happened to me. Getting my best friend and my lover back can only be positive. Maybe things do happen for a reason, and the reason is to get us all together.

Turning back, I walk back to the house. As I walk in, I can hear the TV playing, making me head to the lounge. Dan and Carter are lying together on the large sofa. Carter is in front and is cocooned by Dan's arms. They look good together. I wait for them to see me. Carter spies me first and shifts out of Dan's arms and sits up. He looks wary. His dark-blue eyes are filled with worry. Dan follows suit but stands up, then pulls Carter up to him again.

I look at them and feel my heart beat faster and the butterflies in my stomach awaken and stir as my excitement builds.

"I really don't think I can turn away from you. Either of you, hell, both of you. Shit, I'm going to do this with you." A broad smile spreads across my face as I watch Carter flush, his face pink with happiness. Dan grins and clutches Carter against his chest, kissing the top of his head. "Hey, I want some of that too."

Carter pulls away from Dan and rushes to me. His arms wrap around my waist as he buries his head into my neck, then turns to kiss my neck. The sensation that races through my body is like an energy surge. I feel myself come alive again. As he turns his face up to mine, I must have his mouth. As our lips touch, Carter moans loudly. I swallow it down before matching it with my own. I feel Dan stand behind me, and his arms encase me. His mouth is on my neck. Shudders rack through my body.

Carter's tongue slips over the seam of my lips, dipping inside my mouth. As much as I want to taste him, I know we must pull back. Dan senses it too, and we separate. Carter does the same, and as his thumb swipes across his plump lip, he sighs.

"I'm going to put a suggestion out here." Dan waits for us to listen. "I think you two need to spend some time together. I want you to spend the next couple days, when I need to be at work, to get to know each other again. I don't mean fuck. I mean get connected again."

"Hmm, really? No sex? Where's the fun in that?" Carter pouts.

"C'mon, Car, this whole get to know each other was your idea." Dan sighs, pinching the bridge of his nose when Carter bites his neck.

"I think we all know each other. Maybe I was wrong," he teases. Laughing along, I watch as he pops a quick kiss on Dan's mouth, making them both smile.

I'm surprised when he does the same to me and gives me a wink to go with it. We're soon all grinning like loons. I can't remember being this happy, or I can, but it seems it was in a different life.

"When do you want me to start work, then, Dan?" I decide it's time to change the subject; otherwise, we'll end up fucking each other.

The rest of the already late evening passes quickly. Carter lounges on the large sofa, talking animatedly about work, making us laugh at the shit they all get up to.

"Do you think you'll stay there or look for something so you can use your degree?"

"What degree?" Dan looks at Carter, obviously unaware of his education. I see Carter flush, and I know I've spoken about something he hasn't mentioned.

"I've got an engineering degree, top of the class." He laughs drily. It hurts my chest at the opportunities he's left behind. "And no, I haven't thought about it. I like what I'm doing now."

"But Carter, why not?" Dan asks.

"Leave it, Dan. I'm not interested." The edge to his voice keeps us both from responding but not from passing each other a glance, but Carter sees it. "I'm going to bed."

Getting up from the sofa, he has to walk between both me and Dan to reach the door. We each grab one of his hands.

"I'm sorry, Carter. I spoke out of turn. I didn't mean to upset you." I push myself up so I can hug him. He stands stiffly for a moment, then relaxes into me, his hand resting on my back. "I'm sorry, sugar." I feel him nod and step away.

"Maybe we should all hit the sack?" Dan stands and kisses Carter's temple. "I won't mention it again."

When we reach the top of the stairs, I let go of Carter's hand and walk towards my room.

"Where are you going?" Dan and Carter ask together.

"Bed, I thought that was obvious." I shrug.

"Uh huh, no way. You sleep with us now. If we're doing this, we're starting right now. We don't have to fuck, but we need to be together." Carter frowns at me and beckons me to them both.

"You sure?" They both nod. "Okay, I'll go change and come through."

Grabbing a pair of loose sleep shorts, I strip off and step into them. My fingers run over my scar on my thigh, and I feel self-conscious again all of a sudden. I know Dan has seen them, but Carter hasn't. I really don't want to put him off.

"Don't forget your toothbrush!" Dan hollers at me, making me smile, and I wander into my bathroom to collect it.

When I get in their room, Dan has lowered the lights, and I'm instantly grateful. He understands, and I appreciate it. Walking into the attached bathroom, I find them both in shorts brushing their teeth. I step up and snatch the toothpaste from the side and copy them. The stupid grins are back again as we stare at each other in the mirror.

When we're done, I follow them back to the bedroom, and we all look awkwardly at the huge bed.

"Oh, for fuck's sake, get into bed," Carter mutters and clambers in and lies down. I climb in behind him, and Dan sandwiches him from the other side.

Carter lies on his side facing Dan, allowing me to lie behind him. I want to tuck him into my body, the way we always did before we were torn apart. When his arm reaches back and pulls me closer, I do exactly as I wanted and curl myself around him. My lips find the back of his neck, and I kiss him softly.

"Night, honey," I whisper. My hand curls around his waist and rests on his stomach. Dan's hand rests on Carter's hip. This feels right. This is how it should be.

Why do they want me here? I don't understand. I don't know. But tonight, the act of lying with them, talking, laughing, and joking makes me feel more alive than I have since before the accident. Since I kissed Mallory goodbye and left for work. I have no fucking clue where tomorrow will take me. I simply hope it takes me somewhere with them. Resting my head back on the pillow, I feel the warmth of my lover's body against mine, and soon I feel myself slip into sleep.

I can feel movement around me and some quiet words being exchanged. Then it all goes quiet again, and I fall back to sleep.

I wake slowly, not wanting to leave the dream behind. The dream of Mallory being with me, loving me again. I've had so many of them, but this one feels more real. As his hands stroke over my body, his mouth covers me in kisses. His tongue slides over my heated skin. So damn real, so damn heartbreakingly real.

I don't want to open my eyes as I can still feel his mouth moving down, his nose skimming over my groin, ignoring the thick, throbbing, and achingly hard dick so close to his mouth. Then his mouth is on my leg, sliding up and down the length of my scar, lapping on the sensitive skin and dropping kisses as I tremble.

Wait! That's not right! Mallory doesn't know about my scars. My eyes snap open, and I look around the unfamiliar room, then I feel Mallory's smile against my leg.

"Hmm, it took you long enough to wake up." He kisses my thigh again as his long fingers slide up the inside of my sleep shorts, getting teasingly close to my junk.

"Fuck! I thought it was a dream! Carter, should we be doing this?" I croak out, emotion thick in my throat.

"Yeah, baby. I'm here, and I'm real, and I really fucking want you." His gravelly voice giving his need for me away.

"Really? Fuck, Carter, are you sure?" Please be sure, please be sure, I chant in my head.

"I'm so damn sure." He drags my shorts down my legs and swipes the flat of his tongue from my sac, up the length of my solid rod, then covers the crown with his hot wet mouth.

My hips buck, punching me deeper inside his mouth as my back arches on the bed. "Fuuuuuuuuck! Oh, God! I'd forgotten how much I love your mouth." I pant out before clenching my teeth together to stop from coming straight away. As he slurps up and down my length, the sound of his wet mouth lavishing attention on me has me seeing stars. I know I'm leaking into his mouth as he laps at the slit. I open my eyes and look down and see his dark-blue irises shining like sapphires, gazing at me.

My hands reach down, and I weave my fingers into his long, dark hair, gripping him tightly, holding him but not guiding. This is his show. I'm just here for the ride. He gives me a wink before bobbing up and down my length again, sucking harder and faster. I feel the telltale tingle of my orgasm in my spine and tug on his hair.

"I'm gonna come, honey. Fuck, you feel so good." I punch my hips up again as he sucks hard, his cheeks hollowing. The fire spreads up my spine, forcing me up from the bed. As I flood his mouth and throat, he's swallowing everything I've got to give. As I collapse back down, Carter sucks gently over the ultrasensitive glans, making me twitch and squirm.

Climbing back up my body, Carter drops kisses on my abs and chest before plundering my mouth. I taste myself on his tongue, but it's the flavor of him that breaks through my defenses, and I feel my emotions bubble up, and a sob breaks free.

"Archer, baby, don't cry. We're good, we're together, it's over. No more loneliness, just lots of love and joy from now on."

"I never thought I'd see you again. Even through all the pain and surgeries, nothing compared to losing you."

"Tell me what happened. I want to know all of it, not just your injuries but every part of your recovery. I hate that I wasn't there with you. I hate how we were torn apart." He runs his fingers over my rib cage. "What is this one from?" He shocks me by kissing it.

"My lung collapsed. They had to put a chest drain in to inflate it again. Twice. Plus, my spleen ruptured so that had to be removed." I sigh as his finger traces over the smooth skin.

I get lulled by his soft touch and kisses as he travels over my body, running his mouth over my shoulder and down my left arm. "How about here?"

"Both bones in my lower arm and my wrist, plus my collarbone." More kisses follow his touch.

He doesn't stop peppering my skin with featherlight kisses. I tense as he moves down to my legs. I'm grateful when he chooses the right leg first. Maybe he realizes I'll be done for when he reaches my left leg and my thigh.

Sliding his fingers softly over my skin, he reaches my ankle and kisses it, raising his eyes up to mine silently asking me the question.

"Both ankles broke. This one was trapped under a foot pedal, and all three bones were broken. The other is about the same. There's a lot of metalwork in there holding them together. I wasn't sure if I'd manage to walk again. They were so painful." I see Carter's chin wobble as he swallows hard to control his emotions.

"And here?" His voice quivers as he tries to hold back his tears.

"A broken femur that had to have an external fixator to hold it all together. A lot of damaged muscle and tissue, but my recovery was hampered when an infection developed, and they had to open me up again to clean it all out and fit new metalwork." I can hear the flatness in my voice. I've had enough of telling this, and I know this is the hardest, but also the last time I must tell it. I hope we can both move on together from this.

He covers his face in his hands for a few moments. Then he looks at me, his face fierce with determination. "I fucking hate your mother!"

"Yeah, you and me both."

Chapter
Thirty

DAN

Why is today going so slowly? I've got so much work piled up, with court dates just around the corner. But all I can think about is what Archer and Carter may be getting up to, I wanted them to talk things out, get to know each other again. But there's no way they will be able to keep their hands off each other, and I can't blame either of them. Hell, if I was there now, we'd be fucking and that's for damn sure.

At five-thirty on the dot, I race from the office. When I walk back into the house, it's all quiet. Maybe they've gone back to Carter's. I walk through the kitchen, and I see them on the decking in the garden.

FUCK!

Archer is lying on one of the loungers as Carter rocks his hips over and over. I know that Archer is buried deep inside him. Carter's eyes are closed, and his mouth is a perfect O as he embraces all the feelings coursing through his body. Archer's hands rest on Carter's ass. There's no pressure, just a need to keep hold of him. His palms stroke softly, caressing him as he continues to rock.

The two men I love look even more beautiful than I could ever have imagined. I take a step forward. My movement alerts Archer. He turns to look at me in surprise, but he gives me a lazy smile. Not what I expected, but then he starts to move. His hands now grip Carter's ass and lift him up a few inches. Then with long, slow and oh-so-deep thrusts, Archer moves his cock in and out of Carter's ass. My dick is rock hard in my pants. I rub my palm over it, hoping to calm it down, not encourage it further. I feel a damp patch on my briefs as I start to leak. God, this is so hot!

Archer whispers to Carter something I can't hear. Carter nods as his hand wraps around his dick, and he matches his strokes to Archer's. They are so in tune, even after all these months. Archer increases the tempo but still pulls the length of his cock all the way back to Carter's entrance before plunging deep inside. No shallow thrusts to bring them both to climax quicker. This is lovemaking at its finest. I strip out of my clothes. I'm not missing out on being a part of this. In seconds, I'm naked.

I watch, fixated on their bodies as the late afternoon sunlight catches on the sleek sweat covering Carter's chest and back. Archer pumps inside him rapidly. I watch as Archer's lips move again. Carter's eyes fly open, and he looks at me. As our eyes lock, he reaches out to me. Stepping closer, I tug on my aching length. Carter wraps his hand around it, taking control, pumping me with long, firm strokes.

I lean into him, pushing myself closer. "Suck me, baby. Get those plump lips around my cock."

Archer lets go of his hold of Carter's ass and moves to change positions. Kneeling behind Carter now, Archer enters him again. I kneel in front of Carter, my dick in line with his mouth. On all fours, Carter looks so wanton, his eyes black with desire. Sliding the weeping head over his lips, I watch as he licks them, then parts his lips. I slip inside his hot, wet mouth and groan as he sucks.

Archer holds onto Carter's hips, keeping him still as he pumps his cock inside him. "I have never seen anything so fucking hot as this. Carter, you are divine. I worship you." His words are hushed as he pants, taking him deeper and deeper.

"I'm not going to last. Keep still, baby, let me do this." I stroke my hands through Carter's dark locks as I pump into his mouth. I thrust further into his throat, watching him all the time. As he looks up at me, his lips tight around my length, he sucks hard, hollowing his cheeks. Fuck! I'm going to come.

"Oh Shit! Baby, yesyesyes." I come hard as Carter sucks and swallows, his eyes still fixed on mine. I pull out of his mouth and kiss him. "Your turn, baby."

With Archer's arms wrapped around Carter's body, he pulls him upright, still plunging inside him as I kneel to take Carter in my mouth. As soon as I suck, I feel him tremble, and I know he's going to come. Taking him deep, I swallow around him. That's all it takes before he's bucking his hips, crying out as he comes. I hear Archer's groan as he releases inside Carter's body, thrusting erratically as he climaxes.

We collapse down. Carter lies on my chest as Archer leans over him, dragging huge lungsful of breath in as he rests his forehead on Carter's shoulders.

Carter lifts his head and looks into my eyes as he smiles. His tongue darts out to dampen his bottom lip as his eyes drop to my lips.

"I love you, Dan. That was amazing." He kisses me softly, gently, and so sweetly. I know I've fallen even deeper in love with him.

"Carter, you have no idea the depth of my love for you." I kiss his forehead. Then he groans as Archer slips from him.

"I'll get a cloth." Archer grins at us both as he steps around the lounger.

"I'd rather just shower." Carter grins and pushes himself up from my body. "You two coming?"

"We're right behind you." I laugh and give his butt a swat.

After our shower, which involved a large amount of touching and kissing, we saunter into our room to get dressed.

"Have you brought your clothes in here yet, Arch?" I look over my shoulder as I tug some boxer briefs up my legs.

"I'll do it tomorrow." He saunters off to the guest room to grab some clean clothes.

"Did you mind us being together without you?" Carter steps up behind me and kisses the nape of my neck before resting his chin on my shoulder, waiting for my reply.

"I was surprised," I answer honestly. "Was that the first time today?" I feel unsure of myself and wish I hadn't asked now.

"Yes, we messed about a little bit this morning, but we hadn't had sex. I know we agreed not to jump back into having sex, but we couldn't help it. We had planned for you to be coming home to us, to join us I think if you hadn't looked so turned on, we would have stopped and waited for you to be ready," Carter replies and twists me around so I'm facing him. "Please tell me it was okay."

"I think I would've rather waited until we were all together, I guessed you wouldn't be able to stop yourselves, but I'm not going to pretend that it wasn't amazing. We can work out what we want as we go along. I think as long as we continue to communicate, we will be fine." I lean in to kiss him. My hands reach down to grip his hips.

"Mmm, I like this sort of communication." Carter's mouth is a hair's breadth from mine. His tongue slips between my lips, and soon, we are locked together, devouring, giving and taking, locked at the hip and our hands tangling in each other's hair.

I hear a chortle and a cough as Archer walks back in. "I was only gone a couple minutes, and you two are at it again."

✶ ✶ ✶

It's easy here now after that. I'm liking it. I think, the three of us have settled, and any immediate concerns have dissipated. Now we're out in the garden, lounging around as darkness surrounds us, picking at the food they prepared before we got all caught up.

My hand rests on Carter's thigh as he lies next to me. Archer is opposite, telling outrageous stories of our antics at college, trying to prove I was the bad influence.

"Yeah, right. You go ahead and think that, but I remember the time you snuck in your politics lecturer's college and hid an open can of tuna, just before spring break. The room had to be fumigated by the time it was opened up again for the new term." I shake my head. "You were the bad influence. I was just a country boy trying to get good grades."

Archer laughs hard at this. "You were top of the class, you dork!"

"What about you, baby? Did you have a good time at school?" I ask Carter.

"Um, not really. My folks kicked me out, cut off my allowance, and threw me out of my apartment halfway through my time. I had to provide for myself and apply for every student loan and grant I could get. I had to get a job, so it wasn't brilliant." He looks across at Archer who has a loving gaze fixed on my boyfriend. Fuck! Our boyfriend. "Then I bumped into Archer, and my life turned around. I was happy again. I didn't hang around much with my peers because I got everything I wanted from Archer. He saved me, giving me time to work hard and graduate well. I was happy then."

"We were happy, weren't we?" Archer states.

"Yeah, we were very happy. We thought we had the world." Carter sighs.

"Have you two had any thoughts about what happened and who instigated it? Do you want to take any action?" I ask them as they

169

continue to look at each other.

I can tell we have made him uncomfortable talking about our happy times, so I pull his face to mine and kiss him, whispering, "You're here now. I've got you, we've got you." I feel him relax and kiss me quickly again. I wrap him in my arms, keeping him close against my body.

Then I look at Archer who's smiling again, and I know he's okay. "Did you want to do something? You said you haven't spoken since the accident. Do you want to start again now?"

"I've had a couple thoughts, ideas, really. I don't want to speak to her, but I think I might get a friend to do some poking about in her private life. If she could get police officers to approach you, I'm thinking she's got some secrets going on. My mother likes control and will do anything to get it. I'm guessing she's got some dirty little games going on. I want to find out what they are and bring her down." Archer's face is stony, and his green eyes hard and determined.

"Who will you ask?" I ask.

"Lucas Davenport, Mason's cousin," Archer explains. "He runs one of the country's top surveillance and security companies. If there's dirt there, he'll find it."

"I've heard of him." I look down at Carter, seeing him frown. I know what he's thinking, and it hurts me.

"Don't look at me like that, please. I know what you're thinking, and the answer is because I'm a stubborn dick. I was hurting, and I was angry. I know how much I fucked up, okay?" Archer groans

"Okay, enough of the heavies. We're supposed to be excited about what's going to happen for us. I, for one, want a repeat of what went down earlier and maybe more," I joke, trying to break tension.

"Then maybe we should go to bed?" Archer looks at me, his eyes dark and hooded. I feel Carter tense in my arms, and he lifts his head to look at me. The hunger in his eyes has me hardening quickly.

"I think so, too. Come on, baby." We all stand together and walk inside.

Archer grins and heads up the stairs and through the bedroom door into his room. Carter takes my hand, and we race up after him.

When we walk into the room, Archer has the table lamps on, leaving the room in a subtle muted light. When he sees us, he drops his shorts, leaving us both staring at his rock-hard dick.

"You'd better get naked quick." His hand wraps around himself and strokes himself from base to tip.

We quickly strip and join him.

Chapter

Thirty-One

CARTER

It's been four days since Archer joined us and for the first time, I wake up alone, looking over to the clock. It's still early, so I know Dan wouldn't have left for work. Swinging my legs over the edge of the bed, I stand and stretch. I can feel the muscles in my body protesting, but it's a good feeling. I grab a pair of boxer shorts and head to the bathroom. I pee, then turn to the sink to wash my hands and see myself in the mirror. I've got a bite mark on my neck and another on my chest just above my nipple. I smile, knowing they were put there by both men. Fuck, last night was hot!

When I walk into the kitchen, I see both Dan and Archer are dressed in suits and look damn hot! I let out a low whistle, and they turn in smooth synchronicity and smile.

"I could say the same about you." Dan swaggers up to me and grabs my hips, pulling me up to his hard body. His mouth presses hard to mine before tugging my bottom lip between his teeth and giving me a

172

nip.

"Are you finally making it to the office, Arch?" I cock my eyebrow at him before walking into his arms and kissing him.

"Don't be cheeky or I'll spank your ass," he fake-whispers in my ear, making Dan laugh behind me.

"Hey, no picking on me." I snicker, then grab his coffee mug from him and take a swig, before handing it back. "What's for breakfast?"

"You're too late. You'll have to get something after we've gone." Dan smirks but turns his back and opens the oven, bringing out a plate of bacon and pancakes for me.

"Oh, this is why I love you." I smile and pick up a piece of bacon with my fingers. They both take a seat and try to grab at my food. "Hey!"

"What are you going to do today, baby? Will you be okay with us both out?"

I roll my eyes and laugh. "Yeah, I'm sure I'll manage. I have so far." I snort. "Seriously though, I'm going back to work for a few hours, then I'm going to grab some boxes and pack up my apartment."

"Shall we meet you there for lunch?" Archer asks, but I wrinkle my nose at him and shake my head.

"Nah, I'm gonna be busy. I'm sure your partner may have plenty of work for you." I grin at Dan who smiles. "Can I borrow your truck though, babe? Then I can bring my shit over." I try to ignore Archer's disappointment, but he's not going to let it go.

"Don't you want your boss to know about us?"

"Don't be stupid, Archer. I don't care about that. I just believe we should get into a work routine, and I'd like to catch up with Paris if I can. I haven't seen him since the club. I owe him an explanation," I try to explain, but he's still scowling. I look at Dan for help.

"C'mon, Archer, let him get on with packing up. I'm sure he'll make it up to you tonight." Dan nudges him with his elbow. "We do have a shit-ton of work to go through. I'm guessing we'll be working through lunch."

"Fine, but we will be seen together this weekend, the three of us." He huffs and pouts, and as much as I want to laugh, I know he's serious.

"Absolutely. I promise, Archer. I love you, and I'm proud of us." I kiss him, a long, slow, lazy kiss that has him moaning softly. "Now you've got my dick hard. I guess I'd better deal with that when you've gone."

Dan laughs and grips the back of my neck, then leans in. "You keep your hands away from your dick, baby. Consider it your punishment for turning up in just your underwear," he growls.

"I hate you," I mutter as they stand and get ready to leave.

"No, you don't. You love us." Archer laughs and drops his head down to kiss me.

"Yeah, I do. Go on, get to work, you fuckers!" I'm trying to be stern, but I'm laughing too much.

"Bye, baby. Call me if you need me." Dan kisses me too.

I do as I'm told, surprisingly, and leave my dick alone. I clean up of the kitchen before I make my way over to work.

Walking into the bar, I see Kes smiling at me. Letting out a huge cheer, he raises his arm up and hollers. "He's back! WooHoo! Good to see you, Carter."

I feel the heat on my cheeks as everyone in the bar turns to look at me. The locals all cheer, making the tourists smile and looking bewildered at the scene.

"Yeah, great. Thanks for that, Kester!" I use his full name, making him laugh. When I walk back to the office, I pass Shelley who drops a kiss on my cheek and pats my arm. Kes follows me, and as I step in the office, I see why. Denver is in there with their newly adopted little girl. Denver smiles at me while the little girl claps her hands and waves at me.

"It's good to see you, Carter, and looking so damn good, too. How are you?" Denver looks me over, then stands to give me a one-armed hug.

"I'm good. Still can't believe it, but damn, I'd forgotten what it feels like to breathe properly. Things are good." I drop my messenger bag over the back of my office chair and run my hands through my scruffy hair.

"Are you moving in with Dan?" Kes asks with a twinkle in his eye.

"I am. I'm gonna grab some boxes and pack up my stuff. I can't thank you enough for what you did for me. You helped when I didn't know which way to turn or where to go. I don't know what I would have done without you guys."

"It was meant to be, Carter. You needed to be here for when Archer reached out to his friend. You can't mess with fate." Kes smiles. "Denver needed to come home to find his forever with us."

"So how are things? Is there a triad now?" Denver lifts his brow and smirks.

"It's early days, but it's good. Dan has finally convinced Archer to go to work, so I think he's happy." I match his grin and try not to blush.

The phone rings, and Kes leans across the desk to answer it. I don't pay any attention to the conversation until I hear my name, and I look over.

"Hold on, he's here. I can ask him." Kes looks at me. "Paris is going through some shit at home. Can you take his shift tonight?"

"Of course, no worries."

Kes goes back to talking to Paris. I know his father isn't happy with Paris' sexuality and they've rowed plenty about it. I worry for my friend.

"What's going on?" I ask Kes when he ends the call. "Is it his dad again?"

"You know about it?" Kes looks surprised.

"Of course, I do. Paris is my friend. He's crashed on my couch enough when his father's been drinking and gotten too happy with his fists."

"Shit, I didn't realize it had gotten that bad. He says he's going to have to move out which may mean moving away."

"Why doesn't he have my place? I was planning to leave the furniture I'd bought. I've got nowhere to put it. It's only cheap stuff, but it's good." I'd feel good about letting Paris have my place.

"That's a great idea. Why don't you call him, Carter? I think he could do with a friend today. You don't need to be here now if you're back here tonight. Call him and get him over here."

"Yeah, I need to call Dan too." I wonder if they'll be okay with me working tonight at such short notice. But why shouldn't they, this is my job.

"Okay, do you want me to grab some boxes from the store cupboard?"

"That would be great."

Kes and Denver leave me in the office. Dragging my cell from my pocket, I call Dan.

"Hey, baby. How are you doing?" he answers, and my heart swells just listening to him call me baby.

"Yeah, it's good. There's been a change of plans though. I'm gonna be working tonight. Paris is getting grief again from his dad, so I'm going to do his shift. I'm going to offer him my apartment too. I'll be packing up my stuff and then moving him in. It's gonna be a long day. If I don't get it all done, I'll crash here tonight. Just giving you the heads-up now."

"Hold on a sec."

There's muttering in the background, and then Dan comes back.

"Okay, Carter. Archer's here, and you're on speakerphone. There's no one else in the room."

"Carter, I don't think so. Dan and I will be there and will wait for you. There's no way you're going back to sleeping alone," he growls at me, instantly pissing me off.

Dan speaks up. "You're coming back here tonight, Carter. I don't care what time it is."

"You're being crazy, both of you. It could be three a.m. before I finish. You don't get to tell me what to do, Dan. It's not your call. I'm sorry. I'm busy now. I'll call you later." I end the call before either of them can answer. The next call is much more pleasant. Paris is stoked at the thought of taking over my place. "I've got the truck today. Grab your stuff, and I'll come get you. Text me when you're ready."

"I will, Carter. Thanks, man. You're my savior."

"No worries, I'll see you soon." I laugh and end the call.

I spend the next couple hours boxing up my shit and giving the place a clean. I've had a couple calls. One from Dan and another from Archer. I've let them both go to voicemail. I'm not interested in hearing them beat their chests and order me around.

Just as I get done, Paris messages me, and I head out to get him. When I reach his house, he's standing on the porch with a couple duffel bags and a few boxes. He looks like he's only just holding it together. He's got a black eye, and there's a bloom of bruising on his chin and cheekbone.

"C'mon, dude, let's get you settled. You'll like it there, and hey, it's rent free. I'm leaving all my furniture. Let me know what else you need, and we can get it for you."

"Thanks, Carter. We had the cops around here last night. It got as bad as it can. It's not fair on my mom to be stuck in the middle. She's not happy about me leaving, but she knows my dad is getting worse."

"Was it Conn?" I look at him, and he blushes.

"Yeah, it was. Pretty embarrassing for me, too."

I know Paris has had a crush on our local detective, but as far as I know, he's never acted on it. We shoot the shit for the next few hours as we sort it all out for him. Then we load my boxes into the back of the truck.

"Have the night off, Paris. You need to get your head straight. Enjoy the quiet here and get yourself settled. I'm downstairs if you need me." I give him a hug and kiss his forehead.

"Thanks, Carter. I owe you, man." His voice is thick with emotion.

"No, you don't. Just pay it forward when you can. This place is a good place to heal. You'll be fine."

I head downstairs for my shift. Dan and Archer have left me alone, which is good. Sometimes the silence can be worse. I wonder what they're plotting.

We're a couple hours away from closing. It's been busy, but I've managed to fill Shelley in on Paris, and her mothering instinct kicks into overdrive. She's already sorting out what she can do to help.

"He'll be fine, Shell. Stop clucking about." I laugh at her.

"What can I get you?" I smile at a guy I've not seen before. He looks me over and smiles, but it's not a smile that reaches his eyes. His tongue darts out and flicks over his lip. He's dressed expensively and immaculately. Black pants and a light blue shirt. There's not a hair on his head that's out of place, and considering it's coming up to eleven o'clock, I would have expected a more relaxed dress code, but his dark-red tie is still in place.

"Hmm, now there's a loaded question." His eyes roam over me, making my skin crawl.

"To drink, sir. What would you like?" I stay polite but take a very small step back.

"I'll take a single malt scotch, make it a double."

Turning my back, I walk to the top shelf and pick the most expensive scotch we have and pour him his measure.

"Twenty-six dollars, please."

He offers me a hundred-dollar bill. "Why don't you join me?"

"I'm good, thank you." I look up the bar and see Shelley giving me a weird look. "Excuse me, enjoy your drink."

When I walk up to her, she's frowning at me. "Do you know that guy?" she asks.

"Never seen him before, why?" I want to look back over my shoulder, but I know he's still watching me. I can feel his eyes boring into my back.

"He asked for you by name two nights ago. He wasn't here yesterday though." I feel another shiver run through me. Who the hell is he?

Thirty minutes later, the door opens, and Archer and Dan walk in.

Chapter
Thirty-Two

ARCHER

"Did he just hang up on us?" I look at Dan, who's looking as pissed as I feel.

"He did, what was that all about?"

"I'd forgotten about his stubborn streak. He was like this before. He would never let me help him out. We had so many arguments about money and how he wouldn't take any from me. I paid off his student loans for him when he graduated, but I don't even think he knows. The accident happened and, well, shit, you know what happened. At least he had money in his account when my mother ruined our lives. At least he had that."

"Am I treading on your toes here, Archer? I feel like I'm the third here. You know so much about him, and we're still in the learning phase." Dan looks at me. I don't get what he means.

"What? God, no. You and Mallo... I mean Carter, loves you. I can see it. It should be me worrying. Is he wanting me out of duty? Does he feel he should stay with me?"

"I doubt that. As you said, Carter is stubborn, and he gets what he wants. He loves you, Archer. It's written all over his face. I never thought about loving you. I thought we'd lost any chance of that when we were split apart. Then you met Carter. But I do love you. I want this to work. I know it will be so good."

"I guess it's up to him. As always, that man has me wrapped around his little finger. We are good together, Dan, but I think if he had to choose now, he'd choose you. As much as that kills me, I would walk away. I wouldn't fight for him, that's not fair. I had my chance with him."

"Why are we even talking about this? Carter hasn't said he's not happy. In fact, I think having you back has completed him. You've healed him, and that works for me. I get a much happier man. We'll give him a while to cool down and then call him. We need to get some work done."

I go back to my office and look through the files Dan has shared with me and pick one to start on. After an hour, I pick up my phone and call Carter, but the little shit lets it go to voicemail. I can't help but smile. Just the thought of apologizing to him makes me hard.

My phone rings, and I expect it to be him and growl when I answer, "You ready to get your ass spanked tonight, baby?"

"Hey, you're not really my type, but I'll pass the message on to my wife." The caller laughs. I look down at the caller ID and see Lucas Davenport.

"Shit! Sorry, man. I was expecting it to be someone else." I laugh loudly, then get my head in the game. "Thanks for returning my call. I've a job for you if you've got a space for me."

"Tell me more," he replies.

I spend the next thirty minutes filling him in on what went down after my accident and what my mother did to Mallory.

"Shit! Archer, I wish you'd asked me to do this nine months ago. I could've had you back with him in days."

"I fucking know that now, asshole," I mutter. "Mason offered, but I was too pissed to deal. I know I'm a dick. Both Carter, as he's now called, and Dan have told me. Can you help though? That bitch must have a hold on someone to pull the tricks she does. I don't care what it costs. I want her brought down. How many other lives has she wrecked?"

"I'm on it. Do you want updates or just facts when I have them? She really is a bitch, isn't she?" Lucas chuckles drily.

"She's the lowest kind of human, Lucas. Let me know when you've got something. I don't want to be involved with bringing her down. I'm not doing her courtside shows. Let me know so we can put the facts in the hands of the right people to end her."

"Consider it done, Archer. It's good to know you're happy again. Please put my cousin out of his misery and call him." Lucas ends the call, and I feel a weight lift from me, happy knowing someone will take her down.

I try Carter again, but it goes straight to voicemail again. I think of what he's doing today, and how he's helping his friend. I tune him out for the rest of the day and only see Dan a few times when he pops his head around the door.

So, it's a surprise when he walks in with his case in his hand.

"You ready to get outta here?" He laughs as I look up from a file two inches thick.

"Shit, is it that time already? Hell, yeah, let's go." I shut down my computer and lock the files in the tall wooden cabinet behind me.

"Did you get hold of Carter?" I walk up to him and drop a kiss on his mouth.

"No, the little shit didn't answer me." He frowns. "Did you?"

"No, but I figured he was helping his friend and would have focused on him."

"I guess. He and Paris are good friends. I have a bit more knowledge than you though, about why he's helping him."

"You gonna share?"

"Yeah, I got a call from Conn Martinez. He's a cop and a good friend. Don't look at me like That. He's a friend. Anyway, they got a call last night, and Paris' father decided to try to beat the gay out of Paris. He got away before he could hurt him too badly, but he's gotta be hurting today. Carter's a good man. He'll make sure he's okay."

"Are we going over there tonight?" We've reached his car now, and I climb into the sleek leather seat and relax.

"Too fucking right. He's going to be in our bed tonight. I'm looking forward to reminding him how much he likes it there."

"I think I like the idea of that. Hell, I'm horny as fuck. How long do we have to wait 'til we can get him?" I joke, but I know I can't wait to see him.

"Did you get hold of your surveillance guy?" Dan asks as he drives us home.

"Yeah, he's going to sort it. I told him I don't need updates. I just need to know when he's done, and we can hand it over to the authorities. I know there is something she's hiding. She's a cold-hearted, calculating bitch."

"Well, let's hope it doesn't take him long. For all we know, she's known where Carter is and has the whole time. Now that you're here too, she might get pissed enough to act on it."

"Shit, I never thought of that. Do you think he's safe?" A cold sweat breaks out over my body at the thought of her harming him, physically this time. I know she'd never lift one of her own hands against him, but she has plenty of people that would do it for her.

"I don't think we should mention this to him, but maybe you need to call your friend again. I could be completely wrong, but if she hates him that much, maybe she's capable of hurting him."

"I'll call him again when we get home. Fuck, why won't she just leave me the fuck alone?" I know I could be wrong about her, but I doubt it.

By the time Dan comes back downstairs from his shower, I've spoken to Lucas again, and he says they have already managed to get into a private bank account and a personal email account. I'm impressed at the speed he works. I guess that's why he's one of the best.

While I bring Dan up to date, he grabs us both a beer from the fridge and cooks dinner. Just a simple steak, baked potato, and salad.

"Did he tell you if he's found anything?" Dan asks as he cooks.

"No, but he thought watching out for Carter was good, so maybe he has. I hate keeping this from Carter, but if it turns out to be unnecessary, why worry him too?"

"I agree. We have to carry on as normal and let him get back to being Carter again."

Finally, it's time to meet him. I wonder if he'll still be pissed at us?

Chapter
Thirty-Three

DAN

When we walk in, we scan the room and see Carter watching us. He still looks pissed and wants to know what we are doing here. He nevertheless offers us a beer.

"After you hung up on us and refused to answer our calls, we decided we needed to come and remind you what you'll be missing at home."

"You shouldn't have bothered. I've got the truck. I can make my own way back when I'm done." I'm not giving into them.

Shelley walks over and grins. "Ahh boys, are you missing your man?" She laughs. I grin at her, but Archer chokes on his beer, only just managing not to spit it all over me.

"Oh, boys." She smirks. "I watched what went down with Kes and his men. Don't play innocent with me." She waggles her finger at us but is smiling so damn hard.

This immediately lightens the mood between us, and I grin, blushing.

"Shelley, please for the love of God, pack it in." Carter pleads, but I can't help laughing hard.

"You can pack it in, or you won't be getting anything from me tonight." Carter tries to act stern, but I know he's forgiven us.

Shelley walks behind him and sniggers quietly. "Which one were you talking to, sugar lips?"

Shelley laughs at us, but it's a fair assumption. Carter begs for her to stop embarrassing him and berates Archer for encouraging her.

We chat quietly while Carter works through his shift, but soon it's time to close down for the night. I watch him as he stares at one man as he leaves. The guy turns and gives him a nod and a smug smile, but it wasn't a pleasant interaction. Carter stares at him as he leaves and walks down past the windows.

"You okay, baby?" I'm not happy with that little standoff. He breaks away from looking through the window and puts a smile on his face, but it's not genuine.

"Yeah, sorry. I'm good." Shelley has locked the door and walks back to the hallway at the side and brings out a broom.

"Hey, Shelley. Give me that. I'll do that for you. Let me walk you to your car." I take the broom from her and smile, but she gives me a strange look. I lean the broom against a stool and walk with her to the parking lot.

"Thank you, Dan. It looks like you've got a lot going on there, sweetie. Be careful, they have a past to deal with." She strokes her hand down the side of my face, and her smile is a sad one.

"I know, Shell, and thank you for caring. We're just getting to know each other again." I keep my voice low. I love Shelley. I've known her all my life, and she has a heart of pure gold.

"That's not what it looks like, Dan. It looks like you've fallen hook, line, and sinker for them both."

"I'll be careful, I promise." I kiss her cheek and wait for her to get in the car, start the engine, and back out of the space.

Walking back inside, I see Archer has Carter in a tight embrace and is kissing him so damn hard I can feel my dick swell.

"Okay, lover boys. Pack it in. It's time to go home." I clap my hands together and watch as they lazily pull apart. Archer runs his thumb over Carter's swollen lips and smiles so tenderly I feel the tug on my heart. Archer strides up to me and kisses me. His tongue slips quickly between my parted lips. Just as I close my eyes, I see Carter with his eyes are locked on us. His hand rubs against the zipper on his pants.

I let Archer control the kiss, but then I feel another set of hands on my hips. I break away and look at Carter. Archer reaches for him and brings him in closer to us. He kisses me, then Carter. I smile when Carter sighs softly.

"You ready to go home, baby?" Archer asks him.

"I'm ready for all of us to be together," Carter whispers, his eyes on mine. "I'm sorry I was a dick this morning. Don't gang up on me. We need to be equal and respect each other."

"I know. I'm sorry, too." Archer kisses him again.

"I need to close down the office. It will take me a few minutes. Can you sweep in here?"

"I'll do that," I tell him, Carter nods and rushes through to the office. "Is he serious?" I ask Archer as he watches him.

"I don't think he would say it if he didn't mean it. We must have really pushed him today."

We then quickly sweep the floor and wipe down the tables. Time seems to have frozen, and it feels like a lifetime before Carter comes out of the office and switches the last lights off.

"I'm ready." His voice is low and gravelly, making me think he really is ready.

The drive home is quick and silent. Archer seems lost in his thoughts, and I'm looking through the rearview mirror, watching Carter follow behind in the truck.

Pulling up on the drive, I switch off the engine and wait for Carter to pull up alongside of me. "Come on, we need to be inside."

Opening my door, I slide out of the car and hold my hand out for Archer to take. Without any hesitation, he grasps it and smiles.

Carter takes three long strides to reach me. His mouth hits mine as his hands reach around and grab my ass. As his tongue plunges into my mouth, he squeezes my cheeks hard, pulling my hips up to his. He then pulls back. His blue eyes have turned black as his irises blow.

"We need to get upstairs and get naked, like now," he growls at me, then turns to Archer. "Let's go, baby."

Archer grins and heads up the stairs and through the door into his room. Carter takes my hand and races after his boyfriend.

When we walk into the room, Archer has the table lamps on, leaving the room in a subtle muted light. When he sees us, he pulls his shirt over his head and drops it to the floor. As he pulls at his belt, releasing the buckle, Carter catches up and rips his work T-shirt off and unclasps the button at the top of his tight black pants. He toes off his shoes and pushes his trousers down his legs, leaving him in just a pair of tight black briefs.

"Fuck!" I whisper and then follow suit. In no time, we're all standing in just our underwear. I can see the strain of both men's erections pressing against their waistbands. I rub the palm of my hand over my own hard dick.

Carter drops to his knees and drags Archer's briefs down then takes his dick in his mouth. His cheeks hollow as he sucks him deep. I step out of my boxer briefs and kiss Archer. My tongue slips between his lips, lazily stroking his tongue.

Then I feel Carter's hand wrap around my dick as he pumps it.

"Fuck!" My eyes go wide, making me look down as I feel his hot, wet mouth close around my dick.

Chapter
Thirty-Four

CARTER

Fuck, his dick is divine! My lips close around the swollen crown, and I flick my tongue over the slit, tasting a burst of his precum. I hum as I take him deeper and look up. Archer watches me as his hand strokes through my hair, gripping and tugging on the length. He holds my head still as Dan pumps his hips, pushing his length deeper into my mouth.

"Oh, God, you look amazing. Fuck, I love you. Take him deep, baby," Archer croons at me, then loosens his grip on my hair as I suck Dan deep in my throat. His deep groan excites me as I suck him hard. My nose hits his smooth groin. I love a shaved cock and balls. I gag and swallow around him, then pull back and off him. I turn to do the same to Archer; swapping between the two of them feels so empowering as their moans get louder.

"Fuck, you need to stop. I'm gonna come." Dan moans as I swallow him again.

"We need to get on the bed." I stand and kiss both of their mouths. "Come on."

Archer runs his hands over my chest. His fingers pluck at my nipples, teasing them into hard peaks. His mouth covers one, flicking it rapidly before biting down.

"Arghh, God, that feels good!" Then the sensation intensifies when Dan sucks on the other one. Someone's hands slip under the waistband of my briefs, cupping my ass, before pushing them down my legs.

We stumble back and collapse onto the bed in a heap of arms and legs. I burst out laughing. "I would've thought we'd got better at this threesome malarkey by now. We're not very graceful at this yet."

"Oh, Carter, baby, we can practice this every fucking day." Dan laughs and kisses my neck.

Archer untangles his legs and pulls me up to the middle of the bed and kisses me again, Dan's hands roam up my legs, followed by his mouth, leaving a trail of long, wet kisses in his wake. The sensation of having so many hands stroking my body drives me higher and higher. Something I hope I never get used to. As Archer travels down my body, his teeth scrape over my abs, making me writhe as he gets closer to my dick.

"Oh, God, feels so good." I pant. "Please, oh, God, please."

"What, baby, what do you want?" Archer's hot breath washes over my skin. "Tell us what you need."

"More, I need more! Your mouth on me, suck me, Archer. I need your mouth on my dick before I come." I beg, and I don't care. My dick is pouring a stream of precum onto my stomach. I'm so close. I cry out as Archer slides his mouth down my whole length, but it's the feeling of Dan's mouth on my heavy sac that has me screaming. His tongue swirls around my balls before sucking them into his mouth. My hips buck up as my back arches off the bed.

Archer lifts off my dick and fists it, pumping it hard. "I want to see

Dan bury his cock deep in your ass, Carter, do you want that? Do you want his big, fat dick inside you?" His eyes bore into mine as Dan lifts my ass before sliding his tongue down over my taint and down the crease to my hole.

"Fuck! Yesyesyes!" I cry out as Dan's tongue spears my pucker. His hands spread my cheeks, opening me up to him. As he spits on my hole, Archer sucks me again. I can't bear it any longer. I grab hold of my legs and pull them up to my chest.

"Oh, baby, you look so beautiful." Archer moves up to look at me. "I love you so much. You look amazing with his tongue in your ass."

Dan spears me again, then adds a finger inside me too. I can feel the burn as he stretches me, ready to take him. Then two fingers are in my passage. He pumps them in and out, scissoring as he goes. His tongue slides down my taint to dip into my ass as his fingers stretch me. Then slide further up my crease just to come back and repeat the action. His fingers slide out, making me groan at the empty feeling. His tongue takes their place and stabs inside my hole. I have never been eaten out like this before, and it's driving me wild. My eyes flash to Archer, and I see his hand working over his dick as he stares at my ass. He senses me looking and leans over to kiss me.

"You are the sexiest motherfucker alive. Fuck, I love you."

"I'm ready, fuck me! Dan!" I cry out, then moan as he pulls his tongue from inside me, only to replace it with his fingers. The torture continues as my dick leaks, making a pool on my stomach now.

"You are so fucking sexy, Carter." Dan moans as he looks at me, taking a bottle of lube from Archer I hadn't even noticed him getting. The cool liquid dribbles down over my balls to my pucker. Dan adds two fingers back inside me as he lubes up his dick.

His fingers pull out, and then I feel the head of his dick press up to my hole. Dan has taken hold of my legs and has them stretched up straight. I let out a groan so deep it hardly sounds like me as he slides all the way in.

"Fuck! You are so tight. I fucking love your ass." Dan holds still. I can feel his balls on my ass.

Archer kneels by my head. "You look so beautiful." Leaning over, he kisses me, but it's his dick I want in my mouth. I reach out to grab him, but he has other ideas and swings his leg over my face so he's facing Dan. I open my mouth and let him feed me his dick. As I start to suck, Dan pumps in and out of me. Moaning around Archer's cock has him spurting precum over my tongue.

This feels like something so unreal yet so perfect. The heat of his cock stroking against the highly charged nerves in my ass sends bolts of lightning through my body. His hands grip my ankles tight as he pulls his solid shaft to the tight ring of muscles at my entrance. I can feel the rim of his crown as he slips free, only to plunge back inside. I mutter a cry of sheer ball-aching pleasure around Archer's cock, making him tremble in my mouth. The slick-slick-slick sound of Dan's cock sliding in and out as it glides through my lube-coated channel, mixed with the moans of both men, is heightened by the extra sensations of touch, sound, taste, and smell. My eyes are closed, and I know I won't last much longer. Archer leans over me and takes my dick in his mouth. Dan pumps faster and harder. I can feel my climax building as I tremble.

"Christ, I'm not going to last!" Dan cries out. "Come, baby. Come for me!" His hips fire like pistons, making the head of his cock pound my prostate. Each punch sends a tsunami of pleasure through my body.

Archer moves off my cock and kneels next to me again. He jacks himself with one hand and me with the other. As my spine tingles and stiffens, I come. I cry out their names as my cum fires from my body, My ass clamps hard around Dan as he cries out and comes as well. I feel him fill my ass, the white-hot heat of his release scorching my insides.

As the white ribbons of my cum paint my stomach and chest, Archer comes too, covering my chest with his hot spunk, crying out my name. We stay still, all panting hard. Dan reaches forward and trails his fingers through the ropes of our cum. He lifts them to my mouth, painting my lips with the salty-sweet mixture. He does the same to Archer and himself, then we kiss.

Three mouths joined together, each of us tasting each other, moaning at the flavors. Dan pulls back and leans away. I feel his dick slide from my ass and the slick slipperiness of his cum dripping out of me.

Lazy fingers slide up my rib cage as I lie back, my chest still heaving. Archer leans over me and kisses me. His tongue dips inside my mouth and slides languidly over mine before he sucks my tongue into his mouth. I feel shivers over my body, and my dick twitches but stays limp and spent.

I hear a chuckle from the other side of me. "I thought you were going to get hard again then, baby." Dan nudges Archer and takes my mouth.

"I'm sure we could go another round in a few. I fancy myself in your ass, Dan, while Carter's in mine."

"Fuck!" I groan, and my dick does plump up at the image that conjures up.

"Let's get cleaned up." Dan moves off the bed and stalks away to the bathroom. I hear the water gushing as he turns on the shower.

"I think you must have had a premonition you'd need a shower this large, Dan." I step into the huge glass-walled enclosure. The back wall has a bench built in, and there are shelves and nooks for soaps and shampoo bottles. "I think we could get another three men in here."

I laugh when both of my lovers growl. "Calm down, tigers. I've no plans of letting anyone else touch you."

"I think we're doing well enough with the three of us." Archer kisses me softly. "We still have so much to learn. I'm sorry we hurt you today, Carter. I will try my best to let you be the person you are now. I'm loving the new Carter. As much as I hate the reason why we got separated, I'm so happy be back here with both of you."

"This is meant to be, Archer, I love having you back in my life. I don't want us to be apart again. You need to be here with me and with Dan." I kiss his lips softly as Dan crowds behind me. The water pounds down on our heads as we kiss, the three of us together, just how it's meant to be.

Breaking apart, we wash up and soon are back in bed. I lie between them, and I quickly fall deeply asleep, wrapped in the arms of my lovers.

Chapter
Thirty-Five

ARCHER

"How was last night for you, babe?" I reach past Dan to grab the coffee mugs, managing to snag a kiss on his lips as I do.

"Really? You have to ask that? Fuck, Archer, last night was the best we've had so far. Every touch and sigh imprinted on my heart. It was amazing." He kisses me this time.

"Do you think we're topping too much? I know Mall… fuck, Carter likes to top but…"

"Hey, I don't give a shit who tops or bottoms. Jeez, Archer. Last night was amazing, but if you're worried about not getting your ass tapped, I'll do it tonight." Carter swans past us in just his boxer briefs. He seems to make a habit of not dressing at breakfast.

"I love your choice of clothing for breakfast, honey. It fills my mind with wicked thoughts." I let him kiss me as he walks up to Dan.

"And, Archer, I know you think of me as Mallory. I get that it feels weird for you, but Carter fits me now." He gives me a sneaky look and smirks. "Although you called Mallory out last night when you came over me."

"Shit! Did I? I'm sorry." I look at him guiltily, which makes him grin.

"I'm pretty sure I'll cope." He turns to Dan who has his arm wrapped around him now. "Did you notice or mind when he called out Mallory?"

"Carter, my love, I don't care what you're called as long as you're happy with it. I love you, and so does Archer." Dan puts a finger under Carter's chin and kisses him. It's a slow, burning kiss. After a moment, I chuckle, and that breaks them apart. I guess I'll have to get used to it.

"Dan, sweetheart. I think you're getting him too excited, especially as we're about to leave." I grin and look down at Carter's very prominent erection in his boxers.

"Crap, you did this to me yesterday, Archer. Go on, go to work, the pair of you are nothing but trouble. I'll see you tonight." He shakes his head and makes his way past us.

"Hey, where are you going?" I ask. "I was only messing with you, baby." I reach out to him.

"Oh, I know that, Arch. Just think while you two are at your desks, I'll be lounging in bed with my hand around my cock." He swaggers away from us with a cocky grin and a wink as he looks over his shoulder.

"What are you working today, baby?" Dan calls out.

"Two 'til ten. I'm going to see Paris first though. I'll see you here tonight. Love you," he calls as he takes the stairs back to bed.

"Love you, too," we call out to him, then head out to work.

✵ ✵ ✵

"Shall we go for a beer?" I ask Dan as we walked out of the office. "It's been a long day."

"You mean, you want to see our man?" Dan laughs and claps me on the back. "C'mon, let's go."

We walk into the bar, and it's busy. There's a definite crowd of white-collar workers who have the same idea as us. A cold beer and a chill-out is needed to decompress after being stuck in an office all day. Carter looks up as the bell chimes and gives us a wide grin. His dark-blue eyes sparkle.

It's time to claim him. I nudge Dan forward, and we make our way to the bar. "Hey, sugar, have you missed us?" I lean across the polished mahogany bar and capture his mouth with mine.

Dan catches on and does the same. I hear a chuckle from further up and see Kes looking at the three of us.

"Yeah, I have." He sighs, smiling shyly, a faint blush on his cheeks. "You want a beer?"

"Please." I look around the bar. There are a few strange looks, but most people don't pay us any attention. I see a poster on the back wall promoting an open mic night. "Are you playing?" I turn back to Carter.

"Um, that would be a huge no." He looks horrified.

"You play?" Dan looks surprised. "What do you play? You've never mentioned it."

"He plays piano. He's amazing at it. Why do you look so horrified? You love playing." I don't understand his aversion.

"I just haven't. Anyway, we don't have a piano here. It's mainly just acoustic guitar. A few bring other instruments." Carter quickly ends the conversation and walks away to serve someone.

"You know so much more about him. I wonder if he would ever have told me that. How good is he?" Dan looks miserable.

"Hey, c'mon, you're the one who made him happy again. He would have told you when he was ready. He's really good."

"Why don't we ask Kes to get a piano here? I bet he'll be up for it. Denver plays guitar here regularly. Maybe Carter would join in." Dan smiles at the thought.

"Yeah, let's ask." I look over at Carter who's busy serving and talking to the other patrons.

We walk together to the back office. Dan knocks on the open door. Kes looks up and smiles.

"Hey, guys, come in. Is everything okay? Is Carter okay?" A worried look spreads over his face.

"Yeah, everything is good, but it's something to do with him." Dan smiles. "Did you know he plays piano? And apparently very well."

"No, I didn't, but it doesn't surprise me. We have one at home now. Denver plays too. He prefers his guitar but messes about with it with East's daughter, Ellie. I've seen Carter eye it up a couple times."

"Yeah? Well, we'd like him to play at the open mic night. Maybe not the next one, but soon. Maybe if you had one here, we could coax him out of his shell again. He really is that good. You wouldn't want to miss it," I tell him, hoping to persuade him.

"It's funny you bring this up now. I had an inquiry from someone wanting to play here but was unable to bring a keyboard with him. I've already got one coming tomorrow." Kes laughs and leans back in his chair. "I want to start organizing a gig night where we have a different group or artist get the chance to play a full set. Having some of the gear here would help. I'm not going to ask him to play though, guys. This has to be up to him." Kes looks us both over. "Can I be frank with you?"

We both nod, although I'm nervous as to what he's going to say.

"Okay, you both seem to have a dominant side. Be careful not to overwhelm him. He's not as much of a pushover as you seem to want him to be. Let him be him, the man you both seem to love. Don't try to mold him into something that you, Archer, used to know, and Dan, something you want him to be. Let him love you the way he wants. He isn't a third. Don't make him feel like one."

I feel the tension build up in me as he speaks. Why does he think he knows Carter better than I? I was engaged to him. My back stiffens as I get ready to bite back, but Dan recognizes it and runs his hand down my spine, relaxing me again.

"You have nothing to worry about, Kes. Carter is most definitely holding his own." Dan chuckles.

"That's all I needed to know. As for the piano, I'm sure he'll find his way back to it."

"C'mon, babe. Let's get back to our drinks. Thanks, oh and, Kes, this has to come from you." I nod, and he smiles openly at me.

"Anytime."

As we walk back through to the bar, Carter bumps into us both. His eyes narrow suspiciously, but there's a small grin hiding under a scowl.

"What are you two doing back here? You better not have been meddling."

"I don't know what you're talking about. We just wanted to say hi to Kes." I bite the corner of my lip to stop from grinning.

"You want to be on my shit list, Hawkins?" Carter quips back at me, his eyebrow cocked.

"Hmm, that depends on what you're gonna do to me?" I laugh this time.

"Archer, baby. I can think of a shit-ton of things I could do." He smiles wolfishly this time.

"I'll look forward to every single one of them." I lean over and murmur in his ear, "Especially if it has something to do with your cock and my ass."

"You bet. Now get back out there. This is a staff-only area." He smirks and slaps my ass.

We don't stay long after that, just enough to finish our beer. Dan gives Carter a kiss goodbye as I pay for our beers.

As we leave, I step aside to let a man through the door before we exit. He gives me a deep, penetrating, dark look before thanking me noncommittedly, making me uneasy.

"Do you know him?" Dan asks as he looks over his shoulder at the stranger. "He gave you a weird look."

"He was here the other night. I saw him watching both me and Carter." I look through the window and see him at the bar, watching our man. "Do you think Carter's okay?"

"Do you want to stay?" Dan is watching him too.

"No, it's probably nothing. He's not on late. He's got the truck again. I'm not going to baby him. He's a grown man."

"Yeah, the guy may have been having a bad day."

"Yeah, you're probably right. C'mon, I'm ready to shower and get into some sweats."

I head upstairs as soon as we get inside. Dan wanders into the kitchen, talking about finding us something to eat. I strip off and get into the hot spray of the shower, tipping my head back under the water. The image of Carter and the stranger fill my mind. What was it about him that set off the alarm bells? He gave off a strange vibe as he looked at me. Something wasn't right about it, but I can't put my finger on what.

As I soap my body, I decide I need to tell Carter about the guy tonight. Feeling slightly better when I finish, I switch the shower off and grab a towel. Looking down at my legs as I dry them, I still feel shock and discomfort when I see the scars. Even after all this time, anger surges inside me at the hurt and pain my mother caused us both. The possibility that she could still be a threat to us makes me seethe.

I drag my sweats up my legs and go back downstairs. Dan has taken off his jacket and tie and has his shirt sleeves rolled up to the elbow. He's stirring something that already smells delicious. I step up behind him and kiss the back of his neck.

"You want me to take over so you can go get showered?" I murmur.

"Nah, I normally wait for Carter to get home when he's on this shift. We shower together." Dan twists his head around to kiss me, but I step back and look at him amazed.

"What?" Dan puts down his wooden spoon and turns to me. "Why are you looking at me like that?"

"Why didn't you tell me?"

"What? I guess I didn't think about it. What difference does it make?" Dan frowns, confusion written all over his face.

"I would've waited and showered with you both." I'm pissed about this as a wave of jealousy washes over me. This is something they do. Something private that I didn't know about. They have a routine. They have the relationship I used to have. I run my hands through my still-damp hair, trying to calm my feelings down.

"Hey, Archer, baby, I'm sorry. There's no law to say you can't have another one." He winks and moves to kiss me. I know I'm being a dick, but I step away again. "What's going on, Arch? Why are you acting like this? It's just a shower."

"It's more than that, Daniel. It's the life you two have, that you are building together. That used to be mine." I sigh and move over to the fridge. I need a beer.

"You sound like you're jealous. Y'know that's crazy, right? I love you. Carter loves you. So, why does one shower bother you?" Dan turns the heat down on the stove and copies me and grabs a beer from the fridge. "Don't you think I have worries about you two and the past you shared? I think I've got more reason to be jealous than you, but this isn't a competition about who knows Carter best. I think we both know him, but I know a very different version of the man you know."

"How would you know? You didn't know him then." God, I can hear the petulance in my voice. When Dan rolls his eyes, I know it's gotten to him too.

"Are you seriously turning this into a pissing contest, Archer? Just listen to yourself!"

He crosses his arms over his chest and stares at me, his eyes penetrating, searching for an explanation.

I shake my head, trying to clear it and find a reason for my shitty reaction.

"Yeah, I know. I'm a dick. I'm stressed to fuck. This crap with my mother is getting to me. Just the thought she may be after him still drives me crazy. One minute, I'm thinking I need to go back home and confront her. The next, I want to never see her again, to let Lucas do his job. I'm shit-scared that Carter will get hurt." Running my hands through my hair again, I sigh, almost relieved to get it off my chest.

"Oh, baby, y'know, she may not be doing any of this. She may have walked away, like you told her to. I am seriously against you going back and seeking her out. She will hurt you, Archer. Let Lucas do what you're paying him to do. He'll find out any dirt on her. She's got to have some shit sticking to her somewhere."

When Dan walks towards me this time, I let him step between my parted legs as I lean back against the counter. His arms drape over my shoulders, and he presses his hips up to mine. A small smile creeps over his rugged, handsome face.

"It will be okay. You know that, don't you? We don't put up with any shit, Archer. We will face any problem, and we will face it together, the three of us. We are a team, baby. Don't lose focus of that. We are in this together." His lips touch mine. I relax into him as his tongue drifts over the seam of my lips, nudging for entrance.

As the tips of our tongues touch, Dan knits his fingers into my longish hair, gripping tight as he deepens the kiss. His tongue explores my mouth, lazily caressing the roof of my mouth before sucking on my tongue. My fingers dig into his hips as I grind up against him, our dicks growing harder with every nudge.

A ringing sound breaks us apart. Dan unlocks his fingers and drags them out of my hair.

"What was that?" I ask, looking around.

"The oven, dinner's ready." He smiles and steps away, back to the stove.

I match his smile and pull myself together. I'm here, and I'm loved.

But the niggle is still there. Do I want Carter to myself?

We eat and laugh and chill out until Carter walks in the door. We take a shower. My second of the night.

Chapter
Thirty-Six

CARTER

I stop in the doorway of the bar and look at the stage area in the corner and scowl. A fucking piano! I knew it. I knew they wouldn't leave it alone. The problem is the flare of excitement that flashes through me at the sight of it. A baby grand in gleaming black-lacquered wood.

I turn when I catch movement on the other side of the room. I see Kes standing there, watching me. I tip my head in the direction of the corner. "What's with the piano?"

"Thought it would look good here. Someone wants to play on the mic night and couldn't bring theirs. Den likes to play sometimes too. Why? You play?" Kes walks over to the offending article.

"I used to, don't anymore." I shrug and saunter over to the office.

"Why not?" God, he's not going to let this go.

"I dunno, just stopped wanting to." I drop my coat on the hanger in the office, then walk slowly back out. "You want me to go to the bank for you? We need to get change as well as bank yesterday's takings."

"No, I'm going to do it, then head home again. East's there with Phoebe. God knows what trouble they'll get into. He's a bigger baby than she is." Kes beams at the thought of his lover and their child. I wonder if I'll ever want children. I shake my head at the thought. I'm still trying to get my head around having two boyfriends.

"Have a fun afternoon while I slave away here." I laugh as he grabs the bag with the money in it.

"I'll be back with your change before you open." He waves and walks out.

I sit behind the desk and get to work on the ordering, but I see Kes has done it all. I needn't have come in this early if I'd known. Leaning back in the chair, I prop my hands behind my head and enjoy the quiet. I hear a loud bump from upstairs. Looking up, I wonder if Paris is okay. Shit! What if it's his dad? Jumping up, I race out the back. I'm not using the internal door now. I don't live there anymore, and that would be rude.

"Paris!" I call out as I knock hard on the door. "Paris, you okay?"

I hear muffled voices, then the door opens. He's standing in his jeans that aren't done up all the way, and his chest is bare.

"Shit, are you okay? I heard a crash when I was in the office. Christ, Par, what the fuck?" I take in the multicolored bruises mapping his chest and abs. These are much darker than the couple on his face.

"Huh? What? Oh, yeah, I'm okay. Sorry to worry you." He looks over his shoulder, and I realize he's got someone with him.

"Crap! Paris, I'm sorry. I thought maybe your dad had shown up. My bad." I back away, shaking my head, but a laugh breaks out. "I'm sorry to have interrupted you. You'd better get back to him." I give him a wink.

"Fucker!" Paris grins and shuts the door.

I go back down and into the bar. The first thing I see is that damn piano! I find the tightness in my chest building again. The memories of playing for Archer flood my mind. The nights I would play for him, and he would make love to me. Sometimes on the thick rug by the piano, other times he'd carry me to our bed. For this reason alone, I can't play for Dan. It isn't fair to him, or to me.

Not when I'm wondering if I've made the right decision. Not when I'm feeling so much confusion. But when Archer called me Mallory as he climaxed, I was immediately back with him in our apartment. Even with Dan with us, I felt separate.

Fuck! I can't believe this is happening to me. Two men love me. I love them both, too. I stare again at the damn piece of wood in the corner. Maybe I need to make memories for the three of us. I weave my way through the tables to reach it and lift up the cover. My fingers lightly stroke the keys. Not enough to make them press down and emit a sound, but enough to make my heart race again.

Pulling out the stool, I sit. I can feel my rapidly beating heart and the sweat breaking out on my top lip. The room around me fades as I place my fingers on the keys.

Closing my eyes, I let my fingers play their own tune. I take a deep breath in and hum quietly to myself as the lyrics from Halsey's *Eyes Closed* burst to life in my mind. I find myself singing along quietly. I've never let myself think too much about the lyrics because I love Halsey's voice, but the chorus hits me hard in the chest.

Lyrics that I've tried not to relate to Dan and Archer because I don't feel that. As I whisper the words, I realize maybe it's me that's different. I don't even think I'm replacing Archer with someone new. I think he's a new Archer. He looks the same, he feels the same, but he's changed. Just as much I guess, as I have. We aren't the lovers we were. I'm just not sure if we are doing this to find our old selves again. In which case, where does Dan come into this? I can't hurt him. I won't hurt him. God! I'm so confused.

Shit! I really do not need to be thinking this sort of crap. My voice hitches, but I carry on singing, managing to voice my pain and fear. The worry I have for keeping both Dan and Archer, for them to understand how broken I would be.

I carry on playing but stop singing, keeping the music in my head. My hands fall off the keys as I finish playing, and I close the lid before resting my arms across it with my head falling on to them.

There was something going on between them last night, something had been said. I don't know what, but there was a tension between them. We didn't make love. Archer spooned behind me, his arms around me while Dan faced me, both whispering soft words of love. I'm not convinced they aimed that at each other. What the fuck is going on between us? Are we falling apart already?

I sense a movement to the side of me. Lifting my head up, I wipe the stray tears from my face. When I turn my head, I see Kes, his stricken face watching me cautiously.

"What's going on, Carter?" He steps up to me. "I'm not gonna lie and say you weren't amazing, but the song? The lyrics? Damn, they were powerful. You know you can talk to me if you need to. I won't judge, you know that. I sure as hell won't share it with anyone else."

"I don't know what I'm doing." It's the first thing that blurts out of my mouth, way before my brain catches up and I can tell him I'm fine. Shit, I shake my head, trying to dispel the budding tears again.

"With your men? Is it not what you expected? Not what you want?" Kes pulls a chair over to me and sits. He waits for my answer, and I'm trying to think of the right words.

"I love them. I really do, but it's different. I think, I sometimes feel we're together because neither of them will give me up." I drag a deep breath in my lungs, embrace the pain as my lungs inflate too hard. I didn't mean to say that. "Fuck!" I gasp and shake my head. "I didn't mean to say that."

"Are you sure?" Kes questions, his eyebrow lift. "Or you didn't mean to say it aloud?"

"I don't know. Something happened last night before I got home. I don't know what, and they didn't say. It just felt different."

"Carter, without thinking about it, who do you want to be with?"

"Dan." I look up at Kes, surprised at my answer.

"You look surprised, Carter. Did that come as a shock?"

"Yeah, I mean, I guess. It's because we just got serious. We told each other we were in love and it's true. Dan has helped me find who I am after Archer died. I like the Carter I am now. This is a great place to be. I love it here. I just… it's difficult to explain." I pause and look around the empty bar, trying to gather my thoughts. "Hell, I want the silly part of just falling in love, the parts where you learn so much about each other. When all you do is talk in the dark, in the middle of the night. The chance to make our story, to find the things we love doing together."

"Do you think you've lost that because of Archer?"

"Yeah, I mean the shock of finding him alive and that he's Dan's best friend shocked the crap out of me. The stark reality of him standing in front of me blew me away. I couldn't believe it. Then my heart connected back with his but… It's not that it didn't feel right. It simply felt different. I love him, but I'm not the man I was when we were together, and neither is he."

Kes reaches across, and his hand rubs my shoulder. "You're allowed to feel like this, Carter. You have a right to decide who you share your love, as well as your body, with."

"Yeah, that's where it gets more complicated because the sex is amazing, like out-of-this-world fantastic. I feel we've jumped in too fast and it will burn out. Or they will decide it doesn't work and want to end it. What do I do if they ask me to choose? Or what if I'm not what they want after all? And they want each other again? Where do I fit in with two lawyers and me running your bar?"

"You know that doesn't matter. You're great at your job, Carter."

"I know, and I don't mean to cause you any offense. I love it here. I'm proud of what I've achieved here. I'm just so confused."

"I can see that. So, tell me about this." He waves at the piano. "Why the aversion? And why that song?"

"The piano? That's easy. It reminds me too much of what I had. What I lost. We were engaged. Did you know that? I got the marriage license the day he died."

"Shit, Carter, that's tough."

"Yeah, I know. And now he's calling me Mallory again, although not all the time. I think he's just looking for a way back to what we were and that's not fair."

"You know you're going to have to talk to them. They want you to play, you know that, right? Maybe it would be a good way to open the discussion. Denver manages to reach us through his music. He's a little shit sometimes." Kes smiles, and I can see the love he has for his partner.

"Am I being silly about this? Could I be reading too much into a situation that isn't there? Dammit, Kes, I'm so confused."

"I think you're like Denver. You bottle it all up inside you until you find a way to vent. I think music is the key for both of you. Look, open mic night is tomorrow. There will be a space for you if you want it. It's that simple. Please don't keep this inside you for too long. It's not good for you, and not fair to the men who love you. Even though you're struggling and have your doubts, don't ever forget how much they love you."

"I know. Thanks, Kes." I give him a smile as I push myself from the piano stool.

"Anytime, Carter. You're family, I've told you that." He squeezes my shoulder, then walks out the front door.

I grab the bag of change and put it in the safe.

By the time I open the door, I've pushed the dark thoughts away and just put it down to melancholy after seeing the piano. Paris breezes in, looking very content, and if I'm not mistaken with a hickie on his neck. I know it's not a bruise his father gave him, but I'm not going to tease him. He'll share when he's ready.

I'm busy serving some lunches when I see Dan and Archer walk in. They both look so damn hot in their suits. Archer winks at me and makes his way to the bar. Dan looks at me with a long, lazy smile spreading over his face.

"Oh my, I wouldn't kick him outta my bed," the young lady says to her friend. "Or his friend. Jeez, the men in this town are hot!"

I look down at them as I place the tray on the table and watch them both blush when they realize I heard.

"You wanna share your digits with me, sugar?" her friend says to me with a wink. "We could meet up later."

"Sorry, we're not allowed to give out our numbers." I smile, giving them a wink. "Enjoy your meal."

"He's so cute," she whispers loudly as I walk away, making me grin even harder.

"Hey, baby," Dan says to me as I make it back to the bar. "D'you mind us having lunch here?" He runs his hand down my back, letting it rest at the base of my spine. "I think your admirer is disappointed now," he whispers huskily in my ear before dropping a kiss on my neck.

"She said she wouldn't kick you outta her bed. So it's you she's after." I laugh and pinch his ass before jogging back to the other side of the bar.

Archer watches me with a wry smile. "You must leave a trail of broken hearts behind you, sugar." He slicks his bottom lip with the tip of his tongue, then leans over to peck my mouth.

"Stop embarrassing me. Go and sit. I'll bring you some drinks over. What do you want?"

"We'd better stick to soft drinks. I'll have a mineral water, and I guess you know what Dan drinks."

"I'll bring them to you." I shoo him away.

Paris steps up behind. "Go have lunch with them, if you want. I can hold it down here. You only ever see them in here when you're working. Enjoy their company for an hour."

"You sure?" I like the idea of this.

"Yep, go on. I'll bring you a platter of club sandwiches." Paris saunters off to tell the kitchen, and I wander over with three drinks instead of two.

Chapter
Thirty-Seven

DAN

"Hey! Are you joining us?" I beam a wide happy smile and move out of the booth so Carter can slide in and sit between the two of us.

"I should probably sit on the outside in case Paris needs me." Carter looks over to the bar, but Paris gives him a wink and waves his hands to make him sit.

"It's good to have this time with you, honey." Archer drapes his arm across the back of the seating before pulling Carter in for a hug.

"Paris is going to bring us over some sandwiches, but if it gets busy, I'll have to go back to work." Carter smiles at us, then looks around. "It seems strange from this side of the bar. I'm not normally here in the daytime unless I'm working."

"You do an amazing job, baby." I kiss the side of his head.

"You don't mind that this is what I do?" he asks quietly, a frown creasing his forehead.

"Of course not. Why should that matter? You're good here. It suits you." I smile and give him a wink. "We wouldn't be together if you hadn't worked here."

"Are you doubting it here, Carter? Do *you* feel you should be working someplace else, using your degree?" Archer asks him.

"Nope, I love it here. I just got to thinking you might be embarrassed to have me working at a bar."

"What's going on then? Why are you doubting yourself?" Archer looks at Carter, concerned.

"Archer, don't worry. It was just an errant thought. And you two are on my shit list! What were you doing telling Kes you want me to play tomorrow night?" He smiles, so I know he's not too pissed at us.

"Oh, he told you that, did he? Well, you should be playing. You're amazing," Archer jokes back but has the decency to look a little bit guilty.

I watch as they both stare at each other and can see their closeness. They watch each other, neither wanting to laugh first. As Archer looks away and smiles, the door flies open, and about ten people crowd through, all laughing and joking together.

"I guess that's my cue to get back to work." Carter sighs and nudges my leg to get me to move out of the way.

"Come back once you've served them." I squeeze his hand as he shuffles past my legs. "Please, baby."

"I'll see how long it takes. Your lunch won't be long." He drops a kiss on my mouth, then repeats his action on Archer, unaware or uncaring if anyone watches.

"We are lucky bastards, you know that, right?" I look over my shoulder and see him laughing with the band of new customers. He looks up and gives us a smile.

"Yeah, we are. I find it hard to believe most days; it's surreal. Something that should never have happened. In this enormous country, my boyfriend ends up in the same town as my best friend. Soap operas make this shit up!" He laughs and pops a kiss on my surprised mouth.

Paris comes over with a platter of sandwiches and potato chips. "Here you go, guys. Dig in. I'll send Carter back over to you as soon as I can, I promise." He winks and spins on his heels.

"I agree. I never could have thought of this. I knew when I first set eyes on Carter he was important. That I needed to have him in my life. Now I know why. It was for us to connect again too. We needed him as the catalyst or as the pivotal link to bring our lives back together the way they should be. I'm happier than I could ever have imagined."

"Me too. All I want now is to end things with my mother. I want to know she can't hurt people and wreck innocent people's lives just because she doesn't like them. Like the way she hurt Carter."

Archer picks up one of the sandwiches, his eyes darting around the room. Then I realize why. He's looking for any bad guy that could be out to hurt Carter. My heart eases as I understand his stress. I do wonder why he's worried after Carter has been here for nearly a year now and hasn't had any trouble. Is Archer the catalyst? Is he the one that can tip his mother over the edge of reason? I guess we have some serious talking to do when we get home together tonight.

Turning to him, I grasp hold of his hand. "Listen to me, Archer. We are supposed to be together. We are supposed to have a happy ending. So, stop looking for trouble, babe. We're in this together. Here comes Carter."

"Sorry about that. I should be home by seven, seven-thirty. We'll have the evening together." Carter looks to me. I nod and draw him to me. As he sits next to me, his smile brightens. He drops another kiss on me, and this time he grabs a sandwich and bites down.

"I'm so hungry." He laughs, settling back on the bench, munching on some of the chips now.

"We didn't ask Kes to get a piano, y'know?" Archer grins at Carter, who just shakes his head.

"I know, but you are both a pair of sneaky shits who still pestered him to get me to play." He laughs and points at both of us. "I'm watching you two. There will be consequences if you keep this up."

My eyes light up. "I like the sound of that." I nudge him with my shoulder.

"Yeah, I thought you might!"

I suddenly feel so much happier. Archer chuckles along, making it feel like we're all okay. I look at the clock on the wall and realize our hour is up.

"Come on, Arch. We need to get back to work."

"Yeah, me too." Carter stands, and we follow him across the bar. Carter walks with us to the door, quickly and far too briefly, kissing us goodbye. "I'll see you guys tonight."

As we walk back, Archer looks at me. "We're gonna be okay, you think?"

"Yeah, baby. I really do." I take hold of his hand and give it a squeeze.

I look over at Archer as we hear the front door open. We've got the TV on, but I don't think either of us has been paying it any attention.

Carter walks in, takes one look at us, and grins. We're both still in our suits, although we've lost our ties and the top couple buttons on our shirts.

"Not showered yet then, boys?" He chuckles, then turns on his heel and heads for the stairs.

"I thought we would wait for you. Do you want anything to eat?" Archer calls out to him.

"No, I'm good, but I am horny. So let's go. We're going to suck and fuck," Carter calls back as he continues up the stairs.

Archer looks at me as I let out a whoop of laughter and head after my man. "Come on, Archer. You really wanna feed him when he's talking that dirty?"

"Fuck, no!" Archer shakes his head and follows me.

When we reach our bedroom, Carter's clothes are strewn all over the floor, and the shower is running. Quickly stripping off, I head into the bathroom. I stop in my tracks, standing motionless, looking at Carter. Archer bumps into me and groans.

Carter stands facing us, his legs apart and his head tipped back, letting the water pound down his chest. With his cock in his fist, he strokes himself lazily. Long, deep strokes. His mouth is slack as he embraces the feelings coursing through his body. His other hand runs lazily down his body. His fingertips trace the outline of his taut muscles until he cups his sac, rolling his balls between his fingers.

I find my feet moving towards him as my eyes fix on his body. When I reach him, my hand copies his and traces the hard muscles of his chest.

"You are a fucking God, Carter. I worship you." Leaning in to capture his mouth as he lifts his head and slowly opens his lust-filled eyes.

Archer moves to the side of our beautiful man and reaches out and places his hand over Carter's as he continues to stroke himself.

"My turn, my love," Archer murmurs into Carter's neck as he kisses him on the tender spot under his ear, his hand pumping up and down the length of Carter's rigid shaft.

I move behind Carter. My hands run down the length of his spine, splaying out over his hips before skimming over his buttocks, kneading the firm rounded cheeks. I feel him trembling as Archer kneels in front and takes him in his mouth.

"You look beautiful, baby, so hot." I croon as my finger slips down between his cheeks, heading for his pucker. As my finger circles over and around his hole, Carter's head drops back on my shoulder.

"Take me to bed." He moans.

Archer slowly slips his mouth back up Carter's dick and stands. I reach over and switch off the shower while Archer grabs a towel and strokes it slowly over Carter's chest. I grab another and dry his back before chucking it in the laundry hamper and taking Carter's hand.

When we reach the bed, Archer gets on first and lies down with his head down on the bed.

"I want my cock in your mouth while I suck you, baby."

I watch Carter's eyes light up, and he quickly climbs over Archer, and soon they're locked in the perfect sixty-nine position. With Carter's ass in the air, I move behind him. Spreading his cheeks wide, I swipe my tongue up his taint and over his hole. Taking my time, I lick over and around the tight pucker. As my tongue flicks over and over, I let my finger torture and tease him. Pressing gently over the muscle, I feel him push back, letting me slip inside him. I fuck him with my finger and tongue until I feel him tense up. I know his orgasm is imminent, so I back off and withdraw my finger.

His head lifts from Archer's cock. His lips dark red and swollen, his brilliant-blue eyes now black with lust. As he looks at me, his tongue slides over his lip. "Fuck me, Dan. Fuck me now!"

I'm not going to turn that down, so I reach over and grab the lube, squirting some of the gel on my cock and then tipping it over his hole. I press my finger back inside as I stroke the lube over my cock with my other hand. Then with him still watching me, I push my swollen head against him and push slowly inside. First past the ring of muscle, then holding still.

"Suck him, Carter, make him come as I fuck you," I growl.

As he dips back over Archer's cock, I push the full way in, my hands gripping tightly to his hips. Archer has let go of Carter's dick and is now sucking on his balls.

"Harder, Dan. Fuck him harder," Archer groans. He moves away and twists around so he is lying down with his back on the pillows. Carter takes him back into his mouth and all the way into his throat as I pound him from behind.

I know it won't take me long to come. Shifting my position, I peg his prostate. Over and over, I slide the head of my dick over his swollen gland. Looking at Archer, I know he's about to blow. Easing back, I let him take control and plunge into Carter's mouth until with a hoarse cry he stills and pours his release into his mouth. Slumping down, Carter lifts his head up and wipes his mouth with the back of his hand and kisses Archer.

I pull out, flip him over, and plunge back inside him. More slowly now, I slip and slide deeply inside his hot, tight channel. I can feel every tremor and shudder as his climax builds up again. I don't think I'll be able to last much longer.

"Stroke him, Arch. Let's make him come together."

Archer reaches over him and grasps his dick, his strokes matching my own as we take him higher and higher. Then as his eyes roll back in his head, a deep guttural moan breaks free from him, and Carter comes. Ribbons of thick, white cum pelt from his body. As he fires out, his ass clenches me so tightly I come. I can feel myself flooding him as he milks me dry.

Collapsing over him, I cover his face with kisses. "I love you, Carter Halston," I whisper as my mouth hovers over his lips.

I feel Archer's hand on my back as he leans over to kiss both of us. "That was incredible, just amazing."

Carter smiles, a lazy, satisfied smile. "Yeah, it was. We needed that."

Chapter

Thirty-Eight

ARCHER

I lie back with my eyes closed and let the endorphins racing through my body subside. The bed shifts as Dan pulls away from Carter. I hear his footsteps pad across the floor and then a rush of water.

"Are you okay, Arch? You feeling all right?" Carter's voice is soft as he shuffles to lay beside me.

Opening my eyes, I turn my head. All I can see is the man I lost and the man who replaced him. The concern etched on his face makes me reach out and run my fingers over his stubbled cheek.

"Now? Now I feel blissed out. I feel loved and happy." I twist on the bed so I can face him.

Dan walks back in and smiles. "Here you go, baby." He smooths the warm cloth over Carter's stomach and chest before moving lower to clean up the lube and the rest of the mess we seem to have made.

Carter laughs and squirms as the cloth glides over him. "Shit!" He wriggles away.

"Maybe you shouldn't have made such a mess?" I chuckle and lean over to capture his mouth. I need to pour my feelings into this kiss. I need him to understand just how much I love him.

I need this moment with just him, my Mallory, my Carter. As my tongue strokes over his, I shift so I can lie over him. Leaning on my forearms, my hands tangle lightly in his long, dark locks. His legs open, allowing me to slot between them. I feel his cock twitch and swell as mine slides along his length.

Carter's hands slide so softly, gently up and down my back and over my ribs that shivers tremble through my skin, making me break out in goose bumps. Our tongues continue to dance languidly. There's no rush, no urgency. Just me pouring my bliss into a single kiss. Capturing his moans as Carter writhes beneath me, I swallow them down with my own.

Pulling back, I slowly open my eyes, blinking as I gaze at Carter with his lips, dark pink and kiss bruised, shining with the slickness from my tongue. "This is how you make me feel, Mallory," I whisper his name softly over his mouth. "This is how much I love you."

"Take me, Archer. Take me back." As he opens his legs wider, I can bend my knees and easily steer my dick down to his hole and nudge my way inside him. I feel the ripples from his muscles as I gently push inside him, savoring the slickness inside his channel. I can't hold back the deep groan building in my chest as I kiss him.

With hardly a movement, I just flex my hips, pumping slowly but steadily. I know it won't take either of us long to reach our climax. As his tongue tangles with mine, I sense the shivers running through him as his fingers lock in my hair. Then without any stimulation, I feel his release burst between us. As he shudders through his orgasm, I feel mine build as he tightens around my shaft. Quietly, I moan as I fill his passage; the heat of my release bathes my entire length.

Opening my eyes again, I see the sheen of unshed tears glazing my man's eyes.

"I love you, Archer. Fuck, I've missed you." A tear escapes its confines and runs down the side of his face. I capture it with my mouth, kissing his anguish away.

As I lift myself up and pull out of his body, we hear a moan. Our eyes flash with panic as we turn to see Dan watching us. I'd totally forgotten about him. Is he pissed at us?

"Wow, that was something else." His eyes flash at me, Dan smiles, but there's an edge to his voice that makes me think we've upset him.

Were we too intimate without him? Carter shifts underneath me. Even though I've taken my weight off his body, we're still touching, and the cooling stickiness spreading over his abs feels gross.

"I need to get in the shower. This isn't a great feeling." Carter laughs and wriggles until I roll off him with a theatrical sigh, making him grin. "Come on, I think we could all do with one."

We both clamber off the very messy bed and stumble together to the bathroom. Carter takes Dan's hand.

"Come on, babe. I need you to scrub my back."

"Yeah, give me a minute, and I'll be with you. I'm gonna sort out the bed." Dan gives Carter a sweet but brief kiss and lets us walk past.

Carter looks at me and gives me a questioning glare, making me shrug.

With the shower running and the room steaming up, we both step under the multi-jets. The water cascades like heavy rain beating against our skin.

"Is he okay?" I ask Carter.

"I don't know. He seemed to like what he saw, but he does seem tense." Carter chews on his bottom lip as he ponders our lover's behavior. "Let's get cleaned."

He grabs his body wash and lathers up his body, sluicing away the sticky remnants of our lovemaking. Tipping his head to wet his hair, I grab his shampoo and wash his hair. Running my fingers through the wet locks, I let my fingernails scrape over his scalp. Then as I tip his head back again to rinse the bubbles away, I can't stop myself from tracing their course down his back and over his ass. I dip my middle finger down the crack of his ass and flick over his pucker. I'm only kidding. I know he's taken enough there today, but it makes him wriggle and laugh.

"Fuck off! My ass is out of bounds." He laughs and pushes at me. Grabbing him, I wrestle him down to the floor. We're both laughing and goofing about grabbing at each other when a shadow looms over us.

When we stop and look up, Dan is watching us. His face is closed, and his eyes are tight. He bolts out of the room.

"Shit!" I jump up but feel my leg give way on the wet floor. I fall back down, twisting my ankle. "Fuck, shit!" I look down at my foot and see it swelling. Shit!

"Shit, damn! Archer! Don't move." Carter darts past me, grabbing a towel and calling out for Dan.

I don't want to tell Carter it hurts. I couldn't even if I wanted to. Luckily, my stomach is empty, so I haven't anything to throw up. I hope it's not serious. Pulling myself upright using the shower wall to hold me up, I grab another towel and try to move. I don't have enough strength in my left leg to support me.

Carter comes racing back into the bathroom with his phone stuck to his ear. "Yes, shit, yes! Just get here!"

Chucking his phone on the vanity counter, he rushes back over and throws his arm around me. "We need to get it elevated."

I wince as we stumble to the bed. "Who were you talking to?" My teeth are clamped tight together. "Where's Dan?"

"I don't know. I couldn't find him." Laying me down, he grabs all the pillows, and after gently lifting my foot, he shoves them underneath.

"Can you grab me some boxers? Who's coming over?"

"Denver. He'll be here any minute." Carter lifts the injured leg and gently slides a pair of boxers up over the ankle. He lets me put my other foot through the other hole and shimmies them up my legs. His touch is so tender and careful as he concentrates on not jiggling me about.

"Don't bite your lip, hon." I tease his bottom lip from his teeth. When he looks at me, his eyes swim with tears. "Hey, what's up?" I stroke my hand down his face to cup his chin.

"This is my fault. I shouldn't have messed about with you in the shower. I should've been more careful." The tears fall, making me lean forward and kiss them away. I feel him trembling under my touch.

"Babe, this could've happened at any time. I could slip when I'm in the shower alone. At least you were here to help." I kiss him again, stopping when there's a call from downstairs.

"That will be Denver. I'll go get him." Carter sniffs and wipes his face.

"Carter," I call out, making him turn back. "Put some pants on, please." I look pointedly at the towel still wrapped around his hips.

He grabs some shorts from the chair and pulls them up his legs before he races off down the stairs.

I can hear voices, and there's more than just Carter and Denver coming up the stairs. Crap! This isn't how I wanted to see my new friends again. Fuck it. There's nothing I can do about it now.

Denver walks through the doorway, and I can see the seriousness on his face. He's totally in the zone now.

"Hey, Archer. Let me have a look." Denver's cool, firm hands gently handle my swollen ankle, testing down my foot, checking the pulse point and the feeling I have, making me wriggle my toes. "I think you've just sprained it, Archer. It may be a matter of just resting it, but because of all the metalwork in there, I'm not prepared to risk it. I won't know 'til it's been x-rayed. On a scale of one to ten, ten being the highest, what's your pain level now?"

"It's fine. I've had worse. I'm okay." I can feel the sweat on my body as he carries on with his examination.

"I can give you something if you'd like? You don't need to be brave." Denver smiles sympathetically.

I look past him and see Carter still chewing on his lip. "Carter, babe. Come here, I need you."

He rushes to me and carefully curls up against me, making sure not to jostle my leg. "I'm sorry, Archer. I really am." He turns his head into my shoulder and sobs quietly in my arms. His hand reaches up over my chest to wrap around my neck. I kiss his forehead over and over.

"It's not your fault, honey. Please don't cry. It hurts me to see you so upset," I whisper softly to him. "It's gonna be all right, I promise."

I look up over Carter's head and see Denver on his cell phone. I'm guessing he's arranging transport to the hospital for me. I really don't want to go through it all again. At least I'll have Carter and Dan with me this time.

Looking past Denver, I can see East is here too. I motion for him to come in. He smiles at Denver and walks over.

"How're you doing?" he asks gently.

I chuckle and give him a wry smile. "I've been better. Can you give Daniel a call? He seems to have disappeared, and we're not sure where he is. I don't want Carter alone if I have to have surgery again."

"I'll get on it. Any idea where he could've gone?" East pulls out his phone and searches his contact list for Dan's number. I shake my head. "Okay, leave it with me." Walking away, East puts his phone up to his ear and moves out of earshot.

It's ten more minutes before the paramedics arrive and after conferring with Denver, I'm strapped on a gurney, and I'm on my way to the hospital. There's still no sign of Dan, and I'm getting seriously pissed at him.

"Where the hell could he have gone?" I whisper to Carter.

"I don't know, but I'm coming with you. East says he'll keep trying his cell and will have a look around too. I'm more worried about you, baby." He leans in to kiss me, brushing my hair from my forehead. He'd already fussed about getting me into a sweatshirt.

I think the only reason he's getting away with traveling with me is because Denver has insisted on it. He's going to follow us in his car. I think he realizes how important this is to both of us, not to be apart this time I'm taken to a medical facility. The memories from my accident are still vivid scars on both of our hearts.

Chapter
Thirty-Nine

DAN

My head is in a complete mindfuck; watching the two men I love together as if there is nobody else in the world is fucking hot. The simplicity of it has me growing hard again. I grab my cell phone and turn on the camera to record them. But as I watch them, I see it morph into something so much more. I hear Archer call Carter Mallory, and my head, and my heart, hurt. This is too intimate. This is private. This is them going back to the start.

When I walk in, I see Archer washing his hair. His hands all over him. I watch as Carter pushes at him, making them wrestle. The sight of so much intimacy, seeing how happy and comfortable they are with each other makes me realize they don't need me. Not the way I need them. They will always have each other. They know so much of each other's life that I will always be the third. I know they are up for us being a threesome, but they don't need me to make them happy, to complete them. Not like I need them.

Turning quickly on my heels, I rush from the room, grabbing my keys from the bowl as I reach the front door. I'm out of the house and in my car before I've even had time to think. As soon as I can manage to put the key in the ignition, I'm in reverse and off the driveway.

Driving away, I have no idea what to think or where to go, so I head to the office. It's the weekend, so no one will be there, giving me a chance to work out what the hell to do. When I pull up in my space and switch off the ignition, my phone rings. Carter's number comes up, but I can't talk to him right now. Just one word from him will have me racing back to him and into the confusion in my head. Ignoring it, I switch it to voicemail and get out of the car. Looking down at my feet, I see they are bare. Shit! My head is in such a bad place, and it's been so focused on having something that's not mine to have.

As I unlock the door, I realize this isn't the place to be to think things through. When I come back to work on Monday, it will be the only thing I'll be able to think about. I lock up again, get back to my car, and decide to head out to the lake.

My chest goes tight at the thought of them again. Clearing my mind, I drive away. My phone keeps going off with messages and voicemails, but while I'm driving, I can ignore them. Driving through the trees to the lake and the cabin my folks have, I recall how we used to spend long summer days during the school break here, messing around, fishing, and kayaking. Then drinking and making out as we got older. My sisters brought boyfriends here just as many times as I did. I had my first kiss and, I think, my first blow job here. I never want to know if they did too. Gah, no!

I unlock the cabin and walk inside. The place is always cared for by my mother, so I know there will be some basics in the cupboards and the fridge. I set about making a batch of coffee, not dwelling on my emotions of less than an hour ago. Not yet anyway. By the time I make my way down to the jetty, sticking out twenty feet into the water, the evening is calm and the stars shine so brightly in the clear dark night. I'm ready to think about what to do next.

I've taken two insulated mugs with me, so I don't have to move away when I want another cup. I sit with my feet hanging off the end, not quite reaching the water. I'm a problem solver, so I set about sorting my emotions and actions into the appropriate compartments in my head, ready to work out how to fix each one. The saddest thought is I can sort all of them in one fell swoop and just stop this… whatever this is, with them right now. Walk away and let them keep their forever to themselves. So, if that's the easiest way, why is it hurting my chest and making it hard to breathe?

Because I still fucking want them, that's why.

Okay, so next is to accept being a third and only be invited to be with them when they fancy a touch of something more. I disregard this one straight away. My heart is too invested in this to let that happen. I owe it to myself to find myself a forever man. One that makes me feel as happy as they were. I love the laughter that goes with a good relationship. I found that again when Carter came into my life. I want it again. I want him.

So maybe the lasting point is that I want them. They say they want me. After all, this was my fucking idea in the first place. Another thought springs to life, making me groan. Did I want this with Archer just so I didn't have to make Carter pick? And then maybe he wouldn't pick me? I need to talk to them about how I feel. I bet they're worried about me now. I bet they're going crazy trying to find me. Oh, fuck! What have I done?

I push myself upright and turn to go back to the cabin when I see East's truck driving up and stopping next to mine. What's he doing here?

"Hey, East, what's up?"

"What's up? What's fucking up? You disappearing, that's what's up. For fuck's sake, get a move on. I need to get you to the hospital." East looks really fucking pissed.

"What? How? Who's hurt?" Shit, I can't believe this. I've been ignoring my calls, busy in my own pity party. Shit! What have I done?

"Archer slipped in the shower. His ankle is hurt again. Well, Denver thinks it could just be a sprain, but they've gone to Charlottestown for X-rays. He called for the paramedics, and they've all gone now."

"Oh, Christ! I can't believe it. I've seriously fucked up. Shit, East, we'll take my car. Can you drive for me? I can't believe I've been so fucking selfish." My hands are up in my hair as I hold back a scream.

"C'mon, Dan, let's go." He walks over to my car and opens the driver's door. "We can talk more on the way, but FYI, both were asking for you. Right up to the ambulance taking them away."

"Oh, fuck!"

We pull out onto the road, and East quickly uses the speed of my BMW to get through the traffic and onto the highway. He casts me the odd glance as I chew on the skin by my thumbnail.

"You wanna talk about it? I reckon you've got a shit-ton of questions racing through your head, and I'm guessing they are all about three-way relationships and how they work for me and mine. You wanna share some of them?"

"I don't have a damn clue where to start." I shake my head, still so angry at the way I behaved. "I can't believe I ignored the calls and messages. I just panicked over something and fled. I'm a dick. They are gonna be so pissed."

"I really don't think they're going to be, but you may have a shit of groveling to do when you see them. Carter was frightened, and he needed you. If you're going to be a part of a threesome, you need to man up and take what you want." East glances at me and shakes his head. "Do you think Denver knew what to do or how to act? Fuck no! He ran off a fair few times before he finally got the message into his thick skull that we loved him equally. He doubted himself every step of the way for weeks."

"Really? From what we all saw, he was always very open with you both and never shied away from being with you." I look at East surprised. "I'm so jealous of that," I mutter.

"Hell no! It wasn't like that at all. Look, let me ask you a question, if I may?"

I nod and wait for whatever he's going to draw out of me.

"Are you jealous of them when they are together?"

"Not really. Oh, fuck! I wasn't until I saw them together. Just the two of them and then in the shower just now. They were so happy and comfortable with each other. They were goofing about, wrestling on the floor and laughing so hard. I was jealous. I thought they would never need me because they have so much with each other. After what his mother did to them, I'm wondering if they need more time together alone. It comes down to the fact they don't need me to make them happy, but I need them to do that for me."

"But they both needed and wanted you this evening. They were both worried and concerned where you had gone. They need you now. They want you with them. That should answer your question."

"Yeah, it does. But I think I may have blown it now, don't you?" I ask as I bury my face in my hands.

"Oh, c'mon, Dan. They're not going to think anything like that. They want you there, and if Archer has to have surgery again, Carter is going to want someone to hold him through it all. He never got the chance to be there for his man last time, so he's going to need your help to get him, get them both through this."

"I fucking hope so."

"Daniel, my man, I know so. Trust me, I've seen the look in their eyes before, in the eyes of my men. Trust them and for fuck's sake, trust yourself." East turns right, and we pull into the hospital grounds and head straight to the ER.

"East, I... I mean... shit! Just thank you, I appreciate it."

"Whatever, man. Just get your ass in there and find your men. I'll park and come find you in a few. I need to check in with Kes; he's with Phoebe."

I jump out of the car and square my shoulders to get a grip on myself. I stride in through the doors, immediately looking for my young lover.

"Dan! Oh, thank God you're here!" Carter shouts out to me and rushes over, wrapping his arms around me. He buries his head in the crook of my neck. "I'm so scared. I don't know what's going on. Denver said he'll come and tell me, us. But it's been ages, and I haven't heard anything."

"It's okay, baby. Come on, let's sit. You can tell me everything." I kiss his head, and he turns his face up to mine.

"Where were you? Where did you go?" His eyes fill with more tears, and I lean down instinctively to kiss them away.

"I'll tell you in a minute. Fill me in, Carter, please."

He relaxes into me again as I wrap my arm around his waist and walk him to the seating area. I can feel the tremors running through his body as he clings to me. I find a wide chair and sit. Carter sits on my knee and curls himself into me.

"When you ran out, he stood too quickly and slipped. His ankle gave way. I should have remembered. I shouldn't have been goofing around in wetness with him. It's my fault he's hurt. I called, you didn't answer. Why not?" His dark-blue eyes stare into mine as the anger in myself builds.

"Oh God, this is all my fault. This isn't your fault, baby. I came into the bathroom and saw you both, but I couldn't handle it. Watching you make love with him freaked me out. It was so beautiful and deep. I wondered if we ever made love like that. I doubted what we have, and then the way you were both laughing cut right through me. It made me think you don't need me to make you happy. It's so obvious you're deeply in love with each other. That you will be happy with or without me. I ran, baby. I'm sorry."

"Why? Why... How could you think that after what we have said? You said you wanted it all? We may not have been together as long I was with Archer, but that doesn't mean I love you less. You made me whole again. I love you, Daniel. I want it all with you. Have you changed your mind?" Carter pulls away and looks at me cautiously.

"I just don't understand why you would want me when you have so much together. It doesn't make sense to me. I want you both so much, but I don't trust myself to be enough for you, to make a difference to your already amazing relationship. I'm so sorry, Carter. I'm doubting myself. I'm worried you don't want me anymore."

"I will always want you, Dan. I don't think I would have chosen Archer over you. I want what we have—a new start. I think that's what we're getting with Archer. Neither of us are the person we were so many months ago."

We sit quietly for a few minutes, locked in our own thoughts.

Chapter
Forty

CARTER

"How did you meet him?" Dan asks me.

"Hasn't he told you?" I wait while Dan smiles.

"Only a little bit. He found it too difficult to talk about you."

"We bumped into each other, literally, nearly knocked each other on our asses when I was rushing to get to work. I'd had to move into a dorm and find a job to pay my way through school. I was rushing to the coffee shop I worked in. I was nearly always running late. Archer was a customer there, and he asked me out every day for two weeks before I gave in. He was a pain in my ass. I only agreed just to get him to leave me alone to work." I laugh at the memory.

"That doesn't surprise me. He's a tenacious bastard. When he sets his mind to something, he doesn't let up. So, it must have gone well, that first date?"

I laugh at this. "Er no, he was an ass at the end. I walked away. Fortunately, that just upped his game, and he waited for me at the back of the coffee shop. He was there when I left in the evening. Quite a stalker, is our man. After that, it was on. It took him a while to get me to move in, and we had a huge row about him not letting me pay my way. The lawyer in him came out, and he had a counterpoint for every one of my arguments. In the end, I gave in and let him be in charge."

"What's wrong with his mother? Why did she take an instant dislike to you? Did you ever find out?" Dan runs his hand softly up and down my back the whole time we talk. It feels so good and so right. I can feel my skin humming.

"She's such a bitch. She wouldn't even look at me. She doesn't like my father, but she must pretend to. Maybe that's why. I think it's more to do with not wanting her precious reputation damaged by having an out and proud gay son. Which makes no sense since Archer has never hidden who or what he is. She just expects him to marry a nice girl and fuck men on the side. Cheating and lying his whole life isn't something he would ever entertain, nor would he let a woman go through marriage based on lies and deceit. Archer is a good man, and he doesn't deserve her as a mother." I relax into Dan and close my eyes. I'm done talking.

"Thank you, Carter," he whispers and kisses the top of my head.

"What for?"

"For loving me, for sharing yourself with me and Archer. The list is endless, baby. You have no idea how much your touch, your faith means to me. I'm so sorry I let you both down this evening."

We stop talking as Denver walks through the doors and over to us.

"Hey, guys. Dan, it's great to see East found you. Carter, how are you doing?" Denver's smile gives me confidence.

"How's Archer? Tell me, Denver, how bad is it?" I speak quietly, but even I can hear the strain in my voice.

"He's okay, Carter. The ankle is going to be fine. It is just a sprain. We're going to strap it up, and he'll have to wear a support boot for a week or two, but he'll be okay. My ex did a damn good job fixing him up, and it's held well. I'll take you through now." Denver smiles again.

"Oh, thank you, Denver. Thank you so much for being there for us." I jump off Dan's knee and rush to hug our friend. "I'm so happy you were able to help us so quickly.

When I let go of Denver, I turn back to Dan. I can see the chagrin written all over his face. "C'mon, Dan." I look at him, and still he's hesitating

"Daniel! Are you in or out?" I bark at him, breaking through his reverie.

"I'm in!" he says vehemently. I grab his hand and drop a sweet kiss on his mouth.

"Never make me doubt you again," I murmur against his lips.

"I won't, I promise," he whispers back.

We follow Denver through a set of doors. He pulls back a curtain. Archer is sitting up. His eyes are closed, and he looks so handsome. It makes my heart ache.

"Hey, baby." I pick up his hand and hold it between both of mine. He opens his eyes slowly, and I can tell he's had some pain meds. His dilated pupils try to focus on me. "Dan's here." I lean over to kiss his mouth.

As I pull away, Dan walks to the other side of the bed and copies my action with Archer's other hand. "I'm so sorry, Arch. I really hate myself right now."

Dan lifts Archer's hand to his mouth and kisses across his knuckles.

"Not your fault, Dan. Could've happened at any time. Happy to see you here. I'm feeling stupid. I should've been more careful."

"It won't be much longer, and then we can get you home." Dan kisses him softly.

Chapter
Forty-One

ARCHER

"Good, I have spent far too many hours in hospitals." I cringe at the thought of having to be here any longer than necessary.

"The nurse will be here to strap your ankle and fit the boot. I'll get the paperwork ready for you to be discharged." Denver smiles at me.

"Thank you so much, Denver. I'm sorry to have wrecked your evening."

"It's no problem. It's what friends do." He smiles. "I believe there's a dinner invitation in the offering?"

"Absolutely, just name the day, and we'd love to have you over," Dan speaks up. "I want a pool in the yard, and I believe your guy is the best around." He laughs.

"He really is the best. In fact, I'm going to find him," he jokes, turning around to see the nurse walk through the curtained area. "I'll get the paperwork done. See you soon, guys. Be careful!"

It's another thirty minutes before we can go, and I get ready to shuffle out with the use of crutches *again*! At least I know how to use them properly. Carter and Dan walk on either side of me but don't offer me any support. I'm guessing the scowl and snarl I gave them when they both jumped towards me when I stood was enough to hold them back.

The drive back is quiet. Dan seems to have something he needs to get off his chest, and Carter looks so lost in his own thoughts, I'm not feeling inclined to break the silence. I feel I have caused a rift between us, and I'm not sure why or how to fix it. My head clunks back against the headrest, and I close my eyes, letting the quiet hum of the engine lull me to sleep.

I wake with a jolt as a car door closes behind me. Carter and Dan talk to each other outside of the vehicle. I watch as Dan bends his head down to Carter and drops a very sweet but chaste kiss on his lips. I notice Carter has linked hands with Dan, but both of their faces are solemn. Dan says something else, and Carter nods before letting a small half smile light up his face.

I pull the handle and open the door, pushing it wide so I can swing my body around. Grabbing my crutches from the floor, I start to stand, or I try to. The car is too low for me to get a decent grip to push myself up. I can feel their eyes on me, but I understand the hesitation to help me. I'm going to have to suck it up and ask for some help.

"Any chance of a helping hand?" I call out, making them both lurch forward with grins on their smart-assed faces. "Yeah, yeah. I know." I grin back. "Fuckers!"

We sit in the back garden now. It's time to sort out what the hell happened this evening with Dan. Carter gets up and walks inside, giving me an opportunity to speak to Dan.

"You gonna tell me what went down with you, Dan?" I chug the last of my soda and put the glass on the ground next to my lounger.

"I was a dick, that's all. I've sorted it out, and it won't happen again," he replies as he looks down the length of the garden.

"Not really enough information there, babe." I scowl at him again.

"Look, I got jealous of you two when you were making love and then again when you were fooling around in the shower, and I bolted. I feel like a prick and don't want to talk about it." Turning to face me now, he looks so troubled.

"Does Carter know?"

"Yes, and he put me right. I'm sorry, Archer."

I raise an eyebrow at him, not settling on that answer.

"Fine! I want this between us, but I'm worried I'm not going to be enough for you. That you don't need me as much as I need you. I can see me with you 'til I'm old and grey, but I'm not convinced you see that with me. That was why I ran off this evening." Dan lets out a long sigh and looks back down the garden.

"Then I guess we'll have to prove it to you then, won't we?" I reach over to grasp his hand, and when he catches mine, I feel the slight tremors in his fingers as they grip mine.

Carter looks over at us as he walks back out from the kitchen and frowns. "Is everything okay?" he asks.

"Yeah, I'm just trying to let Dan know we're here for the long haul."

"Good. I want to go to bed, and I want us to be together and happy. I want this shitty fucking night to be over." He turns on his heel and stalks away.

"Shit! Now he's pissed! He's right. Let's go and write this evening off." I stand and wait for Dan to copy me. "Come here, baby." I pull him close, pressing my lips firmly to his. I kiss him hard. "No more doubting us, let's just grow into this together."

Dan nods and lets me step through the doors so he can lock up for the night. I manage the stairs and head to our room.

"At least the bed got clean sheets before all this happened. Otherwise, we'd have to sleep in the guest room." Carter snorts and gets his ass swatted by Dan.

"I can't believe this went down this evening. Thank God Denver was home tonight. We really do owe them dinner," Dan murmurs, then runs his hands down my back, sending shivers all over me.

"Let's get into bed." Carter strips off his hastily shoved-on shorts and T-shirt.

"I don't think I'll be up for much with my foot all strapped up," I grumble and let them undress me.

"I'm sure we can come up with something," Carter mutters as he kneels in front of me, his mouth against my abs. His hands slides my shorts down my legs as he drops kisses further down my body.

As my head tips back, I feel another set of hands roaming over my body, sliding down over my ass, squeezing my cheeks hard before pulling them apart.

"I think we need you lying down now, baby," Carter purrs.

Chapter
Forty-Two

CARTER

I lie on my stomach in with my head on Archer's chest while Dan runs his hands up and down my spine. Featherlight that make me purr with contentment. Archer has been home for a week now, and I have never been so happy. His foot is on the mend. He just has to heal and get some physical therapy. He says he's a pro at this, so we're letting him do what he thinks is best.

"I don't want to go to work." I moan as Dan's hand moves down to my ass, stroking serenely over each cheek.

"You don't have to be there for a while, honey. Just relax here with us." Archer runs his fingers through my hair. I can feel my dick throb beneath me, trapped between the sheet and my stomach.

"I need to cover Shelley's shift. She's got a doctor's appointment, and it's the only day they could see her." I try to move, but Dan now has his mouth on my ass, leaving wet kisses as he traverses the curves.

"No! Let me up!" I laugh and wriggle my way out of their clutches.

"Oh, baby, you know you want to." Dan sniggers at me as he rolls over to show me his hard dick.

"Of course, I do, but I have to get to work. I'll take a rain check and let you two play." I head over to the bathroom and switch the shower on.

Ten minutes later, I'm dry and dressed. Leaning over the bed, I kiss Archer and then Dan. "Call me later if you feel up to it, Arch. Dan, don't let him overdo it."

Unlocking the door to the bar fifteen minutes later, I let myself into the silence, reveling in the calm before the storm. I love the quiet times as much as the heady rush of the manic hours, the ones where I'm rushed off my feet and never feel like I'll be able to take a load off again.

The bar looks good. Paris and Hunter, our newest bartender, stocked up well last night, and the place looks clean too. The cleaner will be here in an hour to get the floors mopped. We found it easier to get someone in early in the morning rather than the guys closing doing it. My walk around has me feeling good. I love this bar. To me, it's more than just a place to work. It became a home to me. Kes, East, and Denver became my family, my brothers. For Kes to hand me a job and a home at a time I needed them most in the world is something I will never be able to pay back to them. Maybe one day I can pay it forward. I often forget the life I planned to have, the life I expected with Archer. I'm an engineer. That's all I ever wanted to be, but not anymore. Nope, now I'm the manager of a really cool bar and the boyfriend of two amazing men, and I wouldn't swap it for the world.

I get busy in the office, working through the paperwork. All the mundane shit I know Kes but, but I get a kick out of sorting. I hear the clatter of chairs being moved around and look up at the clock. I hadn't realized how much time I'd spent in here, and it's almost opening time.

"Hey, Car. How's it going?" Kes walks in and drops his leather jacket on the arm of the sofa against the wall.

"Good, it's good. I wasn't expecting to see you here today. You been kicked out?" I joke with him.

"I thought I'd show my face. I haven't seen you for a while. How's your man?"

"Archer's good. Moaning about being bored, so I think Dan is going to get him to work this week. His ankle is doing well, thanks."

"We're looking forward to coming over for dinner."

"Yeah, it will be good. Dan's good in the kitchen." I smile, thinking about what else he's good at.

"Are you feeling happier than when we spoke last week? You seem a lot more content."

"Was it only a week ago? It seems like longer. Yeah, it's much better. I hadn't realized Dan and Archer were having the same worries as me. I think we've learned to communicate better. I know it's early days, but it's good. I think we've all stopped trying to prove ourselves so much and have learned to just be." I sigh and look around the office, knowing how much work I must do. I see Kes look at me.

"Do you want me to stay for a while? I've got a couple hours free. East is working, and Denver has taken Phoebe over to his folks' place?"

"Yeah, that would be great. Just do what you want." I like working with Kes.

Kes ends up staying for most of the day, as we had a group of women come in, taking up three tables. They all wanted to have a long, lazy lunch. They were loud and fun and very flirty.

Paris comes in at five and looks around at the still-busy room. "You should've called me, Car."

"Nah, Kes was here. It was fine." I watch him walk away to the office to put his jacket away and grab a clean apron. When I look back at the bar, the smartly dressed man is in front of me. His smile is broad but doesn't reach his eyes, and he gives me the once-over.

"Hello again, Carter. I haven't seen you in a few days." His voice is low and off-key. There's definitely something about him that makes me uncomfortable. I hate the way he speaks my name, almost lasciviously.

"Nope, I had a few days off. What can I get you?" I just want him served and away from me.

"I think I'll take a scotch again. Will you join me this time?" His steel-grey eyes bore into mine.

"Thanks, but no drinking on the job I'm afraid." I smile as much as I can, but I know he sees it falter as his tongue darts out to dampen his bottom lip.

"Shame. Maybe on one of your days off? Would you like to come on a date with me?" Again with the staring.

"Um, thanks for the offer, but I'm in a relationship. Let me get your drink." I turn away before he has a chance to reply.

"With the two gentlemen I saw you with before?" He's seriously giving off some freaky stalker vibes. I push his drink across the bar, making sure there's no physical contact. He takes his drink and moves over to the table in the corner, the same one he took last time I saw him. Paris walks over to me with a worried look on his face.

"Is he causing trouble?" he asks, not looking at the guy. "He's asked for you a couple times. I don't like him."

"No, I'm not sure who he is, but he seems to know me. He's just asked me on a date." I shake my head at the thought of him.

"Yeah, he's a creepy dude, for sure."

I'm tired out, but the shift is nearly over. Creepy guy has had another couple drinks, but Paris took his order, and he left me alone.

As I wipe down the counter, I feel his presence and look up. He has an envelope in his hand, and the creepy smile is back.

"Let me know your answer, my number is inside." He slides the envelope over the bar, then taps it twice and looks at me. "I'll be waiting for your call."

I look at the expensive-looking paper on the counter and see my name on the front, typed in large print.

I look at him, stunned. "I'm not interested in anything you have. Please take it away with you. You have nothing I want." I push the envelope back to him, but he ignores it.

"We'll see, Mallory Halston. We'll see." He turns and walks away, leaving me staring at his back.

My mouth drops open as my blood freezes inside me. Fear runs through my body. He knows who I am. Why?

Paris looks at me. "Car, what the hell is going on? Who is that dude?"

"I have no idea, but he knows me. He's given me this." I point at the envelope like it's a bomb about to explode.

"You gonna open it?" Paris looks as freaked out as me.

"I don't know. What would you do? Shit! I don't know what to do."

"Take it home, show it to your men. That way you can decide together. I would take it to Co..." His voice trails away as he looks at me anxiously.

"You and Conn, eh? Nice one, Par. Go for it. He's a nice guy." I smile at my friend as he blushes crimson.

"You don't think I'm too young for him?"

"Hey, no way! You're twenty-one, Paris, and if you work well together, it's right. Age is just a number. Be happy with him, Par, you deserve someone good."

"And there's no way my dad will try anything with a cop." He snorts, making me chuckle too.

I look back down at the letter. I snatch it up and fold it in half, shoving it in my back pocket. I'll see what Dan and Archer think.

Thirty minutes later, we're closing the doors behind the last customer. After locking the door, I cash up while Paris and Hunter clean. It doesn't take us long before we're ready to go.

"See you later, guys." I wave as I climb into Archer's new truck. He finally took the rental back and bought one for himself. I smile as Hunter slings his arm over Paris' shoulder. Hmm, is there more to their friendship? I laugh to myself as I wonder what the town is turning into.

The house is in darkness as I pull up on the driveway. The only light is the one on the porch. I know they've gone to bed and can't blame them. It's getting close to one a.m.

I lock up behind me and tread quietly upstairs. When I get into our room, I see Dan's head resting on Archer's chest. He's fast asleep with his hand around Archer's waist. I need a shower but don't want to wake them. I turn and walk down to the main bathroom. After a quick wash up, I tiptoe back in and slide in next to Dan.

"Hey, baby. You okay?" Archer whispers softly.

"Yeah, sorry if I woke you."

"I wasn't really asleep. Kinda waiting for you to get back."

"Get some rest, Arch." I can feel sleep washing over me already. "Love you," I mumble.

Chapter
Forty-Three

ARCHER

"I need to talk to you guys." Carter stands on the other side of the island in the kitchen as Dan and I make breakfast.

I turn around and see him flicking an envelope over and over, his finger nimble but shaking slightly. Chewing on his lip, I know he's stressed about this, whatever it is.

"What's that?" I point at the paper in his hand.

"There's been this guy. He's been in the bar a few times now." Carter looks at me. "He always asks about me when I'm not on shift and he... shit. I don't know, he made me feel uncomfortable. Just over-familiar, y'know."

I look at Dan and see how angry he looks. I feel it's only a mirror of my own features.

"What does this asshole look like?" Dan demands. "I bet it was that dick we saw the other night."

"Has Kes got the bar on CCTV?" I ask as I move around the island, my hand outstretched for the envelope. "You gonna let me have that, babe."

"Of course he has. Do you want to take a look?" Carter holds onto the envelope, reluctant to hand it over. "I don't want to know what's in here. Y'see, he called me Mallory Halston. He knows me from before."

"Shit! We need to go over the video from last night. C'mon, let's go," I bark at them.

"No, not yet," Carter replies defiantly.

I scowl at him and start to speak, but he shuts me up with a glare.

"I want coffee and food before we go anywhere. He's not going anywhere. He's waiting on my call. He asked me on a date, too." Carter smirks at this and accepts the mug of coffee from Dan with a smile.

"He better fucking not have!" I snarl. "Let me see the envelope, Carter, please."

"No." He looks at Dan who shakes his head at me before dropping his head down to kiss Carter. I watch as he leans into Dan's body and wraps an arm around his waist.

"Why not?" I'm confused. "Why show it to us if you don't want us to see it."

"Because, Archer, we don't have secrets. We never have, and I'm not starting to now. Plus, I'm not sure I'm going to open it. I don't want anything to do with someone from my past, someone who used my old name as a warning. I don't need anyone from the past back in my life. I have you two, and I have my friends, and that's all I want and need."

I relax when he smiles and reaches out to me. Walking into his space, I drop a kiss on his upturned face, his mouth soft and willing.

"Okay, but we're going to find out who this fucker is. The rest is up to you. What do you say to handing this over to Lucas to follow up? He'll alert us to any danger. Don't look at me like that, Carter. I'll keep you safe, and if he has anything to do with my mother, it might be more sinister than a check for 50k."

Carter continues his scowl but nods. "Fine, we'll find out who he is, and if he has anything to do with that woman." He shudders as he thinks of my mother.

"Y'know, we could find that out by just opening the envelope, baby," Dan says as he runs his hand up and down Carter's back.

"Look, let me eat before I have to make any more decisions."

I move away and get back to the breakfast. Pouring the eggs into a skillet, I stir as Dan stays with Carter. He whispers something I can't hear, but it's okay. Like Carter said, there are no secrets, but we're entitled to be private with each other. Minutes later, I pile eggs on top of hot, buttered toast and add some bacon to the side and slide it over the counter in front of Carter.

Groaning, he picks up his fork and digs in. "This is perfect. Thanks, love." He winks, then threatens to stab Dan's hand with his fork as he reaches for some bacon. "Mine!"

The tension dissipates, and I'm reminded of all the times he would do that to me. His eyes latch onto mine and soften as he remembers it too. "Archer would try that all the time too, and it never worked."

We chat about more mundane subjects while Carter eats and try to work out when is the best time to get Denver and the others over for a meal.

"We need to work around his hospital shifts. If we speak to Kes this morning, we can get him to check. I know he's strict about his hours now that he has his daughter to look after, but Kes knows exactly when he's around." Carter smiles as he finishes eating.

"Thanks, Arch, that was perfect. Shall we go? I'll give Kes a call on the way over to let him know."

"Do we need to do that, Carter? Can't we keep it to ourselves?" I look at him as he loads his plate into the dishwasher.

"No, Arch. Think about it. This is someone, a stranger, harassing his bar manager. He has a right to know what's gone on in his premises and that we are going to look through his CCTV recordings," Dan answers. "Also, I think Kes would want to know about Carter's safety. He's like family to him."

"Okay, I hadn't thought it through. I just want it to be under our control, not some unknown, unnamed man. I don't like being in the dark."

"Let's go," Carter states.

Dan drives as I sit next to Carter with my hand resting on his thigh and listen to him talking quietly to Kes.

"Yeah, he's been in a few times. Shelley told me he's asked for me." Carter goes quiet as he listens to Kes. "No, you don't need to do that. Yes, they are. Oh, okay. See you in a few. Yeah, bye, Kes."

"What's he saying?" Dan asks.

"He's going to meet us there. He wants to see what's going on." Carter sighs and leans his head back.

Gripping his thigh, I give it a squeeze. "It will be okay, honey. We've got you. Whatever and whoever this is, we have you."

"I know." His voice is quiet, and I hate it when he feels like this. I know he's riddled with confusion and uncertainty. The confidence he has found here makes me proud. I wonder if he would have had it if we'd stayed together all through the accident. Or would we have been the same people we were? I guess we'll never know the answer. What's done is done.

I wish I knew what was in the letter. He's still got it in his hand, and it's getting folded and unfolded constantly. I know he's warring with himself, but I must respect his decision and let him open it in his own time.

Pulling up outside the bar, Dan switches off the engine and sits back, waiting for Carter to make a move. We sit silently for only a couple minutes before he shakes out his shoulders and reaches for the handle.

"Let's get this shit over with. I want to spend the day naked with you two without some asshat's words hanging over us." Pushing the door open, he jumps down from the cab, pushing the door closed firmly behind him. Striding over to the door, Carter pulls the keys from his pocket, unlocks the door, and steps inside.

Dan walks up to me and takes hold of my hand. His eyes are fixed and focused as he watches our lover walking ahead. With a tight smile, he speaks, "This is going to be okay. It may take a little while and cause a few headaches, but he's our man, and we fight with him."

"I know, but my gut is telling me this is my mother's doing." I cast my eyes up and down the high street. It's a busy morning, so the chance of spotting the guy I saw all those nights ago is nonexistent, but still I can't help but look.

Shutting the door behind us, I make sure it's locked. Kes will use his own keys when he gets here. Looking around the large room, it looks strange seeing it empty and silent. Our footsteps seem loud on the wooden floor. When we reach the office, Carter is on the computer, his fingers flying over the keys as he stares at the screen. Paying us no mind, he keeps his eyes fixed on the computer as we move behind him. Each of us rest a hand on his shoulders and lean forward. I can't keep up with the speed he runs through the video from last night's CCTV. The timer races away unnoticed by Carter in the top corner of the screen. He is focused, knowing exactly who he is looking for.

I pull my cell out of my pocket and call Lucas.

"Hey dude, how's it going? Look, I'm going to be sending you a visual of a guy. He approached Carter... Yeah, Mallory. He's Carter now." I feel Carter tense under my hand. I run my hands through the hair at the nape of his neck, and he relaxes again. "He handed him an envelope and said he'd be waiting for a reply. The fucker also had the nerve to ask him for a date!"

Dan growls next to me, making me chuckle. "Yeah, that's Dan. He's about as happy as I am." Suddenly, the screen stops racing and comes to a stop. It is the fucker we saw at the door. No wonder he looked so smug. I hate bastards that think they have one up on me.

"We've got a visual, Luc. You ready for me to send it over?"

"Sure, Arch. I'll get on it and send it over to Ben. It won't take us long. You wanna stay on the line, or I can call you back?" Lucas asks.

Just then, Kes walks in with both of his boyfriends. There's a moment of bro-hugs, and then Kes moves up next to Carter.

"Call me back, Luc. Carter's family has turned up. Yeah, he has good people here. Gimme a couple minutes, and you'll have it."

Kes is bent over next to Carter as he whispers into his ear. Everything inside me wants to shout out that it's me he should be talking to, but I tone it down and let them finish.

"This is him, Arch. I guess you want to send it over to your guy?" He looks at me, and I see the strain he's under. At home, he seemed relaxed and easy, but now he looks tense and so unhappy that my strength crumbles.

"Oh, Carter, hon. It will be okay, I promise." I run my hand through his hair as he turns to me and smiles sadly.

"I know that, Arch. I just hate this is here. Whatever this is, I know the three of us can deal with it."

I move in front of the computer and send the images to Lucas. He pings back that he's received them and will be in touch. Turning around to lean back on the desk, I take in the people around us. Paris has joined us, and I'm surprised to see Conn Martinez is with him. I've only spoken to him a couple times, but I like him. I didn't expect to see him with Paris, but they look good together. The main image I see is one of family, the family Mallory made when he became Carter. These are good people. They are his people, and I like it.

"What next then? How do you want to proceed when we find out who he is, Carter?" Dan is still holding onto Carter's shoulder, his fingers trailing a soft pattern over the exposed skin at the juncture of his neck and shoulder.

"I guess I should read whatever is in this envelope." Carter sighs heavily.

"Why don't we just call him and get him to come here? All of this seems very cloak and dagger when a simple call could have it all over with?" Paris looks at me bewildered.

"I want to see if my mother has anything to do with this guy before we speak to him. I've already got Lucas investigating her. I feel she is a threat to Carter and could be out to harm him," I explain. My phone rings, making us all jump. Carter looks up at me, his handsome face pale. "It's okay, honey." I answer the call, "Lucas, what have you got?"

"The guy's name is Leon Dukas. He's a lawyer, and it seems he is working for Carter's brother, Roman."

"What? Why is he contacting Carter? He hasn't seen him for years. Hold on, Luc, let me tell Carter." I lower my phone down, keeping my eyes on Carter. He chews on his lip nervously. "Carter, he's a lawyer, and he's working for you brother, Roman. Do you want to talk to Lucas?"

Carter's eyes go wide, and I see a sheen of tears build up. Nodding his head, I hand him the phone. I reach out for Dan who seems to be in shock. He walks into my arms. I can feel him shaking.

Chapter
Forty-Four

DAN

I feel totally out of my depth here. Carter has a brother? I never knew this. I realize I don't know him at all. When I look at Archer, I know he understands how I feel. Opening his arms, I step into his embrace.

"I didn't know. I know so little about him. I feel so useless," I murmur into Archer's ear as he holds me against him.

"I know, baby. I felt the same when I met him again. I look around this room and see so many people who know the new him. People who care for him, and I feel alien amongst you. We will get through this together. We're a family, and we can learn together," Archer speaks quietly, then brushes his mouth across mine. "Okay?"

I nod. "Yeah, okay." Twisting around, I lean my back against his chest and watch Carter as he talks quietly to Lucas.

It seems like everyone in the room is holding their breath. Carter says goodbye and hands the phone back to Archer. The tears in his eyes build again as he shakes his head, trying to clear his thoughts. We all watch as he reaches for the envelope.

"Carter, baby. Are you sure?" I ask him. I reach my hand out for him, and he grasps it.

"Yeah, it's my brother. I love him. I need to know what's going on." Carter slips his finger under the edge of the envelope and slides it across the top, opening it raggedly. Then with a deep breath, he pulls out the sheet of paper. A card falls out and drops, making me reach forward to pick it up.

The card is that of Leon Dukas, the lawyer. I hand it to Carter, and he lets it drop onto the table. He opens the folded letter and starts to read.

"It's from Roman, my brother." Carter gasps as he continues to read it. I see his hands shake as his eyes fly across the paper. "It's my father. He has cancer and is dying. Roman wants me to go home and see him. He says he's been asking for me." He looks up at me, and at Archer in complete shock. "Roman says he misses me and wants to reconnect."

"Shit! Carter, what do you want to do? Can you really see yourself back there?" Archer steps away from behind me and kneels in front of Carter. "What do you think?"

"I don't know. I can't think straight. Why did he go to all this trouble? If he knew I was here, why didn't he just come to see me? Hell, I haven't seen or spoken to my family for, what, over three years now? What does my father want to do? I can't imagine him apologizing. He's never been sorry for anything he's done." Carter runs his hands through his hair and looks back down at the letter. "I can't think straight. This is crazy."

Standing, Carter paces. "I don't trust my father a fucking inch, so he's suddenly got a conscience? I doubt that."

"Maybe you should think about it for a few days. Does he say it's urgent? How long does he say your father has left?" Archer steps in front of Carter and stops his pacing. "Carter, look at me."

He waits until Carter lifts his head and stares at him. "We will come with you. You don't need to do this alone." He pulls him into a hug and holds him until Carter relaxes against him and wraps his arms around him too.

I look at the others. They nod and file out of the room, giving us the privacy I think we need. The door shuts softly behind Kes as he's the last to leave.

"Carter, baby. Come here." I reach out to him, and he steps to me. His head rests on my chest as I stroke his back, soothing him the best I can. "Archer's right, we will come with you. You never have to do anything alone anymore. We love you, baby."

I feel his shoulders shake as he sobs. Lifting his head up, he looks at me so broken and hurt. "I have missed my brother and sister so much. I have thought of them so often. I was told to never contact them again, that I was disgusting, an abhorrence, and I would twist them into my own evil ways."

"Carter, you are an amazing man. A strong, brave, intelligent man, and it's your father that is sick and twisted. Your siblings should be proud to have you as their brother, and I'm sure if you get to meet them again, you will rekindle your love and friendship."

Archer stands behind Carter now as we keep him close to us. "Why don't we arrange a meeting with this Dukas dude? We can have it in the office so it's an official meeting and find out more. I'm just as intrigued as you to find out why they chose this clandestine way of reaching out to you. What do you say?"

Sniffing and wiping his nose with the back of his hand, Carter nods. "Yeah, I think that's a good idea. I'm not sure what I want to do yet. This has come as a complete surprise. I really was expecting some shit blackmail from your mother." Carter lets out a dry chuckle. "I think I would have preferred that. At least we could throw the big guns at her and tell her to get fucked."

We all chuckle at this, and I feel Carter relax. He looks around the room and sighs. "Where did everyone go?"

"I think they realized it was a private moment, and that we were better off alone, I'm sure you'll want to call Kes later."

"You're not working today, are you, Car?" Archer asks and looks relieved when he shakes his head. "Good, let's go back home. I think we could all do with a rest."

"Yeah, I could go along with that." Carter nods. He looks drained, and I'm guessing he'll be asleep as soon as we can get him into bed. "What about this?" He picks up the letter.

"I'll call Dukas, and the rest is up to you when and if you're ready," I tell him.

I tip his chin up and drop a kiss on his mouth. He leans into the kiss and moans. His tongue slips into my mouth and strokes against mine before breaking away and pulling Archer's mouth to his. Kissing him with as much fervor as he did me, I can feel the urgency build up in him.

"Let's go, baby. We'll take care of you." I scrape my teeth up his neck as he pants into Archer's mouth.

"I need you. I need you both so much." His moan hits my heart and my groin equally.

We walk out through the bar as it's opening. Paris walks up to Carter and hugs him. Carter reciprocates and bunches his fists in Paris' shirt. I'm happy to see him with his friend. He's a good man. When they separate, Paris says something, and Carter nods as Paris strokes his cheek in a sweet gesture of friendship.

I get back in the driver's seat and let Archer sit in the back with Carter. He holds him close against his side, and Carter rests his head on his shoulder, with his eyes closed. The drive is quick, and as soon as I pull up on the driveway, Archer kisses Carter softly and whispers to him.

We lead our weary lover upstairs and into our bedroom. "Get undressed, babe. Then you can get into bed."

"You coming, too?" His voice is muffled as he pulls his T-shirt over his head, kicking off his shoes at the same time.

"Yes, baby, of course." I shed my clothes as Archer does the same.

We climb in together and cocoon Carter between us. His head rests on my chest, and as Archer's body presses against his back, we lie quietly, my fingers stroking through Carter's hair and Archer's hand stroking along his ribs down to his hip, soothing him as he shuts down. I feel him settle into sleep.

Archer looks up at me, his face troubled as he frowns. "What should we do?"

"Nothing yet, he needs us here. The lawyer can wait. I'm so pissed at him. He should have come clean straight away, not playing games with Carter and sure as shit, not asking him on a date," I whisper angrily.

"Yeah, we'll sort that. Let's give him an hour here, then we'll give the asshole a call." Archer snuggles into Carter and closes his eyes, and soon he's asleep too.

I find it harder to settle, my brain racing at the discovery of his family. Of course, I knew he had to have one, but he had never mentioned them. I'm positive we would have shared more about ourselves had it just been me and him for longer. This has rattled me. I want to know more. I want to know everything. With a sigh, I slip out of the bed. Carter stirs but turns his body into Archer's and sleeps again. I slip on some sweats and a T-shirt and pad downstairs. Carter dropped the envelope and the business card on the console inside the door. Leaving the letter, that isn't mine to read, I pick up the card and head down to my office.

"Dukas," the deep voice answers my call.

"My name is Daniel Mortimer. You've overstepped the mark,

Dukas. Be in my office in an hour."

Chapter
Forty-Five

CARTER

I wake up alone. The sun has moved, giving off a late afternoon glow across the room. I can't believe I have slept for so long, then I remember why. Roman. My heart squeezes as I think of my younger brother. I wonder what he's doing now. He should be finished with college soon, if not already. Does he work with my father? Does he share the same opinion of me? I doubt the latter or why else would he want to reconnect? And why in such a shady way, such an unorthodox way? Was the overly confident and brash lawyer testing me? Or is he just a dick?

The house seems unusually quiet. I would've thought I could hear at least one of them. I slip back into my clothes and go downstairs. Immediately my eyes fix on my brother's letter. I need to read it again. Picking it up, I walk into the kitchen and grab a bottle of water. It seems like I'm alone here, making me wonder if they have already gone to see douchebag Dukas. I should be pissed, but I don't care if I never see him again. He's a dick.

I head out into the garden. I love the quiet tranquility of it here, and I think I can pay more attention to my brother's words if I'm calm. Opening up the letter again, I take a deep breath.

Mallory,

God, I hope this gets to you. I can't believe it's been so long since I've seen you, spoken to you, asked you for advice and hugged you.

I don't know where to start. Maybe I should just say I'm sorry. I'm sorry for so much.

I'm sorry I sat at the dinner table like a mute and didn't stand for you.

I'm sorry I didn't look out for you after our father threw you away.

I'm sorry I have never said I'm sorry.

But now I'm sorry for why I'm contacting you. I don't expect an answer. Hell, I don't know if you will ever read this, but I have to try to reach out to you.

Father is dying. He has lung cancer, and after two attempts of chemotherapy and radiation therapy, the doctors say there is nothing more they can do. His stubbornness is matched by his irascibility!! Recently though, he has started to talk about you, about how wrong he has been. How he should never have banished you. His words, not mine. About how he would like to see you again. Mother is as much use in this as you can expect. Pippa is no help at all. She hasn't coped well with family life for a long time now. She is busy with school, and I try to keep things neutral.

I don't expect you to come. Like I said, I'm not expecting to find you, but if you can find it in your heart to reach out to me, that would be great. Even if you tell me to fuck off, I will understand. I wish I could have a few moments to tell you how proud I am of you. You stood for yourself, you were proud to be a gay man. I'm proud of you. I love you, my brother.

Ro
Xxx

Ps. This is my cell number (241) 567-4973

I wipe the tears away from my face for the second time today. I reach for my phone and find my pocket empty. Standing, I know I must act quickly before I back out and retreat. I race upstairs and find my phone on the floor. Grabbing it, I look down at the letter again and dial the number. I hold my breath as it rings, once, twice, and then picks up.

"Ro?" The word comes out strangled in my throat as tears flood my eyes.

"Ry? Shit! Mallory, is that you?" Roman answers, his voice deeper than I remember. I hear a male voice in the background, and my brother shushes it.

"Yeah, it's me." I wait. The silence is palpable. Just as I'm about to hang up, I hear him again.

"Oh, God, thank you. Thank you for calling me. Christ, Ry, I've missed you." He sighs, and I'm sure I hear him sniff back a sob. He calls me by the nickname only he has ever used, I'd forgotten all about it but it feels good to hear it again.

"Yeah, me too, Ro. Me too. How bad is it?" I listen as my brother fills me in on all the details. Even between his sobs and his disbelief, I can tell how much he needs me

"Ro… Ro… Ro! Stop talking. I'm on my way." I can't believe I've just said that, but this is family. This is my brother.

"Oh, thank God. Thank you, Mallory, thank you," he cries down the phone.

"It will take me a day or so, but I'm on my way," I answer him.

"I'll send the jet," he comes back with. This makes me chuckle.

"No, you're okay. I'll be with you soon. I'll be in touch." I end the call. Looking around the room, I try to work out the easiest way to do this. Do I just jump on my bike, or do I get a decent rental car? No, I shake my head. I'll take my bike.

I pull my large backpack out of the cupboard in the walk-in closet and pack some clothes. From the bathroom, I add toiletries to the bag. With a quick glance around the room, I make sure I have everything I need for the journey.

When I get downstairs, I find a notepad in Dan's office and leave them a note.

I've gone home. I need to sort this.
I won't be long, and I promise I'll
be okay. I promise to come back.
I love you both
Xxxx

Next, I send a message to Kes,

I've gone home, Kes.
I'm sorry to leave you like this.
I need to get closure.
Thank you for everything.
See you soon.
Carter
Xx

I climb on my bike, start the engine, and head out of the town I now call home.

Chapter

Forty-Six

ARCHER

I wake up and look at my watch. I've had about thirty minutes sleep. Carter is sleeping soundly, so I ease myself away from him and watch as he burrows himself deeper in the duvet. Sleep is the best thing for him right now.

I get dressed and go in search of Dan. When I look in his office, he's sitting at his desk. His geeky black-framed glasses on his nose make him look fucking hot as he stares at his computer screen.

"Whatcha doing?" I walk over and run my hand through his messy hair.

"I'm looking up this Dukas dude. We've got a meeting with him in thirty minutes. I want to know what he's been playing at. That letter should've been handed over to Carter as soon as he met him," Dan replies angrily.

"Then let's go. Carter is sleeping soundly. I'm guessing we can be back before he wakes. You can fill me in on the way."

"I need to change. I can't wear sweats." Dan laughs but rather than heading upstairs, he wanders off to the laundry room and finds a pile of clean, folded jeans. Pulling the soft denim fabric up over his bare ass, I let out a low whistle.

"Commando? I like it." I smirk and run my hand over the firm swell of his ass.

We use Dan's car, and we quickly make our way through the town to his office building. "Tell me more then, Dan."

"His company is sound, and he is the head with two partners. They've been practicing as long as we have with a good reputation. He's mainly a corporate lawyer and works with Halston Commerce, as his main contract, but has other companies on his books. It doesn't make sense for him to have behaved the way he has, and that's what I want to get to the bottom of."

"I agree. He's a shifty bastard for sure."

We get into the office and have ten minutes to spare. We sit together and look again at his profile. The buzzer rings at the exact appointment time, and I move to the door to let him in.

The same smug look on his face appears as I recognize him from the bar. Stepping aside, I let him in.

"Good afternoon, Mr. Hawkins, Mr. Mortimer. I'm Leon Dukas." He offers his hand, and we shake firmly.

"Take a seat, Mr. Dukas." I lead him to the sole chair in front of the desk.

"Please, call me Leon," he smarms. I really don't like him, but I put on a smile.

"I think you need to explain yourself, Dukas." Dan skips any pleasantries.

"Why? What business is it of yours? I had my instructions from my client, and I acted them out accordingly. I had to be sure that I was actually speaking to Mr. Mallory Halston. I had been given a visual, but you have to agree, Mr. Halston looks different than he did over three years ago. Add to that the fact he no longer calls himself Mallory. I had to make sure he was who I believed him to be."

"You have to admit, it was underhanded, asking members of staff about him. Why didn't you introduce yourself and hand over the letter immediately?" I can't believe how cocky this guy is. I think I may have to remind him who I have been working with for the last five years. "Do you feel that asking him on a date was appropriate?" I snap.

"I admit, I overstepped the mark there, but he is a very attractive man. I couldn't resist. I had my suspicions the three of you were together, but if not, why shouldn't I take a chance? It's unusual to find two sets of threesomes living so closely together, even more so in such a conservative small town. Tell me, do you share?"

"Shut the fuck up, Dukas. I mean it, not one more word about our private life," I growl.

"I'll take that as a no. Pity." He smirks again. "Let's get to the point of this pissing contest. Is he going to answer the letter? Or am I going home empty-handed, so to speak."

"Carter hasn't decided yet and trust me, he will never be traveling anywhere with you." I look at Dan, and he gives me a subtle nod. "We're done here. You've handed over your letter. Your job here is done. I suggest you leave quickly. This is a small town that looks after its own. Carter is one of them, and you aren't welcome here."

"I think my instructions from my client are to wait until I hear from Mr. Halston."

"Then I will pass my instructions to my lawyer regarding your harassment of my partner. Mr. Mason Reynolds will be quick to act and have a restraining order against you in no time. You won't be able to talk to him about pissing competitions."

I take pleasure in watching him blanch at the name Reynolds. Such is his power.

Dan stands and looks at Dukas. His eyes narrow but he holds his tongue for now. "I'll show you out. I hope we don't have to meet again."

As he walks out, he turns. "Well played, Hawkins. You are most definitely your mother's son."

Dan locks the doors behind Dukas and lets out a sigh. "He really is an asshole."

"I'm nothing like my fucking mother. That dickwad better stay out of my way."

"No, babe, you're not. He just didn't like your threat of Mason." Dan walks over and wraps his arms around my neck. Leaning in, he captures my mouth and kisses me, then bites on my bottom lip, tugging it between his teeth.

I groan as he releases it, only to thrust my tongue into his mouth. Grabbing his hips and pressing my groin up to him, I rub my hard-on against his through the fabric of our jeans.

"Come on, let's take this home. Carter should be awake by now." I pant as I break away.

We get back to the house, and it's still quiet. We kiss and stumble our way upstairs, heading straight to our bedroom. I let go of Dan so I can take my clothes off when Dan looks around.

"Carter's not here." He looks around again as if he's expecting to find Carter hiding somewhere.

Striding out of the room, I call out to him before racing downstairs. I check the kitchen and the garden, but both are empty. As I walk back into the hallway, Dan stands with a sheet of paper in his hand, and I know what he's done. I don't need Dan to tell me.

"He's gone home, hasn't he?" My voice bland and monotone. I

already miss him.

"Yeah, he says he needs to get it sorted. He loves us and will be back soon."

"Fuck! I knew he'd do this. Why couldn't he have waited for us? We would have gone with him." I hate this. I hate him leaving again.

"He needs to do this. He needs to settle things with his father. We have to let him do this. I don't expect him to stay silent. We can talk or Skype or FaceTime."

"How do you know this?" I'm confused as to how he isn't only so calm but so sure.

"Because the letter from his brother is here too, I can totally see why he needs to do this. We are his, Archer, he won't ever forget that. It's because of the love we share that lets him do this. He knows he's good enough. Good enough for anything, and he needs to tell his father this." He looks at me, his face pained at the loss of his love, but strong and proud of the man he loves. "Okay?"

"Okay. I hate it, but okay. I'm sure he will call us later, but I'm going to leave him a message. He needs to know we understand and we love him. He needs to know he only has to call us." My hand rubs against my chest as I realize the loss of my lover.

I know I'm going to be a wreck the whole time he's away, but deep down, I'm so proud of him. I open my arms, and Dan steps into them. We stand quietly, clinging to each other, holding on tight.

Chapter
Forty-Seven

CARTER

I'm glad I had a nap this afternoon because I know I can ride for a long stretch now. I hit the road and concentrate on riding. My head clears as I embrace the open road. I expected a cacophony of voices, of doubts and regrets. Yes, I feel like I've left a piece of me behind, but I know I'm going back. It's not like the last time I got on my bike and drove away. This time I know where I'm going and what I'm going back to.

After long hours on the road, my stomach growls, and my arms and legs ache. I need to find a decent place to stop for the night. I don't need to pick some shitty motel, so I keep going until I find a decent place with a diner alongside it.

The receptionist hands me my keycard and with a smile says, "Have a good stay, Mr. Halston."

"Thanks." I make my way down to the room and step inside,

dumping my bag on the bed. I've made good time, and if I get up early, I can be back at the house by lunchtime. I pull my leathers off and go into the bathroom for a quick shower before going for food.

The diner is busy, but as it's just me, I get a seat quickly and accept the offer of coffee. I pull my phone out of my pocket. I know there's going to be a message from Archer. Maybe from Dan too. I just hope they understand. My frown turns to a smile as I read their messages.

Honey,
I love you, please be careful.
I get why you need to do this,
but it doesn't mean I wish we hadn't gone together.
Call us when you can and don't be away too long.
My heart won't take it.
Xxxx

The next is from Dan.

Baby,
I love you.
Take the time you need.
Your brother loves you, but not
as much as me ;). That's not possible.
We will be here for you.
Xxx

The pretty young waitress comes back with coffee, and I order a burger and fries. My stomach rumbles again as I talk to her, making her laugh.

"I'll rush the order through for you, babe." With a wink, she sashays away.

She does as she says, and it's only minutes later that she brings a loaded plate over. I groan at the sight and dig in. My phone vibrates on the table next to my plate, and another text comes through. Swiping my finger over the screen, I open it up. It's from my brother.

Mallory,
I can't wait to see you again.
I'm hoping you will stay with me at my place.
I have someone I want you to meet.
I will be with Dad tomorrow, so come straight to
the house.
Roman
X

I finish my meal and head back to my room. Undressing, I clamber into the large and surprisingly comfortable bed. As I close my eyes, I realize just what I'm about to do. The images of the last time I saw my father flash through my mind. I don't know if I'm strong enough for this. I should have Dan and Archer with me. I grab my phone and call Dan. My heart races as I wait for him to answer.

"Hey, baby, you okay?" Dan's voice calms me.

"Yeah, well, maybe… fuck, I hope so. Am I making a mistake, Dan?"

"Baby, you're on speaker. Archer's here. Talk to us, Carter."

"Hey, Carter, honey. You need us with you?" Archer's voice soothes me.

"No, I'm just fucking scared. I'm scared of what I'll see. I'm scared he isn't really sorry. I'm dreading meeting my mother. She let him send me away. She turned her back on me. What if she still feels like that?"

"Carter, listen to me. The second you feel they think like that, you turn and walk away. You have the family you want now. You have us here. You have Kes and his family. You have your friends. Friends that will never turn their backs on you. You are loved. You are loved for who you are and by so many people. You hearing me?" Dan speaks firmly, but it's so heartfelt I can feel myself breathing again.

"Yeah, I hear you. Thanks, Dan. I needed that." I smile.

"Carter, I've told Lucas you're on your way there. If you have any trouble, you call him. He'll be straight to you," Archer tells me.

"Thank you, Arch." I sigh and feel sleep coming over me. "I'm gonna crash. I'll call you tomorrow. I love you," I mumble.

"We love you too. Night, babe." They both speak. I end the call and quickly go to sleep.

I turn the bike in through gates I never wanted to see again and drive slowly up the long asphalt drive to my parents' home. The ride over this morning has been long but uneventful. I'll be happy to get off the bike. It's been a long time since I've ridden this much, and my back and legs ache.

As I switch the bike off and remove my helmet, I scrub my hands through my hair and shake it out. I turn to the door as it opens and hold my breath waiting to see who steps through. Then he's there. Roman, my brother. He's much bigger now. He's grown and filled out. There's a lot of muscle under his well-fitting T-shirt. He smiles, but I can see the tension in the set of his jaw. I must remind myself he's feeling as nervous and awkward as I am.

Throwing my leg over my bike, I straighten my aching back, then take the first step forward. As soon as I do, he rushes up to me. Throwing his arms around me, he holds me so tight. I can feel him shaking, and I find myself holding him just as hard.

"Christ, I've missed you," Roman says as he steps back, using the heels of his hands to wipe away the tears streaming down his face. "Come inside. You can get out of your leathers and get a coffee."

I stare at him, then smile. "You grew up good, Ro." I nudge him with my shoulder. "Not so much of a shrimp anymore." He laughs at the name I would tease him with.

"Yeah, I guess I had to." He looks at me, and a wave of sadness washes over his eyes. "We can catch up later at my place. You ready to do this?"

"Nowhere fucking near ready, but I'm here now, so let's get on with it."

Roman reaches back to lift my backpack from my shoulder. When I go to take it from him, he smiles. "I've got it."

Letting me step in through the large solid oak door, I tread reluctantly over the threshold, my heart beating wildly in my chest. My brother rests his hand on my shoulder, reassuring me.

"It's just us here." We walk towards the kitchen, but he stops. "You want to get changed?"

"I only need to strip these off. I've got jeans in my bag." I slide the zipper down and shrug out of the soft leather.

"I guess you want to know what happened?" Roman asks as we sit opposite each other at the kitchen table.

"What, with Dad?" I raise an eyebrow. "I'm guessing he knew he was ill and decided to do fuck about it until it was too late."

"Well, yeah, that's about it, but I meant after you left." He looks at me, his jaw tight again.

"I didn't leave. I was thrown out. And no. I really don't give a shit about what happened here. I know how bad it was for me, and that's painful enough to think about." I don't take my eyes from his, and I keep my voice low and level. "It's done, Roman, it's in the past. Leave it there."

"I will, for now. Let me tell you about him." Roman goes on to tell me about the treatment he has had and the pain he's in and how it's regulated. "He sleeps a lot now, but he's due to wake up soon. The afternoon is the best time to catch him at his most lucid."

"Why now, Ro? Is this so he doesn't die with a dirty conscience? That he'll get his place in heaven? I don't think he has a right to atonement. Right now I'm thinking karma's a bitch for him."

"I know, trust me, Ry. I know." He looks at me, and I see something that makes me gasp.

"You're gay," I bark out at him. I laugh hard, then square up. I can't help the bitterness in my voice. "And yet you're still here." I shake my head and push myself upright. I was wrong to come here. I need to go home.

"Yeah, I'm still here. I only told him a few months back, and by then, he was already ill. I have a boyfriend. We met in college, and while I have never been in the closet, so much, I just chose not to tell him. I'm guessing Dad chose to ignore it. I wasn't brave like you, Mallory. I wanted to work with Dad. I wanted to be a part of his company, so we just played the denial game. I hated it. Marcus, my boyfriend, nearly left me over it, but I did what I had to do. Look, can we talk about this again tonight? Dad will be awake now if you're ready?"

"I guess I have to be. I'm here now." My head is now full of even more confusion. Roman is right, though. We have time later to talk it through.

We walk together down the long hallway towards Dad's office. I look at my brother in confusion.

"He wanted to be in his office. We've turned it into a bedroom for him." Ro shrugs, puts his hand on the door handle, and looks at me. "Do you want to do this by yourself?"

"Bro, I don't want to do this at all," I answer gruffly but balance it with a smile. "C'mon, let's see how it goes."

When we walk in, my heart seems to stop. The man I have hated for so long now seems to have disappeared, and in his place, is half a man. He's so small and fragile looking. Where is the domineering tyrant I grew up with? His skin's so pale it's translucent as it stretches over his bones. It looks like fragile paper, easily torn and crumpled.

"Dad, you've a visitor. You awake yet?" Roman speaks clearly. I expected hushed whispers, but he talks normally.

"Hey, Dad," I say as loudly as I can, considering it feels like I have a tourniquet around my throat. His eyes fly open, and he gazes at me.

His lips tremble as he tries to find his words, but it's his eyes that have me fixed. His tears swell and spill over before I can even blink.

"Mallory? Oh, Mallory, my son, you're here." He reaches out to me with a very shaky hand, and I find myself stumbling towards him. "I'm sorry, I'm so very sorry."

"It's okay, Dad. It's okay," I say without even thinking about it. I realize that, actually, it is okay. I sit in the chair next to him as he clasps my hand in his, his grip tighter than I thought he'd be capable of.

"No, it's not, son. Don't forgive me that easily. I don't deserve it. I was wrong, and so very cruel," he gasps. Panicking, I turn to look at Roman to check if this is okay, but I'm alone.

"What do you need, Dad? Would you like some water?" I look around and spy a cup with a straw sticking up from the lid.

"A whiskey would be good, if you can sneak one in for me." He chuckles ruefully

"Yeah, that's not gonna happen." I shake my head and reach for the cup. I hold it up to his mouth, and he sucks weakly on the straw.

"Thank you for coming, Mallory. Thank you for letting me make my peace before this bastard disease carries me off." His eyes close, and he leans back on the pillows. I place the cup back on the table and rest back in the chair. I feel much more peaceful than I should, than I ever thought I would.

I think he's gone back to sleep, but then he speaks again. "Are you happy, Mallory? Did you find a good man to love you?"

"I was, and then it all fell apart. I picked myself up and started again. I seem to have had to do that a lot," I answer ruefully. His eyes open to look at me again, sorrow pours from them. "But I'm in a good place now with good people around me. I'm happy. I'm very happy."

It goes quiet again.

"I thought you were with the Hawkins boy," my dad says, sounding confused.

"Yes, I was. We were together for nearly two years. How did you know that?" I wonder just how much he knew about my life after he threw me out. Not that it's important anymore. "He asked me to marry him the day I graduated." I love that this chapter no longer causes me pain, that I have him back in my life.

"So why didn't you marry him?"

"Um, it's complicated," I answer, not really wanting to get into this now.

"I'm sure I'll keep up. It's my body that's dying, not my brain."

I smile at him and his attitude. "Yeah, he had a really bad car accident."

"Well, that's not a reason to end an engagement. So, you going to tell me what really happened?"

"His mother told me he had died. She sent some cops to our apartment. Then I was banned from the hospital. She turned up at the apartment later and told me to get out. That's what happened. The woman always hated me being with Archer. She got her own way in the end."

What shocks me is the hard bark of bitter laughter that breaks free from my father.

"I'm glad you find it funny. It nearly killed me. The grief, the pain of losing him made me want to be dead too. Nothing hurt as much as losing him, not even you hurt me as much as that bitch did."

"No, son, that's not why I was laughing. I'm sorry, but that woman has no heart in her body. Nothing she does ever surprises me."

"I thought you must have known each other. She guessed I was your son when I first met her." I begin to think there is a story here, one I'm not sure I want to know.

"Unfortunately, I know her very well. What else happened, son? What else went on?" He sounds angry, but I can also see he's struggling to breathe properly.

"Not enough for you to tire yourself over. Maybe we can talk more later, or tomorrow?" I pat the back of his hand.

"Yes, Mallory." His eyes shine as he looks at me. "I can't believe you came back, thank you." He lifts my hand and places a kiss on the back of it.

"I'm gonna go find Roman. I'll be staying at his place. I think we've got a lot of catching up to do."

"You do that. He's missed you, so much. I hate that I forced you apart. I guess I'm paying for my sins now." He gasps in a breath that causes him to cough painfully.

"Don't talk like that, Dad. I'm here now, and I'm not going anywhere."

The door behind me opens, making me turn. My brother walks back in. He smiles and looks in surprise at my hand being held by my father.

"He's getting tired again, Ro. I think he's had enough excitement for today." I look at my dad and smirk as he snores softly.

"Yeah, he doesn't stay awake very long. Do you want to hang around here, or shall we head out?"

"Will he be okay by himself?" I can't believe I'm worried about him now.

"Yes, his nurse is here now. He's not left alone, Ry. The nurse knows to call me. C'mon, you look beat."

Letting go off Dad's hand, I lay it down softly on the blanket. Standing, I feel the creak in my spine. The tension from over nine hours on my bike plus the mental overload has me suddenly exhausted.

We walk together out of the room and head down the hallway again.

"I've put your bike in the garage. I thought I'd drive you to my place. You've probably had enough of concentrating on the road."

"Yeah, that's great. I could do with a shower." I give him a sly look. "A beer wouldn't go amiss either," I joke.

"Mallory, there will be a meal, a beer, and a bed with your name on it when we get home. It's not far. Grab your bag, and we can go."

When we walk through the kitchen and into the four-car garage, I grin. My brother always had a passion for cars, and I see a very nice Shelby Mustang sitting in the middle. "I can guess which is yours!"

"Yeah, I love my car. What do you drive?" Roman asks.

"I don't have a car. I just use my bike. Dan has a very nice BMW, and Archer has a fuck-off-size Ford pickup. Seriously, you could live in the fucker, it's huge." I suddenly realize I've mentioned both Dan and Archer. I don't look at Roman as I dump my bag in the trunk and sit next to him. "I need to call home when we get to your place. They'll be worried about me."

"Yeah, no problem. Take all the time you want. You wanna tell me about your life now? What do you do? Did you finish college?"

"Yeah, I finished top of my class. It was hard work to begin with. I had nowhere to live and no money to buy anything." I ignore my brother's sharp intake of breath. "I got a place in a dorm and then maxed myself out in student loans and grants. I got a small scholarship too. I found a job, and I met Archer, and everything got better after that. For a while anyway." My voice trails off.

"You must be very proud of yourself, bro. I feel like a fake and a fraud now. I've taken everything that's been handed to me. Yes, I had to work hard through college, but I didn't have to juggle a job and money worries to get good grades. I had it very easy."

It takes us fifteen more minutes to reach Roman's place. We park in an underground parking lot and take the elevator to his apartment.

I chuckle when he presses the button for his floor.

"What, no penthouse and a private code for the ride up to your floor?" I cock my eyebrow at him.

"Fuck, no! We've got a good-sized place, but I'm not a penthouse type of guy."

"I used to be. Archer had, well, he still has, one of those apartments." I grin.

The ping sounds, and the doors slide open, letting us out. We walk a short way down the corridor to his door.

"Hey, Marcus?" Roman calls out as we enter his place. I look around, taking in the layout. It's not small by anyone's estimation. A large hallway that has its walls covered in photographs of all sizes in black or white frames. I can see into the spacious living area. "Come on in, Ry. Meet the man that keeps me in my place."

I laugh as I see a tall, broad, and incredibly handsome man walk towards me. He smiles widely as his dark eyes twinkle.

"Mallory, it's good to meet you. Roman has spoken about you so much. It's good to see you two together again."

"Marcus, it's great to meet you, too." I hold out my hand for him, but he just laughs and drags me into a big bear hug.

"Okay, Marc, let him go." Roman chuckles and pulls me back. "I'll show you to your room. You can shower and phone home before we eat."

Leading me back into the hallway and to a door on the left-hand side, he pushes it open. I walk into a decent-sized room with a large bed covered with navy blue and white bedding. The walls are painted a soft grey. I like it, and like the hallway and lounge there are photographs on the walls and surfaces.

"Marcus is a photographer, so we have masses of pictures everywhere," Roman explains as I look at some of the ones on the dresser.

"They're really good. He's very talented." I grin when I hold up one of my brother pulling a goofy face. Just then, my cell phone rings, making me jump. "I'd better get that. I should've called by now. They'll be pissed at me."

"I'll leave you to it. There's no rush."

I grab my phone and answer. "Hey, Archer."

"Hi, honey, how are you doing? We've been worried," he asks quietly. I can hear the tension though.

"Are you together?"

"Yeah, you're on speaker," Dan answers. "Please tell us how it went. Did you meet your brother?"

"Sorry, it's been a crazy day. Yes, I met Roman, and it's, hell, it's amazing to see him again. We've just got back to his place. He guessed I wouldn't want to stay at the house. I've just got into my room after meeting his boyfriend, Marcus."

The phone goes quiet, so quiet I think I've lost connection, making me pull the phone away to look at the screen.

"Your brother is gay?" Archer's voice is dangerously quiet. I can hear his anger simmering just under the surface. Dan shushes him.

"Carter, how do you feel about that?" Dan asks. He sounds calmer.

"It was a shock for sure, but hell, not much I can say really. He chose to never confront our father with it, and my father chose to ignore it. Maybe that's what I should've done." I let out a dry laugh.

"No fucking way! You could never have lived your life as a secret. We wouldn't have met if you hadn't come out to your family," Archer says, still sounding pissed.

"Archer, calm down. It doesn't matter. It was years ago, and I know

I have you now. I have both of you for reasons I could've lived without, but we make our own journeys, and I chose to be honest to myself. I don't regret it, and I doubt my brother would choose to do it differently."

"What about your father, Car? Did you see him today?" Dan asks gently.

"Yeah, yeah, I did. It's not looking good for him. But, shit, it was hard. He cried. He cried when he saw me. He wouldn't let go of my hand. He just kept saying he was sorry. It was hard for me, but dammit, I needed to hear that."

"Oh baby, that's so good. I'm happy for you. What about your mom?" Archer sounds more normal now, which makes me happy.

"Y'know, she wasn't mentioned. When we left, Roman said dad's nurse was there, not that my mom was. Weird! I'll have to ask him. Anyway, what've you been up to?" I need to talk about something else, something that doesn't make me tense.

"East came over, and we've agreed on a swimming pool, so he's going to make a start on that for us. Apart from that, not a lot. We went to work and then had a beer at the bar. Kes and the rest send their love to you and tell you not to stay away too long."

I can hear the smile in his voice as he shares his day with me.

"Yeah, about that. I don't know how long he's got left. I'll talk more to Roman about it tonight, and I guess I'll make a decision then. I really don't want to be away from you, not when we were getting it together. I just think I need to be here a little while yet."

"You want us to fly up on Friday? We can do that," Dan asks hopefully.

"Yeah, maybe. Let me see how the next couple days go. I might be needing you both by then."

"Just say the word, Carter, and we're with you," Dan says, then chuckles. "Does your brother know there are two of us?"

I laugh. "I think he's guessing it. I let a couple things slip." I keep laughing and go on telling them I told him about both of their cars and how they'd both be worried. "I'll tell him all about you tonight. I can't wait to talk about you." I look at my watch and sigh. "I'd better go. I need a shower, and I know they are waiting for me so we can eat."

"Okay, call us anytime, day or night. We can be with you in a couple hours if you need us," Dan pleads.

"I will. I love you."

"We love you too. Night, hon." They say together.

Rushing through a shower, I towel off and pull on some clean jeans and a Henley and search out my brother.

Chapter

Forty-Eight

CARTER

"Two? Wow! I'm impressed." Marcus grins unabashedly. "I have my hands full with just him." Then he blushes when he realizes how that sounds. That just makes me and Roman laugh louder.

"It's early days for us, and it isn't easy. There's a lot of history between us that has made it hard at times, but we're learning to talk more. Plus, the whole name thing didn't make it easy."

"What name thing?" Roman asks as he lifts his wine glass to his lips.

"That's what made the whole thing such a fucking mess. I go by Carter now, not Mallory. I needed the change when I was forced away. It felt easier for me to start over. If I had stayed as Mallory, Dan would maybe have remembered me from when Archer and I were together."

"Why would Dan know to connect you and Archer together?"

Marcus frowns. I know how confusing this is without factoring in the two bottles of wine we've gone through over dinner.

"Because Dan and Archer are best friends. Hell, they dated through college." I sigh at how bad it all sounds.

"Fuck!" they both say before laughing hard.

"It's like daytime TV," Roman says, wiping his eyes, but stops laughing when he sees I haven't joined in.

"Yeah, grieving for your fiancé, being banished from your home for the second time, and running scared, only to hope you've found someone good to take the pain away, made me think that too. I'm gonna crash." I stand. "Thanks for dinner, Marcus."

Before I make it to the door, Roman is by my side. "I'm sorry, Mallory. I didn't mean to hurt you or belittle what you went through."

"Okay, thanks for letting me crash here." It seems I'm not as ready to forgive everyone in my family as I thought. Exhaustion takes over, and I'm asleep as soon as my head hits the pillow.

Next morning, I wake up and can't work out where I am. I know it's a very comfortable bed, and I know it's not mine, but my brain isn't awake enough to remember where I am. I shove the duvet from over my head and blink as I take in my surroundings. Oh yeah, Roman's place. Fuck, I've got to go back to see my dad again. I think the adrenaline running through my body yesterday has burnt out, and I'm left with the hollow feeling of hurt, or that I'm about to hurt again. He's going to die, and after Roman talking me through it last night, I'm guessing it's going to be soon. As in, damn soon.

I think back to his comment on Valerie Hawkins and wonder if he's able to talk about her again today. He may have something I can tell Archer. Something he could use against her.

I don't bother with a shower and pull on my jeans and the same Henley from last night. I need coffee. Walking down to the kitchen, I can hear the sounds of breakfast being made as well as the scent of very decent coffee brewing. When I step in, Roman looks at me, chagrin still all over his face, and as he opens his mouth to speak, I stop him.

"Stop shitting bricks, Ro, it's fine. You've always been a dick. I should've remembered." I slap his shoulder as Marcus laughs.

"Coffee?" he offers.

"Please." I lean back against the door frame and smile as I accept the proffered mug. "Ro, where's Mom? Shouldn't she be helping with Dad?" I watch a glance go between the two men.

"Mom left Dad last year. She just said she'd had enough and walked out. The divorce papers came through, and he signed them and hasn't mentioned her since. She got the New York apartment and the house in Aspen, but nothing else."

"She didn't get in touch when he became ill?" They both look at me as if I've missed something, then it clicks. "He already was ill. That fucking bitch!"

"Yep!" Roman looks at me and shrugs. "You ready?"

"Yeah, I guess. What about Pippa? You said something about school?"

"Yeah, she went with Mom. C'mon, I'll tell you the rest on the way. Bye, hon." He kisses Marcus, and we head back out. "Are your guys okay with you being here? I was surprised when you said you'd be coming on your own."

"I. um, left them a note." I scrub my hand around the back of my neck as he laughs.

"Shit! You getting any grief from them?" I shake my head. "I wasn't surprised it took you so long to answer the letter, but I had just about given up on you getting in touch."

"What do you mean? I only got the letter the night before. Your lawyer gave it to me when I was at work."

Roman looks angry. "You need to tell me what happened, Ry. Do you want me to call you Carter? I can. I don't mind."

"Nah, let's not confuse Dad with that. He's got enough to deal with. I still can't get over Mom." I shake my head. "I thought she'd be ready to get her hands on all his money."

"She knew she wasn't getting any. I guess she thought at least she'd get the houses by divorcing him. Anyway, fuck her. Tell me what went on with the letter."

The rest of the ride over takes that up, but he's still shaking his head. "He told me he'd done it when he first got there and was waiting for your reply."

"Oh, well, he didn't, and I'm guessing after I turned his offer of a date down, he thought he might as well hand it over." I laugh at this. "I think Archer and Dan had gone to see him, which is why I didn't tell them I was on my way here. Maybe you need to call him back before they rip him apart."

"Oh, I'll be calling him all right," he snarls.

Walking in the door, we meet Dad's nurse. He's about forty years old and has a kind, smiling face. "Hey, guys." He looks at me and holds his hand out. "You must be Mallory. He's been talking about you. He seems happy to have you back here. Roman, he says you're to get the black leather wallet out of the safe in the study and bring it in. He's restless this morning. I'm guessing it's important for him to speak to you, but don't let him tire himself out. He's really not doing all that great anymore. I'm going to speak to his doc and bring him up to date, but I don't think you have many days left with him."

"Thanks, Rudy. We'll see you this afternoon." Roman says with a grim look on his face.

"Yeah, be kind to one another." He smiles and heads out of the door.

"You want coffee before you go in to him?" Roman asks, but I shake my head.

"What's in the black wallet?" I ask him, wondering what's so important that he must have it now.

"No idea. You go in. I'll get it."

I tap on the door but don't wait for him to reply. I don't want him to raise his voice.

"Hey, Pops." My kid name for him comes out of nowhere, but I see he smiles when he hears it.

"Hey, son. Good to see you again. Where's your no-good brother?"

"He's gone to get the wallet you asked for."

"Ah, that's good. Now listen to me, Mallory. I know I don't deserve you back here, and after I tell you this, you may not come back to see me again. I wouldn't blame you." He looks at me fiercely, his eyes glittering with grim determination.

He sighs as Roman walks in with the wallet and walks up to him, dropping a kiss on his forehead. "Where do you want this, Dad?"

"Hand it over to Mallory. You want to get some coffee or something, Ro? Give me some time with Mallory, please."

"Uh? Yeah, okay, sure." Roman frowns and looks at me. I shrug, having no more idea than he does.

When the door closes behind Roman, my dad reaches for my hand.

"Listen, Mallory. I want to tell you something I wanted to keep from you, but you have a right to know. I think my actions have caused you a great deal of harm and hurt. Don't interrupt me. Let me say my piece, and if you've any questions, everything I know is in that wallet. I'm guessing you and your man Archer will know what to do with it."

I squirm uncomfortably in his gaze and wait for him to talk.

"Valerie Hawkins hates you because she hates me. I had an affair with her a long time ago, from before you were born. It lasted a long while, five years or so. Your mother knew and didn't care as long as she had me. But when Valerie began to make noises about divorces and us marrying, I ended it. But, as I guess you learned, she is a vindictive woman and doesn't like to lose. I think she took out my dismissal of her out on you. When you showed up on the arm of her son, she knew she had found her time to hurt me, but even more so you. She contacted me again, threatening to tell you about me. Again, I dismissed her and said you wouldn't care about me. So that stopped that plan of hers. It took the worst kind of accident to really get her revenge. If she couldn't keep her son, you sure as hell weren't going to have him."

I look at him, not sure what I'm hearing. Is she really that much of a bitch? Oh, hell yeah, she is. Then another thought crosses my mind, one that makes me sick. Archer!

"Dad, for the love of God, please tell me Archer isn't your child?" I can feel the coffee in my stomach sloshing around, getting ready to make its appearance.

"What? Good God, no! She already had him before she sank her talons into my arm." He sounds almost as horrified as me.

"Thank fuck for that!" I murmur and then start to laugh. "Shit, Pops, I almost brought up my breakfast."

"Anyway, Mallory. I'm sorry I caused her to hate you, but please make very good use of what's in there. It's all documented, and copies are with my lawyer, but every bit of what's in there is true. I hope it brings you and Archer some peace of mind."

"Okay, you gonna say any more than that?"

"No, go and get your brother, we can talk for five more minutes, then I'm going to close my eyes for a while."

He pats my hand as I stand up, and I smile and brush the hair from his forehead, feeling how clammy and damp his skin is.

When I reach the kitchen, Roman is raiding the fridge looking for something more than the toast he had at home.

"Come on, he says he's got five more minutes left in him."

I let Roman sit closest to him this time and try to keep my eyes from staring at the wallet on the table. They talk quietly about something to do with work and move on to stuff that happened when we were kids. We joke and laugh quietly for a while, and then his eyes droop, and he falls asleep in midsentence.

Neither of us are ready to leave him. We stay close and talk softly. I tell him what he said, and Roman just shakes his head.

"That bitch had better watch her back," he grumbles.

He sleeps for the rest of the day, but it seems more than that. It feels like he's losing consciousness, drifting in and out of a deep sleep. Sometimes he recognizes us, other times he's confused as to who we are. When Rudy comes back for his nightshift, we decide to stay here for the night. Roman calls Marcus to let him know our plans. He offers to come over, but Roman declines. We both know our father isn't going to last much longer and prepare ourselves for a vigil through the night.

At least we are in comfortable chairs, rather than the stiff hospital chairs, which raises the question of why here, and not the hospital.

Roman laughs. "He was adamant he wanted to die at home. He said he wouldn't take his last breath in a place that smells of illness and disease, where you don't get a decent night's sleep because someone keeps waking you up to check if you're still alive."

"Sounds like Dad." I chuckle. I reach out and take his hand in mine. I get lost in the thought of him taking his last breath and me not being here, not making the rift between us disappear. I'm grateful for the time I have with him now.

"Did he ever mention me after he threw me out?" I don't know why this is important to me now.

"Not for a long time, then I caught him looking at the photographs of you. He looked so lost. I questioned him, and he told me that sometimes in the blink of an eye, you make the worst decision of your life. When I tried to push for more from him, he had already shut down, and the subject was closed. I'm sorry I didn't look for you. It was very selfish of me. When I realized I was gay, I balked from telling him. I took the coward's way out and left for college with my mouth firmly closed. I wasn't in denial, but I knew I wasn't as strong as you. I couldn't own up and be proud. I wouldn't have known where to start surviving without the financial support, not like you did. I admire you so much. I'm so proud you're my brother. I'm not sure I deserve to be yours."

"Don't think like that. You did what was best for you. You're here now, and that means everything. You could've taken his money and left with Mom."

"I could never have done that. I owe him everything. He has given me the chance to be successful, to be good at my job. It's not the money I earn or the luxuries I can have; it's the pride he has for me. I can never pay that back to him. I want him to know I love him and he's not alone."

"Is that why you reached out to me? How did you find me?"

"I needed to have you with me. I knew I wasn't strong enough to do this alone. I put your picture on all the social media sites, asking if anyone had seen you or knew you. A woman contacted me and said she had seen you working in a bar when she was on vacation. She told me where and when she had seen you. I sent Dukas down to hand you the letter."

"He's a dick. You know that, right?" I sigh, wondering what Dan and Archer said to him.

"Yes, and he has been reprimanded and has lost his contract with us."

We sit silently now, each holding our father's hands. Rudy comes in and checks on him, dealing with the medical side of his care. His smile is kind as he watches us say our goodbyes.

I can feel sleep trying to take over, making me shift in my chair, sitting upright again. Looking over at Roman, I can see he's asleep. His head rests on the bed. I watch them both sleep and feel a sense of calm wash over me. I was right to come. I settle back down in the chair and close my eyes for a moment.

Dad coughs in his sleep, making us both wake up. Straightening up again, we lean forward. I smooth the hair from Dad's forehead. He calms again but soon coughs again, struggling for breath. He opens his eyes and looks at us both. His eyes are so clear as they focus for just a second, with a sweet smile on his lips. "My boys, you make me proud." Then light fades from his eyes as he slips away.

"Oh, no. Dad, no!"

Chapter
Forty-Nine

DAN

"Archer, calm down." I place my hands on his shoulders and turn him around to face me. "He will come home."

"Yeah, you sure about that? I'm fucking not. His father died three weeks ago. The funeral was ages ago, and we've not heard fucking shit from him for days. Lucas isn't fucking helping. He just said to leave him alone; he's with his brother. If I don't hear from him by tonight, I'm fucking going there and dragging him home." He sags against me. "I can't be here without him for much longer. We've been apart because of my shitty mother; now his shitty father has done the same thing."

"Archer, stop being a dick. His father died. Your mother did something much fucking worse. Now come on, we promised Kes we'd show up for Denver's gig tonight." I kiss him softly, then hold him close and deepen it. My hands fist in his hair as he groans into my mouth. I pour my feelings for him into this kiss. I know how stressed he is because I am too, but one of us must keep some edge of reason, or we'd both be going bat-shit crazy. Sex has all but been forgotten. We've had a couple nights we've both needed it, but without Carter, it's not the same. We miss him too much.

Breaking apart, I wipe my thumb over his swollen lower lip, then kiss him chastely one more time. He smiles and smacks my ass.

"Come on. We'd best be going." Like it's been him nagging me all afternoon.

The bar is packed when we get inside, but Kes told us he was keeping a booth for us. Both Kes and East are working, but I know they'll be over when Denver starts to play. Paris waves at us and points us to the corner. We wave back and squeeze through the throng. Archer looks around, so he doesn't notice Paris whisper something to Shelley and nod over to us. I caught their badly hidden smiles.

Hunter comes over with two bottles of beers and drops them off swiftly, smiling as he walks away. We sit and talk for a few minutes when Kes walks over.

"Hey, guys. Glad you could make it. It's crazy in here tonight. I'll be over soon. East isn't being any use behind the bar. I'll send him over with a couple more beers. He always gets twitchy when Den is playing." Clapping Archer on the shoulder, he wanders off again.

East turns up just as Denver sits up on his stool. He's got his guitar on the stand next to him, and in a few minutes, the whole place goes quiet. As he starts to play, I look around the room. I watch as Kes leans against the pumps, his eyes fixed on his lover. No one dare order a drink while this is going on, I don't even pay attention to what Denver is playing. I'm so transfixed on Kes and the love that pours from him. Christ, I miss Carter. We were getting there. We all were on our way to having that. The three of us together. But now, as much as I castigated Archer over his doubts, I am having them myself.

Then the room darkens. I can hear hushed voices and a scuffling of chairs. The next sound isn't a guitar; it's a piano. Archer lets out a moan and stands, rocking the table, making people shush him. We still can't see anything, but I can make out the melody of Tom Petty's *American Girl*. Then a voice starts and fuck! I'd know that voice anywhere. Carter, it's Carter playing. I cling onto Archer's hand as I stand next to him, as my man sings not about an American girl, but an American boy. The song so slow and sweet, I feel my heart beating properly again. I have missed him so much. Archer sniffs as tears roll down his face. This version isn't new to him; he's heard it played before. We cling to each other as Carter sings and plays so brilliantly. The lights are back on but still low, allowing me to see him now. I can tell he's nervous though. He has his eyes are either fixed on his hands, or he has them shut. As he comes to the end, I expect him to finish, but even as the clapping and the cheers continue, he starts another.

It's one that he's had on his iPod, and I know he likes it. It's one of the few I've heard him singing along to. X Ambassadors *Unsteady*. I hold back a sob this time because I know I'm feeling more than a little unsteady. Denver joins him, and they sing beautifully together, making me wonder if they have practiced this. If so, when did the little shit get back here? I snort at the thought of being pissed at him. I may be pissed at Kes for keeping this from us. I look at him and see he's as emotional as both Archer and me, so maybe I'll let him off.

When it finishes, Denver stands and holds out his hand for Carter, and the bar goes crazy. Cheering, stamping, and hollering out. Paris is crying and being held by Conn, who has the hugest grin on his face. Standing next to him are two men I don't know, but one of them has to be Carter's brother. They are clapping along with the rest of the crowd. It quiets down as Carter finally looks at us. His face is tense, and his eyes wide as he waits for our reactions.

Taking hold of Archer's hand, I drag him up on stage. I stop in front of Carter and lift my hand up to his face.

"Good to see you again, baby." I pull him against me as Archer wraps himself around Carter. We stand for a few moments before Archer breaks away and kisses Carter, so tenderly.

"God, I've missed you two." Carter sighs and falls into our arms. "I've missed you so fucking much. Do you forgive me?"

"What for?" Archer asks.

"Everything, leaving you behind, not letting you come to visit. Not telling you I was coming home, for this little stunt." He looks up at us sheepishly, but there's a playful glint in his eye.

"Y'know what, I think you're good. As long as you're back for good, I'm happy. I'm so fucking happy," Archer says and then pounces on him, his mouth devouring Carter's, pulling back after a minute to drag me in.

As soon as my mouth touches Carter's, I moan. I get lost in his taste and his scent. My hands can't stop roaming over his body.

"We need to go, like right now. C'mon, I need you in our bed." I moan.

"But my brother…" Carter stammers.

"Your brother will understand." I take hold of his hand and lead him through the parting crowd. I look at Kes who has his arms around Denver and East. He nods and smiles as we walk out of the bar.

Carter sits between the two of us in the front of Archer's truck. I'm still holding his trembling hand, and Archer has his hand resting on Carter's thigh. No one speaks, but there is a sweet calmness surrounding us. Then the quiet is broken.

"When did you get home?" Archer asks. There's tension in his voice.

"This afternoon. I wanted to surprise you. Did I get it wrong?" Carter sounds wary.

"No, honey. I've missed you, and I need you. I hate that you went to somewhere else before seeing us, but to hear you play again was something special. Thank you."

"It's been a really hard time. I'll tell you everything tomorrow. Right now, I need you. I need your bodies to claim mine back again." Carter's words come out as a plea that shoots straight to my dick.

"I think we can do that, Car. We need you just as much," I murmur to him, whispering in his ear.

Archer pulls up into the driveway and kills the engine. When he turns to face Carter, his emerald-green eyes are dark and hooded. The desire blazing from them makes Carter gasp.

"Let's go," Archer's voice is low and husky, full of dark promise.

We rush up the stairs. Archer makes it to the bedroom first, and all but rips his shirt off his body. We match him and face each other.

"This feels like the first time. Why am I nervous?" Carter sighs, his hand reaching down to fist his rock-hard dick.

"Because you're different. You've changed, your life has shifted again. You've found your family and then lost a part of it. You're bound to feel different. It's not a bad thing, baby. I changed after my father died. I became a stronger man. You have too," I say.

Archer moves in behind Carter. His hands rest softly on his shoulders before letting them travel lazily down his arms. His fingers trace his inner arms as he works his way back up. Carter's head drops back, resting on Archer's shoulder. A deep shudder ricochets through his body. I step in front of him and smooth my hands over his collarbone and down his chest. His nipples harden under my fleeting touch, but I carry on caressing his torso. My fingers slide over his heaving chest and down to the six squares that flex, contracting as I leave featherlight strokes.

Archer follows my pattern over Carter's back until our hands meet at his hips. Mine slip behind him and grasp his butt cheeks, Archer reaches forward and traces the groove of his oblique muscles. Carter moans heavily as he pants. Then I let my mouth graze over the flushed, heated skin. Sweat breaks over him as goose bumps bloom under my tongue. Rocking himself between us, I know Carter struggles now as his senses overload.

"What do you want, Carter? Tell me where you want me," I croon to him, then flick the tip of my tongue over his pebbled nipple.

"I need your mouth on me. Take me deep. I need it," he keens.

Archer moves us over to the bed. I think Carter is so far gone now, he doesn't notice us moving. Laying him down between us, I move down his body, dropping long, wet kisses over his body. I let the heat of my breath wash over his beautiful cock. I want nothing more than to lick the thread of precum that hangs down, pooling on his stomach, but I need him begging. I look up and see Archer has claimed his mouth. With his hands in Carter's hair, he pours his everything into his kiss. Carter continues to writhe, desperate for me. I lick down the crease between his thigh and groin, then slip between his parted legs. His hips punch the air as my nose nudges his tight sac. I hear the moan break free from him as he cries out.

It's time! I lick over his sac, making him cry out again and thrust against me. My tongue then slides up the length of his dick. I don't think he's ever been this hard for me before. I know he won't last long.

Archer has his mouth over one nipple, and his fingers pluck and tease the other. Carter's hands fist the sheet as he pants. When Archer looks at me, I wink before taking the swollen head of Carter's dick in my mouth. Sucking hard, I twirl my tongue over and over the satin-smooth skin, drinking down the burst of liquid as it weeps from him. My teeth gently scrape over his frenulum, and this makes him punch inside my mouth. I draw him deeper, letting him nudge the back of my throat before pulling off him, only to blow cool air over the head.

"Fuckfuckfuck! Don't stop! I'm close, I'm so close," Carter begs, his eyes screwed tight shut, his neck long as he tips his head back. The tendons are taut, and his Adam's apple bobs as he swallows hard.

"Not yet, baby. I'm gonna be inside you when you come. When you give it all to Archer." I see Archer move away from Carter and reach over to the drawer. He slides it open and takes out the lube. He hands it over to me.

"Take him, Daniel. Bring him back to us," he speaks quietly before kissing Carter again.

Kneeling up, I push Carter's legs up, opening him up to me. "Hold your legs, my love." Carter reaches down and wraps his hands around his thighs, pulling them up to his chest.

My mouth waters at the sight of his tight hole exposed to me. I need to taste him before I enter him. I swipe my tongue over his hole, drenching it before teasing the oh-so-sensitive ring of nerve endings. I feel him relax, allowing me to dip the tip of my tongue inside, stabbing in and out as he squirms. His legs shake as he holds them tight to his chest. Reaching for the lube, I crack the lid and pour the cool gel onto my fingers. I add the tip of my middle finger to his ring, and as my tongue slips inside, I let my finger join it. Fucking him with my tongue and finger makes my dick so hard. I know I'm going to have to be inside him soon. I let my fingers take over, and soon he's riding three fingers, grinding down hard needy for me. I pull my fingers out and quickly coat my cock with lube. With his hole still open for me, I plunge all the way in.

We both cry aloud. Carter lets go of his legs and wraps them around my waist, holding me still inside him, unable to move. But I pull back, leaving just the head of my cock inside him, then thrust hard again. Archer has Carter's length in his fist, and soon, we work in synch, his strokes matching my thrusts.

"I'm gonna come. I can't hold on," Carter cries.

"Hold on, baby. Wait for me. We can come together," I moan. I know I won't last too much longer. The tightness of his ass squeezes me tight as he tries to hold back on his orgasm. I pull out, ignoring his anguish and flip him over onto his hands and knees. I sink deep inside him again. I want Archer's mouth on Carter's dick, so I pull him upright against my chest. I keep thrusting in and out of his hot channel. "Take him, Archer. I won't last much longer."

Archer lies beneath him, so I lower him back down. With his head between Carter's legs, Archer swallows Carter's cock. With my hands on his hips now, I pick up speed and fuck him harder and faster than I ever have before. My spine tingles as my thigh muscles tense. I know I'm going to come.

"Now, Carter. Come now!" I cry out as my own orgasm fires from me. I feel the exact moment he comes as his muscles clamp around my ass, holding me in a vise-like grip. Archer sucks him harder as he takes every drop of his release. I feel his muscles relax, allowing me to slide out of him and collapse next to Archer, my head near his dick. I can see how tight his balls are in his body and know he's close to coming. I move my mouth up and lick his length.

As Carter pulls his now softening dick from Archer's mouth, he falls to the other side of Archer's body. I expect him to add his mouth to mine, but he doesn't. Pushing me gently away, Carter swings his leg over Archer's waist and grabs his dick, then he slowly sinks down on him.

The noise from Archer as Carter slides down his painful length makes my dick twitch again. I move between Archer's legs and spread them. Licking my fingers, I slide them into his asshole. As Carter rides him, I fuck his ass with my fingers. I reach forward and swipe over his sweet spot. Archer's hips buck up violently as I relentlessly torture his prostate.

"Fuuuuuuuuuuuuck!!!" he cries out and stills. His ass clamps on my fingers as he comes, pouring himself inside our lover.

Carter collapses on top of Archer, and I see his shoulders shake. I pull out of and away from Archer to move up next to both of their heads. Archer wraps his arms around Carter's body, whispering sweet words of love to him.

Letting them have their moment, I head off to the bathroom and start the shower. I know we need more than a warm cloth to clean with. When I walk back through, the two men I love more than anything in the world are sitting up. Carter is in Archer's lap with his legs wrapped around his waist.

Lifting his head, Carter looks at me and with a wobbly smile and tear-filled eyes, he holds out his arms for me.

"I love you, Dan. I love you so fucking much." He hiccups, making me smile.

"I love you more, baby." I hug him and kiss the top of his head. "You ready to stand? I think we should clean up."

"Yeah, I'm okay. I think I have a gallon of cum in my ass." He laughs, then squirms on Archer's lap.

"Hey, don't dump it on me, Halston," Archer joins in, and suddenly the mood is so much lighter.

Leading Carter under the hot spray, I grab the sponge and his shower gel to wash down his body. I laugh when he squirms as I run my soapy hands down the crack of his ass. "Stay still. You said it yourself you were leaking."

"Eww, you're gross. You know that, right?" His nose wrinkles, but he laughs, making me kiss his nose.

"Head back, hon." Archer laughs and kisses his neck before washing his hair for him.

"I've missed this," I say quietly as I finish washing him off. "These little moments. I've missed them." I capture his mouth, kissing him soundly before turning my attention to Archer. "I feel whole again, do you?"

Archer nods and swallows hard, then kisses me. "Yeah, I love you, Dan. I couldn't have gotten through this without you."

"Come on. It's happy time. We're together again," Carter interjects as he wraps his arms around our shoulders. "Let's get back into bed. I want to tell you what went on."

Chapter

Fifty

ARCHER

Oh, God! The feeling as Carter slid down my cock was sublime. The heat of his ass, mixed with the slickness from Dan's orgasm almost had me shooting my load before he'd fully gone down on me. I wanted to rip him away from the stage the moment I heard the first bar of *American Girl,* or Boy, as he always sang when we lived together.

I had to let Dan take charge when we got into the bedroom, or I would have pinned Carter down and fucked him hard, not caring how he felt. I just needed to be inside him. Dan's way was the right way. I never expected the earth-shattering, heart-stopping, mind-altering connection I felt from both of them. If I ever doubted we were supposed to be together as a threesome, that moment cleared my doubts.

Now, as we lie together, in a quickly changed bed, under crisp sheets, I'm ready to hear Carter's news. "You gonna keep us guessing, hon?" I joke with him as he lies between us.

"I'm trying to find the right words. My father and I made peace with each other. It was easier than I thought it would be. He admitted his mistake. I realized I've moved on. I've grown up. I've lived through pain and emotions so much worse than my father's rejection. The what was it, ten hours ride back? That gave me a lot of time to think about myself. Who I am. Who I am when I'm alone. Who I am when I'm with my buddies at work. Who I am when I'm with the men who have become my family. But mostly who I am when I'm with you.

"When I stood in front of, first my brother and then my father, I realized I'm still Mallory Halston. A good man, a man worthy of the love of the people who surround me every day and a man who loves and is loved. So, I forgave him. It was worth it to see the love shine from his eyes again. We talked, we joked, and then the day he died, he gave me, gave us." Carter looks at me at this point. "He gave us the chance of freedom, of clear consciences, and a brighter future. For that I am grateful."

Dan speaks, and his words sound forced, painful. "You said you're Mallory Halston, not Carter, but Mallory. Have I lost the man I fell in love with?"

"Oh, Daniel, no. No way. I am the man you helped me become. I am the man who took a deep breath of fresh air in and cast out the bad, because of you. I love you, Daniel. Call me Carter, that's who I am to you. But I just feel the man I used to be has finally caught up with the new man I have become. Don't ever doubt my love for you. You are the catalyst, the man that brought the three of us back together."

"What do we call you now, honey? It's going to confuse a hell of a lot of people that your name is Mallory, not Carter."

"I think I want to still be Carter. I don't feel like I've lost the part of me that was Mallory anymore, if that makes sense to you. I'm just happy *I* know who I am."

"What was the freedom your father promised you?" I ask, trying to take in everything he has said, making sure I don't focus on just his epiphany.

"Well, that's something I'll be able to fill you in with soon." He smiles and leans across to peck my lips.

"Nuh-uh, that's not going to work, Carter, and you know it." I'm happy he's chosen to still be the new version of him.

"It will all become clear soon, like, really soon." He smirks, knowing I'm not going to stop.

"Mallory Carter Halston, quit your shit and talk," I snarl at him.

I watch as he looks to Dan for reassurance. Dan just shrugs. "Babe, if you want to sleep tonight, you need to spill."

"Fuck! Fine!" He sighs and turns to me. "I'll tell you this, and the rest has to wait. Okay?" He stares, waiting for my acquiescence.

I nod.

"Well, it seems my father and your mother had an affair. It started before I was born and lasted about five years or so. And before you look at me all horrified, you aren't my half-brother! You had been born before they started their relationship. Part of your mother's hatred of me may be due to the fact my father refused to leave my mother and marry your mom. After she threatened to expose him, he reminded her she had more to lose. A woman never comes out well from an extramarital affair. Would her career survive the scandal? So, she left him alone but, as you know, your mother doesn't forgive and forget. That's why she hates me so much."

"Shit! Wow! My poor father. I need to contact him. He's a good man. He doesn't deserve this any more than we do."

"That's all fine and dandy, Carter, but where does our future happiness come into this? Dan asks.

"Well, y'see, my father kept a dossier on your mother's antics and behaviors in her personal life, but more importantly, in her work and her rise through the ranks. He handed this to me just before he died, telling me to do the right thing for me and for you, Archer. Something to settle the scores and to give us peace and satisfaction."

"What have you done with the information, honey?" I dread to think who he may have handed it over to.

"Oh, ease up, tiger! I gave it to Lucas. He'll be in touch." Carter's smile quickly morphs into a smirk.

"Oh, Carter, sugar, you are in so much trouble." I dive on him as he shrieks with laughter. They soon turn to moans as the three of us take pleasure from each other again.

This time it's my turn to have my ass filled and dammit! I don't think I've ever felt happier.

As we settle again, I hear Carter's sleep-laden voice. "Love you both, so very much."

I think he's asleep before either of us can answer him.

❋ ❋ ❋

"Really? Fuck, what time? Okay, yep. Sure, yes, I'll tell him. Thank you, Lucas. Okay, I'm sure he'll call you. Yep, bye."

The name Lucas wakes me up more than Carter talking. Shifting over onto my side, I look up at him. He's sitting up, but the call must have woken him because his face is still crumpled from sleep and his hair is everywhere. To me, he has never looked more gorgeous.

"What's going on, Car? Where's Dan?" I push myself up and peck a kiss on his mouth.

"He's gone to make coffee. It looks like everything is going or has gone down. Where's your iPad?" Carter looks around the room and can't see it.

"It's downstairs. Carter, what's going on? You're freaking me out."

"Put the TV on, get the news channel up. You're *so* gonna want to see this."

Dan walks into the room carrying a tray with three coffees. "What's going on?"

"That's what I'm trying to work out." I take a coffee from him and hand it to Carter before grabbing one for myself. Then my jaw drops. I nearly let go of my cup as I stare at the TV. Or more at the ticker that's running along the bottom of the screen.

Supreme Court Judge Valerie Hawkins arrested on charges of blackmail and extortion.

Press release from chief of police at 10:00 am.

I look at Carter who has a smug smile on his face. "You did this?" I ask him.

"Well, theoretically my father did it. He was planning to do this himself, but his illness got in the way. He left instructions with his attorney, so it would've gone to the police after he died. I think he wanted to do this for me, for us. When I handed the dossier over to Lucas, he did the rest."

"Fuck! This is huge! Shit, I need to call my father." I surprise myself by thinking of him. "Is he involved?"

"I don't know, Arch. I'm sorry. Maybe you should call Mason?"

I don't know what to do. I always knew my mother was a bitch, but I never expected it to be this bad. "Did you read it? The dossier, did you read it?"

"Of course, I did." He's really grinning now.

"Then fucking tell me."

I listen for the next hour as Carter tells us both how she had accepted money for both putting and keeping people in and out of jail. She had bribed and blackmailed individuals, including police officers, lawyers, and other judges. I can't believe the depths she went to rise above others.

"How has nobody come forward before? This really doesn't make sense. Hell, I'm not surprised, after what she did to us. That's probably how she got the cops to tell you I'd died. Shit! I can't take this in."

At ten o'clock, we watch as the statement is read. The chief of police explains the charges and the ongoing investigation. Then my mother's attorney reads out a statement from her, refuting the charges and proclaiming a witch hunt against her. He says she is ready to fight to prove her innocence.

We all laugh aloud at this. I can't believe the bullshit this guy is talking. Then another statement is read. This time it's from my father's lawyer. I clutch Carter's hand tight. Dan is next to me, his arm around my waist, holding me against him. I feel safe between them, cocooned in the bed, and held tight as I watch my family fall apart. Not that there was any love lost between me and her, but I have missed my dad.

This statement is perfunctory, issued from my father's home in Florida. I look at Carter, confused. "When did he move there?"

His lawyer speaks, saying Mr. Hawkins has no involvement with his ex-wife and no knowledge of any of the charges held against her.

"When did he divorce my mother? I'm going to call his lawyer and find out what the hell is going on!"

The screen flicks back to the anchorman. I've had enough. Picking up the remote, I switch the TV off and lie back down in the bed. Closing my eyes and covering my head, I try to block out all the sights and sounds around me, but it's the voices in my head that need quietening. I'm not sure how to do that.

My cell phone rings, and I ignore it. I don't need to speak to anyone. I can hear Dan talking, but with the covers over my head, I can't hear the words.

"Archer, it's Mason. He needs to talk to you." Dan pulls back the duvet.

"No, not now. I'll talk to him later," I mumble.

"Best to do it now, Arch."

Next thing, Carter is under the covers with me. His hands cup my face, and he looks worried.

"I fucked this up, didn't I? I should have told you, warned you what was happening. I'm sorry, Arch. I thought I was doing the right thing. Lucas told me you didn't want the ins and outs of it, you simply wanted her brought down."

"No, honey, it's not you. I promise you. It's just overwhelming. I think the biggest shock is my father. If he divorced her, why didn't he contact me? I thought we had a good relationship."

"Maybe he wasn't sure how you would take it. You had banished your mother. Could he have thought you didn't want him around?"

"Fuck!" I push myself up to a sitting position and run my hands through my messy bed hair. "He did try to see me. When I was in the rehab center, he came. He tried to see me, and I refused him. Shit! Okay, it's time for action."

Chapter
Fifty-One

CARTER

"I need to see my brother. He's at Kes' place. I'd like him to stay here, if you don't mind?" We've made it out of bed and are making breakfast.

"Of course. I can't wait to meet him. He looks a bit like you. Not as gorgeous, obviously, but there's a definite similarity." Dan smiles and runs his hand down my back, making me lean into him.

"Do you wanna call him and invite him over for brunch?" Archer asks.

"Yeah, but I'm guessing we'll get Kes and his guys too. You'd better make more pancakes, Dan." I swat his backside, then grab my cell.

Twenty minutes later, the room is full of people, all of them my family. All laughing and kidding about as if they've known each other for years. Dan walks over, his eyes are fixed on me, and there's a huge smile on his face.

"You look happy." He smiles, dropping a kiss on my mouth.

"I am. This is more than I ever imagined. When I moved here, I was so lost and broken, but the people I met helped me heal. I made friends, who became more to me. They became my family. Then you came along, always flirting, making me feel something again." I look at him as he listens. "You gave me a chance to be happy again. I love you, Dan. I don't think you realize just how much."

"Trust me, I do. The faith you had in me, the trust you gave me, made me fall in love with you. I love seeing you so happy, with me and with Archer. And now with your brother. It's wonderful to see *and* to be a part of."

Roman looks up from his conversation with Denver and East. He smiles and excuses himself from the conversation. He saunters over and slings his arm over my shoulder.

"Have you told them yet?" he asks me, then grins at Dan.

"No, and I don't see what difference it would make to them knowing. Leave it, Ro."

"What? What haven't you told us?" Dan looks at my brother, who looks smug.

"Nothing, it's not important." I shoot daggers at my brother, but he just laughs, and I know he's going to say it.

"Yeah, not important," he snorts. "Leave everything to the two of us. You're looking at the Forbes Thirty Under Thirty list headliners."

I watch as Dan's eyes widen, and he swallows hard. A pink tinge flushes on his cheeks.

"Nice one, asshole." I push past my brother, who at least has the decency to look uncomfortable. "That wasn't your news to share."

"Carter…" Dan starts to speak, but my brother interrupts him.

"I thought you were going by Mallory again?" Roman still hasn't put a lock on his damn mouth.

"Oh, for fuck's sake, Roman. Please stop talking. I don't mind Archer calling me that. It's who I am to him," I snap, my voice louder than it should be. Archer looks over and frowns. I can see him looking between the three of us. I shake my head, but it's too late. He's making his way over.

"What's up? Carter, you look like death warmed over. What's going on?" Archer frowns at my brother. I'm guessing he's not forgiven him yet. He still has issues over Roman's choice of lawyer and the way he behaved towards me.

"Nothing. Roman was shooting his mouth off. He's always done it." I try to lighten the mood even though I can see Archer's not buying it and Dan still looks like he's going to be sick.

"We'll talk about this later. C'mon, let's take this party outside." Archer takes my hand, leading me through the packed kitchen.

Everyone follows our lead, and soon we're all enjoying the warm weather. We know the temperatures are going to drop soon and the mountains around us turn white as the snow falls. The ski vacations will start up soon, and the bar will have a new influx of customers.

Archer keeps hold of my hand while Dan has his arm around my waist. Neither of them show any sign of letting me go. Roman has found his way back to Marcus after a silent mouthed apology. He knows he fucked up.

After another hour, the guys make a noise about getting back to pick up Phoebe from Denver's mother.

Kes makes his way to me and smiles. "It really is good to have you back. Will you be coming back to work?"

"Of course, why wouldn't I? Have you given my position to someone else? Jeez, Kes, I know I've had a lot of time off lately, but everything is done and back to normal. I can be back tomorrow." I never thought that Kes wouldn't keep my job open.

"Carter, or is it Mallory now?"

"I don't mind, whatever you want." I've got my arms wrapped around my waist, something I haven't needed to do for a long while now.

"Okay, Carter. I haven't given your job to anyone else. I want to have you running my bar. I didn't know if you'd want to. You've had a massive change in circumstance. I don't want you to feel you have to come back."

"He told you, didn't he?" I shake my head. The little fucker!

"Yeah, but it was more about him and how he felt about it. He's a lot younger than you and not just his age, but in experience too. He didn't have to grow up fast and learn to live in the real world. He hasn't felt the pain and grief you have. I know his father, the man he had a good relationship with, has just died, but that's not the same as losing the love of your life. Be patient with him. He doesn't know how to do this with you any more than you do."

"I guess so." I scratch the back of my head as I work through what he has just said. "But to get back to the point, when do you want me back at work?" I laugh now.

"Tomorrow is fine. Just pick up your normal hours unless you'd like to lose some of your late nights. Paris is happy to pick up more shifts. I think he could do with the money now he's out of his parents' house."

"I'll talk to him and see what he wants to do. I'll see you tomorrow. And thank you for yesterday, it was perfect."

"You were amazing. The stage is yours whenever you want it." He laughs as East wraps his arm around my waist, kissing my cheek.

"Hey! Keep your hands and lips off my man!" Dan shouts and grabs me out of East's clutches, laughing and hugging me close to his body. I don't think I've ever seen him this happy, and it fills my heart.

Archer walks up behind me as we stand in our doorway, waving our friends goodbye. Roman and Marcus are here but have decided not to stay. They understand the stress Archer is under. Roman walked up to Archer and Dan while they were speaking to Denver, and I'm sure by the look on both of their faces, they listened and accepted his apology for being so flippant earlier.

"You want to talk or are we good?" I whisper into Archer's neck as he pulls me close to him.

"Carter, hon, we are so good. Is what your father left you going to make a difference?"

I shake my head, unable to answer him. Mainly because I'm angry with my father that he thought this could make it better. But after our private conversations, I know this isn't an apology. It's what I would've had anyway.

What I will do with it, I have no idea. I have no need for private jets and holiday islands. I'm not saying they wouldn't be good, but not what I'm looking for in my life.

"Then nothing changes. Things are going to be weird enough with all the shit going on in my family, without adding yours to the mix."

"I guess so. Enough thinking about that. I think we need to clear up the kitchen." I step back and stroll down the hallway. I smile as my brother and Marcus have cleared most of the detritus away.

"Whoa! Thanks, guys." Dan smiles and pats them both on their backs. "Awesome job."

"We're gonna head off. Marcus has an idea for a shoot he wants to scope out." Roman laughs. "He never stops working. We'll be around for a couple more days, then I need to get back to work."

"You got somewhere to stay?" I ask, feeling guilty about them not staying here.

"Yeah, we got a cabin down by the lake. Your man Denver sorted it for us." He gives me a sad look. "I'm sorry I was a dick. I shouldn't've done that."

"Hey, no sweat. I would've told them, but with all the crap from Archer's mom, I decided now wasn't the time." I pull him in for a hug which he reciprocates fiercely.

Then they are gone, and the house is empty. I wander off in search of Dan and Archer, wondering where they have disappeared to. I find them in the lounge. Archer is perched on the edge of the sofa watching the news on the TV. His mother is still the hot topic, and the debating has started over how someone in a position of such authority has managed to get away with this for so long.

"How bad is it?" I sit next to Archer. Dan is on his other side.

"About as bad as it can be. More and more people have come forward, all citing her for blackmail. Some incriminating themselves in the process, but it seems they may be doing a deal with the police. Not so much an amnesty, but only time will tell what happens to them. The police are asking people to come forward with any evidence, and it's pouring in. She doesn't have a leg to stand on here. It will go to trial, but it will take months. There's no way they will let her slip through on a technicality."

Chapter
Fifty-Two

SIX MONTHS LATER

ARCHER

"Are you ready?" Carter asks, knowing it's a pointless question and he's simply looking for something to say to me. I love him for it.

"No, not in any way, but I have to do this; this is closure." Running my hands through my already messy hair for the thousandth time, I automatically reach out and smooth it back down again. Carter smiles at me again, then runs his hands through it, messing it up again.

"You look so much better with it all messy, babe. And it will irritate your mother even more." He gives me a wink and a peck on the cheek. "It will all be over soon."

We've been coming to the courthouse every day for the last two weeks, hearing the full extent of her deception and the extreme levels she went to secure her position, but today is it. The jury has made their decision. They have been deliberating for over fifteen hours now, which I guess is only fair. To give her legal team credit, they put up a good fight, feeding confusion and lies to the jury. In my eyes, there's only one way they can go.

Then there's a knock on the door, and a clerk of the court calls us. We're only in the gallery, but as we're family, we have been given a private room. I nod in acknowledgement.

Dan moves next to me and takes my hand. "Let's go." He kisses Carter's forehead and smiles. "It'll be okay."

Then another man moves up next to me, my father. "Come on, son. It will be over within just minutes."

Getting the call from my dad was a wonderful surprise, even though know I would've sought him out if he hadn't. Dan and Carter understood my need to meet him alone. It was a bittersweet reunion. I worried it would be awkward, but I had no need. My father embraced me, apologizing over and over for allowing her to control our lives. To hear I was with Carter again made him beam with happiness, which quickly turned to amazement when I told him about Dan being with us too. After a cough and splutter, he accepted it, happy to know I had found the loves of my life.

Now, he is a welcome part of my family and has visited a few times in the six months running up to this day. Dan and Carter love him as much as I do.

We file back into the courtroom. All eyes are on us as we take our seats. Then the room is quiet. Valerie Hawkins sits between her lawyers, and their heads are together as they whisper. I can't help but stare at my mother, still unable to believe we share the same DNA. As I keep my eyes on her, she turns and looks at us. I keep my chin up, upholding the strength and stoicism I've managed to maintain through the whole trial. Lifting Carter's hand that is clasped tightly in mine, I kiss the back, proving to her that nothing she did would keep us apart. The look of abhorrence and hatred etched over her stony face has me smiling.

Her lawyer whispers something to her as he looks at us, narrowing his eyes before facing the front again.

We're ordered to rise as the judge enters the courtroom, then we sit silently again. The clerk goes through all the protocol. Then I find myself holding my breath as the lead juror stands and reads out the verdict.

"Guilty."

As he carries on through the long list of charges, he reads "guilty" out for every count.

Slumping back in my chair, I bow, afraid to show my emotions, Then I feel my father's hand on my shoulder, giving me a squeeze, giving me the affirmation I need to believe that it is well and truly over.

"You okay, Arch?" Carter leans into me, worried.

Lifting my head, I smile strong. It's a smile I haven't found inside me for a long time now. Unable to hold back my chuckle, I shake my head in wonder. Turning to my dad, I pull him into a deep embrace. I can feel his shoulders shaking, filled with the same emotions as me. Breaking apart, we both must wipe our eyes.

Turning back to Carter, I answer him, "Yeah, I'm good. I'm real good." Then I kiss him long and hard.

The room is barely lit by the candles surrounding us. Dan kisses Carter as I lie prone on our bed. I can see the sheen of sweat covering their bodies. I can't hold back the groan that builds in my chest. Carter looks at me. The huge, blown pupils hide his dark-blue irises. Licking his kiss-swollen lips, he leans over me.

His tongue licks the crease at the top of my thighs. He travels up over my body, licking and biting at my taut skin. Dan follows his lead and tongues my nipple, capturing it in his teeth. He tugs hard, making my back arch off the bed. When they reach my throat, I feel the bites and licks as they mark me, leaving purple bruises on my skin. Carter reaches my chin, and his teeth scrape over the stubble before licking over my mouth. His tongue dips inside and flicks against the roof of my mouth. Moaning hard, I thrash on the bed.

"Carter, hon, please, God. Please get inside me." My hands are fixed above my head, tied tight to the headboard by a black silk ribbon.

"No, not yet, baby. You're not ready yet." He grins before kissing me again. His mouth travels down my neck to my chest. Dan moves back down my body, and while my kiss-fogged brain tries to decipher all the feelings coursing through my body, I feel his mouth on the swollen head of my iron-hard dick.

"Arrrgh!" I cry out as he slides up and down my length. The heat of his mouth as he hollows his cheeks sucks me deep into his throat. Feeling the muscles constrict around me as Dan swallows, I groan, "No, no! I'm gonna come. Fuck!"

Dan pops off my dick and slides his tongue down to my balls. He sucks on one, then the other, as his finger circles my tight pucker. Christ, I want something inside me.

"Please, baby, please. I need you," I keen.

Carter stops sucking on my nipple and moves down the bed. Sliding between my legs, he pushes them, making me bend my knees, I put my feet flat on the bed, spread wide. I know he can see my hole. His eyes lock on me.

"You ready now?" he asks, his voice so fucking deep and husky. I feel a burst of precum drip onto my stomach. Reaching for the lube, I watch him coat his finger and then his cock. I love having him inside me. He strokes my pucker with two slippery fingers, then one slides inside me, pumping in and out. Two or three times before a second finger slides in, the twist and stretch of them relax my muscles. I know I'm ready for him, but he adds a third. I'm writhing, squirming, panting, and cursing him until they slip out, leaving me empty and bereft.

With the head of his cock pressed against my entrance, he lifts my legs up and hooks my feet up on his shoulders. In one long stroke, he enters me. Filling me in one thrust, holding still while I adjust before really fucking me. This is what I need, what I've been craving. Someone to take me higher, away from all the crap that has happened.

Carter picks up speed as Dan wraps his hand around my dick, working me at the same speed. I know I'm not going to last. As the fireworks explode behind my eyes, I come. Fuck, it feels good. My stomach is pelted with streams of my release. Opening my eyes, I see Dan fisting himself. The tendons in his neck are tight as he cries out my name and comes. He paints my chest, thick ribbons of cum mixing with my own.

Carter picks up speed, and I know he's about to come as he goes rigid. He pulls out and pelts me with his cum. Some hits my chin and lip, making me lick it up. He slumps over me, panting hard. My legs drop to the bed as he leans down and cleans me. His tongue slides through the mixture of our spunk, making him groan. When he reaches my face, he licks my chin, then slides his tongue in my mouth. I suck hard, tasting the flavor of all three of us.

Then sitting back on his heels, he laughs. "Fuck! Archer, I needed that as much as you." Dan joins in as his fingers trace through the mess on my chest.

"Is someone gonna untie me? I really need a shower." I look over to Dan.

"Yeah, okay. I thought about leaving you like that. I like submissive Archer." But he reaches up to untie the ribbon. "I think we'll be keeping these though." He winks.

Carter has slipped off the bed, and I hear the shower start. Coming back to me, he takes each arm and massages the muscles, making me feel cherished.

After a shower, we lie back in bed. Carter has his head on my chest, and I'm resting in the crook of Dan's shoulder.

Today, my mother got sentenced for a minimum of thirty-five years in prison. The judge didn't waste any time condemning her and ordering her incarceration. I wanted to see her in prison orange. I needed to see her once more. Dan and Carter understood my need to do this alone, so it was just my father and me in the gallery this time. She stood in front of the judge, a man she had probably socialized with many times, and looked him straight in the eye. Only when he delivered her sentence did her shoulders droop. As she was led away, she turned to look at us. There was no remorse or apology anywhere in her face or demeanor. Then she was gone. I know I will never see her again. Dan and Carter were waiting for me when I got home, ready to take care of me, and now I'm lying in the afterglow.

"It's been more than a year, y'know," Carter speaks quietly. He lifts his head. "Since the accident. It was over a year ago. Our lives changed irrevocably, all because of one woman's hatred. I can't believe how little she cared, how she only ever thought of herself. We lost each other at a time that should've been so special."

"But she didn't win, Carter. We made it. We found each other and more. We have Dan with us, too. I've never been happier."

"I know. I wish neither of us had had to go through the pain and grief. She broke me, Archer. She stood in front of me and lied, with no remorse. She told me you were dead, and I had to go. She told you, while you lay in a hospital bed, that I had left you. We would be married by now, Archer."

"I found our marriage license. I still have it in my wallet," I murmur and kiss his temple.

"So, I've been thinking." Carter pushes himself up and sits facing us. "I know we can't get married, the three of us, I mean. But I want us to show our commitment to each other."

Dan and I shift until we're both sitting up now. I can see how nervous he is, and I know what he's going to say.

"Dan, you brought me back to life. In a time when I thought I had nothing to live for, you showed me how to love again. Archer, I thought I'd lost you. I grieved for you. My heart broke for you, then you came back again. You didn't run from us, you embraced us and made us whole. So, to both of you, I'm asking if you will marry me. I want to show the world who we are. I want us to have a commitment ceremony." Carter takes a deep breath, and with his hands twisting the sheet over his lap, he looks at us.

"Mallory Carter Halston, I want nothing more than to spend the rest of my life with you. I love you so much. Yes, I will marry you." Dan's voice is shaky as he reaches for him. His mouth hits his, and this is a chaste kiss, but so powerful. His lips press up to his as his fingers tangle in his hair.

Breaking apart, Carter looks at me. His eyes are blazing, the look so potent I gasp. "Carter, we have already chosen to be together forever, this time seems so much more. I want you and Dan to be with me for as long as I'm still breathing. Yes, I will be proud to stand with you and commit to be together."

"Thank fuck for that because I've done something." Carter looks at us and blushes, then scoots across the bed and reaches to the bedside table. Sliding the drawer open, he grabs hold of something I can't see. Sitting back in front of us again, he opens his hand.

Three pale-blue velvet bags, each tied with a different color ribbon—one gold, one emerald green, and the third a deep sapphire blue. Dropping the gold one in Dan's trembling hand, he then gives me the green one and holds onto the blue one himself.

"One for each of us," Carter murmurs. His body buzzes with nervous exhilaration. "Open them."

I see my fingers struggle to undo the bow as they tremble, but soon the ribbon slips free, allowing me to tip the bag up.

I gasp as a heavy platinum ring falls into the palm of my hand, a row of three gemstones nestled in the center. Mine has three emerald stones. So beautifully crafted, yet still so masculine. It's perfect. I look up at Mallory. I try to speak, but words fail me. Instead, I look at Daniel. He has his fingers clenched tight around the ring, tears falling down his handsome face.

"We each have one with the color of our eyes in the center, and the inscription inside is the same for all of us." Carter looks nervous again. "Have I got it wrong?" His jaw tightens as he waits for at least one of us to respond. I look at the others and see sapphires for Carter and amber for Dan.

I twist the ring so I can look inside. *Here With You – Forever.* I can't hold back anymore. I grab Dan and him and drag them against me. We collapse back on the bed, and I bury my head in their chests. "You sure know how to make a bad day good. Hell, it's perfect. I love you."

"So, we gonna do this?" Carter asks as he holds his ring to me. Then he takes Dan's from him. "Give him yours, Arch. We'll put them on each other at the same time."

Scrabbling back upright again, we sit in a triangle and with very shaky hands and huge grins, we push the rings down the fingers of our forever lovers.

Flopping backwards, Carter covers his eyes with his arm. I watch as he laughs. Deep belly laughs that soon have him doubled up.

"Baby?" Dan asks when Carter calms down.

"This wasn't supposed to be done like this. I had it all planned. Y'know, beautiful location, good food, and wine. Definitely with clothes on. This isn't a story we will share with our kids." Then he dives on us again.

Chapter
Fifty-Three

DAN

It seems when Carter decides to do something, he does it quickly. The confidence he has in himself and us leaves me breathless. He really has found himself again and making peace with his father has given him his identity back as well as his brother.

For the last four weeks, his focus has been on our commitment ceremony. Trying to find the perfect location has proved difficult and frustrating. Nothing is right for his very fussy taste and sitting here now at the end of the day, with a cold beer, Archer and I watch him stomp about the garden.

"Why is it so fucking difficult! We live in one of the most stunning parts of the country though nothing is right!" His hands are in his hair, making it even messier than usual.

"Carter, the last three places have been stunning. You may be looking for something that isn't here." I chuckle when all he does is scowl at me.

"Don't be ridiculous. Of course, the right place is out there," he snaps.

"Okay, honey, tell us what you want. What do you see when you visualize it?" Archer tries to placate him.

"I want somewhere simple. I want trees and a large open grass area, and there must be a lake or a pond. Something for a great backdrop but not to take away from what we're doing. Big enough to hold a marquee for the reception, but still have plenty of outside space." He sighs exasperated.

I look at him pointedly, and he just stares back with his hands on his hips. "What? Why are you looking at me like that?"

"Because, my love, you have just described exactly where you are standing. You just pictured this garden."

He looks at me, then around the large backyard, with the trees in the background surrounding the freshwater pond.

"Fuck!" Turning back to look at me, his eyes wide. "How did I not see this? Shit! Can we have it here?" The look of joy on his face makes my heart beat faster.

"Why are you asking? This is your home. Do you still think of it as mine?" I frown. "Carter, you've lived here for nearly a year now."

"Of course, I think of it as home. I was simply questioning if it's feasible. I wasn't asking for permission."

"Then yes, I think we should have it here. Archer, what do you say?"

"I think it's perfect, but even though we love it here, do you want to live here forever? Is it going to be big enough for us to raise a family? I was an only child and don't want that for us. I want a horde of kids. I simply think if we get married here, we will never want to move."

"That's easy. We can rebuild here if we need to. I don't think we'll be rushing into having a family. We have so much to do together, so many places to see, I don't think we need to worry about the house yet," Carter replies.

"How long do you want to wait?" Archer sounds annoyed.

"I don't know. I hadn't really thought about it too much. Maybe two or three years." Carter looks confused at the turn in the conversation.

"I think we should leave this conversation for another time, Archer. Let's get back to whether having the ceremony here is something we all want."

"Yes, I think it's perfect. I know Carter will make it an amazing day for us." Archer looks up at Carter, who is chewing on his bottom lip, a sure sign he's upset. "Hey, sugar, come here." He stands and steps up to meet his fiancé. "I'm sorry. I know we have plenty of time for a family. I'm excited for what the future holds, and children are a part of that. I love you two, and that's what we should be focusing on now."

Carter leans into Archer's embrace and lifts his face up for a kiss. It's a sweet moment that I capture on my phone. When they separate, they are both smiling again.

Standing, I join them. "Shall we have a walk around?"

We spend the next hour coming up with ideas, laughing at the outlandish ones Carter has discovered as he's researched it. By the time the darkness has closed in, we've come up with a plan. Now it's time to make it happen.

"Who's going to be your best man?" I ask Carter as we lie in bed.

"I don't know who to ask. I want Kes because he's done so much for me, but I don't know if that will upset Roman. Do you think he will expect to be it?"

"I think you should go with your heart, not with your conscience. If you want Kes, then have him. Roman is back in your life, and it's working well, but he won't expect it. I'm guessing he'll be thrilled to be included in any way you will have him." I kiss the top of his head as he rests between my legs, his back against my chest.

Archer lifts his head up from the pillow beside us. "I would go with your heart on this one, honey. Kes will be honored to stand beside you."

"Who are you having, Archer?" Carter asks as he twists the beautiful ring around on his finger.

"Mason Reynolds. He's my old boss, but he's more than that. He's a good friend. He helped me through so much when I was recovering and let me stay at his place when I couldn't bring myself to stay in our old apartment."

"I always liked Mason. I'll be excited to see him again." Carter strokes his hand down Archer's face, so softly. "I hate I wasn't there to help you."

"Everything happens for a reason and look where we are now. My mother's gone from our lives forever, and we're together despite her." Archer leans into Carter's hand and kisses his palm. "Who are you having then, Dan?"

"I'm going to ask Conn. We've been friends for a long time."

"Just friends?" Carter smirks.

"Yes, just friends. Well, that's all it's been for a long time now. He's a good guy."

"Yeah, he is. He's been good to Paris. I don't know how serious they are, but they seem happy together," Carter replies.

Archer yawns and pulls the covers up higher, giving us the hint he needs to sleep. "I've got a full day of meetings tomorrow."

"I've got a wedding to plan." Carter smiles before moving between us. He kisses Archer, then turns to me to do the same.

Chapter
Fifty-Four

CARTER

It's all done. Everything is in place. After six weeks of planning and organizing, we are ready. The backyard has been turned into everything I wanted and imagined. The platform with the arbor down by the edge of the water is lit with so many tiny white lights entwined with jasmine, the heady scent in the heat of the evening fills the air. The rows of chairs covered in midnight-blue fabric with a silver silk bow are ready for our guests. Over one hundred people will watch us take our vows.

The marquee is perfect. The tables are laid with the finest bone china plates and crystal glasses. White roses and calla lilies mixed with tall candles decorate each table. All I need now is for Dan and Archer to be here. They left for the airport this afternoon to collect more of our guests. They haven't seen the final results. I'm nervous and excited now. This time tomorrow, we will be married. Not in the eyes of the law, but our commitment to each other is strong and true. This for me, is till death do us part.

I hear someone walk up behind me. "This is breathtaking, Ry, so perfect. I know who I'll come to when it's my turn." Roman throws his arm casually over my shoulder. "I'm so happy for you, bro."

"I can't believe it's going to happen. I never thought I'd find love again."

"I admit to being surprised and skeptical when you first told me, but after seeing the three of you together, I can see how well you work together, that you've got it right."

"I fucking hope so. This cost me a damn fortune!" I laugh and take one more look around before heading into the house again. I'm sure the guys will be back any time now.

"It's good you have a fortune, then." My brother laughs back at me.

It's another fifteen minutes before I hear the cars pull up in the driveway. Having to pick up five people, they went in two cars. I hear the doors slam and lots of laughter as I open the front door.

"Hey," I call out a greeting as Archer grabs hold of luggage from the back of the truck. "You want some help there?" I step down from the porch and over to the truck.

"How you doing, Mallory, or should I call you Carter?" Mason steps up to me and pulls me into a bear hug. The man can give huge hugs. He's six and a half feet tall and swamps me.

"Mason, it's good to see you. I'm good. Nervous, but I'm good," I answer him, smiling.

"You look good. You've both had such a tough time. It's good to see you happy again."

Dan comes around from his car. He collected Archer's dad, and both of them have arms full of bags and suitcases.

"Let's all get inside."

Mason walks behind me, holding his wife's hand. Lucas follows with his wife Tamsin. These guys look like they've all just walked off the runway, they're so beautiful. They're also some of the kindest and most grounded people I know.

With all the noise of about five different conversations, I sneak out of the room. Archer and Dan find me in the kitchen getting drinks for everyone. Their bodies sandwich me between them as their mouths find my mouth and neck. I moan and melt against them as they deepen their kisses. When we break apart, my head spins, and my legs have gone wobbly.

"Is it ready?" Dan murmurs, his mouth still hovering over mine.

"Can we see?" Archer whispers in my ear as he holds my hips against his groin.

"It is, and it's amazing." I grab hold of their hands and lead them out into the garden.

"Wow!" Dan stops walking to stare.

The night has closed in, and all the lights in the garden shine and twinkle. On the water are floating solar lights. This is exactly how I wanted them to see it. The ceremony is going to take place at dusk. The lights will just be coming out. I've got oil burner lights for tomorrow, but I didn't want to light them tonight and have to refill them again tomorrow.

The marquee has soft electric lights highlighting the crystal glass on the tables. To me, it looks perfect, but now it's up to the other grooms to cast their opinions.

Turning to Archer, I see him looking dumbstruck. "Talk to me, Arch, is it what you wanted?" I speak quietly, watching his expression.

"I... I... Fuck, I don't know what to say. Carter, this is beyond anything I could have envisioned. I don't know what to say." He stops gazing over the garden and looks at me. I can see the sheen of tears glistening, brightening his eyes. As he blinks, a tear breaks free and slips gracefully down his cheek. Lifting my hand, I wipe it away with my thumb. "It's perfect, so damn perfect. I wish we were doing this now."

I turn my gaze to Dan and see he's as emotional as Archer. The tick in his jaw flickers as he brings himself back under control. "You are a genius, Carter. You have achieved something magical. I can't wait for tomorrow."

When we get back inside, it's time for relaxing with our friends and family. Spending time with new and old friends as Kes, East, and Denver turn up carrying boxes and boxes of pizza. The jokes and laughter take away any nerves trying to creep through me.

At about ten-thirty, our guests start to leave. Archer's dad, my brother, and Marcus are staying here. The others have rooms at one of the hotels in town.

Finally, the house is quiet, and we can go to bed.

The house is a hive of activity as guests arrive. With the catering company here, I organized a lazy afternoon buffet for everyone. The garden has tables set up, giving them all somewhere to sit and eat. Waiters wander around with mimosas balanced on silver trays. It's going very smoothly.

"I can't believe you've done all this." Archer stands next to me, looking out the window at everyone below. We can see them, but they can't see us from this angle. "It would've been a few friends and some steaks on the grill if you'd left it up to me." He laughs.

"Is it too much?" I look at him, suddenly worried I've gone too far.

"Fuck, no, this is amazing. I can't wait to be down there." He wraps his arm around me, pulling me close. "I love you so damn much. This is the beginning of a new chapter in our lives."

As his lips touch mine, my hands reach up and grasp his head, tangling my fingers in his hair. I moan as his tongue slides lazily across the seam of my lips, parting them gently. As our tongues meet and slowly stroke against each other, Archer's hands slide down my back and grab my ass. I push my hips into his and feel the solid length of his erection.

"I want you," I murmur against his lips.

"We can't. We said we'd wait until tonight," Archer whispers back.

"I can't wait," I beg, grinding against him.

"What are you two up to?" Dan's voice makes us break apart.

"Carter is misbehaving." Archer laughs. "He doesn't want to wait until tonight."

"Aww, poor baby." Dan steps up behind me, pressing me into Archer. "I promise it will be worth the wait." He bites on my earlobe, tugging firmly. Then moves away. "We need to get showered and dressed. It's nearly time."

"Really? Shit!" I feel the panic rising now. "Christ, are we really going to do this?"

Archer and Dan smile, each reaching for my hands. Dan speaks first, "We are, my love. And if I remember correctly, you asked us. This was your idea and look what you've achieved." He points out to the garden where the tables have been cleared but the guests seem to have doubled.

I take a deep breath and calm myself. "I know, it's just nerves. I'll be fine. Who's going first in the shower?"

"Why are we showering separately?" Archer looks at me, confused.

"Because, Arch, if I get in there with you and we're naked, trust me, there will be fucking." I laugh and step past him. "I'll go first."

Reaching into the shower, I get the water running before stepping out of my shorts and pulling off my T-shirt. Stepping under the hot water, I tip my head back and think of my vows. I'm keeping them simple. I only want to tell them how much I love them and that this to me is forever.

I grab my shampoo and squeeze the gel into my hand and lather up my head. I suddenly feel another pair of hands massaging my scalp.

"You're not supposed to be here," I mutter belligerently. "You said no fucking."

"I'm not fucking you. I'm washing your hair." Archer laughs.

"I hate you. You know that, right?" I snap at him, making him laugh harder.

"I know, honey. That's why there's over one hundred people down there waiting for us. They're eager to hear you tell me just how much you hate me." He kisses my shoulder, then tips my head back under the water.

After my hair is clear of soap and bubbles, Archer steps away to grab his body wash.

"C'mon, Car, hurry up!" He grins at me.

"Asshole!" I grumble.

"Yeah, and it's yours tonight!"

"Too fucking right." I finish washing and step out. Grabbing a towel, I dry off and head out to get dressed. I've chosen midnight-blue suits for the three of us to wear, with pale-grey shirts. Our ties are silver grey.

Dan sits on the edge of the bed when I walk through. As he looks at me, the heat in his eyes leaves me breathless. Standing, he strides over to me.

"Do you have any fucking idea how much I love you, how much I want to worship you? You are the most amazing man I know."

"I love you too, Dan. You are my world." I brush my lips over his and feel his breath as he sighs softly. "Go get washed. We've got a wedding to go to."

It's another thirty minutes before we're ready. We're quiet as we dress. I think we're all nervous now. There's a knock on the door, and then it opens. Our three best men are standing there, each hold two glasses of champagne.

"Don't you three look good." Kes smiles.

"Here you are, take one of these." Mason hands over the champagne, as does Conn. "I'd like to say something, if I may?" He looks at the three of us as we stand close together. "Archer, you have been my friend for many years now. I have been with you through the hardest moments, and now I get to see you at the happiest moment of your life. You have found your soulmates. Having Carter back with you is so wonderful, and to then find love with Dan makes your life complete. I wish you a long and happy life together."

"Okay, let's go and do this." Kes claps his hands, then walks over to me. "Come on, Carter, let's go." I walk out with him first, followed by Dan and Conn, then Archer and Mason.

The timing is perfect. The sun is just going down, the scent of the night jasmine fills the air, and the lights are beginning to sparkle. We chose *Look How Far We've Come* by Imagine Dragons; it's one of our favorite bands and just about the only one we agreed on.

By the time I reach the platform by the lake, I can feel the adrenaline building inside me. I am so ready for this now. I feel, rather than look, Archer and Dan walk up next to me, Finally, I look up at our officiate, and a huge grin breaks out. Denver smiles at me as he enjoys the whole show, and I think back to how we decided he would do this.

"Look, it's not difficult. You just have to stand there and pretend you know what you're doing." I sigh, exasperated at Paris.

We sit in Kes' backyard. Ellie and her friends race around the garden with Missy, Denver's dog. East tries to get them to keep the noise down, but it really isn't working.

"You know you can do this." I give him my puppy dog eyes. "Please?"

"I can't, Car. I love you, dude, but seriously, I've seen your guest list. I can't speak in front of that many people." He looks so apologetic I almost forgive him.

"Who's gonna do this for me, then?" I sigh and slap my hands on my thighs.

"I'll do it."

I look at Denver incredulously. "Really? You'd do this for us?"

"Yeah, why not? I give speeches all the time." He turns and shushes Kes. "I mean, at work, I have to do loads of presentations. I'll just pretend it's as interesting as they are."

"Oh, fuck you!" I laugh and throw a beer cap at him. "But thanks, Den. That's really cool of you."

"Carter, you're family. It's what we do." He gives me a wink. "And I get a chance to embarrass you in a speech."

"Ladies and gentlemen, please take your seats," Denver speaks confidently, and his voice travels over the guests' chatter. "Thank you. Now, I guess you all know why we're dressed up in our finery at the end of a long Saturday. And that is to witness the vows of the three men standing, nervously shaking and about to do a runner, in front of me."

Denver is perfect. I can't believe how good he is at settling my nerves.

"So, the guys have decided to say a few words to each other. We're starting with Dan, so I'm going to do the whole official part and ask if there is anyone here who knows of any lawful impediment as to why these men can't join, to speak now or forever hold their peace."

There's a nervous titter through the guests as if someone may speak up.

"No? Then over to you, Dan." Denver grins and steps back.

Dan takes Denver's place and faces us and the audience. I can see how nervous he is, but he takes a long look at my and Archer's faces and straightens up, ready.

"Y'know, I never thought I would find the day I would be standing here pledging my love to someone I love with every fragment of my heart. So, to be here with two men, men that I must pinch myself every morning to believe this is true, has my heart beating fast." Taking a deep breath, he looks back at us. "Carter, you entered my life as a broken man, a man I wanted to care for. I wanted to take away your pain, but you're as stubborn as a mule and as difficult to capture. Somehow you let me. You showed your true colors and, my God, how they shine. You let me in, you shared yourself, and let me love you. For that, I will be forever grateful, and I will spend every day showing you how much I love you. Archer, my best friend, my first lover. The man I owe so much of my confidence to. You showed back up in my life at a time I didn't realize was so pivotal, to all of us. To find out that you and Carter." He chuckles at this. "Hell, where do I start? Let's just say, it got complicated. But then the storm passed, and I suddenly had two men I couldn't live without. Two men that I would do anything for. Two men I wanted to be tied to for the rest of my life. That is why we're here today. Carter, Archer, you are my life. You are my everything. I love you."

Dan steps back, and I don't think there's a dry eye in the house. Archer steps forward. I'm regretting saying I'd go last now.

"Okay, I'm not sure what to say now. I'm the new boy in town, but not to both Daniel and Carter. We have known each other for a very long time. I knew Carter was the man for me the first time he crashed into me. I just had to find a way to make sure he knew it too. He was a slippery little sucker to begin with. Every time I thought we'd made progress, he would scarper again." This makes people laugh, and Archer looks up and smiles at me. "I got him though, but not for long. We both experienced pain and grief in the months that followed, and meeting again wasn't the movie-style reunion you would want. It was, in fact as much of a car crash as the one that separated us in the first place." Archer looks at me and stretches his hand out for me to grasp. "I learned I wasn't prepared to let him go again. I found myself with the first man I loved and the last man I had loved, and I was sensible enough to realize that life doesn't throw second chances around. I grabbed it, and I'm never going to let go. Carter, Dan, you are the men that make my heart beat, the men that give me a reason to be a good man, one worthy of you. I love you."

Shit! It's my turn. I look at Denver as he smiles and offers the space in front of him and in front of everyone I know. I step up, look past the men I'm committing myself to, and speak out to my father, telling him all the reasons why I should be with these men.

"I guess I should've thought harder about marrying two lawyers. I'm not sure I can match their speeches, but I'll give it a go. A few years ago, I lost everything when I came out to my family. I had to become a different person. I had to toughen up and trust myself. I met Archer when I was beginning to stand on my own two feet, but he tried his hardest to sweep me off them again. For a while, he did. We lived a perfect life. We had everything because we had each other. Then life changed, and I lost everything again." I look past Archer because I know I will break down if I look into his eyes. "I found myself in a strange town with no reason to stay except the deep feeling this was a good place. Here, I found a new family, a group of people so real and so true, it felt like home. I also met a very handsome, very persistent, and very sexy lawyer named Dan." There's laughter from the guests now, making me smile, and I look at Dan. Bad move. I can see the tears shining in his eyes. "It was my good friend, Shelley, that told me he was a good guy and I could trust him. So, I did, and he is. Dan is one of the world's good people, someone who will always have my back, and it didn't take him long to have my heart, too. But then Archer came back, and boy, did he upset the apple cart. I'm going to keep this short because you know what happened next, and that's why we're standing here today. Because I love these men. I want to spend the rest of my life with them and grow old with them. I love you."

Denver lets an emotional cough out and steps forward again. "Okay, I think we've cried enough, so I'll just do the formalities. Daniel, do you take Archer and Carter to be your wedded husbands, in sickness and in health till death do you pass?"

"I do." Daniel's voice is firm and strong.

Repeating the same words to Archer, my body thrums as he replies, "I do."

Then it's my turn. Denver looks at me. The smile on his face and in his eyes has me grinning. "You want me to repeat them?" He laughs with a wink.

I shake my head. Turning to look at my very nearly husbands, I smile and clasp their hands. "I, Mallory Carter Halston, take thee Archer Hawkins and Daniel David Mortimer to be my husbands. I promise to love you, care for you and keep you, in sickness and in health, for as long as we shall live."

"I think it's fair enough to say I can now pronounce you husbands. You may now kiss." He laughs and steps back as we step up to each other, and with our hands wrapped around each other's waists, we kiss. Our three mouths join together in perfect harmony.

The gentle laughter from the seats behind us makes us separate far sooner than we want to, but I'm guessing we can wait for now. We have Dan's cabin down by the lake for tonight, and we have forever.

Epilogue

CARTER

TWO YEARS LATER

I watch as Archer and Dan walk through the door. They still make the butterflies in my stomach stir and awaken. I'm thankful for them every day. We have done so many things, traveled to so many amazing places in the last two years, but today is the biggest adventure of them all.

"Hey, baby." Archer walks up to me and drops a deep kiss on my expectant mouth, moaning when I flick my tongue over his bottom lip. "Hmmm, have you missed us?"

"Maybe." I sigh.

"My turn." Dan pulls me against his firm chest and claims my mouth.

We pull apart, and I lead them into the kitchen. On the table are two gift bags. I watch as they spy them but don't say anything, and neither do they. They look at them like they're bombs ready to explode. I want to laugh, but I think back to how we got to this place.

"I want a baby," Archer speaks quietly in the darkness to us.

"I know you do," I whisper back. I've been waiting for this conversation. In fact, I'd discussed it with Dan after Kes and his husbands had another baby. We know we'd made him wait this long while our lives changed.

"I think it's time, too," Dan says back.

"Really?" Archer replies hopefully.

"Yes, I saw the way you looked at Kes' new baby. You wanted to snatch him and run." I laugh.

"I wasn't that bad," he jokes back. "Okay, maybe I was."

"Do you want a baby or a child? Are we looking for adoption or surrogacy?" I know what I prefer, but this is Archer's choice.

"I want a baby. I want one that we have made." He sounds so excited.

"Then let's do it. We've been selfish enough, Arch, and you've let me do my thing and change my life. I want to do this with you both." My decision to open and run a shelter for LGBTQ teenagers has taken up so much of all of our time, I feel that now I have all my qualifications and am doing something I love, it's Archer's time to get his dream.

"I'll ask Kes for the list of surrogates he had. I know he had a tough time choosing because they were all great," he answers. "And Carter, you haven't been selfish. You did what you needed to do, and it was the right thing. I'm proud of what you have achieved."

It takes us six weeks to find our surrogate. We interview six women. It is the last woman we have on the list that strikes as perfect. Her name is Penny. She's twenty-eight, and she has two children of her own. She has never done this before but has been through the relevant counseling to allow her to make this decision.

The entire process is quick and easy on our part, but Penny has to have injections to stimulate her ovaries. Then the doctors fertilize three eggs each with our semen. We won't know who the father is if one fertilizes, but at least it will be one of us. I really hope it's Archer's child. Today, Penny calls and confirms her pregnancy.

This is my way of telling them. In each bag, there are a pair of the tiniest socks ever and a onesie that says *I love my daddies*. There are two bags because there are two babies. I watch as they move over and pick up the bags.

"Do I really want to know what's in here?" Dan asks cautiously.

"Oh, I think you do."

Archer snatches his and opens it. His eyes fill with tears as he pulls out the socks and then sees the little sleepsuit.

"We're having a baby?" he asks me incredulously.

I shake my head. "Nope, we're not having *a* baby."

"Then what's all this for?" Then I watch as his mind turns it over and the lightbulb moment clicks. "We're having two babies?"

The smile that spreads across his face is contagious as he cries and pulls us both in for a hug. "Thank you, Carter, thank you so much," he cries into my neck.

THREE MORE YEARS ON

ARCHER

I'm watching Nixon and Amalie shriek with laughter as their big brother, Cole, chases them around the yard. Their chubby little legs work hard to keep away from the fourteen-year-old boy that loves them with everything he has.

Cole is Carter's son. He turned up at the center a year ago. Beaten

341

up badly by his father after being caught kissing another boy, he made it to the shelter by hitching a ride. Denver helps at the center and runs a weekly clinic there, but Cole was in such a bad way, he came in to check his injuries. Luckily, he had gotten away without any broken bones, but his ribs were very badly bruised and painful for a long time.

Carter knew he had to make Cole's life better. He didn't know what it was about him over the other kids he'd helped, but he just felt it. So, Cole became one of us, and he's an amazing kid. Our family is now complete.

I hear laughter from behind me and turn to see Carter and Dan stepping through the kitchen doors.

"Oh, it's all right for some, lounging out in the garden all afternoon while the rest of us slave away." Dan laughs and leans over the back of the lounger to kiss me.

"I'll make it up to you later," I whisper against his mouth.

"You'd better," he replies and nips my lip.

Carter sits next to me; his hand strokes my bare arm. "How's your day been?"

"The usual domestic bliss of being a house husband. I've stopped Amalie from trying to water the keyboard in your office because someone didn't lock the door." I scowl at him. "I've done the laundry and cleaned up after the terrible twins, and now I'm letting Cole exhaust them so they go to sleep early and through the night." I give him a wink and watch his eyes dilate as he bites on his bottom lip.

"I like the sound of that," Carter answers, his voice husky at the thought.

"I thought you might." I smile. My life doesn't get better than this.

HERE WITHOUT YOU

THE END

Acknowledgements

Yet again, I have at least one hundred people to say thank you to, and
I know I'm going to forget so many important names, but here
goes…

To Rae and Fee, as always, you two go above and beyond for me.
How can I thank you enough for not only your encouragement, help,
and support when these guys were making it so damn difficult for
me? But for your friendship and love, as always and forever, I will
always love you more.

To Louisa Mae, Megs Pritchard, and Tracy McKay, thank you for
keeping me from chucking this away at least three times.

My Honeys, you are all always so kind and patient as you wait for the
next story. To Rachel Hadley, Tanja, Heather, and Whynter for your
constant promotion and support, I couldn't do this without you.

A huge thank you goes to Kimberly Sewald for beta reading and
getting rid of all the English words and expressions that don't make
sense on the other side of the pond, and to Tanja Ongkiehong for
her proofreading skills

A huge thank you to

Sue Soares at SJS Editorial Services for her mad editing skills.

JC Clarke for another stunning cover.

Everyone on Facebook and Twitter for your constant support.

And to you the readers, who without you I wouldn't be here.

About the Author

Normally found in my living room typing away, with my dog, and a warm fire in the winter. In the summer, I sit in the garden soaking up the sunshine, still tapping away on my laptop, still with my dog. I write hot, sexy, and lovable male romance with men you wish you could keep to yourselves, so much so that I sometimes find it hard to share them. 😊

As a bona fide bookaholic, coffee-addicted, wine-drinking and swear-like-a-sailor type of girl, I have still yet to work out how to act my age!! LOL. And I have no intentions of growing up or growing old gracefully, I live in a small, very quiet village in Lincolnshire, UK, with my husband and my dog, and spend all day dreaming up stories full of really hot men.

Other Books

The Reunion Trilogy
Reunion
Reunited
Elysium

The Troy Duology
Troy Into the Light
Troy Out of the Dark

Narrow Margins

Cooper's Ridge Series
Denver's Calling

The Finding Me Series (M/F)
Rising Up
My Turn
Missing Pieces
Set to Fall

25349511R00195

Printed in Poland
by Amazon Fulfillment
Poland Sp. z o.o., Wrocław